Caffeine Ni

GW00696860

Seven Daze

Charlie Wade

Fiction aimed at the heart
and the head...

Published by Caffeine Nights Publishing 2013

Published in Great Britain by Caffeine Nights Publishing

www.caffeine-nights.com

British Library Cataloguing in Publication Data.

A CIP catalogue record for this book is available from the British Library

ISBN: 978-1-907565-39-7

Cover design by

Mark (Wills) Williams

Everything else by

Default, Luck and Accident

Acknowledgements

It would be impossible to name everyone who has helped or encouraged over the years, so I'll give a general thank you to everyone. However, special thanks go to Karen, Nick Quantrill, 'H' and Darren at Caffeine Nights.

Seven Daze

Part 1

Chapter 1

Jim looked again. They didn't look like killer's eyes. Brown surrounded by bloodshot white. Pale eyelids that flickered. Shifty, nervous as hell. Yeah, they were hiding something; something dark. But they weren't killer's eyes.

He turned from the mirror. The bedside clock still read six fifty-five a.m. It hadn't changed since his last look. He briefly wondered if it was broke, but digital clocks didn't freeze or go slow. When they break, the display just blanks.

Moving, he sat on the hotel bed. Bouncy. Springs long gone from illicit overuse and age. He knew he shouldn't be feeling like this. It was the first day of his new job for fucks sake. He should be happy. It definitely shouldn't have made him throw up. After all, it was the chance to meet new people. The start of a new adventure.

He wondered if that was the problem with contract killing. The only new people you met, you killed. The display changed. Six fifty-six. Waiting was the problem. No one had mentioned that. It was all glamour, high risk and money. He'd spent last night checking and double checking everything. In hindsight that had been a mistake. There was nothing left to do but wait. Just clock-watching, daydreaming and waiting.

His stomach gurgled. That wasn't helping either. God knows what muscle it was, but it had perfected twisting and spinning. He looked back at the clock. No change. Should he leave now? Despite all the planning, maybe something had been missed.

There was the other reason too. It kept filling his head. The room was too small. Walls everywhere; you couldn't walk without being next to one. It reminded him of the cell. Occasionally the walls would creep in and pin him to the bed. First his hands, then his face would feel hot. He'd need to stand. Opening a window didn't help. He had to get out.

Standing, he shook his head. He had to get a grip. Walking the four steps to the bathroom, he took the top off the toilet cistern. Fishing out the floating polythene zip-bag, he dried it with a towel. His gloved hands fumbled with the seal before it opened. He breathed out while looking at its contents. A pistol wrapped in another waterproof layer. This was it; no turning back.

His hands hacked at the sellotaped seam. The gloves were useless; fingers and thumbs worked against each other trying to rip it. The seam wasn't giving. All that planning and he couldn't unwrap the gun. The walls moved in again. The heat came back with a vengeance to his neck. His armpits felt wet. So much for the earlier shower. The hotel room was just like the cell. Even the windows had bars. It was too much. That was where this had started. That cell.

He'd been inside many times. The last stretch was never the last. It was never his fault though. He'd just been unlucky. His home life hadn't been easy, but that wasn't an excuse. Maybe he'd been too greedy. When the older kids on the estate asked him to sell cigarettes at school, he just hadn't thought it through.

Of course it spiralled. Cigarettes became other things: electrical goods, phones, whatever needed getting rid of. Not just to schoolkids either. After being caught, he didn't take the hint and stop. When school ended, his criminal record saw no other options existed. The only option was to keep selling stolen goods. Caught again and again, he did a stretch in a Young Offenders that turned him from borderline scally to hardened criminal. Release was followed by all he knew: selling stolen goods and more prison.

A lucky break was needed to end the circle.

Picking at the tape he found a seam and peeled. The clock now two minutes to seven, he panicked. This had set him back. It was going to go wrong.

Cursing, he peeled some more. The worst of the tape gone, it rolled off like a banana. The gun exposed, he checked the barrel and silencer; just as he'd wrapped them last week. Though the ammo clip was wrapped, he made short work of it. Snapping the clip home gave a satisfying click. Holding it, he looked in the mirror. For a moment he barely recognised the suited gun-wielder staring back.

The suit looked good. Off the shelf, but still the best he'd ever worn. This was London after all, and he needed to fit in. He looked up the mirror towards his face. His eyes shifty and uncomfortable. Out of their depth. He'd seen enough killers inside to know what their eyes looked like. He looked at them again. Still a touch of innocence. He tried to remember the look; he might not see it again.

As breaks go, Jim wasn't sure if his was lucky or not. His cell mate for the past two years, "Fingers Harry", had changed his life. He didn't know if it was for better or worse.

Despite his size and short-fused temper, Fingers Harry had become a close friend. Jim assumed Harry was missing his son who was destined to grow up fatherless during his twenty-five stretch. Harry had a way of glamourising his life that Jim could listen to for hours. His tales of scrapes kept their spirits up during those lonely nights.

It was that cell and Fingers Harry that changed his life. Gave him his break.

One minute to seven. Jim slipped the gun's safety on and placed it on the bed. Picking up his new shoes he squeezed in his feet. Either his feet had swollen or the shoes had shrunk. Pulling on his coat, the stickiness returned. A thick coat in summer, he'd stand out a mile but he needed the bulk. The gun needed to be hidden inside the bulk. Placing the gun in his pocket, he fastened the coat and walked to the mirror. Did it show through the coat? Was there an outline, a bulge just above his stomach? He closed his eyes and told himself he'd been through this before. The gun couldn't be seen. There wasn't a bulge. His brain was playing tricks.

He told himself again, no one will notice the gun.

Throughout the stretch, Fingers Harry hadn't been happy. One of Harry's relatives had gone down because of a witness. This plucky member of the public had refused to be scared, intimidated or bought off. This, according to Harry, was a very poor show. "After all, what would happen if everyone witnessed crimes and all the criminals were locked up?" Harry would say. "Anarchy, that's what it'd be."

During the lonely nights, Harry wanted one thing: the witness's head. A contract went out and when some lag took the job Jim was amazed by the amount of money. Ten grand. Ten big ones for a few minutes work. Sure, it involved killing, but from what Jim had heard, it was no great loss; the witness would have drunk himself to death anyway. Rumours abounded he hadn't witnessed anything; a bent copper had paid him to lie.

Contract killing seemed so easy.

The clock flicked to seven. He checked his pocket for the keys and money he'd placed there last night. Still there. One last look in the mirror at the suit bulge and he felt ready.

"Gun, keys, money, phone."

Shit. Phone.

He looked at the cabinet crammed between the bed and wall. Sat atop it, next to brochures for museums he'd never visit, was the Pay As You Go mobile. He grabbed and pocketed it.

"Gun, keys, money, phone."

Two deep breaths later, he opened the door.

Over the months, Harry had taught him about contract killing. He'd made it sound so glamorous. On Jim's release he was given a contact, "Pistol Pete", who lived in the Scottish Highlands. Arriving in the northern wastes of nowhere, Jim quickly learnt there was no youth training scheme or apprenticeship for contract killers. All you have is what comes from inside and what you learn on the job. Previous experience wasn't essential, but useful. Jim hadn't killed anyone, but he quickly talked himself into it. After all, how hard could it be? It only took a second.

Pete taught him respect for firearms. Jim favoured the pistol over rifles after realising how hard long range was. Plus, if you missed you lost the target while reloading. Close up was easier, but with ease comes danger. The danger of being caught. The danger of looking into their eyes.

Though the hotel was cheap and cheerful, he'd found the staff were just the former. Emerging from his room, he saw his neighbours walk downstairs. He classed them as both cheap and cheerful, and also too noisy in the bedroom department.

"Hello," she said.

"Morning." Jim took his time locking the door, hoping they'd continue. They didn't.

"Off to breakfast?"

He'd avoided three mornings of breakfast with them by missing it. "No, straight to work today."

They headed down in front of him. Jim wondered if the groaning stairs could carry all their weight and was surprised when they did. The pair attempted conversation at the foot of the stairs, but Jim couldn't do it. His mind was miles away. Far, far away.

Pistol Pete got him a job. A small-time coke dealer named "Bobby the Nose" was owed a small fortune by a city worker. The customer, Geoffrey Morgan, owed far more than he could repay. His reputation in tatters, Bobby the Nose's other customers were taking advantage. A shock to their systems was needed. Jim was offered the job of restoring his reputation. Of course the money Geoffrey owed would be wiped out; unrecoverable. But Bobby's supplier, the source of the coke and who in turn was owed a fortune by Bobby, was a particularly nasty east London gangster. He was more than prepared to take the hit to save their reputations.

Jim had been told little about Geoffrey, bar his name, address and what he looked like. Pistol Pete had said it was easier that way. "It's just a walking lump of flesh," he'd said. "If you don't know them, it doesn't matter." Jim spent many nights convincing himself Pete was right.

Outside, the temperature was rising. The city that half-slept at night was cranking up its speed. Cars, vans and buses going nowhere clogged the streets, while busy, important people walked with determination and purpose. Jim kept his head down and joined them.

Breathing fast, he tried to clear his head. A virgin assassin, that's what he was. Ten minutes until his metaphorical cherry got plucked. What if it went wrong? What would he be? An attempted assassin. No, just a failed assassin.

He stopped. Moving from the curb he leaned against a shuttered chemists.

"Deep breaths," he told himself. "That's what Pete said. Deep breaths."

He checked his watch. Two minutes behind schedule. Sure he had some leeway, but this left no room for further mistakes. With another deep breath he continued. The only important thing was Geoffrey. He'd been following him for four days, spotting patterns in his movements. It was Geoffrey he had to think of.

Geoffrey seemed regular as clockwork. At seven twenty he'd leave his luxury apartment and head for the seven thirty-seven train. He'd walk through the back streets and past the old cinema. Jim had picked the cinema as the quietest place on route. Only a few people took the short cut; those dark corners hid all sorts of low life. Also, as Geoffrey was known for his extravagance and money, Jim hoped it'd look like a mugging gone wrong. The back of the cinema was perfect. The police would think it was a drug related death.

Technically, it would be.

He turned into Market Street. The old cinema apparently disused for years was all but falling down. Its boarded up windows had at some point been breached, and its insides squatted before returning to an empty shell. Walking up the side alley, he stopped at a rubbish-strewn fire exit and knelt behind an upturned cardboard box.

He waited.

He'd been okay while walking. The rhythmic pulse of shoes on tarmac and the tracing in his head of Geoffrey's route had kept him going. Now he could feel his heart pumping. Also his hands, they were shaking. Wiping sweat from his forehead, he breathed in and out. Staring at a damp patch of cardboard, he felt his heart rate reduce.

With only a minute before Geoffrey would walk by, Jim pulled the gun from his pocket. He took another hard look before flicking the safety off. Waiting was the game now.

Waiting.

Chapter 2

As his quarry came into view, Jim's heart rate pumped up again; its bpm resembling a techno record. His stomach gurgled, having wound itself back into the elaborate sailors knot. Taking a deep breath, he saw the face of the thirty-something man approach. This was happening too fast.

He went through the plan. Wait until he was two yards away, jump from cover, one shot to the chest. Bang. Falls down. Another to the head. Bang. Grab his wallet and phone; scarper. Finished. Finito.

That was clear.

What wasn't clear was why Geoffrey had stopped walking. It was less clear why the colour had drained from his face and he was clutching a shaking hand at his chest. As he crashed to the ground, Jim broke cover. Pocketing the gun, he walked to the breathless figure on the floor.

"What's going on?"

Kneeling, he saw Geoffrey struggling for breath. His lips turning blue, he seemed to be saying, "Help."

Jim shook his head. What was he supposed to do? Pistol Pete hadn't crossed this bridge with him. They'd discussed a million things that could go wrong, but never the person you're supposed to kill having what looked like a heart attack. Should he just whip the gun out and finish him off?

He got as far as reaching for his pocket. Another shortcut user; a smart-suited woman screamed as she saw Geoffrey on the floor with Jim kneeling beside. Jim knew he had to think fast. What would Pete say?

His heart now resembling a Drum 'n' Bass record played at 78, Jim's eyes met the woman's. "Help," he croaked. "I think it's a heart attack." Though her screams had stopped, panic had frozen her to the spot. Resembling a frozen turkey in a trouser suit, she opened and closed her mouth but no words came.

That was a setback. He hoped she'd take charge, manage the situation. He appeared to have picked the wrong bunny. This one had got caught in the headlights. Options whirred round his head, but two stood out: Kill her then Geoffrey.

Messy. Second option to save the life of the man he'd been paid to kill.

"Quick," he shouted, "get an ambulance or whatever."

Jim laid Geoffrey's head back in an attempt to make him comfortable. He then did what Pete told him not to do: looked into his eyes.

The hunk of meat, the walking money cheque Jim had persuaded himself Geoffrey was, had become human. A flesh covered and living - well dying - human being. How the fuck could he have thought of killing someone? He was Jim the lad. A crap thief. He wasn't a murderer.

Before his eyes, the woman defrosted from her ice-cage. Fingers and thumbs, she pulled a phone from her pocket. A latest model touch screen. Jim caught himself eyeing it in between saying, "You're going to be alright," to Geoffrey.

"What's the number for an ambulance?" Her cheeks were red and her shoulders seemed to move up and down involuntarily. He guessed it was shock.

"Ummm," said Jim.

Though on the tip of his tongue, the number for the emergency services was hiding somewhere between his teeth. Thinking hard and deep, his mind flicked through his mental phone book. Scanning the A's, he forced himself to concentrate. Eventually, the page found, the number stood out.

"Nine nine nine," he said.

Shaking her head, she pressed the phone screen three times.

Looking at the man he should have killed, Jim noticed a milky film over his eyes. It reminded him of the dull white marbles he'd played with as a kid. His lips now more blue than red, he didn't appear to be breathing. Devoid of anything helpful to do, he undid Geoffrey's top shirt button. He'd seen them do it on *Casualty* so it could only help.

The woman talked into the phone. Jim couldn't hear what, just a wave of soft voice replying to unknown questions. He looked at her again, taking her in this time. Late twenties or early thirties and power-suited. He thought she was good-looking. More than just good-looking. Fresh-looking, yet red-faced from discovering Geoffrey. Her hair stylishly clung to her head with a little patch wiggling down in front of her eyes. She was far-far away from his league, but he could dream. He wondered why he was dreaming when a man lay dying on the floor.

Jim found certain parts of being in prison hard. He figured that was probably half the point, but there was always help at hand. The lack of freedom could be combated through friendship and alcohol. Drugs could be bought, sometimes easier than on the outside. The one thing he couldn't buy was the thing that after three years became an obsession. Female companionship. Sure sex was a large part of that, but there was companionship too. He'd often kid himself he missed companionship the most.

Of course other companionship was available in prison, but Jim wasn't that kind of boy. Not that that mattered to some inmates. He'd seen the hardest, women-loving men turn while inside. They'd turn back again on release, but it was something Jim knew he'd never do. He often wondered if he was facing a twenty-five stretch his mind might see it differently. He hoped he'd never be in that position.

Straight after his release, he'd been whipped off to the Glens to learn his new craft. There'd been no time for carnal pleasures. Of course he'd thought about women, but the deal was clear. Job first, women second. He needed to focus. It would become the reward he'd want above all others. This afternoon, after his hit had been successful, the plan was to hit Soho in a big way.

All his and Pete's plans were crashing and burning. What was much worse was a man was dying, and all he could think about was a mystery woman on a phone.

Geoffrey's facial colour was blending towards purple. Jim knew he had to get this woman out of his head. He'd just messed up a hit, he was carrying a gun in London and soon more people, ambulances and probably the police would arrive.

He breathed in and out three times, as Pete had said.

The woman shuffled forwards and bent down behind Geoffrey, her phone stuck to her ear. Her position afforded Jim a generous view of her generous cleavage. As hard as he tried not to look, he was always going to fail.

Three more breaths.

"His face looks purple and it doesn't look like he's breathing," she said, her voice growing stronger. He looked back at Geoffrey. His face seemed to be changing colour by the second. Before long he'd look like a radish in a suit. Jim reached towards Geoffrey's throat and undid another button. Again, it had to help.

As he reached for the button, the gun in his pocket bounced off his chest. Paranoia hit. Could she see the outline of the pistol this close up? He knew it couldn't be seen in the mirror, but he was kneeling down; his coat would have changed shape. Maybe it was hugging his body differently. He could see down her top, so maybe she could see down his? He pulled his coat tighter and moved his elbow, trying to cover his chest.

"Can you check his airways?" she asked.

Jim double checked she was talking to him and not the phone. She was. He looked at her face and thought through what she'd said three times before it made sense. Shrugging, he moved his gloved hands towards Geoffrey's mouth. He saw her frown. The gloves. Leather gloves and an overcoat in June?

Pushing Geoffrey's purple-brown lips apart, Jim pushed a finger in his warm mouth. Though he had gloves on, having his finger in someone's mouth still made him gag.

Looking up, he nodded. "Tongue's okay."

"Is he breathing?"

She was closer now, kneeling just behind Geoffrey's head with her handbag beside her. Sitting upright and with a good posture, he realised she was younger than he'd thought. Or maybe she just spent a lot on anti-aging products. Either way, she was good-looking. He knew three years inside could cloud taste buds, but no, she really was good-looking.

Coyly protecting the gun with his free arm, he moved his head towards Geoffrey's mouth and listened. The traffic noise and early morning bustle filled his ears, but he couldn't hear breathing. Holding his own breath and blocking the surrounding noise out, he waited for what felt like minutes until his lungs burned. Nothing. No breathing, just nothing. The sound of nothing.

Moving up, his face inches from hers, he looked into her eyes. Green and blues fought in random; swirly patterns. Moving away, he saw tears at their corners. He shook his head; the words wouldn't come out.

"I don't think he's breathing," she stuttered. She nodded her head in reply to something the phone said. "The ambulance should be here soon." That was definitely meant for Jim. "Here, hold this." After putting the phone on speaker, she handed it to him.

Looking at it like a charged hand grenade, he held it at distance. Three years ago, hell three weeks ago, the offer of a free phone would have had him running. Her handbag was so near too. She was practically begging him to rob her.

Moving so she was on Geoffrey's right hand side, she leant towards his chest.

"Okay, what do I do," she shouted at the phone

"Form your hands over his left breast and make four compressions," the phone said.

Sat there lemon-like, he watched for five minutes as she gave chest compressions. Jim's only movement was to grab her handbag nearer as another city worker walked by, apparently oblivious to them. He wasn't sure if he was protecting her bag or making sure no one else had it.

During those long minutes, Jim watched in awe as she defrosted further. She'd coped better than himself. He knew he had his mouth open and couldn't close it. The bunny in the headlights had become a cool, city kitty.

Sat there, minding a phone and handbag containing God knows how many gold credit cards along with its plethora of lipsticks and tissues, Jim knew the odds were on him doing a runner.

He didn't.

Chapter 3

The five-minute wait for the ambulance dragged. Jim held the phone throughout, his palms sweating as the morning sun heated his gloves. He heard the siren long before he saw the ambulance. Traffic was backing up and mounting kerbs to let it pass, but all the time she kept up her rhythmical massage.

The ambulance on scene, the first paramedic rushed towards them, green bag in hand. Swiftly joined by the driver, Jim watched the scene unfold while still holding the bloody phone and keeping an arm and eye on the handbag. The paramedics took over the massage and applied an oxygen mask to Geoffrey.

The woman, who introduced herself to the paramedics as Charlotte, knelt back to give them room as they continued doing the impossible. As she wiped tears from her eyes, Jim moved towards her holding out her phone and handbag. The cool city kitty, confident in her job as lifesaver was fading fast. She took her phone, but shaking hands struggled to place it in the bag.

The chest compressions continued as the other paramedic got a stretcher from the ambulance. In the space of a hectic minute, Jim helped them put Geoffrey on the stretcher before they wheeled him into the ambulance, continuing the heart massage the whole time. In itself, he found it a spectacle to watch.

As the ambulance roared into heavy traffic, Jim found himself and Charlotte standing by the old cinema, a crowd of onlookers staring at them. Jim placed a hand on her shoulder. "Thanks." He'd no idea what he was thanking her for. Turning her mascara-blotted cheeks towards him, she attempted a smile and nodded.

As the crowds dispersed, Jim noticed she was still shaking. He guessed it was shock. He knew he was shaking himself so asked if she was alright.

"Yeah, I'm." She paused. "I'll be fine."

"Do you want to get a tea or coffee or something. You know, help calm down?"

She nodded and they walked through the thinning crowd towards a coffee shop.

Jim queued on wobbly legs as she went to the toilet to check and possibly redo her make-up. His head buzzed with adrenalin and failure as he looked round. The place was unlike any cafe he'd ever seen. Comfy couches, low tables and the fresh smell of roasted coffee beans played with his senses. It reminded him more of a New York coffee shop than a south of the river cafe. Three years inside felt like ten the way things had changed.

Approaching the front of the queue, Charlotte emerged from the toilet looking heavily made-up. She took a comfy single-seat chair and waved. He waved back, unable to stop himself smiling.

She'd asked for a double-shot frappuccino with caramel, but Jim's mind and legs were all over the place so her order got lost in a series of internal Chinese whispers. Ordering something similar, he chose tea for himself.

"Camomile, green or rose petal?" the heavily suntanned server asked.

"Just tea. Just a cup of normal tea," he replied.

As the drinks were made Jim noticed Charlotte on her phone. She was either ringing the police to tell them he'd a gun and had kidnapped her, or she was ringing work to explain why she was late. The way things had turned out, he was past caring. Despite Pete's training, seeing what'd happened had shaken him.

After paying over six pounds for two drinks, his head joined his hands in shaking as he took them to the table. Charlotte, fully made-up, had regained her attractiveness, yet she'd never really lost it. Even with blotchy panda eyes and smears down both cheeks, she'd turn heads at twenty yards. Jim decided she was definitely early thirties rather than old and the product of a vat of magic youth cream. Also, she was good at talking. Very good. Within five minutes he found out she worked for some American investment bank on the Mergers and Acquisitions desk, whatever that was, she'd been divorced for three years and had a cat called Bilbo named after *The Lord of the Rings* character. He was more than glad she'd taken the lead. His mind didn't feel like stretching itself or searching for small talk. When she asked what he did for a living he paused.

"I err, work for the government, civil service, you know." His cover had been a clerk at the Office for National Statistics. Recently moved to London, he'd spent the last five years at its offices first in Northumberland then Wales. In a split second he'd decided to use his cover. He could hardly tell the truth.

She nodded, looked genuinely interested. "Whereabouts do you work?"

"Erm, Whitehall." He didn't know if people even worked in Whitehall or if they ever had. Her face remained its pale, yet smiley same so he presumed he hadn't dropped a clanger. "Where's your bank?" he asked, hoping she hadn't already told him during her earlier tirade.

Luckily, she hadn't.

Over the next five minutes she talked about the Docklands, the credit crunch - apparently it wasn't her fault - and the university she'd been to as Jim sipped his sugary tea. Her world of finance and London living was intriguing and alien, so he didn't have to feign interest. He did wish though, that she'd talk slower. Or occasionally pause.

Finishing her coffee, she wiped her lips with a serviette. "I need to get going. I rang work, told them what happened, but there's only so much sympathy isn't there?"

Jim nodded. She paused and smiled before standing up.

Usually useless at reading signs, he wasn't sure if that was one. Should he ask for her number? Considering his reason for being in London and what had happened he knew he shouldn't. But he was helpless; something other than his common sense was in charge.

"Can I have your number?"

Her smile grew. "Yeah of course." Reaching into her handbag she pulled out her phone. "Ready?"

Jim pulled the cheap mobile from his pocket, but even with the steadiest of nerves his fingers would have struggled to operate it. "Sorry, I'm useless with these."

"Here." She took it from his hand, and typed furiously. "I'll add myself as a contact."

Jim shivered at the thought of her going through the phone. He'd never used it, had never even typed a number in, but he was certain she'd find something. Something that would give him away. Feeling his face redden, he waited for the inevitable.

"I'll ring mine; make sure I've put it in right." She pressed some keys then her phone sprang into life, playing the start of Abba's "Dancing Queen". Handing back the phone, she fiddled with hers again before returning it to her handbag.

"Well, thanks then."

"Thank you," she replied as she left.

It was half nine in the morning, and he was a failed assassin with a loaded gun in his pocket. There was only one option: get drunk. The leftovers of his three-grand advance were running low. Just under four hundred left, stashed at the hotel. Supposedly, it was for tonight's Soho blow-out. Well, fuck it, he'd nothing to celebrate now, but the money could buy drinks. God only knows what was happening after that. The seven grand in used twenties he should be picking up wasn't going to happen. As of midday tomorrow, he'd be homeless, penniless and hotel-less.

The gun dug in his side with each footstep, reminding him it was there, almost begging him to use it. You don't have to shoot anyone, it was saying, just point it at a bank clerk or a few city workers. Get their wallets and move on. Easy, it was saying. It's so easy.

"Nothing's easy."

Despite the hotel receptionists' surprise at seeing him back, she smiled and told him the cleaner would probably be in his room. Luckily, the cleaner had been and gone. Removing the gun from his pocket, he froze when he realised the safety was off. Slumping to the bed, he retraced every footstep and movement. The gun could have gone off at any point killing himself, Charlotte or anyone else. Jim shook his head. Unloading and rewrapping it in the zip-lock bag, he replaced it in the toilet cistern. Returning to the bed, he removed the gloves and let his hands breathe for the first time in days.

Smiling, he thought what a waste all the effort had been. Geoffrey had had the last laugh. He'd probably ruined his life too.

He'd been trying to ignore something on the way back, but it kept popping back into his head. Had Geoffrey survived? He hoped so, but also realised if he was alive the contract might still be active. Would he be expected to kill someone he'd just saved? That would be cruel.

His thirst for alcohol and Soho had waned. Taking a bath seemed a better and cheaper option. Four hundred quid had to last the rest of his life. A life he knew couldn't involve contract killing. It just wasn't him. He couldn't do it.

After a long soak, he lazily dressed and went for a walk. Completely avoiding the cinema, he instead headed for the river then the city. Walking for hours, it surprised him just how big London was. Most of his travelling had been underground, so he'd formed a mental image of every landmark and station being fifty yards from the next. The bustling reality was so different.

For the last four days he'd followed Geoffrey via tube to his workplace. Both the city and its financial heart were alien to what he'd grown up in. Raised on the outskirts of Coventry Jim knew city life, but the city blitzed by the Luftwaffe was worlds apart from the capital. Jim knew all of Coventry's estates, both upper and lower class. In London he was lost. The financial heart, the place he'd followed Geoffrey to each day, felt like the only place he knew. He couldn't convince himself he belonged anywhere, but the skyscrapers, wall to wall bistros and bustle of expensively suited workers drew him like a magnet.

Crossing Tower Bridge, he hugged the river passing London's highlights before reaching Canary Wharf. His legs ached; he didn't dare think how many miles he'd walked as he found a bench outside the Gherkin and sat down.

Studying life as it passed, it didn't take him long to remember why he hated the city and its workers. It wasn't just because they'd ruined the country. The whole area stank of money, both inherited and newly created. It wasn't a good smell. Not a healthy, wealthy smell, but a vile odour of greed and backstabbing to make more money. He knew people all over the country were destitute, some nearly starving. They spent their days in damp, overcrowded houses living off microwave chips and special brew with no hope of change. But these bastards. They wasted other people's money on flash clothes, lifestyles, drugs and champagne. And when they messed up, who was it that bailed them out? Normal working taxpayers like himself.

He paused. Remembering he'd never paid any tax, he reconsidered his rant. The injustice was there though. The greed and expectations of others to sort your bad times and let you keep the good times angered him. They'd gone back to paying bonuses already even before the problems were sorted.

Remembering his own youth, and how his mum had struggled to bring him and his sister up angered him further. They had nothing but each other but unlike the *cliché*, they weren't happy. Fucking miserable most of the time. Would things have been different if they'd had money? He wasn't sure.

Looking up and tracing the towers stretching to the sky, he pondered it all. He'd been here the past few days, scouting round, becoming invisible and trying to spot a corner that wasn't covered by cameras. Trying to find a murder spot.

Today he'd seen it differently. Time and a need to push away this morning's failure had shown him the true city. The brown stinky stuff it ran on.

He thought back to what he'd nearly done. What he'd nearly become. How could he have put himself in that position. Killing someone. How had he accepted killing another human being? And for money too. Surely he'd become worse than his quarry. He'd become the underworld equivalent of a merchant banker. And he didn't need Fingers Harry to tell him what that was slang for.

Disgusted, he left his bench and headed for the tube. His destination east, in search of a proper pub and proper people.

Chapter 4

Four tube stops was enough to rid him of the city and enter the relative warmth of the under-city. The Queens Arms was the nearest pub to the tube and possibly the only pub left in east London where you could still smoke, drink a warm pint and have a fight with a builder. Half deserted at lunch time, he approached the bar.

"Yeah?" said the barman.

"Pint of best."

Pulling a chipped glass from under the bar, the barman pulled the pint, avoiding eye contact. In jeans and t-shirt, Jim felt he fitted this part of London more than the city, but he wasn't known. He could be anyone from anywhere and this was a local's pub. Occupants of local's pubs never welcomed newcomers; they always looked for an ulterior motive. Jim just wanted a drink and the company of others. Earning their trust was the first step.

Paying half the price he would have four tube stops earlier, he took the pint and sat on a bench near the pool table. Two builders, probably a plasterer and chippy, playing pool nodded at him. Jim nodded back and took in the rest of the bar.

The pub was old. He reckoned the term rising damp had been invented with this pub in mind. It had been built a hundred years ago and redecorated only a few times since. Two pensioners with red noses and half-pint pots sat round a rickety table reading their papers, occasionally stopping to moan about foreigners. An old television above them beamed out racing from Chepstow through a dust-covered grille. The barman sat on a high stool pretending to wash glasses while he fiddled with his mobile phone. At the end of the bar a family of flies hovered over stale cheese sandwiches sweating in a Tupperware box.

Taking a glug from his pint, he rested it on a ripped beer mat. Breathing deeply, he pulled out the fags he'd bought earlier. Despite no smoking signs everywhere the whole pub was at it, including the barman. Even the flies seemed to be enjoying the second-hand smoke.

He'd been to east London before, though not this pub. After getting friendly with a few people inside, they visited London on release five or six years ago. The intent of the trip was mugging tourists. After all, they didn't think it fair that London's thieves got to bag all the American's and Jap's wallets. No one ever visited Coventry on sightseeing tours. The lads from the provinces should be given a chance. They'd booked into a cheap guest house further up the road, drunk themselves stupid in a West End pub then bottled it when it came to the actual robbing. Though he returned with less than he came with, he still remembered it as a good night.

"Wanna play the winner, mate?" asked the plasterer. He'd more plaster on his clothes than any walls he'd ever been near.

"Yeah, go on then." Jim flicked a sausage-shaped lump of ash from his fag and waited for one of them to lose.

Five hours, six pints and two cheese sandwiches later he left the pub. Though a tense start to the game of pool, the atmosphere soon defrosted. After Jim had bought a round of drinks, the plasterer and chippy opened up with questions and jokes flying round. It turned out Jim had been in Hewell Prison the same time as the chippy, though neither recognised the other. Jim tended to keep his head down when doing a stretch but the chippy, a serial grievous bodily harmer known as "Tim by Four", was a more social inmate. Their joking and shared stories about the screws, prison food and Fatty Fred's shower room antics had the desired effect. By the time he left he'd forgotten all about Geoffrey, Charlotte and contract killing. For some reason, he didn't know why, this pub felt like home, or the nearest thing to it in London.

Squinting as he re-entered daylight, he walked along the road remembering the fun he'd had in London last time. He reckoned it was the nearest he'd ever come to a lad's holiday. Of course they all lost contact. Most of them, like himself, ended up back inside within a few months.

He found himself walking towards the guest house. He'd never have found it on a map, but his subconscious seemed to know the way. Soon finding it, he looked the place up and down. Tired, peeling paint coated in city grime. The curtains hadn't been washed, the sign was still missing a H from House, and the "Vacancies Tonight" sign hung in the window where it seemed destined to spend its life.

Maybe he could stay here a while. He couldn't go home. Having broken his parole terms, all the usual coppers would be queuing up to put him away. This had to be cheaper than the hotel. Of course, he needed money to pay for it, but he reckoned he could get by. He'd find the right contacts, he always did. Yeah, maybe he could. The Queens Arms seemed like a good pub, the builders friendly enough too. Stay here a while, under the radar, make some money then move on.

He sighed. It wouldn't work. Perhaps he should just give himself up now. What was the point of waiting for that knock on the door. They'd find him. He could go back inside and serve another year. At least then he could go home. Not that there was anything in Coventry for him.

He turned back to the road. A Range Rover with blacked-out windows pulled up, its back window level with him. The eighty-grand car stood out immediately. From the corner of his eye, Jim noticed people looking. A few even dived into the nearest shop.

He stood rooted to the spot as a large, absolutely huge man with a crooked nose and gold teeth stepped out. Catching Jim's eye, he nodded for him to get in the back.

In Jim's experience of big blokes asking you to get into cars, he'd discovered it was best to do as he was told. After all, if they wanted to hurt you, they'd just hurt you. They wouldn't ask you to get in the car first. As far as Jim could see, someone wanted to talk to him. Someone who drove expensive cars and hired seven-foot thugs.

He thought he knew who it was.

He sat in the back next to the big-muscled lump as the Range Rover sped off. In front, sitting next to the equally large driver was a small, wiry man. Gold bracelets and cufflinks told his wealth in case it had been overlooked. His suit not Burtons or Top Man, but made to measure. The scent of expensive aftershave soured the air.

The man turned, his well-tanned face not via spray can or sunbed. "Well." He spoke in a quiet, measured tone. "That didn't go to plan, did it?"

Although a question, Jim knew it didn't need answering. Questions like that didn't. It said shut up and listen. "You see, I'm in an awkward position after what happened." He spoke confidently and fast, as if reading from a script. "I believe our contract was three thousand up front with another seven on completion. Now, I know the circumstances surrounding this morning's events. It's been on the fucking radio all day; you could hardly miss it. Fact is, he's alive."

Jim felt relief leap across his face. He knew this wasn't a smiling occasion but was unable to stop his muscles forming a grin. Clenching his fists and biting his bottom lip, he hoped the smile hadn't been noticed.

"Now of course he's on life support, but even if he does die it doesn't get the message across I paid for. You see," he turned back to the road, "I'm a businessman. I take risks. Calculated risks. The credit crunch has hit us all hard you know. Certain decisions and risks had to be taken. Writing off twenty gees with another ten in costs may sound foolish, but it was necessary to release other funds I'm owed. Funds that I need urgently for an ..." He paused. "An opportunity."

Jim knew that despite this man loving the sound of his voice he wasn't someone you could actually talk to. You couldn't criticise or disagree. Just yes, yes, yes. Whatever he needed the money for, and it didn't bear thinking about, Jim knew he'd messed up the plan.

"You see," he continued, "the interesting world of accountancy has a term called the opportunity cost. To me, the opportunity cost of everyone paying me now offset, in quite a large way, the cost of employing you. By our mutual friend having a heart attack, I now have to reconsider my plans. In short, the opportunity I've missed has cost me."

Jim nodded. He hadn't said a word since getting in the car and they seemed to be halfway across London already. The traffic, usually gridlocked, seemed to part in their path.

"Now to the nitty-gritty. In my opinion, and obviously you're entitled to yours, but my opinion is you should have finalised the contract yesterday. You watched him for two days and did nothing. For all I know today was a trial run too. I have no proof of that, but as I say, in my opinion, it should have been yesterday."

He had a point. Jim himself would admit he'd made too many dry runs. He'd struggled with the physical part of killing. The theory was easy - pull the trigger - but the practise? He'd bottled it yesterday. At the last minute he left the gun in the toilet. Somewhere inside, he knew he'd have bottled it today. Tomorrow too.

The car went silent. This was where it got nasty. He took a deep breath, and tried to prepare for what was coming.

"The result is this. I believe I'm owed money from you. The three you were advanced and also an amount for, well for want of a better term, compensation for the loss of opportunity. As I say, feel free to voice your own opinion on this."

He turned round and looked back. Jim found his head nodding and his mouth saying, "I agree."

Turning back to the front, he continued, "I'm glad we're in agreement. Under different circumstances we could have enjoyed a successful business relationship for many years. However, things weren't to be, were they?" He paused again. "Anyway, how about we make it a round ten? That's three for the advance and another seven for the loss of opportunity."

Jim nodded again. Of course it wasn't a question. The man in front wasn't expecting an answer, and had neither turned nor looked in the mirror.

"Good. Now, I'm a reasonable man and as time is no longer of the essence, you'll want some time to sort your affairs out. Shall we say payment is due this time next week?"

Again, not a question. Again, Jim nodded.

"If you plan on leaving London, please let me know in advance. Ralph will give you a card. Please only ring from a call box, not a mobile. They're so insecure these days."

Jim thought the ogre next to him was more a Knuckles or a Harry than a Ralph. Still this funny old world took all sorts.

The Range Rover skidded to a halt at the kerb. Ralph exited then held the door open. As Jim got out, Ralph pushed a business card into his hand. Not looking at either the card or Ralph's eyes, Jim pocketed it and started walking.

He appeared to be near Westminster beside the Thames. For a summer's early evening, it made for a pleasant if highly polluted setting. Unfortunately, there was nothing pleasant in Jim's head, it having been fried both by the thought of owing ten grand and also by a knuckle scraper called Ralph.

He stopped at the railings and took a deep breath.

"Where am I gonna get ten big ones?"

His phone rang.

Checking the display, it showed his one and only contact. Charlotte.

Chapter 5

Charlotte could talk. After five minutes he had both a hot ear and a detailed breakdown since she'd left the coffee shop. She'd gone to work, but hadn't done much having spent the day either talking or searching the internet for news on Geoffrey. As Ralph's boss had pointed out, it had been a big news story. She told him the term "two mystery city workers" had appeared regularly when describing them. On reflection, Jim thought someone helping a stranger in London was big news. A community spirit long gone had made a temporary return. Charlotte was so obviously buzzing after her good act that her voice and brain were speeding away. In other circumstances Jim may have felt the same. But he needed ten grand in a week. And his plans had gone up the swanny when his new life failed. She was the only person he knew in London. And, he had to find ten grand in a week.

He couldn't.

Could he?

When her first pause came, he made an effort to speak before she restarted. "I didn't go to work."

"Right," she said. Her opening tirade finished, he felt she was giving him time to respond.

"I don't know." He'd never been good at thinking on his toes. Besides, he'd taken in so much this past hour his mind was chucking stuff back out. "I just didn't feel up to it."

"Right," she replied. "I needed to go in, I mean I probably could have worked from home. They set up a home office last year in case of tube strikes or well, the other strikes, you know, terrorist ones. Anyway, I've got a deal ongoing with a client in the Emirates and you know Arabs, they don't like half measures. Everything's got to be done right. It's important for them that they hear the trading floor in the background. I mean, I'm stood there, trying to get Gerald opposite me to make as much noise as possible and ..."

Jim stopped listening. Her attempt to give him time to word his sentences was very noble but she was obviously too pumped up to come down to his level. There was far too much noise in his brain for this. Was she nervous and this a release? Or was this a normal London thing? Either way his psychology skills were worse than his thinking skills so he conceded defeat.

Trying to picture her stood on the platform waiting for her train, iPhone crammed to her ear alongside all the other lonely people, he wondered why and when London had become so unfriendly. They all had so much in common yet they'd be in isolation, almost scared of talking. What a city. What a shite city.

"... but it's only because my sister moved out, she's getting married again next summer by the way, but I had to get rid of the car. I mean, I'm far too old to be sharing flats these days. And after the divorce, money's been tight ever since. I'm sure you know what I mean. The cost of living in London's terrible isn't it? I've got a friend in ..."

Why, he thought, why is she talking to me about money? It's got to be a nervous thing. Maybe Geoffrey nearly dying had pushed her near the edge. They say death or near death does that. How near the edge was she? Or, how close was she before?

"... but after she came back from Peru all her flatmate's stuff had gone. This flatmate had just cleared off in the middle of the night and not paid two months rent. She'd taken her espresso machine too, which Jenny said was meaner than not paying the rent. I've got this other friend, Katie, she ..."

Definitely nerves. In Jim's slightly drunk and sex-starved view of the world, he thought maybe a few bottles of wine and male company could cure her nervous disorder. If he got a word in edgeways, he'd ask. Nothing too heavy. Just meet for a drink. After all, she must live near the hotel, she was going towards the same tube as Geoffrey.

Of course there was a problem. He couldn't meet her, he was already drunk, though the drive in the Range Rover had done a fantastic job of sobering him. Also, he was wearing his casual, scummy clothes which transformed him back to the no-good scrote he was.

Maybe he could meet her later. She was waiting for a train; he could go back to the hotel for a quick shower and a change of clothes. Considering his recent business dealings with the East End entrepreneur, he could do with being sidetracked.

She never paused long enough for him to suggest it. After what may have been ten minutes, she got on her train. To his surprise, the one-sided conversation continued another twenty minutes. She'd barely stopped talking as she got on and tried to find a seat.

As her train rattled on and Jim watched the river peacefully, she at last appeared to be nearing a natural pause. Whether she'd run out of things to say, or thought she ought to include him wasn't clear. Her sudden question, "Where do you come from?" caught him by surprise. His head was so fried he was unsure whether to use his carefully thought out cover, or his own, real and murky past.

"I was born near Coventry." It wasn't a lie.

"Really," she continued, "I used to know someone from Warwick when I was at college. That's quite near, isn't it? Like most friends at college we lost touch. What brought you to London?"

The truth felt good while it lasted, though it was just one short sentence. "After college I moved to Northumberland to work for the Office of National Statistics. A few years ago they moved me to Newport in Wales. Then, six months ago, the chance to move here came. You know, I thought, come to London, make a million, get out of small town life. You know, hit the capital."

"Doesn't really work like that does it?"

Watching a particularly rowdy launch boat go by, Jim looked at the Houses of Parliament then the luxury flats south of the river. "They've put me up in a hotel at the moment, until I can find somewhere to rent."

"Finding somewhere decent is so hard isn't it? I mean ..."

And she was off.

As the train reached her stop so she could change to the tube, they said goodbye. Curiously, Jim thought it was a very quick goodbye considering the length of the call. There'd also been no mention of future calls or contact. Again, curious. He expected at least, "I'll ring you tomorrow," or maybe even a pause so he could ask her out. But nothing.

Starting the long walk back to the hotel, Jim wagged his hot ear trying to clear his head.

How do you make ten grand in a week?

The waiting and wonder of Charlotte's swift entry and disappearance was soon over. A text message buzzed onto his phone less than half an hour after her call. He retrieved it with a smile.

We've just been on news again; they called us mystery heroes :)

Though disappointed by the smiley, he was glad there was no *lol* or *omg*. He wasn't quite sure what either of them meant. The whole mobile phone and texting phenomenon had passed him by on his last stretch. Everyone seemed to have sprouted a phone from their forearm and be constantly sending and receiving messages. What was so important that had to be read there and then? He didn't get it. If you had something to say, something important, why not ring?

He reconsidered. If your name's Charlotte then a text is fine. Pausing midway across Lambeth Bridge, his drunken, chubby fingers took ages to type the small phrase, *Thanks. I'll put telly on.*

The rapid car journey, his newly acquired ten-grand debt and Charlotte's earbashing had made five pints feel like two. As a preferred method of sobering up, he'd take strong coffee any day. Despite being a memorable day, it had to be his worst ever. Perhaps more alcohol was needed. Evening was drawing in and he'd walked miles, yet he felt more awake than ever.

Thinking again of Charlotte, sat opposite him in the coffee shop, talking to him, apparently enjoying his company, he shook his head. What was going on?

After walking the final mile to the hotel, he went to his room for a wash before dinner. He was hungry. Two cheese sandwiches and miles of walking left you empty, but he'd gone through and out the other side of hunger. Still, evening dinner was included in the price so at the very least he'd waste it to get his money's worth.

Before leaving his room, he paused. The couple next door didn't sound like they were in. He really hoped they weren't in the dining room. He could picture it now. "Oh, come and join us, you must join us." He didn't need a couple of randy middle-aged probable swingers talking to him while he ate his pie and chips. He decided if they were in the restaurant he would about turn and walk out, and find a burger joint or fish and chip shop, if such things existed in London.

They weren't in the dining room. Relieved, he sat at the lonely one-chaired table that had loser written all over it. Surrounded by travelling salesmen, conference attendees and even the odd holidaymaker who'd booked on the cheap, they were a pitiful combination. Jim had no previous experience of budget hotels, but he'd bet his granny they were all like this. Soulless, yet functional beds for the travelling fraternity with a tasteless meal added. Looking again at his co-dinees, a forty-something balding man, a thirty-something receding man and a couple of jolly looking holidaymakers, the male not having the fullest head of hair, he wondered if the hotel offered a discount for the follicly challenged.

He sipped the tap water provided. No doubt they'd let the water stand all night so people would instead buy their vinegarish house red. Gazing at the other diners who had hair, he wondered if any of them owed ten thou to an East End wannabe Kray brother. No, they were all spoon salesmen, insurance execs and yokels from the sticks visiting head office and sampling the finest Soho had to offer while their wives thought they were in late meetings.

Soho.

He should have been there now, blowing a fortune on coke, hookers and champagne. A night of celebration after a hard day. The first contract would have led to another then another. Pretty soon he'd have made enough to quit. He could have bought a farmhouse somewhere in Devon and made goat's cheese or grown organic vegetables or some shite. There was supposed to be no more buying and selling. That had ended. No ripping off old ladies, either. Or young ones. No ripping off city workers. No ripping off youngish city divorcees who talk a lot.

No ripping off Charlotte.

Shaking his head, he sighed and looked at the kitchen. The saloon-style swing doors revealed a waitress attempting to carry four plates at once. Whether she was trying to look professional or was just lazy wasn't clear. Offloading her plates of brownish stew at two tables, she returned to the kitchen for more. Beef stew in summer? Jim wondered what delights their winter menu would contain. The waitress returned with a plate for him and a short grunt. He thanked her and asked for a drink.

"The bar's open." She walked away.

He worried the stew with his fork, but ate less than he thought he would. Ten grand wasn't very appetising and though he'd tried to push it aside, it was always there niggling away in his brain's trying-to-forget compartment. Every five minutes or so it would return and remind him he was in the shit.

Leaving the restaurant, he headed for the bar and ordered a pint of flat beer. Quietly supping it at a table, the only other noticeable drinker was a sharp-dressed city worker talking loudly on his mobile about profit projections. He was so obviously booked into the wrong hotel it was embarrassing. Hidden in the shadows was another balding forty-something civil servant or executive. Jim considered going over and introducing himself, but that would mean talking pretend shop and he knew he wasn't good company. The guy didn't look too interesting either. He looked happy alone and in the shadows.

He finished the pint in three long mouthfuls; the city worker was really that embarrassing to listen too. Leaving the glass on the bar, he went upstairs.

Next door were still out which was a small blessing. A lack of anything to do, and the dull headache he recognised to be an evening hangover made him switch the telly on.

Geoffrey was indeed mentioned on the London news. Jim again put it down to London's lack of humanity that it could be newsworthy. Like a talking dog or a town mayor who's walking backwards for charity, the item made the light-hearted part at the end of the program, just after the daily count of murders and muggings. In a short, ten-second piece, showing file film of a hospital, the reporter did indeed refer to them as mystery heroes and good Samaritans. Apparently, Geoffrey was recovering well and Jim thought no doubt looking forward to his next line of coke.

Sighing again, he channel-hopped. Avoiding soaps and documentaries, he found the film channel. An old action film was on with the swearing and killings dubbed out to convert it into a PG. This proved a distraction as he lay on his bed, willing sleep to come.

Chapter 6

The text message startled him. He'd been drifting off, his mind in some film-inspired daydream. Accessing the message, *Just had my tea; burnt the pasta lol,* he wondered again what the fuck was going on. Maybe she was lonely. She must be to send complete strangers details of her culinary disasters. Jim wondered just what she'd be doing now. She'd probably be in her luxury flat sat on some hugely comfortable fluffy sofa with her legs tucked under her. An explosion of cushions would surround her; maybe her cat was asleep on one of them. Fresh from the shower she'd be in a dressing gown applying polish to her nails, or maybe plucking at her thin eyebrow strands in front of a mirror. There'd be a documentary on the television, but she wouldn't really be watching it. Her mind would be thinking of tomorrow's meetings or who to send a text to.

Jim sighed as he typed, *Bet it was better than mine. We had beef stew.*

Now fully awake and with the time nine o'clock, the rest of the night lay in front. While inside, he'd been waiting for this evening. Three years of pent-up frustration that should be being released had been cancelled. The moment had gone.

He thought again of Charlotte. Alone in her flat, surrounded by the trappings of luxury. What would ten grand be to her? A month, two months wages? It couldn't be far from that. After tax, rent and everything else he supposed it would be nearer six. It could be even more. He'd heard of these Londoners supposedly on huge wages, but after removing the cost of living in London they were poorer than a Glaswegian bouncer.

He couldn't do it anyway. That caring woman who'd overturned all sense of London tradition by helping someone; she didn't deserve what he was thinking. Their chance meeting shouldn't lead to her having a broken heart or wallet.

Beef stew. Omg. What sort of hotel is it? her text said.

He smiled but knew she'd come to her senses. Today had been a huge shock; her mind hadn't rationally dissected what she was doing. The messages would end tomorrow. He knew that. And then he'd really be alone.

It's not the Ritz that's for sure, he replied.

Lol, her quick reply.

They'd end tomorrow. Definitely. She was good-looking though. He remembered once more looking at her face in the coffee shop while she sipped that coffee and milk mutation. Clear complexion, confident. He also remembered the horror on her face as she saw Geoffrey, the tears when she thought he was dead.

She'd got in his brain. Nothing was going to happen between them, it couldn't. She'd come to her senses tomorrow. Even if she didn't, how long could he keep up the pretence? How long before he slipped up? All she had to do was ask him a question about statistics and he was a goner. No, this ended tomorrow.

In the meantime, he needed sleep. Though his head was in full hangover mode, his mind was whirring. Sleep was far away.

Alcohol was the answer. Lots of it. Picking up a jumper, he headed downstairs. The bar was similar to before: quiet, brightly lit and impossible to relax in. The city boy had scarpered, probably to more livelier surroundings and the balding civil servant had also gone to wherever those creatures go at night. The only drinker was a suited and well-rounded middle-aged man reading the evening paper. The restaurant waitress was also sitting at the bar sipping from a bright red bottle of alcopop, while the barman wiped glasses with his towel occasionally making conversation with her.

Armed with a pint and a scotch, he took the far table. His neighbours still hadn't appeared. Jim didn't like to think what or who they were up to. Downing the scotch in one, he shuddered as its fiery goodness burned. Sipping the pint, he looked again at the barman and waitress.

She was totally absorbed in her phone, fiddling with buttons while he occasionally whistled or strutted like a peacock round the short bar area. His obvious attempts to impress her lost while she sent or received messages. "Are you going out over the weekend?" he asked her. She shook her head as a reply, her eyes not leaving the phone.

Jim pulled his own phone from his pocket. His eyes cloudy, from both the long day and drink, he scanned through the phone menus. He wondered again what made these little things such coveted gadgets. Soon enough his brain on autopilot commanded his chubby fingers to open a new text.

Having a drink in bar. His thumb hovered over the send button. It's over tomorrow, he told himself. Maybe, just maybe, the mention of a drink might force something before she realises what's going on. He pressed send. If she replied saying she could do with a drink, he'd ask her out.

Placing the phone down, he looked back round the bar. The barman was trying a different track to his chatting up, while the girl typed some unfeasibly long message.

Taking another glug from his pint, his fingers started itching. Pubs did that to him. A drink needed to be accompanied by a smoke, and they'd banned smoking in pubs just before he'd last gone down. He'd been amazed when he came out by the amount of beer gardens and alleyways converted to smoking dens. Even the smallest pub where once there was just a car parking space now had a lean-to or open-sided shed crammed full of smoking drinkers while the pub itself was empty. Draining his pint he headed to the bar for a top-up. The barman was still fighting a losing battle and after Jim paid for the drink, he headed for the open fire exit which contained the helpful sign, "Beer garden this way".

The tiny tarmacadamed courtyard was surrounded by a high brick wall. Rubbish bins and a skip stood in one corner, with a weather-beaten plastic white table opposite. Placing his glass on the table, it wobbled, one of the legs being badly bent. Sighing, he moved the glass to the opposite side and sat on a plastic chair under the hole-ridden umbrella.

His phone next to the pint glass, he willed it to buzz or even ring. The first scotch and pint were turning the hangover into a thick head. He sighed and rolled his head round his shoulders as he pulled out a cigarette. The ciggy lit, he exhaled loudly and leant back. The chair creaked a protest.

Six more heavy draws from the cigarette and his head felt lighter. The kick that only a part-time smoker can feel combined with his headache to create an almost euphoric state. It reminded him of the pills he'd sometimes taken inside. Of course, he kept them hidden from Harry. Harry was very anti-drugs. Anti-taking them mind, not anti-the profit from the sale and distribution of. "That shit rots your body and mind, son," he'd say, "give me a bottle of whisky any day."

Wondering what Harry would be up to took him back to the cell. Would Harry have a new cellmate? Would they get on as well? His mind jarred as he wondered if Harry knew he'd messed up. "That little sap's fucked up bad," he imagined him saying. "Let me down he has. The lad's let me down."

He flicked the near burnt-out fag at the rubbish skip and lit another. He hadn't just let Harry down; what about Pete? All that training gone to shit. He'd probably sullied his good name too. Maybe he'd be next in a blacked-out Range Rover wanting ten grand.

The phone buzzed. *I don't really drink midweek. Work and that, you know.*

That settled that.

Stubbing out the second half-smoked fag, he downed the rest of the pint and pocketed the phone. The barman was still trying to pull. Jim was impressed with the effort but wondered if he did it every night. Maybe he was just practising his moves. Perhaps he'd read it wrong and they were just mates.

The stairs weighed heavy on his legs. Just how many miles had he walked? In the bedroom, he was glad his neighbours still weren't back as he lay on the bed. Struggling with the remote, he chose a comedy program then opened his mobile again. *Me neither, I just felt like a drink,* was his message back to her.

The comedy program wasn't funny and as he got beneath the covers, he wondered if she'd reply to the last message.

After half an hour, she did. *We've just been on the late news. Off to bed now.*

Turning off the television, he sent a reply. *Goodnight*, then switched off the light.

Chapter 7

The night was the longest he could remember. He'd dropped off quick enough, but something woke him after a few hours. His head thumping, he wished he'd bought some tablets. He should have seen a headache coming. Sleep didn't return and the hours ticked by until sometime after six. Every minute the LED alarm clock ticked off brought another calculation of how little sleep he'd get. He'd set the alarm for eight. Breakfast, included in the price, finished at nine and checkout was half ten. The calculation haunted him as he thought through his options.

By two a.m. he'd narrowed the options down to either run, rob a bookies or post office, or just give in. How else could he possibly make ten grand in a week? Of course he could phone Ralph and admit defeat, maybe ask to work off his debt. An entrepreneur such as Ralph's boss would surely appreciate extra help. Problem was, if he said no a couple of broken kneecaps or concrete wellies were guaranteed. If he said yes, he'd be the gangster's bitch forever, the debt would never be paid.

What he definitely was not considering, what absolutely was not going to happen, was ripping Charlotte off. Sure she had money, that was clear. She was also a divorcee, maybe lonely and the conversation so far had convinced him that despite him being more Mario than Lothario, he could fleece her if he wanted. He didn't want to. He didn't want his kneecaps rearranged either. There had to be another way.

Back to a post office or bookies. The problem was, Jim had told himself at four a.m., CCTV cameras. They're everywhere. It's not like the old days. He'd met enough armed robbers inside to know that. Sophisticated security alarms, silent connections to police and hidden cameras so powerful they could tell whether you've shaved or not weren't to be messed with. The honest thief's job was so hard these days. As Harry would say, "If they put us out of business think of all the unemployment. Think of the children. Why doesn't anyone think of the children?"

By five he knew he'd be staying at the hotel a few more nights. His only real plan was to do what he failed at last time in town: rob tourists. Though something he'd never tried before, he knew how easy it was. Inside, they practised wallet snaffling during the quiet times. Some of the country's best pickpockets had shown him their techniques. Stealing had never been his thing though. Not his career path he supposed they'd call it these days. Someone would bring him a vanload of gear to get rid of - no questions asked - that was his job. That was what he knew. Still, at the very least, a couple of wallets of cash could pay the hotel bill while he came up with a ten-grand job. Maybe more. Anything above ten was his. The difference in robbing ten and twenty grand wasn't huge. Similar security, similar sentence if caught. An extra ten would keep him a long time. The rest of his life he hoped.

By six, the biggest weight in the gym was being lifted. A haze of clarity told him he didn't need to solve the problem tonight. He had six days. Planning them was the key. He'd wasted the last six, hung-over hours tossing and turning in bed. There was no point. Everything would become clear in the morning. If it didn't, rob a few tourists for pocket money and see if the idea came the next day. Relieved, he closed his eyes, sleep certainly seemed nearer. His mind, like his legs were exhausted. His mind wandered to Charlotte. Had she fallen asleep straight away? Slowly, as his eyes closed and concentration drifted, Jim fell asleep. His last thought was he was definitely not going to fleece her.

It wasn't going to happen.

His throbbing head struggled to comprehend the grating noise that had woken him. Looking at the source, the alarm clock buzzed merrily, announcing to the world eight o'clock had arrived. Jim sighed. What time had he got to sleep? Slamming his hand on the snooze button, he slid a paper-thin pillow on his face and screwed up his eyes.

His head hurt. He'd barely drunk for three years and the two-stage drinking session had created a monster, two-stage hangover. Through the depths of his mind, two names were appearing, pushing themselves to the top. The names became clear: Geoffrey and Charlotte.

Throwing the pillow off, he moved towards the edge of the bed, his head pounding hard. Picking up his trousers and retrieving the phone, he looked at the display. A yellow envelope showed a new message.

Can't sleep, how about you? the message said.

"Shit."

How had he missed it? He was awake ninety per cent of the night. Perhaps it hadn't buzzed or the trousers had muffled it. The time stamp read just before one. Just before he woke up. Maybe her message woke him. Shrugging his shoulders, which increased the headache, he took his time replying.

Sorry I missed your message. I slept off and on. Hope you got off eventually.

Sending it, he went to the bathroom and filled a plastic glass with water. The stale and stagnant water greased his furred tongue as he drank. Hitting his stomach, it gurgled. He imagined his dehydrated body instantly using the water, carting it off to the most drought-ridden areas. A glance in the mirror revealed a badly hung-over thirty-year-old with bin-liner sized bags under each eye. Beard stubble was showing and tufts of his hair were at right angles to his head. The headache was still pounding, but he was getting used to it. He breathed out heavily, his rank breath clouding the mirror. Filling the basin with tepid water, he washed his hands and face.

Less than five minutes after his message, the phone beeped a reply. Unable to help the smile crossing his face, he ran to the phone.

Eventually got off at three. I've rung hospital. Geoffrey doing well. Off to work. Catch up later :)

The smile grew as he returned to the bathroom. "So." He cocked his head and pursed his lips to a pout. "Catch up later, eh?" Winking at his hazy reflection in the mirror, he finished washing then got dressed.

Walking to the empty reception, he rang the imitation bronze call bell. The dull ping didn't help his headache. Each step down the stairs had felt like a crisp packet bursting behind him. Last night's waitress and bar proper-upper walked from a rear office in a fairly clean uniform.

"Yeah?" She looked confused already before Jim had even said anything.

"Have you got any headache tablets?"

She shook her head immediately though appeared to take longer to digest the sentence. "No. There's a shop down the road."

"Oh. Okay."

"Was that it?" She scrunched her nose up. Whatever she'd been doing before was obviously more important than this.

"Yeah. Thanks for your help."

Opening the outside door, a rush of polluted morning air and noise knocked him back. His head pounding, he walked to the shop and bought some painkillers. Nearly five pounds lighter, he returned to the hotel and headed for the restaurant.

Most of the people from last night were there and in various states of dress and hair loss. Though none were in pyjamas or dressing gowns, some had obviously slept in parts of the clothing they were wearing. Feeling a bit overdressed in jeans and t-shirt, he picked the single man, sad bastard table and sat down. His mouth still Sahara dry, he coughed as he tried to dry swallow a tablet. Eventually getting it down, he chewed the other instead. The powdery sharp taste filled his mouth and removed what little saliva he still owned.

Waiting, he picked up the menu and read it again, the sixth time so far. Looking round, his neighbours still weren't about. Perhaps they'd left yesterday afternoon. He'd only met them a few mornings when his head was still buzzing and his plans were clear and simple. They'd talked to him for ages, most of which he didn't listen too, but he was sure they'd booked in for a week.

Eventually, the waitress cum receptionist appeared and took orders. Jim ordered the full English - you got to get your money's worth - and a cup of tea. After two minutes of looking round the room, politely smiling and checking his watch, he was bored. Everything was so slow in the hotel. It had to be intentional. Take your money then leave you high and dry waiting all day. Compared to London's fast pace, the hotel felt like it never moved.

The problem for Jim was most of the other guests had someone to talk to. A few of the other single guests were also breakfasting; possibly late starts to their working day in the city. Most of the suited and booted brigade he'd seen in the bar or at meal times had probably eaten earlier. Their toast would have still just been warm, unlike the cold and soggy toast Jim knew he was going to get.

Picking up a free paper from the windowsill next to a dying plant, he attempted to read the two-week old local news. The breakfast arrived twenty minutes later. The chef was a genius, managing to both burn and undercook sausages simultaneously. The nearest he'd come to Michelin was a calendar. Jim presumed it was a he, but chances were it was the waitress-receptionist all-rounder.

Crunching through the burnt shell covering the pink sausage meat middle, Jim dunked his cold toast in his runny egg and shovelled it in his mouth. Despite everything else, the eggs were perfect. The headache tablets now working, his appetite had improved. He had a long day ahead and breakfast was the most important meal of the day. Just what his long day involved, he wasn't sure. But if he ended the day with less than two grand in his pocket, the next five days would be harder. Much harder.

The breakfast finished, he wandered to the deserted reception and rang the bell. This time the ping just made him wince. The tablets were doing a grand job, they weren't worth a fiver, but they were working. The waitress appearing, now dressed as a receptionist, wasn't a shock.

"You again?" Her scowl was set at full mast.

"Can I stay a few more nights, please?"

She sighed, heavily. "What room?" She shook her head in case there was any doubt of the extra work he was causing.

"Room twelve." Jim looked at the London Eye leaflet on the stand next to the desk. He would admit that despite his slight fear of heights, he fancied a go in it. Sure it was just seeing London from up high, no chance of making ten grand, but it just seemed like a good experience.

Retrieving a piece of paper from a file, the waitress looked for a pen. "I don't know where they disappear to. Ah, there's one. Right." She sighed again. "How many extra nights?"

"Two, maybe three."

She sighed again. It lasted a few seconds. "Shall I write down two or three?"

"Two."

"Oh, hang on. You paid cash, didn't you? We'll need payment in advance." The first smile Jim had seen cracked its way across her face. She was hoping that would scupper him. She was expecting a fight. Expecting him not to have any cash on him. Her smile grew in anticipation.

"Yeah, that's fine." Watching her face drop gave Jim his own smile.

She looked wounded and briefly struggled for words before finding them. "That's a hundred and twenty-eight pounds then."

Handing over nearly half his remaining money, Jim tried to keep his smile. He'd bought himself two days bed and board. Two days in this city to make or break himself. Technically, the making would be for someone else's benefit. The breaking would be all his though. All his.

Back in his room, he was surprised Charlotte had rung twice and sent a text since he'd gone for breakfast. He still hadn't got the hang of carrying the damn thing everywhere. It was like some traceable identity bracelet. Everyone needed to carry one. To have the means of being tracked and contacted twenty-four hours a day. He reckoned his Granddad had fought a war to stop that sort of thing, but it'd been ushered in through the back door.

The message: *My lunch meeting got cancelled. Are you near the city at one today? The table's already booked.*

Smiling, he typed, *Yes. Where can I meet you?*

After a brief celebration he took his crumpled suit back out of the suitcase. Turning his nose up at the state of it, he opened the trouser press operating manual.

Chapter 8

Taking the tube to the city, his last hundred and fifty quid in his pocket, Jim felt a twinge of optimism. Being skint was nothing new; he'd spent his life without money. It felt like an old friend returning. In some ways, he was glad the way things had gone yesterday. Glad he was back to skint old Jim.

Glad he wasn't a murderer. Shaking his head, he stared at the tube map. Three stops to go. Why did she want to meet him? They barely knew each other. He'd convinced himself last night that sleep would bring her to her senses. Obviously it hadn't. He wanted to see her, but wondered where this could possibly go. What possible common ground did they have?

For a summer's Friday lunchtime, it had turned surprisingly warm. The tube caught the full stickiness of the subterranean metropolis. The passengers in his carriage, mainly tourists, had smiles on their faces. Capital smiles, he called them. Their hearts captivated by the bright lights and tall buildings, they wandered from spot to spot taking photos and enjoying themselves, but deep down secretly glad they were only visiting and didn't have to live here.

Today's plan was forming well. Meet with Charlotte for dinner and hopefully get a few words in edgeways. Then maybe, hopefully, arrange something for the weekend. The longing he'd had for a roll in the hay with Soho's finest had gone. He wanted more. He wanted someone classier.

The other benefit of meeting Charlotte in the city was he could spend the afternoon visiting pubs. No doubt he'd find some bladdered stock brokers or bankers and relieve them of their wallets. Today, Jim had decided while struggling with the trouser press, would be old school day. No guns or armed robberies. No, today he'd examine the art of pocket pilfering. Wallet stealing was the game, maybe even the odd mobile. If he was really lucky, a laptop. Keys to a car? As the tube clickety-clacked over poorly maintained tracks, he pictured himself driving someone else's Porsche, spending their money and using their phone.

Allowing himself a smile, his dream continued as the tube worked through London's labyrinth. Ten grand in a week was a serious ask. What made it really hard was the nation's love affair with plastic. So few people carried money anymore that even finding ten thousand in notes might take longer than a week. He briefly wondered if there was even ten thousand pounds of paper money actually in existence. Of course, he knew from his day job that everything had a cash value. Every piece of plastic, every phone, laptop, even car keys had a black market value. Problem was, it was between a fifth and a tenth of the actual worth. The other problem, he didn't know anyone in London to offload gear onto. This wasn't a big problem. The Queens Arms yesterday had stolen goods written all over it. Even with his poor mathematical skills, he knew he'd need to steal upwards of sixty phones a day to get anywhere near ten big ones. Cash was the way. Some places must have cash. They were the ones to hit.

Jim loosened his tie. He always felt uncomfortable in a suit, it reminded him of court. This afternoon would be a bit of fun, no serious money could be made, unless by a one in a million chance he found Ferrari or Porsche keys lying round. Just a bit of fun, a chance to earn some pennies to pay the week's hotel bill. Maybe enough to take Charlotte out - if she agreed, obviously.

He checked the tube map again. Still three stops away. His watch showed he was nearly an hour early. But, he told himself, that was good. Being early gives you time to get your bearings. He'd have a quick shufty round; find side alleys in case a quick exit was needed. The amount of CCTV cameras in the city was worrying. In a suit and wearing shades he wouldn't look too out of place. He reckoned he looked like a proper merchant banker.

Smiling harder, he looked at the dusty floor. Next to his left shoe was a grubby five pence piece. Picking it up, he pocketed it to the disgust of the woman opposite.

Just that little bit closer. Ten grand was getting nearer.

Leaving the station, he walked round looking at bars, coffee shops, sandwich shops and restaurants. The square mile felt bigger when travelled by foot. People and traffic everywhere, side streets, back alleys, similar looking landmarks. Everything conspired to make you lose your bearings.

A half hour walk made him comfortable with the layout. But it was the people he wasn't comfortable with. They had too much money, and with it too little respect for anything.

Charlotte had texted him the address of the restaurant earlier. She'd offered to send him GPS coordinates, but Jim had said there was really no point. Whatever the hell GPS was, he doubted his twenty quid throwaway phone could use it. The restaurant was actually quite easy to find. Being half an hour early he went for another walk, keeping his bearings and location all the time.

The restaurant itself was expensive. He stared at the window menu with horror. He had a hundred and fifty in his pocket, but that was supposed to last him more than one lunch. Some of the main courses were nearly a hundred. Add to that wine and he was looking at an embarrassing afternoon of washing up. He hoped, really hoped, that she'd be both a light eater and feminist enough to insist on going halves.

He stood outside the restaurant with five minutes to go, the streets thronged with what appeared to be every city worker. People walked round him at their quick London pace. He almost felt seasick stood still. Busy people wanted busy sandwiches or wraps or whatever it was they ate, and they wanted them quickly. They wanted them yesterday.

He almost didn't recognise Charlotte in her light brown suit, Gucci shades and tied back hair. When he did recognise her, it was too late to hide his smile. She was good-looking. More so than he remembered. He immediately wondered what she was doing looking at him. The suit, he convinced himself. You're wearing an expensive suit. Don't forget that.

She walked the last few yards to him, a slight smile on her own face. "Sorry I'm late," she said.

Jim was surprised the sentence had stopped so soon. "You're not. Late I mean. I'm early."

Smiling, she stepped the final half yard bringing her to his side. A wave of expensive and slightly floral perfume scouted out an advance party. Breathing in the freshness, Jim's eyes opened more. She seemed more dominant and confident. The constant talking gone. He hoped so anyway. That scared bunny in the headlights yesterday was now a confident, slick and slightly intimidating woman. Jim couldn't help but feel like a kid in junior school. He was well out of his league.

"Shall we?" she asked.

Jim nodded and walked towards the restaurant, holding the door open for her. Chivalry may be dead, but it at least gave him an excuse to smell her perfume again.

The table had been booked in Charlotte's name, Rathbone. Jim thought it the sort of name that oozed money. It had big house in Cheshire and private school written all over it. The *maitre d`* welcomed her with a theatrical cheek-kiss and ushered them to a small table in a recess. Charlotte took the rear seat giving her a view of everything behind Jim's back. Jim had only a wall and Charlotte to stare at; the wall was never going to win.

A sparse conversation, possibly in French, between Charlotte and the *maitre d`* told Jim this wasn't her first time here. She was well known. This was also her table and the *maitre d`* had been well tipped in the past.

As they were left to their menus, Jim peered over the top of his. Her eyes were scanning the menu she probably knew by heart, while her left hand traced a figure of eight over the top of a spoon.

"Sorry about missing your message last night," said Jim. "I walked so much yesterday I just sort of collapsed."

"It's okay." She flicked a wayward lump of hair that had fallen in front of her menu back onto her head. "I didn't really have anything to tell you. It's just, you know,   sometimes ..."

"I know," Jim interrupted. He sensed she was gearing up for a speech and thought he'd nip it in the bud. "I woke up about oneish, but couldn't get back off."

She smiled and her eyes returned to the menu.

Looking at his menu, Jim tried to put on an "I'm not that hungry" look. "How was your morning?" His eyes flicked briefly towards hers.

She placed her menu diagonally across her cutlery. Taking a quick scan round the nearly full restaurant, her eyes met his. "Quiet really. I mean, I was supposed to have a meeting with a client, but he cancelled so that was two hours and a lunch appointment gone. I'd already booked here and well, you can't waste reservations here, they're just so hard to get, you know."

Jim nodded.

"Apart from that a fairly normal day. I haven't seen any heart attack victims yet either." She smiled at what could have been a joke.

Jim smiled back in case it was. "Just a normal Friday for me. In the boring world of statistics nothing exciting happens."

She nodded then returned to the menu. Her face wasn't as smiley as yesterday. Maybe she'd realised him for the chancer he was. Looking at the menu, his eyes hovered over the starter section, not going anywhere near desserts.

"What do you fancy?" she asked.

You, he nearly said. "The mushroom tagliatelli sounds nice." It was also the cheapest.

"That's a starter isn't it? I'm not sure I can manage a starter and a main."

Jim knew this was where things could get out of hand. He could barely afford a starter, let alone eat more than one course. "Erm, what do you want?"

"The lobster's fantastic." Her smile half returned.

Jim nodded and forced himself to look at the price. It ought to be more than bloody fantastic for that. He knew his eyes were bulging, but was helpless to stop them. This was almost torture.

An idea formed in his head. He'd later admit to having no clue where it came from. Though not strong enough to turn a man from crime and towards religion, it was damn close.

"I err." He paused for effect, trying to look more nervous than he already was. "I don't eat meat."

"Oh no." Her face fell; the smile disappeared. She looked mortified. Jim felt his own face drop too. "I'm sorry. I mean, I just assumed you ate ... Oh. My. God. I just didn't even think. I mean here we are in the 'meatiest' restaurant in London, and you're ... Oh I am so sorry ..."

He wanted to interrupt and stop her, but couldn't. The vegetarian wheel had been set in motion and no amount of mung bean salad was stopping it. The cute city kitty had morphed back to the scared little talky bunny.

"... I should have asked. We could have gone to Bellini's or that really nice Japanese place off ..."

"It's okay," he interrupted.

She stopped talking. Putting the menu down, she held her forehead in her hand.

"Seriously." He knew he'd mess it up but before they'd even ordered. That was quick. "Look, it's only food. I can have the, umm, green salad or the nut and seed roast." As impossible as it was to say that with enthusiasm, by God he tried.

The waiter, maybe sensing the need to interrupt, walked over. "May I take a drinks order? *Madam, Monsieur?*"

Charlotte said, "A bottle of," then added three words Jim didn't understand. Charlotte nodded at him for approval. He nodded back and forced a smile.

"Are you ready to order your food, Madam?"

"Not quite," she said.

Jim laughed as the waiter walked away. "I'm sorry."

She shook her head, the stray piece of hair flopped off her forehead and returned to her cheek. "It's me who should be apologising."

"You have lobster, I'll have the mushroom pasta."

She shook her head. "We'll both have tagliatelli. It'll be a nice change."

An embarrassed silence ensued, during which time Jim remembered he'd eaten beef stew last night and had told her. She obviously hadn't remembered. She would though. A different waiter offered the bottle of wine to Jim. Testing it, as he'd seen posh people do in films, he was surprised by its smoothness. It almost didn't taste like wine. He was used to best bitter and prison Hooch. He'd rarely drunk wine, and what he had, had been cheap plonk. But this, it excited taste buds he never knew existed. He thanked the waiter and confirmed to Charlotte it was very nice. Very, very nice.

"How long have you been a vegetarian?"

A little voice in his head said two minutes. "Not forever. A few years."

She nodded. "What made you convert? Sorry, that's not the right word is it?"

"Erm." Think Jim, think. "Money at first. I mean I'd never really liked the way animals are, erm, farmed and all that. Intensive farming, yeah, you know. But, yeah, it was lack of money really." He felt his cheeks growing red. He knew that sounded as transparent as a jellyfish.

The main waiter returned, just in time to save Jim.

"Are you ready to order now, *Madame, Monsieur?*"

"Yes," she said. She proceeded to give the order in French, and added a long burst afterwards. By the look on the waiter's face, Jim guessed she'd either told him he was a vegetarian or a child killer.

The waiter removed some cutlery and walked away. Jim gulped back some wine. The conversation had lulled. He wanted to talk more about her than himself. He wasn't comfortable lying; it could only trap and catch himself out.

However, he was struggling to pick a topic. If he asked about her past or her family he knew the question would come back at him. He had to pick something just about her. Something she couldn't reuse.

Charlotte seemed reluctant to make conversation too. Maybe she'd realised this was a stupid mistake. Jim had the feeling this was going to be a long, fruitless and expensive lunch. Maybe he should quit now, before it got really expensive. But, that little voice in his head returned. How many times was he going to be in this position? A woman opposite, who was sort of interested. It wasn't going to happen again. He should at least make the fucking effort. He had to keep her talking. Talk about her work. If he got her lost in conversation, this might not be a disaster.

"So," he started, "how's that deal going you mentioned?"

She frowned slightly. Puzzled, she seemed to think what deal she may have told him about. Suddenly her eyes lit up. "Oh the Dubai deal?" He nodded. "Yeah, we're getting there. Some pull out, others join. It gets quite hectic this close to the deadline. Someone pulled out this morning, hence the reservation. Still, it all goes on expenses, you know." She smiled.

Jim regretted his conversion to vegetarianism. Did that mean she was paying in full? If so, she could have made it clearer.

The stray lump of hair had rolled down her face again. Flicking it back atop her head, she dropped her voice and looked him straight in the eye. "There's so much money involved. It makes you wonder sometimes. I mean, I know it's oil money and oil's running out so they're investing for their future, but just how much do you really need?" She shook her head.

Her piercing eyes had made his stomach quiver. It was probably a good job he wasn't eating meat. He sensed that beneath the high-flying deals, this cookie wasn't the happiest in the packet. Seeing other people's money make more money, obscene amounts of money, can't be easy. He just wished someone would share some with him. Ten grand's worth to be precise.

"I'm not sure I could do, you know, your job. Must be stressful. All that money." He hoped his lie wasn't too see-through. What he'd give to spend ten minutes in a room with an Arab.

She shook her head, the lump of hair coming free again. "It's not stressful really. It's just organising. As long as you're organised it sails through." Her voice dropped to a whisper. "To be honest, being nice to total arseholes is the hardest part."

The word arsehole took him by surprise. The little rich girl opposite maybe wasn't that rich. Sure the name sounded rich, but that seemed too down to earth.

Jim curled his nose slightly. "I'll stick to statistics. I've always been useless with money."

Her eyes grew wide, and it wasn't the approaching mushroom pasta. She shrugged her shoulders. "Money's not everything," she said as the waiter arrived.

Despite the lack of anything dead on his plate, Jim actually enjoyed the meal. Small portioned and intricately put together, it was what he'd always called posh twat's food. Yet it tasted fantastic; each individual flavour seeped out. It wasn't worth thirty-five quid, but he'd always known that.

The dinner was unrushed and chatty. Charlotte's rate of talking had speeded and slowed throughout, the faster bits when she got excited. Jim had eventually run out of other topics and had asked about her family and past. He received a long lecture about her life growing up in Buckinghamshire, her two older sisters she didn't see anymore and her parent's tragic death in a car accident four years ago. There's only so many ways to say I'm sorry, and Jim used all of them at least twice.

"This is actually nice isn't it?" she said. "You don't notice there isn't meat."

"It's not that hard really, to not eat meat I mean." He supposed it wasn't anyway. He imagined you just cooked normally, but missed out the meat bit.

"So where did you grow up?" she said.

"Coventry." He knew he'd told her that yesterday. Perhaps she hadn't remembered everything. Maybe she wouldn't remember the beef stew.

She smiled and nodded. There was no backing out now, so he started his carefully invented background. He hoped she'd find no holes. His real fear was that she'd have once lived next door to the fake Jim.

Luckily, and after ten minutes talking, during which time his pasta got cold, his story was watertight. She seemed to buy every word about his moderately unhappy childhood, his obsession with statistics after failure at sport and his degree at Aberdeen University. Aberdeen had been Pete's idea. Pick the furthest university away, and chances were not many English people went there. The tale finished with his moving to Northumberland then Newport for his work with the Office of National Statistics and finally to London. He even threw a few failed relationships in on the spot to add reality. This new invented Jim had taken him over trance-like. He realised afterwards just what a good job Pete had done. Shame he'd let him down so badly.

Finishing his speech, he offered Charlotte a top-up. She accepted and he finished the bottle into his own glass. The conversation seemed exhausted. Jim went through a mental list of Charlotte's life, looking for anything he hadn't asked or she hadn't volunteered. Work? Done. Growing up, school and university? Definitely done. Her failed marriage? Maybe best not to dwell. Favourite biscuits? Done, bourbons. He remembered the big deal she was brokering. That sounded interesting. He knew little about finance and the city, but he was after money and the city had lots of it.

"You're going to think I've come down in the last shower," he started, "but, I don't really understand the money side of the city, you know."

Her eyes lit up again as she tried to re-stick the wobbly lump of hair back to her forehead. "What part don't you get? There's lots of different areas." She leaned forward.

"All of it." He laughed. She didn't laugh back. "Just a joke. I mean the deal you're about to do. How do they know, the people putting money in?"

"Investors," she interrupted.

"Yeah. How do they know they're going to make money? Surely it's as much a gamble as the five thirty at Monmore?" Seeing her confusion, he clarified, "It's a greyhound track."

Choosing Monmore had been a mistake. He was supposed to be middle-class. He should have said Ascot or Newbury. ONS workers didn't know random greyhound tracks. Unless of course they had gambling problems.

She nodded. The hair slipped again. "There's a limit to what I can say. As I'm sure you know, insider trading's illegal. Obviously, we don't do anything like that. There's regulations and well... It's just obvious. It stands out a mile."

Jim nodded. She hadn't answered his question, but she'd taken the conversation to a different, much more interesting area. The next question he wanted to ask was, can you turn a hundred quid into ten grand in a week. He thought he knew what the answer would be.

"Sometimes," she continued, "with takeovers, the sheer amount of money invested will push up the price with people speculating, and it just becomes common knowledge. It's almost a free-for-all."

She was building up to something but he hadn't a clue what.

"I mean, if people found out what companies the Emirates were thinking of buying, they could earn themselves a pretty penny." Her voice now almost a whisper.

Jim was unable to help the smile growing on his face. "When does the deal happen?"

"About four weeks until it goes public."

His face fell further than a bank share in a crash. In six days he'd be at the bottom of the Thames, his concrete shoes making him look like a Subbuteo-style, life-sized ornament. Another exit had slammed shut.

Aware of just how much his face had dropped, he shovelled the last piece of cold pasta in his mouth. Charlotte made a brief excuse and went to powder her nose. Jim assumed she was using the toilet rather than snorting a line of coke like many of the other diners probably were. Noticing she'd left her coat and laptop on her chair, thoughts ran through his head.

Laptop, eighty quid, coat twenty. Actually, the contents of the laptop could literally be worth millions in the right hands. Millions. No, he wasn't going to do it. Charlotte had never hurt a fly. He couldn't do it.

Returning, she sat down and the conversation moved from finance and deals to Friday afternoons and the lack of work they produced. Jim explained that every day was quiet in the world of National Statistics, but Friday was just a dearth of wanting to go home. Charlotte, on the other hand, had a meeting at four and a few pieces of paperwork to catch up on in the office.

They sipped their after-dinner coffee in contented half silence. They'd both declined dessert, Charlotte for her figure and Jim in case they were going fifty-fifty on the bill. Carefully and not too subtly, he engineered the conversation on a roundabout route from Friday afternoon to Saturday night.

"So, what are you doing tomorrow night?" he said.

Her eyes lit then dulled. The loose piece of hair didn't move. She appeared to have welded it to her scalp during her toilet break. "Nothing."

Trying to word his next sentence to sound non-corny was hard. He eventually settled on, "Really? Someone like you shouldn't spend Saturday night alone."

She grinned slightly, encouraging him further.

"How about we go out?" he said, "A film or show or something?" He hoped she wouldn't pick a show; they were expensive.

She nodded her head. "Yeah. I'd like that. Yeah."

"Okay." He smiled. Fighting back the temptation to shout "Yes", he instead hid his face behind his cup and sipped it.

"I'd better think about getting back." Her heart didn't seem in it, which increased Jim's smile.

Jim took a look at his own watch. Two hours had flown by. Surely ONS workers weren't allowed two hour lunches. It'd be nearer three given the travel to and from his supposed office. Whether she'd thought anything was odd, she hadn't said.

"Can I, umm," she caught the waiter's attention and mouthed the words, "have the bill please?"

Jim made an attempt to go halves, but she insisted lunch was her idea, and besides, it was on expenses. He tried again to go halves, but luckily she wouldn't hear of it. Forgetting himself for a moment, he told her Saturday night would be his treat. She reluctantly agreed and he wondered whether a burger, chips and walk by the river would be beneath her. Sighing as they got up, he followed her out of the door.

As she turned towards him on the now quiet street, an awkwardness had crept in through the back door and was holding them hostage. What happened now? Brisk yet firm handshake, peck on the cheek or a full-on kiss? Jim wished, for probably the first time in his life, he was more European. The quick double peck on each cheek was built for this situation. But, being English, he pushed forward his right hand.

She looked at it then offered her own.

"Thank you." He took her hand and gently shook it twice.

"Thank you, too," she replied, not releasing his flimsy grip.

"I'll ring tomorrow, you know, so we can arrange things."

She smiled and let go of his hand. He knew, or rather hoped, they'd be talking a lot sooner than tomorrow.

"See you." She turned and walked away.

Chapter 9

Walking round the corner, Jim let out the scream he'd been holding back. Getting odd looks from briefcase-carrying yuppies didn't bother him. He'd done it. Got a second date with the most eligible person he'd ever met. Finding his bearings, he headed for the riverside. He needed to clear his head before he started work. His head was now a Charlotte-filled mess recreating every conversation, every smile and every one of his lies. Taking a few deep breaths, he leaned against the dock wall.

"Come on boy. Pull yourself together. Ten grand in six days. Ten grand in six days."

The come down was fast. Impending death usually took the glint off an otherwise agreeable lunch. His mind now in tatters, he hoped it would concentrate him on the job ahead.

He lasted ten seconds before he thought of her again. He was taking her out tomorrow night so that would limit what he could do tomorrow afternoon. That left him needing a wedge of cash to take her out and pay for a few more nights at the hotel. At least three hundred quid. Though keeping Charlotte in the manner to which she was accustomed would probably make it nearer five hundred. Turning round, with just a hundred and fifty in his pocket, he headed for the nearest bar.

Entering, the first words he heard were, "Tarquin, did you see Jocasta look at you earlier?" He instantly knew he was both in the right place and society could only benefit from his forthcoming actions. The place was cool, both air-conditioned and fashionable. White walls were offset by some new trendy artist's painting, while the open-plan bar area left a large standing or mingling zone in the middle. Piped jazz played through decent speakers at a respectable volume, while the occupants sipped cocktails and bottled beers. A clean, fresh smell ripped through his nose, the combination of expensive aftershave and perfume.

Jim approached the bar. After a minute waiting, he caught the barmaid's eye and ordered a bottle of something foreign and lagerish. Robbing him of seven pounds, the barmaid removed the bottle top for no extra charge. Stood next to Jim were two bankers. He presumed they were bankers by their expensive suits, but would admit they could easily have been brokers, consultants or even just plain twats.

"Off to Monaco this weekend," said Twat A to Twat B.

"On your own?" Twat B replied.

"No, the baggage comes with me, unfortunately." Twat A laughed.

Jim smiled. These two would do. He wouldn't lose any sleep tonight.

"Whereabouts in Monaco," interrupted Jim. His false posh accent turned Monaco into Mon-archo.

Pushing his chest out, Twat A stepped aside from his buddy and looked Jim up and down. Red cheeks showed he'd been drinking heavily. Pale and tired, he looked wary of outsiders. After a few seconds, he seemed satisfied that although he didn't recognise Jim, he must somehow know him. "Monte Carlo, of course."

The other twat sniggered at his friend's heroic cheek.

Jim nodded and sipped his lager-style frothy drink. He counted to three inside his head. He wanted to knock the grinning smiles off their faces, but that would come later. For now, he was his best mate. "We stay in Larvotto when we go there," Jim said. "Obviously, we do the casinos at night."

Being bored and in prison had benefits. "Shifty Ted", a roulette whizz and serial gambler of other people's money, had talked for hours about his time in Monaco after robbing a post office. It ended nastily of course. He was caught and extradited. But Ted was such a good talker and explainer that Jim had been given a virtual tour of Monaco and its pleasures. Jim had listened avidly, impressed by all the money and wealth, hoping some day he could go there and give the money a new home.

Twat A grinned then laughed. "Yacht or apartment?"

"Apartment." Jim edged slightly to his right. His plan was to nudge Twat B from the conversation. Every sentence saw him edge further in front of him. "Cressida's father owns it. One of the benefits, you know." He nodded suggestively. The twat knew just what that kind of nod meant. "Shall we sit down, chaps?" He pointed to a empty table.

It turned out Twat A's name was Raif, Twat B had a name too but Jim hadn't bothered to listen when told it. He wasn't important. A plan was brewing in Jim's head, he wasn't sure where it was going or what it involved, but Twat B played no part.

They spent half an hour drinking expensive lager and talking about Monaco, bonuses and money. It turned out Raif's short break was a gift from his company for the best performing twat this quarter. When asked where he worked, Jim gave Charlotte's company's name. He regretted it instantly, but he was thinking on his toes and mistakes were bound to happen. He was sure they'd never remember. They were both well gone.

As they spoke and laughed the plan grew, mutating in his head. What should have been his first venture into wallet thievery was becoming more serious.

"Better make this the last one chaps," said Raif. "Melody's picking me up soon."

"You going straight to the airport?" asked Jim.

"Ya. Flight's in a few hours."

Twat B made his excuses and headed for the toilet leaving Raif at Jim's mercy. This was hard work yet enjoyable. He still couldn't believe just how easy it was to be accepted by wearing the right clothes.

"Which airline?" asked Jim.

"BA, of course," said Raif. He pulled the tickets from his rolled up jacket and waved them around, Chamberlain like.

He'd bitten his tongue for much of the last half hour, but knew this would be worth it. He'd have the last laugh "We went by train once. Terrible journey, took nearly a whole day. Cressida's idea of course." Jim tutted. Placing his bottle back on the table, he accidently knocked Raif's. The bottle rocked from side to side, teasing before it fell, and directed the foaming lager towards Raif's trousers and expensive mobile that he'd displayed advert-like in front of him.

"Jesus. Sorry, chap." Jim reached for the fallen bottle and remounted it, splashing another glug over Raif's trousers. "Oh, clumsy. I am so sorry."

"It's alright." Raif stood up. Drunk yet in charge of his faculties, he headed for the toilet.

With them both out of sight, Jim took a look around. Their corner was quiet and well hidden. The bar was filling; everyone was knocking off early on a summer's Friday. The weekend calling, a few drinks before the tube was one of the benefits of living in London. Though busy, the clientele were more interested in getting served than what Jim was up to. With one eye on the toilets, Jim slipped his hand into Raif's jacket pocket and pulled out the plane ticket. Quickly opening it, he read the name and address. Raif Mortimer, 33 East Street, London N5. Replacing it, he looked round. No one had seen.

Twat B returned first as Jim hurriedly typed Raif's address into a contact on his mobile. All fingers and thumbs, he managed the postcode just as the twat sat down.

"I'm really sorry," said Jim. "Can you apologise to Raif for me. Too many afternoon drinks, I fear." Jim stood, sweeping his hair back with a sticky, beer-filled hand and giving a theatrical wobble.

"Oh, I'm sure it's okay." The twat smiled. With Raif away, he seemed at last relieved someone was talking to him.

"I'll pay for the dry cleaning obviously. Have you got his phone number? I'll ring him when he gets back from Monaco."

Jim pulled his mobile from his pocket, saved the contact with Raif's address on then clumsily typed his phone number into a new contact. Finally, he thanked the twat for the drinks, implored him again to pass on his apologies and staggered out of the bar. On his way out, he saw a pound coin lying on the floor near an empty table. He picked it up.

Outside and leaning against the wharf, he tidied up the contact details in his mobile and checked his watch. Five o'clock. The financial heart had just closed for the week and the bars, tavernas and coffee houses were teeming with the masters of the universe, cheering off the week and spending more money than Jim would see in his life. Though he'd been drinking, he was sober. Sure the buzz gave him an edge, but he was working. Friday night, a summers Friday night, was his best chance of loosening tongues and pockets. He had to work this as long as he could.

Smiling, Jim thought of Raif. What a shock he was in for when he returned with his baggage after their once in a lifetime holiday. Walking towards the busiest of the bars, Jim was determined not to be too greedy. There was enough money floating around. If he just creamed a small amount from the top it'd hardly be noticed. Cream off too much and you drew attention.

The next bar was rammed with a hundred Raif and Jocasta's. Squeezing through a throng of people, Jim queued then bought himself a bottle of beer. He butted into a few conversations and tried to mingle before a lonely misfit latched onto him.

The misfit, Jake, was unlike the others he'd seen so far in the bars. The more they spoke, the clearer it became that he had much in common with the meek young man. He wondered how Jake had ended up working for a bank.

Two young women leaving through the smog of people looked at Jake. "Look, it's him," one said to her friend. Jim noticed Jake's face growing bright red. There was history and Jim was nosy enough to want to know it.

"I didn't know they let your sort in here," the other said. The first laughed as they walked past.

Despite the noise and amount of people, it felt to Jim that everyone was looking at them. He could only imagine how small Jake felt. "What was that about?"

His redness grew, and huge blotches attacked his cheeks. "Girls from the office a few floors down. I was seconded down there. An IT system implementation, you know."

Jim nodded. He didn't know what it meant, but thought he ought to.

"It's the credit impairment section. They're ..." He stopped. Jim nodded to help him along. "They're evil, it's the only word. All these people with houses getting repossessed; they're laughing, more than laughing. They got some sort of kick out of choosing which one to kick out next. A perverse pleasure, you know, the way they pick people. They're playing games with people's lives, you know."

Jim nodded. Jake was bright red. He saw something in him but couldn't put his finger on what it was. Compassion amongst greed? He wasn't sure.

"So what? Did you have words?"

"Doesn't matter if you do. It's like they rule the world with their little cliques. I made what I thought was an anonymous complaint. Next thing I'm demoted and moved to a different office. Whole section's got it in for me. Actually, the whole bloody bank's got it in for me."

Jim shook his head. "Some of the things that go on here ... makes you sick doesn't it."

As Jake's colour started to tone down, Jim looked round. The bar was now rammed as the last of the institutions kicked out for the weekend. Jim started another conversation with Jake while he eyed up prospective customers for the "Bank of Jim". A group of three young brokers stood in shirts to the left, their accents portraying wealth. To their right, two other young women looked lost and hard-faced as they tried to avoid advances and offers of drinks from unhappily married men. Further round he spied a mixed group stood in a circle. Youngsters most of them, but a particularly loud and balding man was ripping yarns while the rest sipped their wine and cocktails. Their boss had taken them out for a Friday drinky. The working week hadn't finished for them. Some looked bored, wanting to go home, while others followed every word their leader said. The next promotion dangling like a carrot. He'd have the fullest wallet of them all, that was without doubt. No wedding ring either. Divorcee maybe. Jim knew the type. He'd take some of them to an Indian after their drinks. Maybe he'd try it on with one of the girls who was keenest for promotion. If he had to rob someone, this was a good place to start.

Finishing his drink, Jim nodded at Jake. "Nipping to the loo."

"I'll get another round in," said Jake.

He'd timed the walk to perfection. The baldy boss had just finished his punchline and one of the others was about to start his own related story. The group had separated slightly, half of them sipping drinks hoping to nick off, while the others listened to their boss. Squeezing through a small gap, Jim bumped into the loud baldy man. Quickly, he heavily placed his left hand on the man's shoulder.

"Sorry," he said. "Bit of a crush in here tonight."

The man shook his head. It wasn't a problem. "Always like this in summer, isn't it?"

"Oh yeah," Jim replied. He patted the man's shoulder twice, again just a fraction too hard, while squeezing past. He nodded, smiled then walked to the toilet.

His heart had been in his mouth as he'd walked away. Thinking any minute he would have noticed and shouted or called the police. But he hadn't. The misdirection trick he'd practised inside actually worked. A hand landing heavily on your shoulder disguises what the other's doing. While watching him earlier, Jim had seen his wallet half sticking out from his trouser pocket. It'd been too easy in the end, not a challenge, but he'd take it however it came.

He sat in a toilet cubicle as he rifled the wallet. Not having gloves, he used the thinnest part of his suit jacket to pull out the identification badge. Martin Charlesworth MSc, a brokerage executive for the largest bank in London, had just lost three platinum cards, a gold Amex, his golf membership card, driving licence and three hundred pounds cash.

Pushing the wallet back into his pocket, Jim straightened his suit then left the toilets.

Jake was still queuing at the bar, but Jim headed the other way for the beer garden. Martin Charlesworth still hadn't discovered his wallet was missing, but Jim knew walking past was asking for trouble. No doubt he'd only realise it was missing when he was at the bar, midway through an expensive order.

"How embarrassing," said Jim, walking out the door into the garden. "How embarrassing for you, Martin. Shame you've only got a gold Amex too, eh. Not good enough for platinum yet, old boy?"

The garden led to a back street which narrowed past bins towards another road. Slipping into the busy streets, he walked for a minute, his bearings clear from earlier. Heading down a side road, he saw a small cafe or bistro as they now seemed to be called.

Sat outside at a table were two young woman. The two that Jake had had dealings with. A newly opened bottle of wine sat between them. They'd just arrived for either a meal or a quick drink somewhere quieter and more expensive. One of them got up and headed inside. Jim pulled out his phone and slowed down.

"No," he said, "just tell me which hospital. Hello. Hello." He'd reached the remaining woman and stopped walking. Blonde, smart and no doubt extremely intelligent too, but an awful bitch to anyone in trouble. Yeah, she deserved what was coming.

Catching her eye, Jim started again, "Hello. Yeah, my battery's dying. Which hospital is she in? Hello, hello."

He held out his phone and furiously pressed a few buttons, the off button being one of them. "Jesus, no. Not now." Looking round, he searched the length of the road both ways before turning back to the table. A pair of eyes looked at him, enjoying the spectacle. "Excuse me." He put on his posh voice. "Do you know if there's a payphone around? Phone battery's packed up." He showed her the lifeless phone in his hand. "My wife's giving birth and I need ring to the nanny quickly."

"Here," she said, "you can borrow mine. Is everything okay?" She genuinely looked concerned as she pulled a touch screen phone from her handbag.

"Oh, are you sure?" He tried to look sincere. It seemed to be working. "My wife's gone into labour. She was visiting a friend so I don't know which hospital she's gone too." She unlocked the phone and handed it to him. "Thank you." Jim stared at the phone screen and winced. "What's her number, what's her number?"

"Can I do anything to help?" She seemed pleasant enough. He wondered for a minute if Jake had given him a false story. No, he seemed genuine too. It was the baby line. It had brought out her best side. Under other circumstances she would have blanked him.

"Ah, my wallet," Jim feigned both surprise and delight. Pulling out Martin Charlesworth's wallet, he dialled the number on the golf membership card. Before the phone had even connected, he said, "Hello, it's me again. Which hospital? You what? What do you mean?" He started breathing in and out heavily. Clutching his chest, he slumped into the seat next to her, cancelled the call and put the phone on the table.

"Oh my God, what's happened?" She stood up, confusion in her voice.

Jim continued his breathing. "Panic." He paused. "Attack." He breathed in and out twice. "Glass ... water."

The woman ran inside the cafe. Jim slumped over onto the table, his hand swiftly entering the open handbag on the floor. The purse inside was huge, too big to steal, so he opened it and removed a small wad of cash and a few cards. Next to the purse was a phone, except it was wider and blacker than most mobiles he'd seen. He pulled it out too, then leant back in the chair. Ruffling his hair, he stood up feigning light-headedness. The woman returned with a glass of water. Jim drank half of it, banged the glass on the table, thanked her profusely then hailed a passing taxi.

Chapter 10

Travel through the city was slow. Every traffic light seemed to be against them. He stared at the black phone. Called a Blackberry, it seemed to have a proper, if tiny, keyboard. He'd no idea what it was for or why the woman had that and a normal mobile. There was no obvious way to turn it off, so he slipped it in his pocket and pulled the battery out.

Now nearly a mile away, he turned his own phone back on. Charlotte must have finished work by now, but hadn't sent a message. Maybe it was a Friday thing. She'd no doubt be in a rush to get home. He typed the message, *On way home now*, but didn't send it. It sounded desperate. They'd had dinner and it had gone well; she'd agreed to see him tomorrow. She was probably stuck waiting for a train or having an after-work drink.

Maybe she'd run out of phone credit. Jim himself was nearly halfway through his ten quid's worth already. Hers wouldn't be Pay As You Go though, it'd be on a contract, and paid for by work with regular upgrades as soon as some new vital way of using a phone got discovered. He locked the keypad, the message unsent, and asked the taxi driver to pull over.

Though on a roll, he had to be careful. Pretty soon two people would realise they were missing wallets, money and a phone. Loads of people mislay wallets and phones. Chances are they'd think it was their own drunken stupidity. However, their first thought could be Jim. They might remember the way he'd walked into them or had a panic attack just at the same time their stuff went missing. It was a chance. If they remembered him, they might remember what he looked like. If both of them remembered him and reported it, his description would be circulated.

Now stood on the edge of the financial district the bars and restaurants were quieter. In the near distance stood the Houses of Parliament, dispenser of the laws that Jim took it upon himself to break. Was there time for just one more? Yeah, maybe just one more. He was on a roll after all.

He walked into a wine bar. Though not as busy as the last, it was still doing a fair trade. Most people were drinking champagne; the air felt richer with wealth. A different sort of wealth. Inherited not earned.

Feeling more out of place, Jim made for the bar and ordered a malt whisky. Looking round, most of the customers were sitting at tables. Sipping the whisky, he found no easy access to any of the groups. Downing the dregs of the smooth tasting but not worth the price whisky, he made for the toilet. In the cubicle, he examined the phone again plus the cash. One hundred quid from the woman. Fresh from the cashpoint, it had a crisp feel. He pocketed it and looked again at the wide phone. Picking out the Sim card, he wrapped it in paper and flushed it down the pan.

Returning through the bar, he left. He stood out like a sore thumb; the place had too much class. Or thought it did. He walked further down the road past a more rowdier pub until he came to another wine bar. Light-headed from the drink, he walked in. Busier than the last, it was still quiet compared to the city. He wasn't sure if he'd drawn a blank or not. Sat at the bar, he ordered a bottle of lager.

It didn't take him long to realise that the bar was as busy as the city, but half the people were outside. They seemed to rotate from outside back in. The whole place reminded him of a Japanese sushi bar he'd once walked by. The sushi replaced by humans. The smoking ban to blame. People were nabbing tables then taking it in turns to go outside for a smoke before returning for a half hour sit down.

One particular table caught his interest. The women had cleared off outside leaving two lads to guard the bags. The lads, more interested in staring at something on a phone than the bags, had missed one on the floor. Looking round again, he saw two CCTV cameras: one aimed at the bar, the other the back door. Downing the lager, he raised his eyebrows at the barman and got off the chair.

The coat stand played its part well. Jim couldn't remember any pubs in Coventry having a coat stand. Anything placed on it would disappear before it'd stopped swinging. Grabbing the least expensive looking coat that was roughly his size, he headed for the door. Dropping the coat near the table, he swore. The two lads looked up, one of them smiling.

"Need some sleep," said Jim.

The lad nodded then went back to his mate's phone. Picking up the coat and the bag underneath, he swapped arms and left. Outside, he cursed himself for not staking the area out. He'd just got in a taxi and got out. He didn't have a clue where the side streets were, or worse where the CCTV cameras were.

The bag was big, maybe too big for a coat to hide. Rolled up in a ball under his arm, he knew it looked suspicious. He'd only a few minutes to get out of the area. Walking quickly past cafes, wine bars, takeaways and restaurants, he guessed this was a refuelling street. Every bit of floor space transformed to keep you full to bursting with food and drink.

He headed for a side street across the road. Full of bins, it was the back way into the food shops. People were mingling in the street, but he hoped everyone was too busy in their own world to notice him. Besides, he reckoned the alley was regularly used as a toilet most Friday evenings.

The bag was mainly full of junk. Women stuff he'd always called it. Tissues, lipstick, hairbrush and the like. Using the coat as a glove, he opened the purse. Two cards and fifty in notes. He shook his head. This wasn't worth it. Risking arrest for fifty quid wouldn't get him anywhere. He didn't really know what he'd been expecting. He supposed he was lucky to find anyone actually holding cash these days.

One other item in the handbag caught his attention. Another large phone that wasn't a phone. This one was like Charlotte's. The Apple symbol on it could only help its resale value. Ditching the Sim card, bag and coat, he re-entered the street, made a point of checking his flies then hailed another taxi.

He went further west, the roads now clogged with evening traffic. With this being the norm for London, he wasn't surprised everyone used the tube. Though everything seemed close by in reality it wasn't. He reckoned everyone would be better off living on the outskirts of Bristol or Nottingham, and drive to work there. But there'd be one thing missing: they wouldn't be able to say they lived in London.

He stopped the taxi after fifteen minutes. Now not having a clue where he was, apart from being past St Paul's, he walked down the street. Again the combination of takeaways, eateries and drinking establishments, but this time interspersed with shops, both touristy and normal ones. Finding a fairly plush-looking wine bar, he entered.

His first thought was he'd drawn another blank. Groups of people either sat or stood round tables, open ground between them. Two men sat at the bar on stools slowly drinking themselves into a weekend daze, while another stood ordering a round of drinks.

Sitting next to the habitual drinkers, he thought of playing the long game. He could stay there for the night. Eventually, as more and more drink was gulped and people became less stable, they'd leave themselves open. The problem was, the longer he stayed, the more chance someone would recognise him.

Ordering a pint and scotch, he settled in and looked round. The two men nodded as he glanced round, taking everything in. Not really in the mood for conversation, he instead watched the barmaid wipe down the bar area. She was thorough, almost obsessive, about wiping drips. Catching her eye and smiling, she didn't smile back. Work, especially on a Friday night, was just work for her.

Looking at the array of optics behind the bar, a mirror reflected the rest of the bar. He looked at the room full of heavy-walleted Londoners. Ten grand was nothing to this lot. Three or four hundred each would be nothing. Maybe he should ask them. Make up some tat that he was dying or needed it for an operation. They'd just shun him. A few hundred quid to save a life wouldn't impress them. Sure they probably all had standing orders to a Third World Charity, but that was different wasn't it? No, they wouldn't be interested.

Sat in a booth, almost out of sight, but reflected between a bottle of Glencadam and Mexican tequila, Jim noticed two people. A balding man in a suit and a good-looking thirty-something woman with a stray lump of hair. His stomach twisted as he recognised the owner of the hair lump.

Charlotte.

Leaning on the bar, he covered his face with his hand and carried on watching. Unsurprisingly she was doing most of the talking, yet that happy beaming woman he'd dined with hours ago was now a stern and efficient businesswoman. The man had a glint in his eye. Even in mirrored-reverse Jim couldn't fail but notice it. His stomach turned again. Had he read this wrong? It was her job to be pleasant and meet people she didn't necessarily like. She said as much earlier. Was he winding himself up, and making something out of nothing? Breathing out heavily, he leaned further against the bar.

It suddenly hit him. He was a wide boy, a no-good thief. Why did he think she'd be interested? They'd saved someone's life together, that's what had happened. Two random people in London pushed together. Friendship was all it was, and that wouldn't last when she found out where he'd spent the last three years.

Or maybe, just maybe there was more. His stomach cramped. Pulling a mobile from his pocket, he realised it was one of the stolen ones so quickly replaced it. Pulling his own out, he turned it back on. Clumsily deleting the last message he'd nearly sent, he wrote a new one.

Just wanted to say thanks for earlier. Really enjoyed it. Taking a deep breath, he pressed send. The barmaid moved further up the bar wiping the clean surface as she went. Now blocking his view, Jim sighed and moved forwards on his stool. He could just see her face. She stopped talking. Reaching into her pocket, she pulled out her phone.

He felt terrible, sat so close, watching her. Waiting to see her reaction, yet he had to do it. It would end this once and for all. Sleeping at night was going to be hard enough without this as well. She pressed her phone screen a few times, her eyes scanning it. He watched, waiting for some acknowledgement.

The reaction came.

His stomach churned harder. Shivering he tried to finish his scotch but couldn't. He felt sick. He needed fresh air. He left the drinks and walked outside. His legs wobbled everywhere; drink had caught up with him. It wasn't just that, it was her reaction. He stopped and leaned against a sandwich shop door, gulping down breaths.

Slightly calmer, he remembered the look. The look when she realised who the message was from. Her face had changed. The sternly efficient gaze melted, a smile taking its place. Her face seemed to lift as her mind absorbed into the phone.

Jim didn't fully understand why his stomach was turning. Sure, he felt something for her. Three years of her majesty's pleasure had left him yearning for other pleasures, but this was different. He'd never experienced or even believed in the L word. He'd had friends that were obviously fond of each other. He'd had girlfriends himself too, but it was always just a laugh. Never serious. He ran out of the bar because watching her didn't feel right. He was seeing things he shouldn't. None of this was right. Being in the city, the heart of London. This was her domain and he was pissing all over her doorstep.

Heading towards a tube station, his stomach in tatters, his phone bleeped.

Chapter 11

:) I enjoyed it too. Just in meeting. I'll ring soon x. As much as he stared at the phone, the x wasn't giving anything away. He knew that x's had become popular. Some women used it for everyone and everything, while others kept it more personal. What sort was she? It was her first, so he doubted she was a habitual x-er. Why now for the first one? Why? In some ways, he wished she hadn't sent it.

The tube chugged electrically towards Victoria. Jim wanted to go east, towards the Queens Arms, but had settled for the first train out to avoid bumping into Charlotte. He was also wearing a suit, which wouldn't go down well in the Queens Arms.

As messed as his head was, he knew the bank cards and mobiles in his pocket needed offloading. Devoid of any contacts, the Queens Arms was the only place he knew. He was sure he could offload them there. Not that they'd be worth much. All this chip and Pin shit was ruining the average card thief. God knows what Fingers Harry would have to say on the subject. Before, it'd take days for stop notices to get round, and if you made small enough purchases you could run up huge debts. Nowadays, you were talking hours, even minutes if you made a large purchase or bought in the wrong place. Luckily, the cloners still wanted cards. Copies of the cards would be winging their way round the world to countries without chip and Pin readers. He'd probably get a hundred for the seven cards, maybe more as this was London. Everything seemed to cost more in London.

Waiting for his stop he looked at the message again. Her meeting must have dragged on. He hoped she'd ring before he arrived at the Queens Arms; trying to talk to her there would be awkward. He was tempted to ring her, but she said she'd ring. He thought of the bald-headed city letch opposite her and curled his fists. A different time or place and he'd have smacked him, and no doubt been arrested or more usually been smacked back ten times harder.

Changing at Victoria, Jim waddled through the crowded terminal for his connection. The next tube was rammed, sweaty and embarrassingly quiet. Though a good opportunity for petty theft, Jim knew that tube trains were notoriously difficult. There was literally nowhere to run. Following the herd off the tube, he walked back to the hotel. Approaching the door, his phone rang.

Charlotte.

"Hi, it's only me," she said. "I've been stuck in a really bad meeting for hours; you wouldn't believe it. The bloke's a moron. Still, that's life isn't it? You have to take the good with the bad ..."

Jim nodded at the receptionist as he walked towards the stairs. She shrugged her shoulders back. Whatever he was doing, she didn't care.

"I mean some people just don't know a good deal when they see it. He almost needed it spelling out. Apart from that the afternoon just sort of flew by. I went back to my office for a bit ..."

Opening his room, Jim started to switch off. He liked her talking, it felt like having the radio on, but it was too one-sided to really listen to. Emptying his pockets he lay down and, phone clamped to his head, properly examined his haul. Carrying the wallet had been a risk. He should have dumped it straight away.

"... but I don't really know about that. I mean, you think you know someone and then they come out with that. That's juniors for you, I suppose."

Her slight pause caught him out while he was fiddling with his gloves. He was trying to pull them on without touching the outsides. A losing battle. She continued. "There's a new mystery series on the telly tonight. Do you like mystery series? Or thrillers I suppose they're called. I love them ..."

Finally getting one glove on, he held the other to get easier access. Pulling the cards from the wallet, he remembered that although he touched them using his jacket, his dabs or DNA may still be on them. They needed cleaning.

Besides the money, credit and other cards, there was also an emergency condom which was just in date. Jim copied Martin's address onto the back of a Tower of London brochure. He hoped having Raif's address would be enough, but it never hurt to hedge your bets.

"... and crime series too. They're so cleverly done, aren't they? Just keep you in suspense the whole time. Some of them are a bit unbelievable. I mean you know there are criminals out there, but if you watch these programmes you'd think everyone was at it ..."

There was no answer Jim could give to that. He just thanked his not very lucky stars she was still talking. Niggling doubts over where this could go resurfaced. He went back to counting his new money. He'd barely made four hundred after the drinks and taxis. He should have made well over a grand. This wasn't a good start.

"... I can't stand adverts though. I sometimes just pause the telly for ten minutes and do something else so I don't have to watch them."

Quietness descended.

After a few seconds, Jim said, "So, is there anywhere you want to go tomorrow? You know, anything you want to do?"

"Oh, that's the other thing. I've got a really early start Sunday; got to work would you believe. On a Sunday. So anyway, I'm going to have to get to sleep early ..."

Jim knew it'd been too good to be true. She'd seen through him. Her next line would be, "you're really nice and all that, but ..."

"So I was thinking," she said, "are you free tomorrow afternoon instead?"

He gasped. Had she really said that? "Yeah," he replied, forgetting about his ten grand debt.

"Good. I was thinking, perhaps, I mean say if you're not interested, but, there's an art exhibition at the South Bank I'd like to check out. I mean, if you don't want to then say. I don't mind. I know it's not everyone's cup of tea, but one of my clients was talking about it and it sounds good."

"No, that sounds great," he lied.

"Excellent. Look I'm just about to hit the underground. I'll have to say goodbye."

"Okay. Shall I ring tomorrow morning then?"

"Yeah. Okay, got to go. Bye," she replied.

A change of clothes, gloves and a wipe down of the cards took Jim fifteen minutes. Within an hour he was outside the Queens Arms. He was concerned he'd bump into Charlotte at the tube station, but luckily he didn't. The East End was different at night. Jim wasn't scared, but he understood how some may be. Daylight still clung to the streets, but the grime and dereliction made it darker, sinister.

Jim wondered what the world was coming to with all these thieves, muggers and fraudsters around. Harry would have a similar view. "Streets ain't safe no more," he'd say. "Was a time when you didn't have to worry about being mugged, but now it's as regular as taking a dump."

The Queens Arms was busier than the previous day. Jim was surprised just how busy considering its other life as a sleepy, daytime pub. Looking at some of the clientele, well-dressed young people, he guessed they'd stopped for a pint before moving on elsewhere.

Seeing Tim By Four and the plasterer playing pool, Jim nodded then headed for the bar. A clear tension surrounded the group in front of the bar. Already half drunk and with plenty of spare seats around, they'd set their stall on blocking other people rather than having a quiet drink. The group of young lads, maybe too young to drink, seemed to gain pleasure in hindering others. Jim almost felt he had to ask permission to get through. Greeted with looks that said, "Not from these parts are you?" Jim held his nerve and struggled through. Things had changed in this country. It wasn't just London but everywhere. Respect had gone.

Feeling old, he got his warm pint and moved to the pool table. The lads at the bar were staying well clear of that area. Maybe Tim and them had had dealings before. Maybe there was some respect left, but you had to earn it. It wasn't just given anymore.

"Alright lads," said Jim.

"Jimbo," said Tim. "Putting your name up then?" He pointed at a chipped blackboard with incorrectly spelt names dangling from the wall. Jim nodded and scrawled his name under the last. The split grain of chalk made it look like jjm.

Though Tim was playing with Mick, someone called "Danny Boy" was up next though the word "boy" had been written with a different hand to Danny.

"How's tricks?" said Mick.

"Yeah, not bad. Mustn't grumble. Yourself?"

"We gave up at lunchtime and came here. Brickies are taking too long; dossing round most of them."

"Not bothered though, are we?" said Tim. "Still get paid, see."

"Can I have a word, Tim." Jim knew it sounded too serious. He should have waited or worded it differently. "Do you know any, er, fences, mate?"

Tim scrunched his nose up and shook his head. "I'm trying to keep out of trouble."

"I know, mate. I won't, you know, involve you. I'm just in a sticky patch. I need pointing the right way."

Tim sighed and pointed his pool cue towards a scabby-faced loner nursing half a mild in the corner. "Terence the Ference we call him. Don't get me involved, pal. I'm on licence."

"So am I," said Jim, walking towards Terence. "So am I."

Jim pulled a barstool from under Terence's table and sat opposite. Closer up, his face was clearer; like a weasel sucking a sour sweet. "Can I get you a drink, pal?"

"Maybe." He swirled the dregs of his mild round, staring at the bar.

"You're Terence? We might be able to help each other."

Terence turned and stared at Jim. He felt his gaze hovering over his face, shoulders and stomach. "Don't know what you're talking about." He spoke with too much pleasure and the dregs of an Irish accent.

"I'm a mate of Tim By Four." Jim knew he was sounding desperate.

Terence looked behind him over at the pool table. Jim guessed Tim must have nodded because he turned back. "First things first," he said, planting the nearly empty glass in front of Jim.

Jim nodded and stood up. A path cleared amongst the youths to allow him to the bar. Jim guessed they'd seen him talk to Tim and Mick. There was something between the lads and Tim. Buying four pints, he took two to Tim and Mick before returning to Terence with his mild.

He took a huge glug as if Jim might change his mind and want it back. "What you got?"

"Seven cards, driving licence and a couple of smart phones."

"Same person?" Terence asked.

Jim shook his head. "Three different ones. The driving licence matches three of the cards."

A smile crossed Terence's thin lips which quickly faded as his brain appeared to hatch a plan. "Not worth a fortune, my friend, but I should be able to do something." Terence took another huge mouthful of mild, leaving a third left in the bottom. "Wait a minute then knock on cubicle three." Standing, he hobbled to the toilets. Flicking a glance back to the pool table, Jim nodded at Tim who smiled briefly then nodded back. After counting to one hundred, he stood up and went to the toilet.

Walking into the damp chill of the toilet block, Jim breathed through his mouth to negate the powerful aroma. Knocking on cubicle three, Jim wasn't surprised when the door opened and Terence ushered him in.

The cramped and smelly office wasn't needed for long. Jim handed over the cards to a muttering Terence and was handed fifty quid in grubby tenners.

"Is that all?"

"Not worth much more, pal. Driving licence is the best. Cloners like them, see. Got name, address and date of birth." His faint drawl made birth sound like both.

Jim nodded. The tube fare and the drinks he'd bought hardly made it worthwhile. "Oh nearly forgot." Jim pulled the Blackberry and iPhone from his pocket, the batteries and cases detached. "How much for these?"

"Yeah. Quite high demand for them. You've thrown the Sims away?"

Jim nodded.

Terence nodded back and pulled five more tenners from his pocket. Jim snaffled them from his hand still wondering what a Blackberry actually did.

"Do you get rid of bigger stuff too?"

"What you got in mind, son?"

"TV's, DVD's, stereos? Maybe bit of furniture?"

Terence did his wily head shake again. "To be sure, but you no going to get rich."

Jim nodded again. "Know where I can get a small lock-up? Just a garage would do."

Terence eyed the tenners still in Jim's hand and stroked his chin. "Oh, I don't really know."

"There's a drink in it."

"Try "Filthy Alan". He's got a tat shop on the High Street."

Jim walked back to the bar, now almost empty, and ordered another pint of mild. More than half the youngsters had disappeared. One of the remaining ones was playing pool with Mick. Dropping the mild off to the smiling Terence, Jim joined Tim and Mick. The lad, Danny Boy was a good player, giving Mick a run for his money, though he kept himself to himself throughout the game. However, his foul on the black after clearing the table was almost certainly deliberate, leaving Mick an easy win.

After some feigned disappointment, Danny Boy rejoined his mates before leaving. Now Jim's turn on the table, he racked up the balls letting Mick break. Halfway through the game, Jim asked the pair whether they'd be up for helping with a little job on Sunday. Though Tim wasn't overly keen at the idea, he soon came round.

After his third pint, Jim's head felt light. Though he'd been drinking all day, it'd only just hit. Feeling a slight swagger in his walk, and a blurriness when lining up a shot, it reminded him of good times, and of Friday nights long ago.

It was only the phone buzzing in his pocket that brought him back to London and a ten grand debt. And Charlotte, of course. Downing his pint, he pointed to the phone, made excuses then left.

Hi. Are you sure the art gallery is okay? :) the message read. Walking down the High Street, the gang of youths had taken up position outside a kebab shop. Now three times more intimidating, Jim pocketed his phone as he walked by. They looked at him differently than before. He'd no doubt some of them were tooled up, but they'd seen him with Tim and Mick and that appeared to give him some kind of status.

A few shops down, he pulled the phone back from his pocket and replied, *Course it* is. *I like a bit of culture.* Knowing the only culture he approved of was fermented yeast, he smiled and carried on walking.

A grubby second-hand shop called "Alan's Emporium" was undoubtedly Filthy Alan's tat shop. Filthy Alan had long since locked up and disappeared for the night. He'd have to come back tomorrow during the day which, given his date with Charlotte and the clothing changes it required, would make tomorrow tight.

The tube station was busy. As it wound through the soil towards central London its clientele changed from working classes, who'd just finished or were starting shifts, to a wealthier class going out for the evening. In the space of three miles, Jim observed the change.

As he emerged above ground, his phone bleeped. *Sure? I don't mind if you want to do something else x.*

He couldn't say no. How could he refuse an x? It wasn't possible. Jim's chubby and slightly the worse for wear fingers typed, *Course. Looking forward to it x.*

The x had been returned over the net. Though it felt too early for x's, Jim felt it the right ball to serve. He wasn't bothered with scoring points. He just wanted her to know he didn't mind where they went. All he wanted was her company.

Her reply, *xxx*. Jim knew he'd read many things into that over the next twelve hours.

He'd missed the hotel's all-inclusive evening meal. Though he'd eaten well earlier, his belly slopping with alcohol needed more. He settled on a burger and chips from an imitation McDonalds round the corner from the hotel. Glad of some processed meat, Jim chuckled while sat in the corner. He wasn't sure exactly how to end the vegetarian flood now the gates had been opened. Then again, where exactly was it going? There's only so long a man can pretend to work for the ONS before getting caught out. Then there was the money. Even if he found ten big ones, how long could he live in London. What could he do, carry on robbing? Nah, he'd get caught. At some point the truth would out.

Finishing his salty burger, he tried to move the sudden sense of hopelessness. His brain, fried by the afternoon's alcohol, was telling him he needed more. More alcohol. Only then could this make sense. Stopping at a corner shop, he bought a half bottle of whisky that'd never been near Scotland and retired to the hotel room.

Next door were still conspicuous by their absence. He did wonder if they were dead; some sex game gone wrong. Slowly rotting next door, the smell would eventually give away their demise. Jim had no doubt he'd get the blame for that too.

He lay on his bed and turned on the television. He wondered, just for a second, if a quick look round next door would be in order. They may have left something behind, practically begging for a new home. He discounted this. Any sign of a break-in and the police would be called. They'd want to speak to him as their neighbour. No, he'd leave them alone.

Downing whisky from the bottle, he watched the television. The program was a gritty new crime show, and he was sure it was the one Charlotte would be watching. A weather-worn, world-weary detective was investigating a series of murders in Lincolnshire. Jim's vision was slowing blurring and the actor's voices lost midway to his brain. A few more gulps of whisky and the room took on a circular motion. He tried to reach for his phone, to send one last message to Charlotte, but heavy eyes beat him to it.

Sleep ended a long day.

Chapter 12

Morning broke with a fierce headache and a text message. Blurred eyes and a delayed brain read the message, *Morning x. I'll be ready about one.* Noticing it was already ten and he'd missed breakfast, Jim walked to the bathroom, phone in hand, and turned on the shower.

See you at one. Where shall i meet u? he clumsily replied.

Leaving the phone next to the sink, he stumbled into the shower. The phone buzzed as he battled to wash the whisky and sleep from his skin. The piddly, quarter-sized complementary soap was soon gone, but Jim stayed under the shower for another five minutes until he was sure the worst of yesterday had been removed.

Drying with the half-sized towel, he retrieved her reply, *Tube station? Or outside coffee shop?*

Wet and slippery hands typed, *Coffee shop sounds good.* He pondered whether to stick an x after, but decided against. Receiving the message, *Okay xxx,* he shook his head and reached for his razor.

As his hour and a half of preparations, coffee drinking and television watching continued, he received two more messages which he replied to. Neither contained earth shattering news but were just a running commentary on whether she'd be slightly late or not. Looking at himself in the mirror, with painkillers finally killing the hangover, Jim thought he looked fairly presentable. Clean clothes were running out, he'd only a few anyway and nearly a week in a hotel had taken its toll. He'd have to visit a laundry soon; somehow squeeze that into his other plans of making ten grand. Problem was, he still didn't have a plan. Street robbery and wallet stealing seemed easy enough, but it wasn't getting him anywhere. Taking a hundred from his stash, he remembered he needed to pay for a few more nights in the hotel tomorrow. That would only leave three hundred.

Next door had reappeared at some point overnight. God knows where they'd been or what they'd been up to. Maybe he should have broken in while he had the chance. He shook his head. What was the point? He may have got a few hundred or some near worthless credit cards, but not ten grand. Plus, it was too close to home.

Leaving at ten to one, Jim walked the heavily-trodden path towards the cinema and coffee shop round the corner. Arriving a few minutes beforehand, he checked inside but she wasn't there. Leaning against the wall, he checked his phone for missed messages: none. Of course, he knew she'd be late. She'd blame not being able to find her strapless shoes or her front door key or something.

He looked again inside the coffee shop. It had a lot to answer for. Selling its near infinite range of unpronounceable coffee-themed drinks, it alone had brought their initial conversation. He wondered how different things might be if she hadn't cried so much when the ambulance left, or if she'd refused the offer of a drink.

He sighed. He'd never know.

He had to admit, this whole idea of dating someone was both new and scary. Not the same variety of scary as walking into a prison dining room on your first day; eyes everywhere trying to catch yours so they can accuse you of staring at them. No, it was different. A more awkward, stomach turning fear of being hurt in a different way. On the inside instead of out.

She arrived ten minutes late. Watching the sun catch her hair and smile, with her flowery summer skirt clinging to each step, Jim felt her entrance couldn't have been better if a Hollywood director had staged it. With ten paces to go, Jim rested his head on his shoulder. The wolf whistle he was desperate to let out held back. Smiling, they walked the last few steps to each other. Unsure again whether to offer a kiss or his hand, he just said, "Hello."

"Sorry I'm late. I couldn't find my strapless shoes."

Jim's smile nearly turned to a laugh as he shrugged his shoulders. "You look fine." He quickly added, "More than fine."

She smiled again as they walked past the cinema and the piece of tarmac that Geoffrey had nearly croaked on. Side by side, Jim thought of taking her arm but didn't.

"Wonder how he is," said Jim.

"I'll ring the hospital later and find out. They said yesterday he was doing well."

Jim nodded.

The conversation stilted as they neared the station. Charlotte hadn't launched into the tirade of chatter Jim thought she would. Jim himself struggled to think of an intelligent topic. Polite conversation about the weather, disappearing shoes and the last art exhibition Charlotte had been to was all he could muster.

Arriving at the tube station, Jim inserted some coins into the machine to buy a one day travel card.

"Haven't you got an Oyster?" She flashed her blue card at him.

He'd seen them around. One of them was in the toff's wallet he robbed yesterday, but he was paranoid enough without having his entire travel details stored on a database. Plus, he could hardly register one without an address or bank account. Charlotte's slight frown told him she was wondering why he didn't have one for work. She didn't look as if she believed he queued up every morning for a ticket.

"Um." His brain was still cloudy from last night's whisky. "I get a weekly Travelcard and work refunds part of it. It's easier just to buy the ticket." He'd no idea if the ONS would actually pay for staff getting to work and back. If they did, he thought the government ought to do something about it.

"Oh." She didn't look convinced. The lump of hair fell from its position on her forehead, snaking past her eyes.

Through the gates and down to the tube, Charlotte told him about her Oyster card and how she couldn't do without it. Jim was surprised when she said it automatically topped itself up when running low and it even worked out the cheapest route and fare for each day. All that data though, all that information on every journey. It had evidence written all over it.

"What happens if you lose it?" The stolen card was still back at his flat. He was considering it.

"You report it stolen and they put a stop on it."

The thought went as quickly as it came. Maybe Terence would give him something for it. They must have some value.

The LED display said the tube was three minutes away, which meant it was actually six minutes away. Jim was getting used to London and its eccentricities. The other passengers waiting were silent, except for a gang of young lads, no doubt going to the city for the day. Conversation still wasn't coming naturally between them. Racking his head for something to say, Charlotte beat him to it.

"Cool down here isn't it?"

Jim knew it was going badly; they were talking about the weather again. She'd probably sussed he was in a different league. This was going to be a long afternoon.

"I always think of the blitz whenever I'm here." He looked up at the CCTV camera pointing at his head. Maybe an Oyster card was the least of his worries. "I've always thought they must have been freezing in the middle of winter."

Charlotte looked round. If she was looking for some evidence of the blitz, sixty years of renovations and graffiti had removed it. "It's amazing everything they went through, isn't it?" She looked back, her eyes locking on his. "To think, the things we moan about today. Hardly bears comparison does it?"

Jim wondered if it could get worse. He'd introduced death and destruction into the conversation. If this was going to work, he had to make one hell of an impression. "I'm sure one of the rights they fought for was for us to sue the council if we fell over a pothole. Wasn't that what Churchill said after 'fight them on the beaches'?"

It was nearly funny inside his head. After the words left his lips, he realised it was less than funny. She smiled, nothing more. A gust of air, forced through the platform, told them the train was arriving. The clock still read three minutes away as it had for the last five. Minding the gap, they took a side bench in a half full coach, sitting next to each other.

Sharing the tube with Saturday shoppers, tourists with cameras and the odd miserable worker, the tube trudged through the relative coolness of the underground. Sat in near silence, which Jim found uncomfortable, he occasionally caught her eyes in the reflection from the window opposite.

Most people disembarked for the main sights leaving the tube quieter as it headed towards the dead-at-weekend financial area. Taking advantage of their near privacy, Jim caught her eye again in the tunnel-blackened window and stuck out his tongue. Her eyes lit up, dimples appeared and the lump of hair dislodged itself from her brow. She screwed her nose up theatrically and returned the gesture. Near laughing, Jim stuck his thumbs in his ears and waggled his hands in a way he hadn't since school. Giggling, she stuck her own hand in front of her nose and waved it. After saying, "Ner ner nener ner," Jim laughed loudly then turned to her.

Removing her hand from her nose, her eyes met his. Her clear blue retinas seemed to peer into his soul, searching for something. He felt himself blushing but kept the gaze, slowly moving his head inch by inch towards her. She licked then pursed her lips. Her own face was moving towards his too. Now just inches apart, if the driver hadn't have said, "Next stop is Bank. Bank is the next stop," Jim thought they would have kissed.

Walking along the sunny embankment, the mouldy Thames beside them, Charlotte led Jim towards the art gallery. She'd already got them lost twice and, laughing and joking around, they'd reverted to giddy teenagers.

The art gallery now just in view, thanks to the help of some GPS mapping app on Charlotte's iPhone, Jim's heart beat harder as he struggled for things to say. The tube driver had a lot to answer for. He'd made a difficult position harder. He considered stopping, taking her hand and moving in for a kiss. This was London though. She'd likely smack or spray him with mace. Instead, he looked at the river. Warm but murky despite all the attempts to clean it up. He wondered how often it was dredged. How long would a body lay at the bottom before it was noticed? He hoped he wouldn't find out.

"What you thinking about?"

He looked round, the midday sun catching the lump of hair that stood ready to fall down. Feeling himself smile, he said, "Nothing. Nothing that can't wait."

With the gallery now in sight, he thought of reaching for her hand. The near miss in the tube was in danger of becoming ancient history. As his hand sneaked its way towards hers, her pace seemed to increase. Unsure whether she'd seen the hand or was just keen to get to the gallery, he shrugged his shoulders, put his hand in his pocket and followed her.

At the entrance, a security guard, or curator as he later learnt he was called, greeted and handed a pamphlet to Charlotte. She thanked him before they walked a few paces towards the middle and tried to get some bearings. Looking round, the gallery was filled with pictures and sculptures made of both stone and what looked like domestic rubbish. White backgrounds and walls made every piece leap out from sharp angles. The pictures and pieces of art themselves were, Jim thought, nothing special. Blobs of paint and old cans stuck together didn't really work in his book. It wasn't art as he knew it. He was no connoisseur, and he could admire the effort and ability it took to paint a landscape, but five blobs of varying shades of red paint on a woman's trainer? He didn't see how that took any ability. He also didn't see what the hell that had to do with repressed slave labour workers. Charlotte seemed to get it though. That was good enough for him.

The hour walking round went too quickly. There was only one piece he could describe as likeable. A landscape in the classical sense, except it portrayed a modern street scene. Muggers hiding in the shadows, ladies of the night advertising their wares while pimps looked on threateningly, and drunks flailing at each other over some pointless argument. He stood for five minutes taking in every detail.

"Good, isn't it?" she said.

"Yeah. It's like the opposite of an old painting, isn't it?" He'd never make an art critic on a late night BBC2 programme, but he hoped he'd got over his point.

"Past meets present." She pointed to the same street scene in the pamphlet by some artist from the 1800s. "Wonder what the original artist would make of it."

Jim nodded. He walked with Charlotte for another ten minutes as she looked at all the works. Quiet, the gallery only had about ten visitors. Some were obviously upper class. Cravats and country clothing worn as emblems of wealth. Maybe they were looking at the exhibits as potential purchases hoping to buy something from the next big thing. Others meanwhile were ordinary but affluent Londoners, here for a day of culture. The artists themselves were few and far between. Charlotte congratulated one on his excellent piece of work, but the young man's lip curl and snarl proved he put more effort into his attitude than he ever did into his attempt at art.

Jim felt he'd been well behaved throughout. There was obvious temptation to make money, but he'd let it go. Charlotte meanwhile had taken a few secret pictures on her mobile even though photography was banned. "You'll get me in trouble," he'd said, the irony lost on her.

After a brief attempt by the curator to sell them some artwork and give them brochures for future events, they went to the coffee shop next door. Buying Charlotte a coffee and himself a tea was not a cheap process. He also managed to nearly get her order right. It was certainly closer than his previous attempt.

Sat by the extensive glass windows, looking over the Thames and its craft chugging by, reality was catching up with him. Time was moving on and although he was enjoying every minute, he had a lock-up to rent and money to somehow make. Conversation had all but died, but occasionally Charlotte would mention the work she needed to do as preparation for tomorrow's meeting. He sensed, or hoped, she didn't want the afternoon to end either but knew it had too. There were other days they could do this. Assuming he wasn't dead in five days.

Catching the tube back to their stop it was too crowded to pull funny faces, so they sat in silence reading the tube map over and over again. When Jim leant slightly on Charlotte's arm she didn't pull away. Leaving the station they meandered through the streets, Charlotte deciding which streets. It was unsaid, but Jim knew she was going home and he was walking her. This whole date malarkey had been easier then he'd thought. He'd been expecting to be constantly trying to entertain or impress her. Without the aid of alcohol, the real and not very interesting him was all he had to offer. Funniest thing of all was she didn't seem to mind.

Nearing a newly converted block of old warehouses, Charlotte started talking again. Not the slow conversation she'd been making all day, but her old style of phone hyper-talking. Her speed increased the nearer they got to the luxury ex-warehouses. He thought her defence mechanism had kicked in.

The non-stop breakdown of what she was doing tomorrow reached a crescendo as she stood by the door to one of the old buildings that had been nearly tastefully renovated. Turning, she faced him.

"This is me then."

"Looks nice."

"Oh, it's okay. Bit expensive to heat in the winter but it just about does, I mean ..."

He wanted to kiss her, not only to shut her up, but also just to make it clear how much he'd enjoyed the last few hours. The near miss haunted him again. Would that be it forever? He'd be kicking himself for the rest of his short life if it was. The mood just didn't feel right to pounce. No alcohol, that was the problem. He didn't want a detailed breakdown of electric bills and why storage heaters may look good but are useless at heating a warehouse. He wanted her.

"... but that's what you get for having so much open space I suppose."

She'd finished.

"Thanks," he said. "I've had a great time."

"Thank you." Her hair flopped down.

"Can we do it again?" He expected her to say no. He didn't know why, but this whole dream, this whole Charlotte thing had to end. Maybe she'd be kind and end it now for both their sakes.

She nodded. "Yeah. I'd like that." Turning, she unlocked the front door and half stepped inside. Jim moved nearer, standing partly on the doorstep. He could see up the stairs and into her apartment. Moving his face forward towards hers, he saw her lips.

The kiss happened. He wasn't sure if it lasted seconds or milliseconds, but he was briefly lost in a world where nothing mattered.

"Bye for now then." Another lump of hair had joined its sibling across her eyes and her cheeks reminded him of a tomato sauce bottle.

"Bye."

Chapter 13

Walking towards the tube station, a spring in his step, Jim hoped he'd catch Filthy Alan before he closed. He reckoned Filthy's flat was above the shop so chances were good. As the tube ground east, Jim hated to think how much he'd spent in fares. Obviously not ten grand, but he reckoned most of the money he'd made had gone straight in the mayor's pocket.

The East End was as inviting as ever. Saturday market stalls were closing down, side streets were full of litter, fishmongers waste and needles, and groups of young hoodies hung around hoping to intimidate pensioners. Finding Filthy Alan's shop was easy despite last night's drink.

Opening the door, a waft of stale air that'd probably seen the blitz greeted his nose. A fragrant mixture of stale urine, unwashed male and mothballs combined with the dust and dim lighting completed the picture. Scanning the shop, Jim noticed the diverse items: old umbrellas, wardrobes, books, cigarette cards. The thick layer of dust suggested nothing had been purchased or moved in years.

Wondering how a shop so obviously a front could have survived without getting busted, Jim called out, "Hello, anyone home?" A small and frail yet dirty man appeared from behind a curtain. Milk-bottle glasses hid a face you'd never trust to babysit a kid. His pot belly extending over undone and stained trousers was as big an advert of his single status as the lack of rings on his fingers.

"You Alan?" He knew he was. It was obvious. The bloke was filthy.

"Who wants to know?" He peered through the murky half-light trying to recognise Jim.

"I'm a mate of Terence's. I'm looking to, er, rent a garage for a week."

Filthy nodded his head. "Terence, eh." He walked to his fifties style till and rung up no-sale. Collecting a few keys, he walked from behind the counter. "I'll need to lock up; it's round the back." He nodded up and down again, looking at Jim as if he recognised him. "What's your name, son?"

"Jim." He didn't offer his hand for a shake. It wasn't clear what decade Alan had last washed his.

Locking the shop, the limping Alan led Jim round the back. The once tarmac-covered road now lay in blotches of grass, weed and nettles. The lock-up, though secure, smelt as bad as the shop. Various nondescript rags, an old mattress and some magazines lay in a corner, while a few empty whisky bottles lined the walls.

"Fifty a week. Two weeks in advance."

"I've only got eighty on me. Will that do for now?"

"Go on then." Alan nodded and bared a few blackened teeth. "I'll trust you, pal."

Handing over eighty, Jim received the key and left the garage, locking it behind him. He only had a few quid in coins left, but luckily he'd bought a zone three travel card so he could take a tube north before heading back to central London.

The tube was busy as it crawled north. Shoppers returned home with bags and smiles. Everyone in the carriage seemed to have headphones on. The iPod was a mystery to Jim. What was wrong with vinyl and cassettes? Apart from the bulk and ease of damage of course. The world just wanted to get smaller and more digitalised every week. He wondered where or how it would end. They were expensive too these music players, and so small. Expensive and small. He smiled as half a plan hatched in his brain.

Finding the road he wanted was hard; he needed a map but his money was at the hotel. He knew he'd look conspicuous asking for the road. Of course this was London, and they had invented the look the other way culture, but he still reckoned with his luck he'd get caught on CCTV or ask the wrong person.

Once he had the street, finding the flat was easy. A tall Victorian house, it'd been split into three or four flats plus a basement box room. Raif Mortimer, or Twat A as Jim still preferred to call him, owned flat two. Jim guessed this was the first floor and rang the buzzer next to the number two. Three minutes later he rang again. Then again. No answer.

Satisfied that Raif was living it up in Monaco with no house-sitters, Jim wandered back to the tube station. Central London and its plethora of tourists, out of towners and drunkards beckoned.

With the time just after seven, and another missed hotel dinner behind him, Jim strolled through Covent Garden between the swathes of well-dressed theatregoers, nightclubbers and general minglers. The wine bar he chose was reassuringly expensive. Pushing through the crowds towards the back, he quickly scanned for unattended purses, jackets, mobiles and bags.

Reaching the toilet at the rear without either incident or other people's property, he waited a few minutes in a cubicle. Though he'd desperately not wanted to do this tonight, he only had enough money for a few drinks. If he wasted that money by buying a drink and scanning the bar, he could lose it all before he even got started. The hope that a better plan would have come to him by now was just hope. Still clueless, the only real thing left was to get a few more wallets to tide him over.

The only thing he'd spotted through the bar was a handbag on the floor next to a table. The table's occupants, obviously from the sticks for a memorable night out, were too engrossed in their conversation to consider anything a threat.

That was too risky. He'd been lucky last night; there were no coats around and the bag's owner was sitting right next to it. As flamboyant as London was, walking out of a wine bar carrying a handbag was going to turn heads. It didn't even look manbaggish as some handbags seemed to.

Manbags. Jim wondered what on earth Fingers Harry would make of them. "It ain't right," he'd say. "A man's got pockets, ain't he? What's he need a fuckin handbag for?" In some ways his life sentence was for his own benefit as well as society's.

Smiling, Jim thought back to those nights. Those long prison nights. An easier life; no one bugging you for ten grand, and no one threatening to kill you. No expensive hotels.

No Charlotte.

Pulling his mobile from his pocket, he thought about sending a message. He hadn't a clue what to type. Anything would do. Anything. Re-pocketing the phone, he shook his head. He'd send one later when he got back to the hotel.

Could he take the handbag? Walk with it towards the front door, clean it out of purse, phone and whatever else as he walked then dump it? Could he? Too risky, anyone could see. The bar was so packed he'd be trapped if someone raised the alarm. No, too risky. Sure he needed money, but silly risks would see him back inside quicker than Fingers Harry could destroy a manbag. No, he'd walk back out, find another bar and start again. He had all night after all; the only thing complaining was his empty stomach.

Walking out he passed a different table of intently talking theatregoers. The programmes on the table and *Les Miserables* baseball caps were dead giveaways. Noticing a jacket slumped on the back of a chair, Jim slowed and brought his left hand near the jacket's hem. Breathing hard, he paused slightly and slipped his hand inside the pocket, using his body to cover the rest of his hand. His hand made contact with a wallet-sized lump of leathery plastic. Swiftly clenching and pulling it out, he palmed it into his other hand then his pocket. It took less than two seconds. Jim was impressed with himself. All that practise inside had come in handy. Feeling a rush of adrenalin, the fear of getting caught he supposed, he realised why some did it time and time again just for that rush.

Outside, and after a brisk walk, he found an alleyway. Rummaging through his new wallet he was annoyed again he hadn't brought gloves. Charlotte was the fault. His brain a mess of art galleries and doorstep goodbyes, he'd lost the plot somewhere.

The wallet had two credit cards, a driving licence and fifty pounds in notes. The owner, Mr Les Hibbert, would no doubt be fairly miserable himself when he realised it was missing.

Something else inside the wallet stopped him. A NHS employee card for a hospital in Oxford. The bloke obviously worked there. Jim guessed he needed the card for security or something. The job title stood out - porter. The bloke looked mid-fifties, yet he was a porter. Maybe he'd been forced into the job, made redundant, the only alternative the scrapheap. Or perhaps he'd always been a porter; not everyone in Oxford could be a professor.

He thought of the theatre tickets. London wasn't cheap as he knew to his own cost. This was their big night; probably been saving all year, and the Bank of Jim had just ruined it.

Shaking his head, he placed the cards back in the wallet and turned round. Walking away, something inside made him stop. A little voice telling him that perhaps this once in a lifetime trip for the Hibbert clan might be just that. Perhaps one of them was ill. The last wish of someone with six months left to live was to see a show.

He found himself back inside the pub. Walking a few steps, he looked at the bar and then round the room twice. When he was sure enough people had seen him, he looked at the Hibberts, opened the wallet then looked again. Walking to the table, he caught Les's eyes.

"Excuse me, I think this is yours."

The man look confused then shook his head. "No my wallet's in my ..." He reached for his jacket, felt the pockets. The groping increased as the wallet-sized lump couldn't be found. His eyes grew wider, panic setting in as he knew it was missing. Looking at the wallet in Jim's hand, he nodded, mouth open. Jim opened it again, checked the picture against the gaping, fish-like Les Hibbert then handed it to him.

"Thanks," he said.

Jim just shrugged his shoulders. "It was outside, on the floor."

Les looked through it, counting the cards then the money. "It's all here."

Jim turned to walk away.

"Wait," a woman, possibly Mrs Hibbert said. "Do you want a drink? Buy him a drink Les. Go on, get up. Go on. Buy the man a drink."

Jim turned back round. "No, it's fine. I've got to go."

"Here." Les himself was standing now, a twenty pound note in his hand. "Have a few drinks, eh. Call it a reward."

"No. Seriously, I've got to go." He felt his face redden. Most of the bar were watching. As he headed for the door, he heard Mrs Hibbert say what nice people Londoners were. He thought she couldn't have been more wrong.

Outside, he walked. He could probably put the last few minute's actions down to stress or even Charlotte, but no, strange thoughts had run amok in his head. He needed ten grand. His life depended on it. What fucking right did he have to pick and choose who to rob? Everyone was fair game. The thieving Jim deep inside him knew that. This week was going to be hard enough without vetting everyone he stole from.

A traditional London Irish themed pub caught his eye. He needed a break and a drink, a chance to get his head back in order. The bar, a mix of Irish, wannabe Irish and people just itching for a fight, was fair company. Sat on a barstool, Jim tried to speak with the man slumped next to him who seemed in a different plane of intoxication to everyone else. The barman, a casual looking shaven-headed Australian, nodded at the man then shook his head. Jim took the free advice and left him alone.

The pint half-quaffed in ten minutes, he pulled out his phone. He'd got used to regular messages. She was obviously busy preparing for tomorrow, but he'd still hoped for a text. Nothing more had been arranged either just shall we do it again. Typing *Thanks again for earlier. How's work going?* he debated with himself for a few seconds before sending.

The barman smiled and nodded at his phone. "Don't know what we did before them, mate."

"Yeah." Jim struggled to think of a follow-up. The Aussie looked friendly enough. On a year off or whatever, supposedly touring the world but actually spending his Saturday nights serving in an imitation Irish pub in London. Jim knew as bad as his life was, there was always someone worse off.

"You just here for the day then, mate?"

"Nah. Working here for a few weeks. Thought I'd check out the bright lights and all that." The barman smiled before serving another customer. Jim quaffed another glug of Guinness. The near comatose man by his side coughed. Spittle covered his chin and he gurgled with every short breath.

Taking another sip, the need to smoke was returning. He knew he wasn't alone. Most of the pub's drinkers seemed to be in the garden. A few coats were dotted round, some of them being looked after by solitary non-smokers. Another desperate half idea formed in his mind. If only he could distract the coat-watchers away. Not in this pub, obviously, but in the busier wine bars. Problem was, it seemed the affluent didn't smoke as much. They were too busy detoxing or going to the gym to have time to smoke. In some ways, he knew it the reserve of the poor and downtrodden. Worse thing was, it didn't even do anything. Highly addictive but with little effect. What was the point of it?

"What about you," Jim asked the barman. "How long you here for?"

"Visa runs out next month. I had plans for visiting Scotland and Cornwall, but they fell apart."

Jim nodded. As pleasant as this was, it wasn't getting him ten grand. The theatregoers would be heading for their performances soon. This was prime robbing time and he was wasting it talking to an Aussie.

"See you, mate." He downed his pint and walked outside.

Street performers were making the most of the evening light to entertain and make money. Whether card tricks, mime or just comedy, they were making a mint from the passing crowds. Jim wondered whether they were doing anything different from himself. Sure, their money was donated instead of forced, but it came down to the same thing.

Stopping at one, a bald-headed man round a card table with various cups and hidden balls, Jim wondered if he could do it. He'd learnt and almost perfected sleight of hand in prison. He'd also learnt a few card tricks too. After all, they were both just cons. It might earn him something. Less chance of getting arrested too. He could buy a few packs of cards, mark them subtly and remember each one. Even get hold of a foldaway table and come down here for a few days. Five days left. Two grand a day.

He sighed as he watched, spotting the man palm a card and shove it up his sleeve as he made fun of an onlooker. Of course everyone had turned to look at the source of his joke. Only Jim saw the card switch. It was easy. Two grand a day was a big ask though.

Jim walked away. The man made some joke about him and his sexuality to the delight of the crowd. Jim turned back, a smile on his face, and laughed.

Rounding the corner. He slipped his hand back into his pocket. The wallet he'd just stole from the man next to him was thick and almost certainly real leather. That was always a good sign. The street performer had seen Jim steal it during his distraction. Jim knew that.

The joke questioning his sexuality as he walked away was a warning. A warning not to queer his pitch, as entertainers had said years ago.

Two streets away, the wine bars were busier. This was the heart of theatreland. A hundred pounds only bought you a mediocre seat; people saved for months, years even to see a show. Jim walked straight to the toilet. It seemed to be the norm for him. Anyone following would think he had a bladder problem. In the cubicle he examined his latest wallet. He knew he'd hit the jackpot when he saw the man watching the entertainer. Wearing a dinner suit with penguin tails, he just fused wealth. Something about him just said upper class.

Inside the wallet, two hundred pounds, four cards, and a double-barrelled named driving licence were joined by a slip of paper with four numbers on it.

"Bingo."

He knew the numbers could have been anything. Car park code, room key code, anything. There was just that chance he was a "Forgetful Freddy" and it was a pin number for a card.

No time to waste, he left the bar. Further robbing would have to wait this evening; he didn't have long before these were reported. In the idealist of worlds, the man would go to a show for three hours, enjoy himself then realise his wallet was gone. By the time he got hold of the right banks another hour or two would pass. Jim knew he could have a few hours of fun. Walking round a corner, he found a cash machine. Covering his face as much as possible, he entered the first card. Pin incorrect so he pressed return card. Again for the second one. The third however, an almost new credit card, worked.

"Yes."

Withdrawing two hundred and fifty, the maximum, he walked away. He knew his face would have been partially caught on camera, but it was a risk he had to take. Unless they caught him in the act of using it, they'd never find him. He was already on the run, having broken his release terms, so another minor crime wasn't really going to make a difference.

Moving away from theatreland, he entered a small shop. Walking round, he picked up a bottle of whisky then asked for sixty fags at the counter.

"Here you go, mate." Jim handed over the card. "Look, I've not got time to nip to the cashpoint. You couldn't give me cashback could you?"

"Can't do cashback on a credit card, pal. They charge a fortune." The shopkeeper shook his head as he scanned the bottle.

"I'm in a real hurry, mate. I'll make it worth your while."

The shopkeeper's eyes seemed to be replaced by pound signs.

"How much you after?"

"Hundred, hundred and fifty?"

The shopkeeper paused. Jim guessed he was calculating how much in charges that would cost. "I'll give you hundred and fifty cash for two hundred on the card."

Jim sharply sucked in a breath. There was a cashpoint just round the corner. He couldn't appear too desperate. However, he had a good idea the shopkeeper had already sussed him out. Fifty quid cash for some small hassle. The shopkeeper had a bargain there.

"Go on then."

Luckily, the card worked. Jim didn't have a clue how much longer he had but he was determined to hit other shops before it was cancelled. Small electrical items were beckoning. However, he knew card companies weren't fools. This was a new card and multiple purchases in a short time would raise flags. It was all computerised; some algorithm based on normal spending patterns. One more shop though, just the one then he'd throw the card away.

Hailing a taxi, he headed for Oxford Circus. Barely a mile away, he was relying on the roads being clearer now night was drawing in. Turned out to be a good guess, the mile only took five minutes to drive.

Entering an electrical shop, Jim headed for the digital music players. With time running out, he picked up two mid-price imitation iPods. Putting them back, he instead picked up two actual iPod's. The banks could afford it after all. All that money they make.

Queuing, he picked up The Story of The Clash Vol 1 CD which was on special offer and waited for an empty till. His hands sweating, he pulled the piece of paper from his pocket and again memorised the four numbers. The till free, he handed over his music players and CD.

"These both do the same thing, you know that don't you?" said the helpful cashier.

"Yeah," said Jim. "Presents."

The cashier nodded and rang up the items. Placing his card in the machine, Jim waited for sirens to start screaming, gun-laden secret police to appear or the door's shutters to close.

They didn't.

Typing the code in, there was a long, deathly wait before it accepted and the sale was complete. Trying not to look relieved he left the shop, another bag in his hand.

The jewellers next door was beckoning. Could he risk it? It would be stupid to now he'd got four hundred in cash plus two iPods in half an hour. No, he'd be stupid to try another so quickly. He turned and walked away towards Carnaby Street and Soho.

On the way he hit a few pubs, but no wallets or bags beckoned. He reckoned he'd had a good day. No point spoiling it now by being greedy. Besides, he had a bag with bottles of clanging whisky and iPods. He didn't exactly fit in.

Deciding on one last pint before he made for the East End, he entered a bar. Bright and recently decorated, Jim reckoned the word plush was invented for this sort of place. The music loud, he noticed the abundance of mirrored walls, vases and plastic flowers. The clientele themselves were lively and young. They were in groups of four to five, same sex mainly. It had a more lived-in feel than the other bars nearby. Those others were just temporary stop-offs, a different crowd each day having a few snifters before a show. This one was a regulars bar, and different to anything he'd seen in Coventry or the East End. These guys were loaded. Or they thought and pretended they were.

Ordering a pint, he scanned the bar. With the time getting on for nine, he knew the night was just beginning. Still plenty of time. Today may end up making up for yesterday.

The pint gone in five gulps, he left the bar. No one appeared to have noticed him either enter or leave. Everyone was so wound up in their own little groups and worlds. Making for the tube, he passed another jewellers. Still open at this hour seemed ridiculous to Jim, but this was London. This was the way things were done. Seeing a bracelet in the window, he almost gasped at the price. A ton for little more than a silver band. It looked like the new thing though. He seen girls wearing them both in the city and in pubs. They seemed to be personalised with beads and gems. Taking a deep breath, he walked into the shop.

The staff looked down their noses but he was less than bothered. The camera above the till worried him, but they were everywhere. The only other way was a face mask and armed robbery. If he had to get caught, he'd take three years over twenty.

Wrapping the bracelet in a box and then a bag seemed to take them ages. He felt his neck get hot; he knew it wasn't the weather. The fading sun was making the air cool. He wondered for a minute if they'd pressed a panic button and were waiting on slow police to arrive. Paying with the card, he expected the worst. Surely it would have been stopped by now? He waited, his hand hovering over the screen, knowing the door was five steps behind him. He'd just run if there was a problem. Catch a cab and head east.

When the machine asked him to enter the pin, he did. Another wait. It seemed to take forever before it read please remove card. He tried not to look surprised as the shop assistant handed him a receipt before he made for the door.

Ambling down the road, he looked for a tube. That was another problem with London: lack of signs. Sometimes you'd see a sign pointing to a tube, other times you could walk for half an hour looking for a sign, only for it to point the way you'd come.

Eventually finding a sign, he moved up a side street. The tube station in front, he noticed a police car fifty yards away. Parked outside a wine bar, he knew it was nothing to do with him. It couldn't be, he hadn't even robbed this street. A little spark of doubt crept into his mind. Maybe they were warning all landlords to be on the lookout for a scabby, thieving Coventry lad.

He shook his head and made for the tube. Waiting on the platform, he was convinced any second the police would come down the stairs. His stomach, though empty, was full of butterflies. He'd a bagful of loot, a pocketful of cards that had probably been reported missing and hundreds of pounds cash, semi-traceable to a cashpoint.

He needed to clean himself up. He'd hide some cash at the lock-up. Sure, it wasn't very secure, but a couple of the bricks looked like they could be removed. The whisky, iPods and necklace; they could be left until he found buyers.

The tube eventually ambled through the tunnel, taking him east.

Alighting in the dark and damp East End, Jim's phone pinged. *Thanks, I enjoyed it too. Work boring and going slow:(* His stomach, now rid of butterflies, was complaining of its near twenty-four hour famine. Jim entered the nearest fast food shop to the tube station. Kebab World, with its one solitary branch in east London, would have to do.

Jim had a system for kebab shops: the slab of rotating meat had to be large. That way he knew it hadn't stood round for days, the bacteria inside being heated then cooled with every shift. Kebab World looked okay, and the slab was huge and the surfaces clean. He smiled as he considered his venture into vegetarianism. Like everything else recently, it had failed.

Waiting for his pitta to be warmed, Jim typed a reply. *Sorry to hear that. Keep your chin up x.* He added the x after some deliberation.

Her reply took five minutes to arrive and came mid-bite of chilli sauce-coated kebab. *Thanks xxx.*

As he walked, he noticed the High Street still bustled with late shops, teenagers and trolley-pushing bag ladies. Jim slobbered his kebab spilling a good third on the floor. Taking the back street by Filthy Alan's, he wandered to the lock-up. In the encroaching night, the back alley had gained a higher degree of seediness. In a few hours, Jim imagined its visitors would include the hookers, drug dealers and gentleman of the road trying to find a bed for the night.

Leaving his loot and most of the cash, he made for the Queens Arms. Not to get drunk, that certainly wasn't going to happen, he just wanted to see Tim by Four to make sure everything was set for tomorrow. He did fancy a pint in a proper pub, but that wasn't the reason he was going there. Also, he needed to see Terence to offload his new collection of driving licences and bank cards.

The Queens Arms was heaving, though most of the customers again looked like they were only staying for a couple. Jim bought three pints and joined Tim and Mick near the pool table.

"You alright, Jim?" said Mick.

"Not bad. Yourself?"

Pleasantries over, he sat and confirmed they were still set for the morning. Mick's eyes were glazed over, the result of all day drinking and tablets that weren't vitamin C or paracetamol. The younger lads were all over by the pool table, apparently enjoying the only night a week when they didn't have to pretend to lose. The stares and sour faces Jim had received yesterday were gone. He'd been accepted. Looking round the dank, stained walls and its inhabitants, he was almost glad. Almost.

Leaving the builders, he joined Terence for a quick pint. The pub was so packed that Terence conducted his business under the table instead of in the toilets. Gaining fifty quid for the cards, Jim wondered if it was worth it. It'd only paid for the kebab and today's drink.

"Know anywhere I can get a fake driving licence?" he asked Terence.

Again, his eyes lit up at the thought of a deal. "Yeah, how realistic do you want it?"

"Fairly good," said Jim.

"I know someone with a machine. Proper one, same as DVLA use. Not cheap though." He shook his head.

"How not cheap are we talking?"

"Usually charges a grand. Might be able to get it for six hundred as you're becoming a regular."

"I'll think on it." Jim reckoned the normal price was five hundred, but Terence had upped it because he knew he was desperate. At least his cash was building up. But at the current rate, and with another hotel bill due, it wasn't quick enough. After saying his goodbyes, he sold a packet of fags to the pool table lads at half shop price then headed for the tube.

Nearly finished prep now x, the new message said.

Good. I'm just watching telly, he replied.

Walking through Piccadilly Circus, Jim was surprised by both the amount of photo taking tourists still out, and also the amount of clubbers out for the evening. He briefly thought of buying some aspirin and trying to flog them as E's, but he knew clubbers weren't that stupid. Sure he might find a couple of twats who'd spend a tenner to cure a headache, but he'd have to leave the club smartish. He'd barely cover the entrance price let alone make money.

What you watching? x

He cursed, knowing he shouldn't have picked watching telly. *Just channel-hopping really,* his reply.

Walking into a pub, he made for the bar and sized the clientele up. The night was getting on, but he had to do something to make money. A mixed group of twenty-something's at a corner table nosily announced to the world their intoxication. They all looked okay to Jim. Nothing offensive or dislikeable about them. Sighing, he ordered a pint. They'd have to do. It was nothing personal, they'd probably understand that. He couldn't afford to be choosy. It was a life or death situation.

When one of them approached the bar through the throng, Jim edged towards him. Nodding, Jim kept his eyes hovering around, but not directly at him. "You alright, pal?"

Up close he realised he was early twenties. He also looked nervous. People kept to their own groups in this sort of pub. People didn't usually do what Jim was doing. Jim could sense the lad was wondering who he was and why was he breaking the unwritten laws of Saturday night drinking. He eventually replied, "Alright."

"Know any good warehouse parties, mate?" asked Jim, supping on his pint. He had the group pegged down as clubbers. Some of them had reflective and fluorescent jackets or t-shirts on.

"What are you? Police?" He laughed and tried to attract the barman's attention.

Jim smiled and took another sip of his drink. "Yeah, right. I'm the chief fucking inspector." He waited for a smile before continuing. "Nah, me pals are at Sonic Sound, but I didn't make it in." He hoped Sonic Sound was still going on a Saturday night. "Cheesy Ted" from prison had told him about it and their stringent door policy. Only beautiful people needed to apply; anyone less than beautiful wasn't allowed in.

He nodded his head. "Yeah, they sometimes let us in, sometimes don't. I haven't heard of them splitting groups before. Normally if a munter's in a group the whole lot don't get in." His face dropped realising he'd just called Jim a munter. Jim didn't mind. It'd make his job easier.

He eventually got served and swapped some small chat with Jim about clubs. They were off to Manhattens for the night which Jim said he hadn't been too. Jim said he'd probably have a few more drinks then head off home, but the lad, Jason, invited him over to the group's table.

On closer inspection, the group didn't seem like the usual crowd of hippies and pillheads. He supposed this part of London was too expensive to be workshy. Then again, maybe they weren't from London. Two of the men looked warily at Jim as he approached. The two young women with them who Jim thought would probably freeze to death later in what little they were wearing, smiled.

"Who are you then?" asked one of the girls.

"Jim. Are you sure you don't mind me sitting here?"

"Nah," said Jason. "Don't worry, pal." He looked at his mates before continuing. "Jim here's been dumped. His mates got into Sonic Sound but he didn't."

Jim screwed his face up. Jason had virtually called him ugly. Again though, it could only help. The girls looked genuinely sympathetic. The blokes tried to hide smirks behind bottles of lager.

An hour quickly passed of Jim chatting about Coventry's crap clubs and how his night in the city hadn't gone to plan. The more talkative girl listened avidly and told him all about their little gang. They lived in south London though were anything but local. The two girls shared a flat above a chip shop, while the lads had a pad just up the road from them. Meeting at university in the city, they'd stayed on, still living the London dream.

Jim was surprised and almost happy to learn that the chattier of the girls worked in the city. An executive of the insurance arm of a bailed-out bank; Jim thought he could remember some scandal about that bank's insurance mis-selling. Maybe not though; there had been so many scandals they all merged into one. Jason was something in IT but didn't really talk much about it, and the other girl, after flunking her degree, was training to be a nurse.

The time approaching ten, they were making moves to leave. Though they'd invited him to the club with them Jim had made excuses saying there were parties in Coventry, plus he'd missed his lift back now and didn't fancy trying to get back on Sunday morning.

"All that talk of chips has made me hungry," he said as they were getting their stuff together. "I might get some before I head back to Paddington."

"The Golden Catch in Stockwell, that's where you want to go. Best chip shop in London, isn't it?" she said.

"It's a bit out of the way though," the other girl said to herself more than Jim.

"I'll probably just get a burger at the station." Jim smiled as he finished his pint.

Standing up, the girls put tiny coats over their tiny clothes while Jim pretended to send a text to his mates. After giving them hugs, high fives and wishing them a good time in Manhattens, he got ready to leave.

"You sure you don't want to come with us?" she said.

It was obvious to Jim that one of the lads had history with her. Maybe they'd recently broken up or had some long-term unreciprocated longing. Either way, daggers had been flying at him for the past hour. His phone had also just buzzed inside his pocket so he pulled it out and shrugged.

"Nah, thanks though. You know, you're really great, beautiful people." He'd been trying not to over-milk the loved-up atmosphere, but reckoned that might have gone too far. "If

I get the next train, I can be back in Coventry for midnight."
He pointed at his phone. "Loads of other mates'll be there."

She nodded, seemingly pleased he wouldn't be on his own for the night. As he left Jason handed him a slip of paper with a mobile number on it. "Give us a call next time you're in London. We can meet up in a club or something."

Jim thanked them all and left after much hugging and talk of being beautiful. He tried to smile but couldn't. Sure, they were loved-up pretend hippies with too much money, but they were genuinely nice. They probably didn't deserve what he was about to do.

Chapter 14

Finished now. Off to bed x, had been Charlotte's message.

Sleep well x, he replied while finding his bearings on Stockwell High Street.

In some ways Jim thought it more deprived than the East End. Graffiti on shutters of long closed shops, dimly lit alleys and pavements with group of youngsters hanging round. Litter placed everywhere but in bins completed the picture. He'd no idea where to start looking for the best fish and chip shop in London, but decided the High Street would be a good start.

A few kebab shops, Chinese takeaways and the odd Indian littered the road. Hard-looking pubs offered little friendship and even less opportunity for crime. Not that he'd feel comfortable robbing in them. They weren't much better off than himself. Okay, they might not have a life sentence hanging round their thick, tattooed necks, but no, he couldn't rob them.

The ravers however, were different. They had money to waste on pills and fifty quid entrance fees so they could afford to lose a few belongings. Nothing that would really hurt, just a few bits. They'd be insured anyway, so it didn't matter. He wondered why they chose to live here and not some upper market area. Guessing that student life had left them poor for decades to come, he figured they'd gone for cheap rent.

The street was long with endless traffic flying by. He eventually found the chip shop off a side street. In the middle of a row of shops and takeaways he wondered just how you actually got in. He stalked past twice looking for small doorways or some communal entrance hall, but found nothing. Realising there must be a back way, he thought he'd lose his bearings once the chip shop was out of view.

Sighing, he walked up the street, counting both the number of shops and roughly the number of flats above them. An alleyway ten shops down gave him the chance to get slightly nearer.

The alley ended soon; the rear of the building was back to back with another main street. A small road, it was barely large enough for a modern car. He imagined it to be the sort of lane police chases on *The Sweeney* was filmed in. Cardboard boxes flying everywhere when handbrake turns were pulled. A high brick wall with broken glass set in the top wasn't welcoming. Walking down the lane, counting as he went, he passed fifteen small wooden doors, some open some locked while others rotted in neglect. Reaching what he thought was their door, the obvious flue from the back of the chip shop snaked into the sky next to a stairwell to the second floor.

The door was solid and locked. Backing down the road, he pushed open one of the rotting ones and entered a small back yard. The second floor stairwells weren't linked to each other which Jim guessed was to keep people like himself out. Climbing over three partition walls would see him cut to shreds on broken glass.

The dark yard, which smelt heavily of urine, had a broken pallet in a corner. Staring at it for half a minute, he was unable to put it to any use. Wishing he'd brought a screwdriver, he was about to admit defeat when he saw a broken spade lying in the corner. Rusty and devoid of a handle, it was almost perfect. Hiding it by his side, he sneaked out and back to the locked door. After a final check no one was around he forced the door open. The crack as the wood split echoed round the enclosed yards. He was convinced someone would have heard it. He'd probably not only end up battered but also deep-fried when they caught him.

Sneaking past two bicycles and up the stairs, he came to the flat's entrance. A very solid wooden door with deadbolts at the bottom wasn't a good sign. Bending down, he opened the letterbox. Though he knew some of its occupants were out, he wanted to check they were all out. No noise came from within. He whistled a few times hoping a high pitch would attract any dogs. No barking. No noise at all.

He saw a piece of string dangling inside just to the left of the letterbox. Jim shook his head. Surely people didn't still do that did they? This wasn't the fucking sixties anymore after all. There were some right nasty buggers around these days.

Pulling on the string, it was just that. String, no key, just string. Maybe they weren't as stupid as he thought. However, it did mean there'd been a key at some point, perhaps they'd been broken into before. What it meant was they were forgetful. They'd locked themselves out a few times and used it as a backup, but later realised it was the obvious place a thieving scrote would look.

Turning round, he looked at the three flowerpots on the small balcony. Probably tomato plants but maybe cannabis. Lifting one, he scraped away some earth. The key was hidden just below the surface of the largest pot.

Using his sleeve, he inserted the key in the lock. It turned easily. Shaking his head, he hoped to God the two girls used a security chain or bolt when they were alone at night. He practically fell inside the house; they hadn't bothered with the deadbolts either. Jim thought of ringing Jason, getting him to tell the girls off. Maybe he'd do it tomorrow.

Inside the flat, he took off his jumper and covered his hands. DNA couldn't be helped but he'd make sure he left as little trace as possible. The flat was small, tiny even. A corridor led straight into a kitchen cum living room. An old electric cooker stood right to the side of the solitary sofa. Against the wall stood an old telly with a pile of clean-looking washing in a basket. Two doors led from the room crammed into the space between the sink and television. Behind the sofa, and crammed against the other wall, was a table and two chairs filled with papers, magazines and more clothes.

The laptop on the sofa immediately caught his eye. While inside he'd had computer training courses. He wasn't bad at it. Finding the right keys was the hardest part. Though access had been restricted, a few diehard techno-freaks found ways round everything. Jim classed himself as a more manual person than a computerised one. The most important thing Jim had learnt about laptops was a good one sold for at least a hundred. For some reason, if it was an Apple, it went for double.

This one wasn't an Apple. Some cheap Taiwanese or Vietnamese brand; it was fairly clean and looked new. Definitely worth a ton. The telly was too large to take; a thirty-inch flat screen would cause some questions on the tube. The Wii and Digibox connected to it were worth money as was the Nintendo DS on the sofa arm. Walking to a kitchen cupboard he found a few Waitrose bags for life, and stacked the Wii, controllers and games in one and the Digibox, DS and laptop in another. A couple of dark coloured, flimsy jumpers from the clean pile of clean washing added to the top made them look like bags of clothes. Though late at night to be walking round with clothes, London had taught him anything went in the early hours.

The two doors hid a bedroom and a small corridor leading to a bathroom and another bedroom. He didn't want to search the bedrooms. The girls were okay, if a little trusting. Some villains would upturn drawers and go through underwear in the hope of a fiver. Jim hoped he had higher standards. He looked briefly round the rooms for anything small and electrical. An iPad was in the bedroom obviously belonging to the insurance exec. The other bedroom had nurses' uniforms hanging from every spare inch.

A small jewellery box also caught his eye. He shouldn't really do it. Inside it, just a couple of earrings and a gold chain. He'd be lucky to get twenty quid. Closing the door, he left the jewellery.

Back in the cramped living room, an iPod in a dock caught his eye. He had two of the things already, but guessed a third wouldn't hurt. Bags packed, he paused, wondering about the nurse. She'd been drinking Bacardi in the pub while the others had bottles of beer or cocktails. He guessed she was the hardest up and wondered if she'd be insured. Going back through the bags, he wondered if the laptop was hers or not. Without turning it on he couldn't be sure. What about the DS? The iPad was the city worker's; there's no way a trainee nurse could afford one. Leaving the DS, he left the flat, locked the door and replaced the key. After walking a couple of hundred yards he hailed a taxi to the hotel.

Lying on the bed, he added up his takings while taking a look at the laptop. He thought he had just over seven hundred quid plus the electricals. Grand total, thirteen hundred tops. Not bad, but he was still a day or two behind. Tonight had been the night too, the biggest day of the week.

Sighing, he went back to the laptop. Definitely the city worker's. Virtually everything was password protected; emails, some piece of bank software and most of the files. A few personal files, letters to their landlord about leaks and a CV were the only viewable things on there. Though he knew it would take ages, he started to uninstall the software and files. Like a twat he hadn't brought the power lead and guessed, with his luck, the power would run out midway. He'd leave the iPad and ask about it first; he hadn't a clue what sort of security they had.

He thought about sending Charlotte another message. It was only twelve, but she'd been quiet for over an hour. He reckoned she must be asleep. He wondered if her lump of hair fell down while she slept. Did she subconsciously move it back up, or was that just an awake thing? Yawning, he looked at the clock. Realistically, there was still more work to do. Pubs would be clearing out soon. People would be milling round the streets either going to clubs or home. A few of them would have overdone it; they'd be lying in a gutter somewhere or taking a few minutes rest on a seat. Their wallets would be nearly empty but easily pliable. However, ten grand was a long way off and petty theft wasn't getting him near it.

He lay back on the bed. There had to be a better way. A way that didn't involve stealing directly from people. Ten grand was a huge ask, and to do it a hundred quid a go was too much to ask. No, he needed to think of something bigger.

Chapter 15

Waking from what felt like his best ever sleep, he hit the shower.

Morning. Off to work. Catch you later x, the text that woke him said.

Have good day. I'm off to bosses house for Sunday lunch. He'd half fed the lie yesterday. It seemed reasonable enough that someone who'd moved to London would no doubt be bored of hotel meals and would be invited by a workmate or boss. He hoped it added realism.

Breakfasting on sausage, egg, beans and toast with the other hairless and hopeless guests, he then booked and paid for another two nights. The receptionist was different but possessed the same customer service skills as her colleague. As Jim went back to his room, he bumped into his neighbours who'd obviously had a late night and even later start.

"Morning," she said. "How's breakfast?"

"Awful," said Jim, opening his door. "At least it's not burnt." Smiling then closing the door, he didn't like to add the sausages were nearly raw if not partially alive.

Rechecking his stash in the cold light of day, which by rights should be approaching five grand, was a gut-wrenching disappointment. He was nowhere near. He could flog the gun for a few hundred if it came to it. But he knew he should keep it until the last moment. Just in case he needed it for an armed robbery.

Pocketing his gloves, he left the hotel to a drizzly Sunday. Taking the tube to Piccadilly, he kept looking in the glass, mirrored by the dark tunnels, expecting to see a face there. A face with a blonde lock of hair that wouldn't stay attached to its head. A friendly face with a big smile.

He had it bad and he knew it.

Sighing, he looked at the tube map printed on the train's side. He wondered just how many people looked at it every day for want of anything better to do. Whether they'd forgotten a book, read the paper too quick or were avoiding eye contact with a psycho, everyone read and reread it. He thought that the map with its simplified and downright incorrect geography must be the most viewed map in the country. Pondering that maybe subliminal messages had been hidden inside, he gave it another look. One definite benefit was everyone knew how to spell Aldwych.

At Piccadilly, he wandered round. He didn't know what had drawn him here. Virtually no way to make ten grand. It might be a good place for wallet filching; everyone taking photos of the pretty lights, heads facing upwards and away from prying fingers. But, he'd given up on that. It was the easy way out, yet it wasn't even a way out. He'd never get enough that way. He needed to think of a big job, not waste his time wandering about.

A touristy smiling couple walked towards him. Resplendent in their waterproof jackets and visible camera, they looked confused at a map.

"Excuse me, sir." The obviously American man spoke with the sort of accent Jim thought only existed in parodies.

"Yeah," Jim replied. He'd made eye contact with the woman, then man. He knew it'd be impossible to relieve them of their worldly, yet heavily insured goods. The crowds were just too thin.

"How do we get to Lye Cester Square from here?"

"You mean Leicester Square? Up the top, turn right for about a mile then you should see it on your left."

As they thanked him, Jim wondered where those directions would lead them. Middle of the Thames probably. Continuing to walk away from Piccadilly towards Soho, the real futility of this came back. He'd only four days left. Wherever time was flying to, it wasn't doing it productively. Finding a coffee shop, he ordered a tea and sat in the dry.

He had to do a big job tomorrow. And the day after. He'd no chance otherwise. This afternoon was different, of course, but he needed to plan what he'd been putting off.

Slurping his tea, he thought of bookies, banks and post offices. No one else held the sort of cash he needed. Banks were a no go. Too many cameras, security guards and do-gooders. Post offices? Maybe. Not here, not London. Maybe borrow a car, take a trip to a village in Buckinghamshire or Berkshire or Twatshire or wherever.

He sighed and sipped his tea. This wasn't going to happen. He didn't have time to find a good place, stake it out and get a second car to swap for the getaway. That was last resort territory. Plus, most post offices had time delays on their safes. The time delay was usually just long enough for the police to arrive.

Back to bookies. An upmarket bookies might be good for a few hundred, but the real money, the big amount he needed, wouldn't be in the till. The big money would be in the night safe, dug deep into the floor. The keyholder or holders wouldn't be around, or in some cases they wouldn't even hold a key. Private security firms did. If he could disable the security alarms and cameras, take in some heavy duty cutting gear, the money would be his. Alone though, with three days to find somewhere and stake it out? No chance.

Back to square one.

His tea finished and the rain nearly stopped, he stood up. Once more he wondered where the hell he could get ten grand in four days.

His phone beeped. Charlotte.

First meeting done, just waiting for next to arrive x.

Jim sighed as he typed, *Good luck x.*

This thing between them wouldn't go anywhere. If by some fluke he did get ten grand, how long before she found him out? A month, two maximum. How would he support himself? Realistically, if he fleeced her, he'd be doing her a favour.

"The girl needed teaching a lesson," Harry would probably say. "It's a tough old world out there, cookie. And the Charlotte cookie needed toughening a bit more. Too trusting, that was that gal's problem."

Thinking again of her smile and that lump of hair, he shook his head. A bookies. It had to be a bookies. Maybe a jewellers. Continuing his stroll, he ended up near Carnaby Street. Finding a party shop that wasn't too expensive, he bought a Darth Vader mask. Though poorly made from Chinese plastic, it did the job of covering his face and the eyeholes were big enough to see out of.

An idea struck him. He'd later wonder where the hell it came from. But, it just appeared like the proverbial bolt from above. Geoffrey. Geoffrey Morgan. The man responsible for this. The man who'd had the nerve to have a heart attack instead of being shot. Why should he get off scot-free?

Fiddling with his phone while avoiding a sudden shower, Jim typed, *Did you hear how Geoffrey is? x* He couldn't work out if the x should go before or after the question mark. Either way it didn't look right. He sent it anyway.

A minute later the reply came, *OMG. Totally forgot. I ring hospital x.*

He shook his head. She was too good to use in this way.

"You bastard," he muttered while hovering in a clothes shop doorway. "Utter bastard."

When the reply came, *Still in hospital, recovering well x,* he thanked her and started towards the tube and the East End. Today had just got busier.

The High Street that led to the Queens Arms was back to its usual quiet dearth after the hustle, bustle and bloodstained antics of a Saturday night. In the pub, Tim by Four and Mick the Prick were playing pool and on their second pint. Despite not having worked for two days, Mick was still covered in a sheen of plaster. Jim got himself a quick pint.

The lads were on good form and looking forward to their outing. As Jim explained the plan, Tim had the most questions. As he was on licence, Jim could only try his best to assure him that the plan was sound. The pint quickly finished, Jim squashed into the middle passenger seat of Tim's work van as they headed towards north London.

"You brought the decorating gear?" he asked.

"It's all in the back."

Mick produced a joint from his shirt pocket as the transit chugged through the streets. Jim hadn't thought of him as a pothead, but he supposed he hadn't really thought of him at all. When Mick handed him the part smoked spliff Jim shook his head. "Paranoid enough already without that."

Mick shrugged his shoulders and passed it to Tim. "Paranoia on a job's a good thing. Keeps you on your toes."

With the van filling with second-hand heavy, earthen smoke, Jim thought he might as well have had a chug on it. He couldn't remember when he'd last smoked; it would have been sometime inside, but because of the smell smoking was always awkward. Harry wouldn't let him bring it near the cell.

The van nearing north London, he felt light-headed. While Mick talked of his previous jobs Jim realised he wasn't as honest as he looked. Only difference was he'd never been caught.

Finding the street proved hard. One-way systems the fault; they made travelling a bigger chore. Eventually finding the tube station, Mick used an A to Z to guide them to the flat. As they waited outside, looking up at the windows, a sicky feeling rose in Jim's stomach. It wasn't second-hand smoke either. His survival rested on this job. It had to be a big one.

The messing round and wallet filching had ended. The big time had arrived.

"We all set then?" asked Tim.

"Yeah. I need a wallpaper scraper and screwdriver," said Jim. His head had returned fully from its half trip to spaceville. The thought of concrete wellies had once again worked.

They hauled the gear they thought was needed to the front door. Tim was carrying a trestle table, several rolls of wallpaper and a toolbox. Mick had another table, a mound of plaster-covered sheets and a toolbox. Jim had two large toolboxes and a couple of power drills. Quickly pushing the scraper under the front door lock, the door sprung open with unnerving ease. Mick nodded appreciation. "Good training," said Jim. Piss poor lock he neglected to add.

Trundling to the second floor as quietly as possible, Jim sighed when he saw the locks. A five lever Yale and two deadbolts, one of them head height. "Gloves on lads," he whispered. Drilling the deadbolts out was easier, if noisier than he'd hoped. So far there was no neighbourhood interest. Jim suspected the other tenants were practising the age-old London tradition of keeping to themselves. That didn't stop them ringing the police. He knew that. He could only hope they wouldn't.

Despite the screeching of drill bit on metal, even at slow speed, they were inside within two minutes. Raif's flat was a typical two bedroomed conversion. The once stunning three storey, five bedroom house has been converted into four flats. Raif's occupied most of the first floor and was probably the largest in the house. The cramped kitchen cum living room had furniture crammed into every available space. Photos of the happy Raif and his girlfriend lined the walls.

Checking the furniture, the two-piece sofa was new, mass produced and not worth selling. The music system however was compact, new and valuable. The plasma telly though almost stunned Jim when he looked at it. It was huge. Tim reckoned it was fifty inches. Even if it wasn't, it was almost as large as the trestle tables.

"We'll think about that," said Jim as he helped unroll the sheets of wallpaper onto the floor.

Walking through a narrow hallway, Jim peeked in the bedrooms and bathroom. Nodding, he suggested they started in the main bedroom first. The planning in the pub had paid off. Within minutes the three of them had emptied almost everything that was Raif's into the sheets, clothes included. Everything belonging to his girlfriend was put to one side. Socks, coats, bank statements, trousers, shoes, the sly *Big Uns* magazine hidden under the wardrobe. Absolutely everything that was Raif's was nabbed.

Working back through the spare bedroom into the living room, Raif's life was laid out on the floor. The pathetic collection of clothes, bills, statements and knick-knacks from his youth wasn't much to show for a life, but he was losing the lot. Filling the empty toolboxes and sheets, there was still room for a laptop, iPad and gold-plated carriage clock. Jim pondered the carriage clock. It could be hers, a family heirloom even. The principle had been made though. Everything male had been removed. If a couple of borderline goods joined the swag, it was bad luck.

Jim raided the drinks cabinet taking a couple of nice malts but leaving the Baileys and Creme de Menthe. The bathroom also produced a selection of shower gels, razors, expensive aftershaves and any soap that wasn't pink or smelt of flowers. The final, and Tim informed Jim rather petty, act was to cut Raif's picture out of any joint pictures on the wall. Jim tried to explain he had to; it would send the police on a different track to just theft, but the pair remained unconvinced.

With everything packed up, including somehow the plasma and a desktop computer crammed between two trestle tables, Jim thought they were ready. He rolled up the wallpaper they'd used as carpet to catch any falling hair or skin particles, and moved the swag to the front door. Fifteen minutes from start to finish. Jim could still barely believe no one had noticed. Adrenalin had pumped throughout, the minutes seeming like two. Surely someone must have noticed? Their plan if discovered was flawed. Pretend to be repainting the house while Raif was on holiday. Another little extra from the boss for being twat of the month. After they'd gone people would notice. Close inspection of the deadbolts would leave no doubt they'd been drilled. But from a distance, a busy neighbour walking past with bags of shopping, Jim doubted they'd notice.

They paused before leaving the flat. Jim's heart floating far above him. Tim had gone pale as well. Though he'd put false plates on the van, he knew just how many CCTV cameras would have caught them on the way. One last check out of the window, and they left, piles of bags, sheets and trestle tables in hand. As they loaded then got in the van, Jim breathed again. He'd expected four squad cars to screech to a halt or a posse of neighbourhood watch with baseball bats and dogs. But no, nothing.

Driving away with a van full of Raif, Tim was the first to break the silence. "I'd give anything to see his face when he gets back."

"Where did you think this up?" said Mick.

"It just came to me. It was the way he spoke about her, his other half. When he called her baggage in that pub. Something in me just ... I don't know. The idea just came to me."

"Fair play," said Mick. "Never thought of myself as a woman's rights campaigner before. Suppose I am now, aren't I?"

"Course you are, mate," said Jim. He shook his head at the smiling Tim before checking the rear-view mirror all the way back to the East End.

Unloading the van into Jim's lock-up took twenty minutes. Jim promised to go thirds on the proceeds when he got rid, but they wouldn't hear of it. Mick said he wasn't bothered about money; it'd been such a laugh he'd have paid to do it. But Jim promised to sort them out. It was obvious by the following silence that in a perfect world they'd take a third, maybe more for supplying the van, but there was an undertone. It was obvious they knew he was in trouble. He supposed his recent dealings with Terence hadn't gone unnoticed. He considered coming clean and telling them he needed ten grand by Thursday or he was going to be propping up the city's latest skyscraper, but it didn't feel right. They knew something was up, and that was all he reckoned they needed to know.

"I'll sort you lads out, I will."

"Come on. You can buy us a drink." Tim slapped his arm. Though hard for a playful slap, Jim reckoned a serial GBHer's slap would always be hard, playful or not.

Taking the iPods he'd bought yesterday, Jim and Mick hit the pub while Tim changed the number plates then took his van back. Buying a round, Jim got some interest for the iPods from the youngsters hanging round the bar. One of the young lads went to the cashpoint for forty quid while another promised to buy it another time.

Playing pool, and nearly winning, Jim bought the second round when Tim appeared. Terence the Ference was still nowhere to be seen. Mick said he always turned up late on a Sunday, but even that didn't explain why he wasn't there. He was paramount to the plan. What use was stolen goods without a fence?

He continued playing pool and joking with Mick and Tim for an hour. The grubby and smiling Terence finally appeared and sat in his chair supping half of mild. Finishing the game off Jim bought another round of drinks, including a pint for the grinning Terence.

"I'm starting to enjoy our little deals," said Terence as Jim sat next to him.

"You'll definitely like this one. I got a few bits and bobs in the lock-up that need new homes."

Terence's eyes lit up before he had a chance to think it through. Pausing, he said, "Quite a lot of supply at the moment. Prices aren't what they used to be."

"I'm sure you'll do your best."

He drained his half then grabbed the full pint, taking a large sip.

Jim shook his head. "That's the only one you're getting today. You should be buying me drinks." He went back to the pool table and waited, watching the smiling Terence savour every sip of free beer. Bored of waiting, Jim played the next game. Midway through a shot, his phone bleeped.

Retrieving the message, *All done. How was dinner? x* he replied with, *Great. Roast beef x.*

It was only after pressing send that he remembered he was vegetarian. "Shit. Come on get with it."

"Shot weren't that bad," said Tim.

"No, it's not that."

"Bird trouble?" asked Mick.

"Something like that."

His phone bleeped again. *Sorry. Did you just eat potatoes and veg then? x* He sighed. He couldn't believe she was still buying this vegetarian malarkey. It had to end. Mind you, everything had to end.

Yeah. It was embarrassing. I'm still here, his reply.

Okay x.

"More hassle than they're worth," said Tim. He paused in reflection. "Actually, it's probably fifty-fifty ain't it?"

Jim nodded. "I seem to dig deeper holes all the time." Lining up his shot, he potted the black and for once the white ball didn't follow it down.

When Terence had finished worrying the pint, Jim led him to the lock-up.

"You got any drink here?"

"Depends what price you give me." Jim thought taking the bottles of malt may have been a good move after all. He walked beside the limping Terence the best he could. Whether he was actually in pain or just enjoying disability benefit Jim couldn't work out. Either way, he moved painfully slow. Opening the lock-up, Jim watched Terence draw breath sharply.

"Sweet Jesus." He started laughing. "There's a pretty penny here."

Terence made a note of everything with Raif's gold-plated pen on the back of a bank statement envelope. Plasma, DVD recorder, cufflinks, stereo, everything was listed except the clothes, aftershave, laptop and any personal or bank documents.

"You got any glasses for that?" Terence nodded at the whisky.

Shaking his head, Jim picked the bottle with least in and held it towards him. "On the house." Pulling it back before Terence took it, he added, "Best prices though."

Terence nodded and finished his list off. "Fifteen hundred, maybe two gees," he eventually said. "I'll get one of my nephews to pop down tomorrow with his van."

Jim nodded. "What about that fake ID? He held up Raif's driving licence. How much has the price dropped since last night?"

Terence rolled his head from side to side. "He owes me a favour, but ..." he paused, eyeing another bottle of scotch, "two hundred. I'll need that plus two passport photos."

"Okay. I'll be here at eleven tomorrow."

Terence left with two bottles of malt in his greasy palms. "Pleasure doing business again, pal."

Jim nodded before putting the last bottle of malt, some clothes and the bank paperwork into Raif's sports holdall.

Chapter 16

By the time the tube had chugged south of the river, six o'clock had been and gone. The day had once more disappeared in a drunken stupor. Emerging from the station, he sent a message, *Nearly home now.* By the time he reached the hotel, her reply was, *Hope you had good time. I just burnt my tea x.*

He didn't bother replying. Instead, he hung up his new, clean shirts in the wardrobe. Splashing on Raif's cologne, he went down for dinner. The receptionist chef had turned spaghetti bolognaise into the most inedible dish ever. Jim was sure it was from a powdered catering pack, but she'd even managed to ruin that. Eating in silence, he was glad to see a single man sat at his neighbours table. Today was Sunday so their weeks' holiday in the big smoke had ended. They'd be home by know with tales of their city escapades. Jim tried hard not to think exactly what those escapades had involved. He was eating after all.

He finished off his tea with a pint in the excuse for a beer garden. Smoking, he wondered how many he'd drank today. Six or seven? Maybe eight. They didn't seem to count anymore. After the initial buzz of the first few it was just topping levels up, like a car in for a service. When you stopped topping up, the hangover started.

With little to do and the hotel room seeming too familiar, he went for an evening walk. After all, nothing finished off a good day better than a walk along the river. The murky, slimy, polluted bloodline of the capital shimmered in the last dregs of daylight. The unfriendly, bustling city was on its Sunday wind down. People were getting ready for their busy lives to get busy again in the morning. Stood there, leaning against a graffiti-ridden lifebuoy, Jim had never felt so alone. As the Millennium Wheel glimmered, reflecting rays into lightless corners, Jim pulled out his phone.

Can I ring you? he typed, and sent.

Yes, her reply.

Despite having only three pounds credit, he rang. He couldn't remember if he'd rung her before. He was sure he hadn't. She'd always rung him.

"Hi," she said.

"Hello. Sorry, you don't mind me ringing, do you?"

"Course not. Why would I mind? I was only watching telly. Hang on I'll just put it on pause. That's the best thing about …"

Listening for a few minutes brought a part of him back to life. Her confident, yet scatty talking gave him the feeling of being needed, if only as a listener. Unsure just what was happening, just what these feelings were, he sat on a bench and waited for a Charlotte pause.

"… most people have cable or satellite, but it's just like Freeview with three hundred other channels you never want to watch." She breathed heavily.

"Have you got a busy day tomorrow?" He knew the question was inviting a long reply, but there was no other way to engineer this to when would they next meet. That was what he wanted to talk to her for. He realised as soon as he'd heard her voice.

"Fairly. Seems weird after working today that I'm free parts of tomorrow, doesn't it?"

"Yeah. Do you fancy going out somewhere tomorrow night? Have that meal I owe you?"

"Yeah."

She seemed lost for words. Jim immediately took advantage. "Good. Look I've got to, you know, get ready. I'll ring you tomorrow."

"Yeah. Thanks," she replied.

Turning his phone off, he walked back from the river towards the luxury ex-warehouse apartments. Towards Geoffrey's in particular.

The swipe card entry system and nameless keypad numbers next to the entrance was a problem. The door itself was just two panes of glass which seemed odd considering the high cost security measures next to them. Breaking in without the swipe card was possible, the door could be forced, but he didn't know anything about the alarm. The numbers one to four stood proud of the buzzers. Jim knew Geoffrey's flat was on the second floor so presumed number two.

"One way to find out."

The buzzer emitted a low distance noise. Jim waited, prepared with his stock phrase in case someone answered. "Hello, I'm a Jehovah's Witness. Have you ever thought there was more to this world than just ..."

No one answered. Giving the door a small but firm push with his gloved hand, there was no give. It was firmly and electronically locked. Walking back towards the river, he pondered the next move. He loved a challenge. Despite the last two days, he was no expert at breaking and entering. It was just another thing forced onto him by the ten grand debt. Housebreaking had never been too appealing. He supposed it was a too customer orientated crime. He preferred the back room job of dealing with its proceeds. A new build, card swipe exterior with God only knows what locks on the apartment door that would be a huge problem to a professional. It was way beyond him. There'd probably be cameras too. This kind of area, redeveloped and highly priced, but just streets away from older and more problem boroughs always had drug problems and teams of young scallies ready to break in.

"Young scallies, eh."

The river was still as brown and untempting as he'd left it. He remembered seeing some archive news footage somewhere; a whole beach worth of sand had been imported so young kids could go paddling and swim amongst the turds and industrial effluent. Wouldn't happen nowadays, no one would want it. The council would probably get sued for even mentioning the idea.

Walking along the bank towards London Bridge, a few evening strollers passed by. Couples arm in arm, both young and old. The odd small crowd of menacing looking teenagers threw stones into the water and swore while trying to smoke stolen cigarettes. A bobby on a bicycle rode along, his eyes searching for trouble.

Jim lit another cigarette and stopped by the railing. The sky reddened towards the west as the sun set over London. The reddy hue in the sky bounced off the skyscrapers and bridges leaving a bloodlike haze on the streets. Crossing the bridge, he walked back along the northern shoreline, the redness in the sky darker with each footstep. Passing a variety of tramps on benches, *Big Issue* sellers and East Europeans flogging dodgy cigarettes, he carried on, unsure exactly where he was going.

Leaving the river and walking north, the streets grew darker. A million ideas flooded round his brain, each fighting for position near the front. Deep down, he'd no idea what was going on. It was like his body was being dragged towards somewhere friendlier, somewhere that wanted him.

He continued walking for an hour, maybe two. The streets all seemed the same. Some crammed full of houses, others shops with flats above. Most of the shops were still open. London didn't stop for Sunday or night-time. Round the next corner he found himself on the outskirts of Soho, his dreamlike walk woken by shining, flashing neon signs advertising the more baser of entertainments. The entrance to a bar, barely more than a doorway, caught his eye. A heavyset bouncer in a tuxedo nodded at him. Beside the bouncer, a young woman in a leopard-skin top and tiny shorts waved a beckoning finger. Being a man of lax morals he couldn't refuse.

The corridor gave way to red-carpeted stairs leading down to a basement room. A bar set in the corner, the lighting dim around the rest of the tabled room except at a small raised performance area. The woman led Jim to a table, her hips revolving in some circular motion that transfixed his eyes.

"Take a seat." Her voice was European, definitely East European. Jim had heard of these clubs while inside. This was exactly the sort of place he would have visited after killing Geoffrey. Sitting down on the cold hard chair, Jim noticed a woman dancing in a bikini on stage. The sign outside the door had said exotic dancers. He remembered that Soho had cleaned up its act over the years. Where once every bar was topless and sometimes bottomless, the majority were now just plain, but skimpy, exotic. She sat opposite, her long dyed-blonde hair covering parts of her brown eyelashes and pockmarked face. Her eyes were wide, some stimulant or deadener the cause.

A leotard-wearing waitress came to the table. "What'll it be?"

"I like champagne, do you?" said the nameless woman.

He'd heard about these clubs alright. Hundred pound bottles of champagne, a bit of flirting then it was, "We can rent a room somewhere, you know." Jim was both half drunk and lonely. Three years inside did strange things to a man. In the back of his mind he could hear Harry say, "Go on, my son, do the business."

He shook his head. "Just a whisky, thanks."

"Are you not going to buy me a drink?" Her eyes pierced his. She was damn good at her job. He felt himself slipping further into her eyes, further into what he knew was coming.

"I can't afford champagne," he managed to say. She looked hurt, mortified. She was gorgeous and spending time with him of her own free will, yet she wasn't worth champagne.

"Rum and coke." Her head turned away briefly before relocking to his eyes.

"What's your name?" He expected her to say Magdalene or something with lots of x's or z's in.

"Cindy, what's yours?"

"Jim." He was out of questions. He looked again at the woman on stage, writhing around and being ignored as the three other customers were being entertained by their own version of Cindy.

The drinks appeared quickly.

"Twenty-five pounds please."

He handed over thirty and didn't expect change. She knocked the drink back in one swift chug. Licking her lips afterwards, Jim looked at his own whisky and sipped it. Cheap and watered down, it'd never been north of Watford let alone the Scottish Border.

"We can rent a room somewhere if you like?" Her hand had crept under the table and lay on his thigh. The gentlest of touches; it still made him shiver.

"I ..."

The phone in his pocket bleeped. Charlotte.

"No. I can't do it. Sorry."

Standing, he turned round. A bouncer by the stairs eyed him suspiciously. He tried to walk towards them, but his legs had grown lead weights. The air was too thick. Not enough oxygen. He breathed in and out a few times, his vision breaking. A heavy hand grabbed him by the side and dragged him up the stairs. His feet barely touched the ground and his shirt collar almost strangling him, he saw the last dregs of daylight appearing through the door. Falling flat on the pavement, his arm hurt, muscles flared with pain. Scrambling to his feet, he had to get out of there. There were two of them; the kicks were going to start flying. Just like the prison showers. He had to get out of there.

He stopped running when his breath ran out. Taking huge gulps of London's finest air, he looked round. Still in the wonderful Soho, though a more upmarket part, the bars no longer boasted exotic dancers but burlesque shows and expensive meals to the passing customer. Soft porn without seediness. Throw in some food and it's respectable.

Jim entered the first bar he found and ordered a pint. The barman explained they only served bottled beers, so he made do and sat down. He pulled out his phone and looked at the text that had saved him. *Going to bed now. Goodnight x.*

He shook his head. How close had that been? Would he actually have done it? He knew the answer and didn't like it.

Goodnight x, he replied.

Looking round, the bar was busy for a Sunday. Tables strewn haphazardly were full of well-clothed Londoners discussing some article in that day's broadsheet. A few people were looking at him. He was on his own, a stranger in their little alcohol serving paradise. Of course, he also had a layer of pavement dust down his jeans. He felt hot too, he knew his face was red. He looked like someone who'd just run a mile. Their eyes burned into him, he thought they could see what he'd nearly done. Somehow they knew what he was in Soho for.

Finishing the beer in a long sup, he left the bar. The grotty hotel and his bed were calling.

Chapter 17

Monday morning broke with the annoying buzz of the alarm and a, *Morning. Hope you slept well x,* text.

Fine thanks. What about you? I need more phone credit x, his reply.

After a quick shower, he discovered that Charlotte too had slept well but she was running late. Eating his breakfast, just plain burnt, he reread the two-week old local paper.

He ate quickly; today was going to be busy. It might even get scary mid-afternoon. He also had a date tonight and that was weighing heavy. Maybe tonight would be make or break night. He still wasn't sure what the whole London protocol was on bases and dates. In Coventry, a ten-minute chat and a packet of pork scratchings sufficed, but London was different.

Charlotte was different.

Leaving the hotel, he headed for the tube. After buying a pair of low gain reading glasses, he paused at a photo booth, giving his best smile as the machine took then spewed out four photos. Heading for the East End, he thought of Terence. As much as he liked him, which wasn't much, he trusted him less. He'd woke in the middle of the night convinced that Terence, nephew in tow, would be robbing the lock-up. He was determined to get there as soon as possible. Terence had the look of a no-good thief about him.

Arriving at the lock-up by half nine, his faith in human nature was restored: the lock was still locked and intact. Sifting idly through the bits and bobs that was Raif's life, Jim wondered if he should have taken the jewellery and her bank details too. Adding her bits still wouldn't have got him near ten grand, but it might have given another gee or two. Principles could prove to be leg-breakingly expensive in three days time.

Terence eventually arrived at eleven in a twenty-year-old transit van and a younger, hoody-wearing driver. "Morning," said Terence, "this is Rob."

"You alright?" asked Jim. The youth nodded and grunted something incoherent.

As the three of them went inside the lock-up, Jim closed the door. The last thing he needed now was some passing scally seeing what was in there.

"I been doing figures all night." Terence pulled out the ripped envelope and another piece of paper. "One t'ousand five hundred."

Jim reluctantly nodded his head. The plasma was nearly a grand to buy. Plus all the other bits. If he could somehow get it all to Coventry he reckoned he could get three grand within a week. Word would get around though, and with the coppers already looking for him he'd be back inside within ten minutes. "You got yourself a bargain. That includes the licence, doesn't it?"

He grimaced before agreeing. "I think we've both done alright here, haven't we?"

Jim half smiled and helped Terence and his nephew load the van. Less than half an hour later, they drove away in a cloud of black smoke. After Jim stashed the roll of used tenners and twenties in the lock-up, he changed into one of Raif's suits with a shirt and tie and left for the city. Lunchtime was calling.

Busy again today x, said her message.

Me too x, he replied.

The city towered above as he strutted forwards. Half past twelve and the masters of the universe were breaking for lunch or a few drinks. The area again teemed with expensively suited men and woman, mobile phones strapped to their ears as they ordered wraps, baguettes and fruit by the bowl.

Settling into a bar, Jim looked round. The usual array of important and well-paid people laughed and joked as they sipped cocktails or bottles of beer. Jim walked through the bar looking for an opening. Reaching the back, he headed to buy a drink. Nothing had screamed at him, but then again he didn't know what he was looking for.

All the hassle of robbing a wallet for a couple hundred quid wasn't worth it. Still, without any proper ideas, he'd hoped coming here might give some opportunity. Car or house keys were the only worthwhile things to take now. He sighed. He needed to up the ante. A little bookies or post office. He had the mask, false moustache and glasses now. And, he had the gun. This would be his last lunchtime in the city. He knew it wouldn't get him anywhere near ten grand.

Drinking his beer, he looked round. Clusters of people, mainly men, basked in their own glory. Finishing his bottle, he brushed past a group of them towards the exit. His hand swiftly returned to his pocket with a new wallet. It'd been easy in the end. These bankers were so busy chatting and drinking, Jim reckoned you could set of a firework and no one would notice. The risk wasn't worth it though. Luck wasn't infinite and was surely running out. Outside, he wondered if the ONS produced the statistics of wallet robberies. What was the percentage chance of snaffling ten grand before then? Smirking, he rounded the corner.

Two police officers were in front of him. They immediately picked up on his nervous double take and misstep. The police were always around, it being the ideal terrorist location, but he'd avoided being this close. To run or about turn now would admit guilt. He had to carry on walking. Walk past them. Maybe even smile at them. He was wearing the clothes after all; he belonged there.

Their eyes burned into his as he approached. He felt his legs turn to jelly, but he forced himself to catch one of their eyes and smile. He felt his cheeks blush and confident smile slipping to a guilty one. He swallowed hard, ready for any conversation.

One of them nodded. Both their eyes were on him. Surely he wasn't the only innocent member of the public ever to look surprised or even guilty when they saw a policeman. Everyone must do it, he told himself, everyone.

"Nice day again," Jim croaked. His voice straddling octaves like he was thirteen again.

The short-sleeved policeman nodded. "Hope it stays like it."

Passing them, he carried on, legs wobbling like a ten-minute-old horse. He expected them to say, "Stop. We'd like a word." He expected a firm hand to appear on his shoulder followed by the words, "Come with me, laddie." He expected everything in the space of two seconds.

It didn't happen.

His chest ached. A fast beating heart the cause. He needed to sit down and breathe for a few minutes, get his head and body back into shape. But, he couldn't. He had to get away from here. Finding another packed bar, he went straight to the toilet. Taking the cash from the wallet, only fifty quid this time, he ignored the cards and driving licence. The whole wallet minus cash went straight in the toilet cistern.

It took ten minutes to calm himself down. He'd had a lucky call. That was close to game over. He'd have been fingerprinted and sent back down for breaking his release terms. Pretty soon, while inside, some of the East End gangster's underlings would have paid a visit.

He sighed. He wasn't even supposed to be taking wallets today. Why had he done it? There had to be an easier way to make money. There just had to be. Maybe he should throw in the towel now, ring up the gangster's knuckle scraper, and admit he had two nearly three grand and could he have another week.

No. He couldn't do that. The quest he'd been given was some kind of perverse head fuck. He knew as well as Jim did that ten grand wasn't possible. The only outcome was Jim getting the kicking of his life. Even if he did pay him off could he trust him to end it there? Or would he say you now owe another two grand for interest?

Jim shook his head. "Where can I get seven grand in four days?"

His phone buzzed. Charlotte.

Finally having lunch now, busy morning z, the text said.

It took him a while to figure out the z should have been an x. At first he thought it was some new smiley. Settling on, *I ate mine hours ago x,* as a reply, he left the toilet and made for the tube.

The East End was busy as lunchtime turned to afternoon. In the lock-up, Jim changed back into his other clothes, popped the mask and glasses into a bag then took a tube back. By the time he got to the hotel it was nearly three. The day was disappearing in a haze of tube trains and failure. At least he'd made some money this morning. But it wasn't enough. Strictly speaking, that was yesterday's money. Back on the streets, he walked round south London, moving slowly, but looking everywhere. The main roads were gridlocked while the side roads a weird combination of one-way streets and dead ends.

The further from the river, the more the city changed. Decay and despair increased by the yard. By the time he got to the outskirts of Brixton, it resembled an alternative reality of the clean and money-filled financial district.

He'd passed a few bookies on the way. Most were well-known chains with low-paid staff and cameras everywhere. Standing outside an independent one, he popped his glasses on and entered. It was only after he opened the door that he realised he needed a hat. He wasn't used to disguising himself. Learning on the job was never a good idea, but what else could he do?

Decayed walls lined the small room with decayed and weary minds filling the punters heads. Three television screens filled the far wall showing a race, results and odds. At the back, and behind thick glass and metal were two men; one huge bloke in his forties and a younger man. The older man stared hard, his eyes burning. Jim wouldn't like to meet him alone in a dark alley, or even a bright alley.

As the screens showed the 4.10 at Monmouth, Jim watched along with the other punters. A selection of long-term sick, the unemployable and pensioners, this was their second home in between a few lunchtime pints and early evening drinks.

A two-year-old, Naughty Bad, romped home by a couple of lengths. Four to one. Jim wished he'd had his three grand on it, but that wasn't the way to riches. The only winners in this game were ones behind the counter.

"Horsey Dave", a fellow crim Jim had known inside, had given him various clues on what to look for in racing. Dave was more interested in winning than robbing shops though, but Jim had remembered the information in case it was needed. Greyhounds were a better bet than horses, that'd been his first tip. Smaller races and no rider to ruin things. Jim picked up a paper and looked at the form for a few races.

Besides a few grunts and complaints from other punters, the shop was silent. Occasionally, behind him, the two men behind the counter would talk to each other. With every other word a swear word, it was distracting in itself. Settling on a Yankee accumulator of four dogs, Jim wrote out a slip and handed it in.

The big bloke behind the counter didn't remove his fixed glare, not even when Jim pulled out two twenty pound notes. Looking at his slip, the man screwed up his nose. Stamping his ticket and handing back the counterfoil, the man stayed silent. Buying a powdery tea from the machine, Jim leant against a high table and watched the first race start.

Lady Lassie came first but that was where it ended. The next dog, Hocus Pocus, seemed to prefer running backwards to forwards, My Little Doggie looked afraid of imitation rabbits and the last dog, Bankers Bonus, fought a good race but failed towards the end. Screwing up his ticket, he shook his head and made for the exit. The large man behind the counter, now full of smiles, said, "Come again," as he left.

Jim left and walked back to the hotel. Maybe choosing a Yankee had been a bad bet. He needed two of them to win to roughly break even. Horsey Dave was right. There was only one winner in a bookies. Only one. Approaching the hotel his phone pinged. *Finished. On way home x.*

I left early today, Jim replied.

You civil servants are all the same x, was her reply.

A few more messages were exchanged as he got ready to meet her at half seven. Picking a woman up from a flat for a date was new, so new to him. A stomach full of nervy worms gnawed at him, trying to upset his poise.

He looked good in one of Raif's blue shirts. Admiring himself in the mirror, he caught his eyes. The past four days had worn him down. Bags hung from weary, almost bloodshot eyeholes. Drink wasn't helping either. He'd been sloshed four days in a row now. He had to give it a break. Maybe just a couple of pints tonight, then a few whiskies when he got back. That would be all.

Assuming he came home tonight.

No. He had to remove those thoughts from his head. Nothing should be expected. She was a proper lady. Proper London ladies didn't do that. He had to be respectful. It had to feel right. It wouldn't happen like that.

He left his room. Though half an hour early, he fancied a walk to fill the time. Being cluttered up inside, his head was wandering around going through options that would never be there. Wandering past Geoffrey's flat, he again wondered how easy it would be to get in. Rock climbing the wall seemed to be the only way. Even then he wouldn't know which flat he was after.

Before long he'd meandered towards Charlotte's. Still quarter of an hour early, he sent a message. *I'm a bit early. Shall I wait in the pub down the road?*

He stood outside the front door kicking his heels for two minutes before the reply came. *No it's okay. I'm nearly done.*

His stomach was a mess of butterflies that never wanted to eat again. Taking a deep breath and checking no lumps of hair were sticking up, he pressed the door buzzer.

"Hi. That was quick." Her voice electronically mutilated through the entry phone.

"Yeah." Was all he could think to say.

"Come in."

The door buzzed as the lock was released. One last deep breath and he pushed it open then walked into the lower stairwell. He'd seen a glimpse the other day, but now actually inside a crisp freshness filled his nose. Flowers or pot pourri seemed to fill every void. There was another smell though, the smell of a new building. Recently plastered walls and the smell of timber settling in. He'd give it five years before major structural alterations were needed, but for now the residents were living the ultimate dream. Spacious flat, good area, exclusive neighbours. What more could they want?

The eight or nine stairs of bare wood led to the lower gallery. In the background, another flight of stairs reached up. Old bricks and bare wooden beams clashed with new door fittings and handrails.

"Come in." Her voice called from round the corner.

As he walked up the stairs, the room opened before him. Large wasn't a big enough word. Three massive leather sofas arranged in U shape stood in the middle, like a field of cows chewing the cud. Facing them, the biggest LCD television he'd ever seen. A small coffee table in front of the chairs littered tidily with magazines, books and remote controls. The evening sun shone in through the large front window accentuating the split level of the galley above. Bookcases and modern prints lined the walls and a Blaupunkt music system took the right hand corner, a small desk occupying the left.

Behind the sofas, a dining table with six chairs was plonked near the far wall. The nearer wall had two doors, one heading under the stairs and barely large enough to be more than a cupboard. At the rear of the room, and under the supported ceiling, Charlotte stood in the kitchen. Jim wondered if the kitchen had been borrowed from a hotel. The ubiquitous central island played host to a sink and work area, while behind it an array of ovens, grills, hobs and oversized fridge filled the wall. It amazed him the sheer quantity of stainless steel that had been crammed into the area. Another door led from the kitchen. Jim hadn't a clue what would be in it. This had been a warehouse, so it couldn't be a garden. The bedrooms were above, so what else could be back there?

Smiling, he walked to the kitchen. In Charlotte's hands were three pairs of shoes, two strapless, one with a lot of straps. He thought she looked stunning, more than normal. Her hair was still damp and a touch frizzy. Make-up had been applied, and the dress, a knee-length black number, suited her.

She held her hands up, the shoes swinging round. "This is my pad."

"Incredible," was all he could say. It was more than incredible; he'd never seen anything like it. He tried to close his mouth aware that his tongue was nearly on the floor.

"Sit down." She pointed at the sofas. "I'll just finish my hair off."

He wanted to tell her she looked perfect, but the words wouldn't come out. Every time he tried, they sounded corny in his head so got no further. He wandered round the middle sofa and sat in the corner feeling lost. The music system was playing a CD at a incoherent volume. Background music. He thought it was jazz or blues, but really wasn't sure. The speakers either side of the television looked powerful enough to blow the poorly renovated roof off. He wondered what The Clash would sound like at full volume.

As hard as he was trying not to, his brain feverishly totted up the contents. It was a lot more than twenty grand, though, at Terence's rates, it would be closer to eight.

That didn't matter though. Charlotte was off limits.

Off limits.

As she went upstairs he flicked through the small stack of magazines. Financial and other highbrow titles. He didn't know where to start. He supposed a glossy gossip mag or puzzle book was not in keeping with the rest of the place. Picking out a copy of *Private Eye,* he sank back into the cow-sided sofa. It seemed to mould around him, keeping his posture yet giving an immense feel of comfort.

Occasional noise and a hairdryer whirring told him she was nearly ready. Beside him in the other corner of the sofa was a laptop. Gripping the magazine closer, he tried to purge his mind of the thought running through it. The details of her deal would be in the laptop. Information on share prices, investors, maybe home addresses. He could set himself up for life by just walking out now.

Off limits.

Sighing, he put the magazine down. The words weren't going in. Where the hell could this go? Just exactly where could this go?

The bedroom door opened, her voice sharply following it. "I'm really sorry."

He turned round. Her face looked hurt again, mortified. He had a good idea what was coming next.

"You don't have to sit there. The chairs at the dining table are solid wood. Sorry, I forgot."

Jim wasn't sure what she meant, but stood up anyway. "Sorry, what do you mean?"

"The sofa. Sorry, I just didn't think."

Jim looked at the sofa. Whatever she was on about, he hadn't a clue.

"Leather?" She looked ready to spell it out. He clicked. Phony vegetarianism had foiled him again.

"Oh. Umm." He paused, looking away as she descended the stairs, her droopy lock of hair leading her way. "It's okay. I'm not that much of a ..."

"No, you shouldn't apologise. God, you must think I'm awful. Please, sit at the dining table."

Jim walked away from the sofa. He was the awful one and he knew it. This whole vegetarian lark had gone too far. He had to find a way of stopping it.

Reaching the bottom of the stairs, she picked a pair of strapless shoes from the pile and squeezed her feet in them. Jim was standing midway between sofas and a table, unable to move either way.

"Are you ready?" he asked.

"Nearly." She smiled. "Handbag and phone." She walked towards the kitchen area and picked up her bag. Scouting round for her phone, she paused, her face confused. "Upstairs."

Jim stood rigid, still midway between the cows and chairs while she went upstairs. His voice had all but disappeared. All the things he wanted to say lost amongst a sea of confusion. He realised his mouth was open again. He felt like an inbred simpleton speaking to a rocket scientist.

She reappeared and walked downstairs. "Ready now." Her face beamed with a glowing smile.

"Okay." Was all he could manage as he followed her outside.

Outside, as she triple-locked the door, Jim looked around. People were still milling around either going home or out for the evening. Turning to face her as she put her keys in her bag, he remembered the last time they'd stood here. Two days ago, but a kiss had sealed the start of whatever this was. Her face blushed before him; maybe she was thinking the same thing. Looking down at his feet he pondered making his intentions clear; taking her in his arms. But it didn't feel right.

"Where are we going then?" she asked.

"Well, considering I'm a bit of a stranger, I was hoping you could recommend somewhere." But nowhere too expensive he thought, but didn't say.

Her face dropped momentarily. He guessed she was looking to be surprised. He'd done that alright. Truth was, he didn't know anywhere. Even if his story was true, how would he have come across somewhere decent to eat so quickly?

Her smile half returned. "Chinese?"

Jim nodded. "Sounds good to me."

"We need a cab then. I know a good one." She stuck her arm up in the air briefly. Though not much traffic seemed to come down the back street, there always seemed to be a cabbie around, just waiting. Within seconds, the cab pulled up to the pavement and Jim opened the door. Remembering his manners, he let her in before himself.

"Where to, guv?" asked the cabbie.

Charlotte said a road name that Jim didn't catch, which was followed by the cabbie tutting and sucking in air. Mumbling something about "North of the river," he eventually pulled a u-turn then joined the queue of traffic crossing the Thames.

Sat next to her, her perfume filling his nose, Jim caught her eyes and smiled. "Had a good day then?"

"Yeah," she paused briefly for breath. "Got another investor in today, which was nice. I thought yesterday I'd got the last one, but it just goes to show there's no harm in looking. Then I caught up on some paperwork that seemed to take forever in itself ..."

Jim noticed the taxi driver looking in the mirror. Catching his eye, he smiled.

"... and then that was it, home time. What about you?"

Her eyes caught him off guard. They seemed to rip the heart from his lies. What could he say? Sold a load of stolen goods, robbed a wallet from some geezer and nearly got caught then went looking for a bookies he could pull an armed robbery on?

"Working on the, erm, GDP update today." He'd seen a news stand earlier guessing next week's outcome.

"Oh," she said. "I thought the Bank of England did GDP. I didn't realise the ONS were involved."

Damn. It had to happen. She'd caught him out. Or had she? He didn't know either way. As far as Jim knew, the Bank of England just printed bank notes. Why would they produce statistics? What was GDP anyway? What the hell did it even stand for?

"It's like a joint thing, you know." He hoped that would work.

She seemed convinced. "It's the talk of the city you know, what some people would give to ..." She stopped midway through the sentence. He followed her eyes to the taxi drivers mirror. What was she about to say that she didn't want him hearing?

"I just crunch figures really," he said. "I don't know what half the people there do."

Silence filled the cab as they stopped midway across the bridge. He hoped he'd sounded genuine. The cabby hadn't looked at him with a raised eyebrow. He was just plodding on trying to go somewhere in a city full of people going nowhere.

Crossing the bridge, it occurred to him where her train of thought had gone. She was going to say people would pay for inside knowledge of GDP figures. He was sure that was what she meant. Maybe he could work on that. Information like that must be worth seven grand.

Off limits. Charlotte was off limits.

He looked out of the window and winced. Would one of her acquaintances count as off limits? There'd have to be no comeback to her. He couldn't hurt her, but some other city slicker? They were prime targets.

"Shall we get out here?" she said.

Jim looked back at the road. Gridlocked. Nose to tail, both directions. The cabby sighed loud enough to be heard in Chiswick. Jammed as he was, now north of the river, Jim couldn't blame him for being miffed.

The fare was ten pounds eighty. Jim handed him a twenty and shrugged his shoulders. Joining Charlotte at the curb, they meandered up the busy street towards what Jim thought was Chinatown.

A ten-minute walk later they were in Chinatown. Having never been there before, Jim was amazed by the shops, signs, bustle and array of restaurants. It was just how he'd imagined, and more.

"You haven't been here have you?"

"No." His voice trailed off.

"If you want Chinese, go to Chinatown."

Jim thought she'd said it snobbily. Perhaps she'd wanted to be surprised by where he was taking her. Either way it was too late. She did seem different this evening. Her whole demeanour. Whether stressed or maybe just bored of him he wasn't sure. As she guided him towards a particularly bright and large restaurant, he thought of taking her hand. Maybe kissing her before they went inside.

"This one here," she said, ruining his chance. Not that he'd have done it anyway.

He reached for the door and opened it. She smiled, but it wasn't her best one. He knew he should have gone for Indian, or something more exotic or trendy.

Guided to a table, they sat down. The waiter handed out menus and took their drinks order. They both had a bottle of lager while waiting for the wine menu. Jim studied the menu. Chinese names with English descriptions afterwards. There were no numbers; how were people expected to order? Try to pronounce the squiggles that were words or just point? Pointing was always going to win. The menu was in the wrong order too. Any normal Chinese was soup, starter, main and then dessert. This one was all over the place.

Jim looked round. Charlotte had the best view again. Her back to the outside wall left Jim with paranoia that someone behind was flicking v-signs at him.

"Quite busy isn't it?" he said.

She nodded. The stray lump of hair finally fell across her forehead but was quickly tidied up. "Weekends are impossible to get a table. I sometimes bring people here for lunch in the week."

Jim nodded. His regular Chinese haunt in Coventry, Wok This Way, didn't bear comparison to this place. He wanted to tell her about its surly waiters and chipped tables, but couldn't. He knew this was where things would end up. He couldn't make her a part of his life. He could never really open up. Always in the back of his head were the lies, the cheating. He wondered how serial philanderers and men with multiple lives and families had either the energy or the brainpower to get away with it.

"There was a restaurant we used to go to in Newport. It was called Wok This Way. Always made me laugh that name." Though he'd managed to twist the lie, it still felt a lie.

She smiled. "There's an Indian in Basingstoke called The Spice is Right. That makes me chuckle."

Jim laughed. "Know any more?"

She shrugged her shoulders.

"Fish and chip shop in Newcastle, Right Plaice Right Time. They spelt it wrong though, which ruined the joke."

She laughed before sipping her lager. "What do you fancy? They do a wide range of vegetarian."

Jim sighed before he looked at his menu. He had to sort out the vegetarian thing, but now wasn't a good time. He'd normally have chicken curry and chips or sweet and sour chicken balls. He was going to have be inventive. "Quite a lot here, isn't there? What are you having."

She shrugged her shoulders. It was Charlotte's choice of where to eat. He took it that he should be deciding what they ate. This could go badly wrong.

"I suppose," he said, "we ought to decide how many courses first. Soup or starter, then main and pudding." He regretted saying pudding. The London word was undoubtedly dessert.

She patted her non-existent stomach. "I don't think I could manage more than soup and main."

Jim nodded. He was relieved. Not for the cost, the place seemed quite reasonable, but just for the number of decisions involved. The wine waiter arrived and gave him a few more seconds thinking time. Jim said Charlotte should order the wine as she knew a lot more than he did. She ordered something French with a long name. Jim nodded, pretending to agree it was a good choice.

"Hot and sour soup?" he asked. She nodded. That just left the main. On the back of the menu was the business lunch section. Three courses for a tenner. Chicken in black bean sauce he'd had before, remembering it was nice.

"Do they do a vegetarian black bean sauce?" he asked while making a show of looking all around the menu.

"There." She pointed. "The vermicelli's also very good. I haven't tried the veggie one but the chicken's incredible."

Jim nodded.

When the waiter returned he ordered the soup plus a combination of three dishes between them. The wine soon appeared and flowed. Jim got brave and told her about the time he spent a month in Coventry for the ONS. At last he didn't have to lie. Turning the conversation round to her, he asked what else she'd done recently besides work. She was not as open as before; talking was jerky, not fluent. Jim wasn't sure if that was normal for a second date or not. He knew so much about her and wanted to know more, but couldn't think where to start. His own lies got in the way. He knew this could only go on for so long. They needed to connect; an embrace or more. He had to remove that thought from his head. Especially the more part. The bit that came after the embrace.

The food was more than worth the money. Jim was more than impressed. It was nowhere near as salty or oily as his old takeaway. Very powerful flavours too. He almost hadn't missed the lack of meat.

The wine nearly finished, and the time approaching nine, the stifled conversation turned again to Jim's job. Charlotte was interested in what he actually did during the day. This was an obvious problem, and his few attempts at playing the fool and trying to shift the conversation didn't work. "Do you know what I mean, though." He tried a different track. "You work there all day and when you think about it later, you think, what have I actually done?"

She smiled. "Yeah. Happens to me too. Sometimes you just firefight all day, but with no embers to show at five o'clock."

Jim liked that line, but had a feeling she'd used it before.

"So the GDP revision figure." She leaned further into the table, her eyes connecting with his. "Do you do any work on that?"

Her eyes so close, she could have asked him to kill a puppy and he'd have done it. Was this going somewhere it shouldn't or was she finding common ground? He thought back to the taxi. He was sure she'd hinted that people would pay for advance information. He wondered both what they'd pay and why she was suddenly so interested.

"Yeah." He paused. " But what you've got to remember is you don't see the whole picture." He paused again. He knew in his head what he wanted to say, but was unsure whether it was believable. "I mean, I see one part of the figures. Finding what the actual figure is from that part. Well, it's bordering on impossible." He realised he'd answered her unasked question: Did he know what the figure would be? He wondered if he could use this at some point. Would the information be worth thousands?

Off limits.

He shook his head. "Sorry, that probably didn't make sense."

Her lump of hair flopped down but she didn't push it back up. "I did this course on sampling at college ..." Jim wasn't sure what sampling meant, but he guessed she didn't mean taking a loop or riff off a song to create another tune.

"Sometimes the sample doesn't have to be large to give an accurate end result." He got what sampling meant, but he didn't like where this was going. She left her sentence hovering, dangling in the wind like her lump of hair. He was surprised as she shook her head. "No, it's a revised figure. Sampling theory breaks down doesn't it?"

Jim nodded, he didn't have a clue what she was on about now. He just wanted the bill. Maybe a toilet break was needed.

"You have to see all the parts or else it's as much a guess as the first reported result." She seemed to ponder this for a minute. "That's quite clever really, isn't it?"

Again, Jim nodded before standing up. "Little boys room," he said, walking away.

The bill paid, and the topic of conversation altered, Jim wondered what was next. A taxi home and a peck on the cheek would see him in bed before *News at Ten*. He wanted more, not more between them, but more time with her. She seemed different tonight, and he was only just working out why. What he'd thought were bored signals weren't. She was relaxed. The motor mouth had gone too. She was herself with no need to talk for the sake of it. He thought he was falling for her too, in a big way, but this wasn't the time for that. He'd be dead in three days if he didn't get rich soon.

"Do you fancy a drink before we get back?" He realised after saying it that it kind of hinted he'd be going back to hers. He clarified, "I mean before I go back to my hotel and you go home." He realised that sounded worse. Her face joined his in going red. He wanted the restaurant to swallow him or the huge Chinese warrior dragon on the wall to come to life and eat him.

"Probably ought to get back. Early start and that. Shall we share a taxi?"

Jim nodded. He couldn't help but think he'd set his cause back a week or so. God knows what Harry would have said on the subject. "Second date? Second date? You should be rutting her in empty doorways by now you big ponce. You've disappointed me again, son. Disappointed me. Again."

The taxi hailed, Jim half leaned on her as their stop-start journey headed south. Turning towards her, her face and lips next to his, he kissed her. Expecting her to pull away or slap him, she didn't.

A minute later, his face numb, and mind pulped to a mash, he breathed. He'd smudged her make-up and lipstick, and the droopy lump of hair was now joined by three other lumps. But he hadn't dislodged her smile. Taking her hand, he held it until the cab pulled up outside her flat.

Another kiss outside her door and Jim was ready to go. He didn't want to go, but he didn't want to stay and ruin it either.

"I'd better ..." He pointed down the road.

She nodded. "Me too, I ..."

One more kiss, then he stepped back. Opening the door, she stepped inside then turned to face him. "Thanks for dinner."

"Thank you. It was your choice."

"Thanks anyway." With one last smile, she closed the door and triple-bolted it.

Walking down the street, Jim looked at the sky. "Why now?" he asked. "Why the fuck now?"

Chapter 18

Jim woke with a curious gurgling in his stomach and a clear head. The first day in many without a hangover, his mind rushed with thoughts of Charlotte.

Morning x, the text said.

Morning. Thanks again for last night x, he replied.

Breakfasting on burnt sausage and partially raw toast, he received the reply, *Thank YOU for last night x.* Smiling, he finished his breakfast, paid for two more nights then hopped into the shower.

Within two hours of waking, he walked the familiar East End High Street towards The Queens Arms. Still an hour from opening, he headed for Filthy Alan's. Inside, the familiar unpleasant smell hit his nose. Filthy, despite his apparent poor vision, recognised him straight away. "I'm trying to get hold of Terence," said Jim. "You haven't got a number have you?"

Filthy did a wily head shake Terence himself would be proud of. "Might have."

Shaking his head, Jim pulled a twenty from his pocket. Filthy's memory now clearer, he said, "No point ringing, he never answers. His flat's just up the road. Floor two, number six, Che Guevara Tower. Just up the road. You can't miss it."

Thanking Filthy he left, spotting an old foldable table on the way out. "Keep that for me," he said. "I'll come back later."

"Always a pleasure doing business."

A ten-minute walk and he realised Filthy was right. It was easy to find. The thing blocked out most of the East End's natural light. Climbing the stairs, he knocked on Terence's door before waiting. After the third knock Jim was convinced he was out, but shuffling behind the door told him he was in luck. Opening it, Terence nodded his head for Jim to enter.

"Who gave you my address?" he said, bolting the door.

"Filthy Alan. It's okay, I'm only after the licence."

Terence leant past Jim and closed the corridor's only door. Inside was the living room and a mountain of goods, some Raif's and some from other unfortunate souls. Like Filthy's shop, Terence's flat had the same musty male smell. He wondered if they were in some way related.

"You're in luck." Terence reached into his pocket and pulled out a card. "Wouldn't know it was fake, would you?"

Jim grabbed it and looked. Though at first not recognising himself with glasses on, it was definitely him. The card was a good copy. Hologram and professionally sealed; he reckoned it would nearly fool the DVLA themselves.

"Nice one."

"Does a good job. If you're after a passport, he can do them too."

"This'll do for now." Jim turned and made for the door that Terence was opening.

"I'll see you for another drink next time you're in," Terence called after him as he made for the stairs.

"Thought you might," he replied.

By the time he'd reached south London again, morning had gone.

Having lunch now x, Charlotte had said.

Me too x, he replied.

Leaving the hotel with two bags for life containing an iPad, Wii, the laptop and Freeview box, he walked further south. He'd always thought the new, modern pawnbrokers were ideal for the criminal. Easy cash. Except for one thing: proof of address. Like everywhere else, cameras seemed to rule the shops too. It took a large pair of *cojones* to walk in with stolen goods and risk all for a few hundred quid.

Jim smiled. He thought the glasses gave him a cultured look. Like a proper civil servant. Though why a proper civil servant would need to pawn electrical goods was a big question. He avoided four chain pawnbrokers before finding an independent one. They'd still do checks, he knew that, but he reckoned he'd more chance of succeeding in a small shop. He'd get less money too, but that went with the territory.

Two days left. That was all. Just two days. He had considered ringing the big man when he woke this morning, telling him how near, or far, he was away. Admitting defeat. But he knew his sort. What he'd do is add on five grand interest and give him another week. He'd be going round in circles for months if he wasn't careful. With every minute the police would get nearer, until eventually he'd owe fifteen grand to the nasty bastard from the inside of a prison cell.

Seven grand in two days. It couldn't be that hard, could it?

Walking into the shop, he immediately spied a camera above and another behind the chicken-wire fronted counter. A large hatch to the side of the wire allowed goods to be handed over and returned. The man behind the counter, small, bearded and miserable, nodded his head.

Walking forwards until he was face to face with chicken wire, Jim held up his bags. "Wii, iPad, laptop and Freeview box."

The man screwed up his nose in a well-rehearsed bartering technique. "Not much cash around these days I'm afraid. How long do you want to borrow for?"

Jim pretended to think for a few seconds; he knew he wasn't ever coming back. "A week, maybe two."

"Let's have a look then."

He pulled a handle, spinning the hatch round so the empty side appeared in front of Jim. Placing the bags of goodies inside, Jim waited as the hatch spun back round.

Muttering and sighing, the man plugged the various items in except for the laptop. "You got a lead with this?"

"No."

He tutted some more, but to his disgust it turned on. Jim realised as the screen turned pink with a yellow smiley face in the middle that he should have changed the background as well as deleting the files. Taking his time inspecting everything, he eventually turned back to Jim.

"Eight hundred the lot."

Jim screwed up his face, but nodded anyway. It wasn't a bad deal. He wished he'd come here instead of Terence with some of the other bits. He might have been one step nearer to ten grand. Handing over one of Geoffrey's bank statements and his new driving licence for ID, he received eight hundred in twenties plus a small, carbon copy chit with a number and the details of his goods on.

"Do you want the bags back?" he asked.

"Nah, you're alright," said Jim.

"Sure? They're bags for life."

"No." Jim walked to the door. "They'll probably only last two days before breaking."

The tubes were quieter mid-afternoon. Jim preferred them that way. Too many suited important people and nowhere to sit made for an unhappy man. Alighting at his stop, he walked towards his next destination. Despite the hospital being huge, it was near impossible to find. Asking in a shop, and being forced to buy a packet of fags in return, he got directions.

Walking inside the hospital, he approached the front desk wishing he'd brought some grapes or flowers. "Excuse me. Which ward is Geoffrey Morgan on?"

"What's he in for?"

"Heart attack."

"Try third floor reception."

The flustered receptionist moved onto the next question asker as Jim waited for the lift. He'd never liked lifts and remembered why as the doors closed. He didn't think it was claustrophobia, but just a minor fear of being hemmed in. Just like the cell walls. No room to stretch or move when you wanted to. Harry had said he was in the wrong game if he didn't like being detained. "You wanna move into gardening or scaffolding or something, lad. Being banged up's part of the deal here. Part of the deal."

The lift doors opened just as he felt sweat drip from his back. Walking out, he breathed heavily. At least he was in the right place if he collapsed. The clear and bright hospital walls and floors reflected the sun into his eyes. Squinting, he made for the third floor reception. The air was thick with a clinical, clean smell, and his head felt woozy from the heavy breathing.

"Excuse me, do you know where Geoffrey Morgan is?" His voice faltered. After all, he was hardly on a mercy mission.

"Ward three. Just down the corridor." She pointed.

Jim followed the signs and red markings on the floor to the Coronary Care Support Unit. He knew the man he was looking for. He'd studied his picture enough, yet he didn't know Geoffrey at all. Chances were Geoffrey wouldn't recognise him. Even if he did, Jim didn't know what to expect. Surely he wouldn't just say, "Thanks for saving my life. Here's ten grand for your trouble."

No. Things didn't happen like that. Not in the real world. Jim still didn't fully know why he was here about to meet the man he should have killed. Maybe that was the reason.

Lying on his back and wired up to various machines, Geoffrey turned from his television to look at Jim as he turned the corner. Jim pitied the man in front of him. Bare-chested, pale and helpless, he looked like the proverbial death warmed up that he was. Jim saw his eyes widen as he stared. He seemed to recognise him. Jim was surprised. After all he was dying, all but dead, the last time he saw him.

"Hello." A weak and frail voice. Like a ninety-year-olds. Jim half smiled and looked away from his eyes and towards the wall behind. Filled with electronic gadgets, wires and gizmos, Jim found himself wondering what he could get second-hand for the copper in the wires.

He looked back at Geoffrey. "How are you?" He knew it was a stupid question, but couldn't think what to say. This had been a bad idea. Surely he'd know what Jim had been planning. It must be written all over his face.

"Been better." He coughed. The bleeps and pulses of light flying across the monitors increased slightly in speed.

"Sorry, I haven't brought you any grapes or anything."

He kind of laughed. "Don't worry, I'm sick of them."

Silence filled the gap as Jim wondered what to say next. He reckoned Geoffrey was wondering too.

"Thanks," Geoffrey said.

That seemed to say it all. Just a small apology. Jim waved it away. He didn't deserve thanks. Charlotte had done most of the work, and besides, if she hadn't have been there, God knows what he might have done.

"It's okay. Anyone would have, you know." Jim stopped and looked again at the monitors. The pulses, peaks and troughs were quite hypnotic. He reckoned he could stare at it for hours checking for each little change or irregularity. If you were hooked up to it, after a while, just watching it would make it change. Would it be possible to change the rhythm yourself to one you preferred to look at by breathing faster or slower?

"Sit down." Geoffrey pointed at an orange plastic chair.

Jim sat down. Geoffrey smelt of hospital and sweat. He'd obviously not had a bath in days. Maybe a bed bath, but they never really got you clean. Jim thought of himself if ever he had to get a bed bath from a nurse. He knew it'd be a fight to not stand to attention. Thinking of Anne Widdecombe or cricket batting averages could only hold off so long.

"What's your name?"

"Jim. The woman was Charlotte; she did all the work."

"I can't remember much to be honest. It seemed to happen in double speed. It was like I was trapped inside a bubble or something. Couldn't speak or move; just this pain."

He paused. His monitors and beeping had increased. Jim was terrified he was going to have another heart attack. Being next to him on both occasions would look suspicious.

"What have the doctors said?" Again he was struggling to find things to say. Why was he here?

"Warning sign. I need to wind it down a gear, take it easy in future." He sighed. "Have to find another easier job, plus somewhere else to live."

Jim thought that in itself was probably more stressful than carrying on working. There was something he'd come here to do, but Geoffrey had just made that ten times harder. Of course it shouldn't matter. He was fighting for his life here too. He knew Geoffrey was in so much debt he'd be bankrupt with or without the contents of his flat. But here, face to face. It didn't make it easy.

"Do you, er," Jim paused, "need anything? You know, clothes, stuff, anything from home." He realised how desperate and badly worded that sounded.

"No thanks. My ex wife's sorting some stuff out." Geoffrey paused briefly and seemed to take in what Jim had said. "You're amazing you know. Seriously, no one helps anyone in London. Yet you and that girl; what was her name again?"

"Charlotte."

He nodded. "You not only stop in the street to help someone, but you actually then visit and offer to get them anything they need. You're not from London are you?"

Jim guessed it wasn't just his accent that gave him away. "Coventry."

"Never been there. Maybe I might now. Maybe I might."

Geoffrey managed ten more minutes of talking before nodding off to sleep. Still sat in the little plastic chair, Jim placed his hand on the bedside cabinet. The bottom part of the cupboard opened outwards. What would Geoffrey have inside? A washbag, house keys, maybe a couple of quid for the telephone? Or maybe not. The telephones and televisions seemed to work off some sort of payment card now. Again, the whole world had gone cashless leaving the honest criminal wanting.

Looking around, Jim opened the cupboard. Squeaking and creaking, it made too much noise for his liking. Geoffrey was still sleeping, along with the other patients, but Jim didn't like this one bit. He looked inside. A brown dressing gown lay next to a few pairs of pants. Behind them, the new washbag, hastily bought from a chemist by his ex. A leather wallet beside was tempting. Very tempting.

Chapter 19

Leaving the hospital, Jim felt a spring in his step. His confidence in something had been restored. It took him a while to realise what it had been restored in. Himself. The leather wallet was still inside Geoffrey's bedside table. Its contents, forty quid and a driving licence, were also still there. Jim had walked away from it. Temptation had been fought back.

He liked to think that if the wallet had two hundred pounds instead of forty and a few credit cards he still would have left it. Yep, it would still be there. If there had been house keys he wouldn't have taken them either. Of course he wouldn't.

Sending a message, *Just been to visit Geoffrey. He's a bit weak but okay x,* he headed for the tube.

Getting off the tube in the East End, her reply came, *You should have said. I would have come with you. What did he say?*

Opening his lock-up, and retrieving the three packs of cards he'd left there, he replied, *He said to thank you. You saved his life.*

You did too, she replied.

After closing the lock-up he went round the corner to the Queens Arms. With Mick and Tim playing pool it felt like time had stood still. He wondered if the pair actually did any work, but Mick's new sheen of dusty white plaster said he'd at least put in an hour today.

Saying hello then buying a round of drinks, Jim headed to the pool table.

"How's tricks?" said Mick.

"So so. Yourselves?"

"Not bad, ta," said Tim, missing an easy pot. "Shit." He shook his head.

"You're losing your knack, pal," said Mick.

Smiling, Jim got out the packs of cards and opened them.

"Bit early for poker, mate," said Mick, potting a ball.

"It's not for poker. Just trying to earn a bit of bread." He separated the picture cards from two of the packs and put them into piles.

Tim walked over and sat next to him. Leaning forward, he spoke quietly, "I can spot a man in trouble. You gonna tell me? Or do I have to guess?"

Jim sighed. Should he tell him or not? He couldn't tell him the full story. How could he tell anyone he was a failed assassin? Maybe an abridged version would do. "Sort of. I owe ten gees to someone you shouldn't borrow money from."

Tim sucked in a mouthful of air and reached for his pint. "How long you got?"

"Two days." Jim avoided Tim's eyes and carried on his futile little task of marking the corners of the queens, kings and jacks.

"Shit." Tim slurped down half a pint as Mick continued to clear up the table. Just a red and the black left.

"I'm about halfway," he lied. He was hoping to get halfway by tomorrow. Really hoping.

"I could probably rustle a grand up."

Jim felt his cheeks redden. He truly was stuck for words. He barely knew Tim by Four from Adam, yet he was offering him a grand to help keep his kneecaps intact. Finally he said, "I can't take that, mate. I don't know if I'd ever be able to repay you."

"As and when, mate, as and when." He returned to the table to try and put Mick off his last pot.

Sighing, Jim practised shuffling the cards then started to rehearse his tricks. It'd been a while since he'd done them, and his head felt blown by Tim's offer. Maybe this would work after all. He still needed a few more big ones, but the nearer he got to ten grand the more working limbs he'd have to make more money with.

The tricks were fairly easy, mostly relying on distraction to perform the switches. It needed a cocky, loudmouth attitude. Though card tricks weren't his thing, he knew he just had to think of that Range Rover and ten grand and he'd do anything.

Mick came over with another pint. "I can get you five hundred, pal. You should have told us the other day. I could have helped."

Jim shook his head. "I can't take your money, mate."

He shrugged his shoulders. "You can. And you will."

"What do you mean helped?"

"Eh? Oh, every now and then word goes about." He paused and looked round before continuing, "Cars. There's a gang see, exports them to Russia and Eastern Europe. They pass the word round on the make and model they're after. If you come up with the goods there's a monkey in it."

Jim nodded. He knew of similar scams in Coventry. Break into a house, steal the car keys and drive to a lock-up. Easy money as long as you changed the plates or avoided the number plate recognition cameras. The people involved weren't to be messed with though. Organised crime from Russia and the Baltics involved nasty people. Getting out once in wasn't easy.

"Thanks," said Jim. He felt himself blush again. He really didn't know what else to say.

Mick nodded and sipped at his pint. "There's other ways too. You heard of that gang doing jewellers?"

Jim paused. "The motorbike gang?" He'd heard about them. Everyone inside had. A high-powered bike pulls up outside a jewellers, passenger gets off the rear and smashes the window with a sledgehammer. A handful of rings and necklaces taken, they get back on the bike. Less than a minute from start to finish.

"Is there anyone you know got a bike?" Mick took a large swig of his pint.

Jim shook his head. The only person he knew who could even ride one lived in Coventry and only had a moped. A getaway driver restricted to 30mph? No, it wouldn't work.

"No. Anyone round here with a bike?"

Mick shook his head. "My brother's been on the lookout for a year. Says he's going to drive one himself one day."

Jim shrugged and carried on marking the cards, getting used to the weight of them while shuffling. Quaffing his own pint, he realised just how late in the afternoon it was getting. There was still a long way to go. That seemed to be the story of the last week. Finishing his pint and thanking them, maybe too much, he left the pub and headed for Filthy Alan's.

The smell was worse than this morning as Jim waited for Filthy to waddle through the shop. The small, foldaway table Jim stood in front of was designed for picnics, but was ideal for a small stall or performing card tricks. It was maybe too low for Jim's height, but by adjusting the legs it would go higher but be less stable.

"How much, mate?" asked Jim.

Filthy sucked in air past his rotten teeth. "Thirty quid new these are."

"This isn't new. How much?"

"I'd be robbing myself if I let it go for less than fifteen."

"It's covered in dust. I'll give you five."

"Twelve's my last offer."

"Ten."

"Go on then."

Filthy insisted on shaking Jim's hand. His sweaty, unwashed palms made Jim shudder. He didn't dare think when they'd been last washed. The table folded up well, and was easy to carry on the tube as it whisked him westwards.

"Now, finding the queen is a very old English trick. I'm going to show you." Jim looked at the assembled small crowd that was building. Mainly tourists, about half of them not having English for a first language made his job easier. The late afternoon sun was heavy and shining in most of their faces, another trick of the trade Jim had quickly learnt watching others. He shuffled a pack of cards with as much flair as he could muster. Most of their eyes were on the cards, searching out his secret, trying to outwit him.

"That's the problem with us Brits. We love our queen. Of course, they have different sorts of queens in your country don't they?" He pointed towards a group of Japanese tourists. Japan was near enough to the Philippines for the joke to work. Most of the crowd turned to face the bemused and curious Japanese pair hidden behind their cameras. Jim took the opportunity to cut the pack and palm a queen from his right sleeve onto the bottom.

The crowd, some of them smiling, some half afraid to smile at a politically incorrect joke returned to him. With his hands constantly moving over the cards, and doing a pretend shuffle that only shuffled the first half of the pack, he continued.

"The job is to find the queen. Anyone can do it. There's plenty of queens about. You been to the East End?" He looked directly at a couple from America.

"No, sir," he replied with a southern twang.

"Ain't no cowboys there, pal." Jim looked at some others in the crowd and smiled. "There are pearly queens though. You seen them?" He looked back at the couple. The man looked ready to rip Jim's head off. He looked like he normally took no shit, but this wasn't his domain. He was alien here. Jim had the upper hand.

"No, I have not."

"You ought to see them while you're here." He stopped shuffling and turned fully to the man. "Their clothes are covered in sequins. Millions of them. You must have seen a picture."

"I've seen a picture," said his wife. A few murmurs in the crowd agreed.

"Worth a look. Right then, sir." Jim still had the American's goat up. "Find the queen."

He spread the cards out into ten small piles. Knowing the queen was on the bottom of the pack, he knew its exact position in the third pile. "Choose a pile, sir."

"That one." He pointed at the furthest one.

"Come a bit nearer, come on. Let the dog see the bone."

He shuffled nearer, his wife now taking pictures on her camera.

Discarding the chosen pile, Jim collected the other cards together and started shuffling again, while incessantly talking and making jokes about Las Vegas. After a minute of choosing piles and discarding them, the American picked the pile the queen was in. Luckily at that moment a few European tourists turned and walked away.

"Where you going? I haven't got to the good bit yet. Don't go please." The crowd turned to look at the people leaving giving Jim the chance to collect up the cards and switch two piles around. He continued for a few more minutes. Now nearly twenty people were around his little picnic table, but he also noticed some attention from another entertainer opposite him. The man was talking to a security guard. The *piazza* had regular guards who doubled as movers-on in the case of street entertainers without a licence. Jim knew he had to hurry up.

He speeded up both by talking and moving faster. He was nearing the endgame of the trick, but he still hadn't had the opportunity to plant the card properly. An idea struck him; it might just work.

"Of course," he picked up the remaining cards and shuffled them again, "the queen isn't in here. It's in your back pocket." He pointed at a hapless man in the crowd. The rest of the crowd turned to stare at him. Obviously, the man checked his back pocket and on finding nothing shook his head. "Well of course it's not in your pocket," said Jim. "How could it be, you're over there." The crowd laughed, unaware what Jim had just slipped into the American's back pocket.

Another minute or so of creating piles and reducing them produced nothing. Jim finally turned over the last card announcing, "You've picked the only queen in the pack."

The card was the four of spades. "Shit." He added. The crowd laughed. Some of them looked ready to walk away. The finale beckoned. "Actually," Jim pulled the last stack of cards the American had split up and turned them over, "all of these are queens and you couldn't pick any of them."

The crowd looked stunned. Mouths open. They'd seen the cards seconds ago, but they'd morphed into queens.

"Finally," said Jim pulling a hat from behind the table, "could you check your back pocket please."

The American, still only a gag or two away from lamping Jim, wasn't buying it. "You're not making a fool of me, pal."

"Seriously," said Jim. "Just take a look."

He did and produced a queen. His face fell in a stunned, open-mouthed trance.

"But ..." was all he could say.

"Thank you very much, folks. My name's Jim, and if you could spare some change I'd really appreciate it. Thanks for watching."

A few left, sneaking off without paying, but the majority dibbed into his hat. The higher sums came from the Japanese tourists. Jim thought that was probably indicative of the exchange rate or world economy or something. The American couple, still bemused and more than confused, slipped a twenty into his hat.

"Thank you," said Jim and gave his wife a theatrical wink.

As the security guard started to move over, Jim emptied the hat, packed up the table and left. Counting the coins he was surprised; almost a hundred quid. Deep down though, he knew this was a losing game. Getting moved on every half hour would never see him do more than four or five tricks a day.

Just outside the main square, he set up his table again and played a variation on three-card monte, not for money, just for entertainment. It had been a while since he'd practised it, so the first few times were failures, but he kept his banter up which the small crowd liked. A quarter of an hour gained him just twenty quid after which he got moved on. Getting moved on twice again got him another thirty, but it was becoming too much of a problem. Finding another spot, he lasted just ten minutes before a couple of policemen appeared from round a corner. Packing away instantly, and with only a fiver, he headed for the tube. Waiting for the train, he considered life as an entertainer. If he could make a few hundred a day, which seemed fairly easy, he could rent a bedsit somewhere south of the river and still keep seeing Charlotte after Wednesday.

After crunch day. Assuming there were any bits of him left after Wednesday.

The table dropped off at the hotel, Jim collected a few bits and made his way to Waterloo Station. A busy evening in the rush hour, the station was split between commuters heading home and people heading for the Eurostar. Wishing he had a passport that would let him travel unhindered across Europe, he waited in a queue at an exchange bureaux.

It wasn't that he wanted to run away - especially not from Charlotte - but he just knew that escaping from this mess and starting again in some French vineyard as a grape picker would give him a decent chance of survival.

The queue was small but slow moving. Edging his way to the front, he wondered how these places still survived. Hardly anyone travelling abroad changed money anymore. Everything was done on card. Every purchase, no matter how small, was done on a piece of plastic secured by a four digit number that most people wrote down or stored in their phone.

Reaching the front, the blonde-haired twenty-something woman screwed her nose up as she asked what he wanted.

"A thousand euros please."

"Certainly, sir." Her face cringed while saying sir. "How would you like to pay for this?"

"Cheque please."

She sighed and pointed at the sign. Cheques were yesterdays news. No one used cheques anymore. The sign clearly stated that cheques must be accompanied by a bankers card and two forms of identification.

"I've got a cheque book, driving licence and bank statement." he offered.

"We need a bank debit or credit card," she happily replied.

"I haven't got either."

She shrugged her shoulders, pleased she'd ruined someone's day.

Walking away, he headed for a pawnbrokers or cheque-cashing shop. He daren't visit the same one twice in a day. That was asking for trouble. Most of the central London ones were chains with good CCTV and even better procedures for identification.

Plucking up what little courage he had, he entered one.

He had considered just going to the bank. Conversely, he knew you needed a picture ID to buy fags, alcohol, football tickets, hire a car and even leave the country. Banks, however, were not as strict. This always struck him as odd. Surely drawing all of someone's money from a bank should be classed higher than hiring a car? All he had to do was satisfy the cashier with a few forms of identification and he could clear out his account.

Well, Raif's account.

Raif had once more proved himself to be a fool. His bank statements showed over two grand in his current account. Two big ones sloshing about just waiting for some lag to do the decent thing. "The lad was asking for it," Harry would say, "practically begging for it." He also had ten grand in an internet only ISA account that Jim had no idea how to touch. Raif was back off holiday tomorrow anyway, but that ten grand … It could have solved all his problems.

The bank idea had been discounted. If he got caught in the act, the police would be round him like flies round shit. It wasn't worth it for two grand. Not when he was sure he could get a grand easy enough at a bureaux or pawnbrokers. When Raif checked his account, not to mention the state of his flat, the police would be after him anyway, but that was a few days away.

He'd found the cheque-cashing shop he was in a few streets from Waterloo Station. Payday loans, said the sign. The very, very small print said 3419% APR. Walking in, he'd been greeted by an orange uniformed, balding man with his name badge, Philip, conveniently placed over his left nipple.

"Hello, sir, can I help you?"

Jim reckoned he suffered from an overkeenness that London had yet to rip from his soul. "I need to cash a cheque. It's a bit of an emergency."

"Certainly. If you'd like to follow me to a booth."

The shop was split in two halves. The front half carpeted with tabled nooks and niches oozed respectability and service. Philip and two other badge wearers walked the floor, meeting, greeting and offering a service. Behind them lay the other half. A chest-high partition, the top half bulletproof glass. In some ways Jim thought it resembled a post office, in others a bank. The cashiers behind the screen were a different breed. Bean counters. Harsh looking men and woman, the fear of being held up always in the back of their minds.

Sitting in the booth, the chair straight backed and hard, Jim looked over the table at Philip as he logged onto his computer. Efficient and friendly, he idly chatted about the weather as his computer fired up. Jim thought the whole atmosphere was designed to make this seem no different than buying a pound of apples from a supermarket. There was nothing seedy or shameful about being here. It was just a business transaction.

"Okay, name and address, please."

Jim fired off Raif's address. He had the statements and driving licence in front of him in case of any mishap. Luckily there wasn't. When asked for date of birth though, he had to pretend a coughing fit while looking down at the licence for the correct date.

Things soon came to the meat of the action. The heat in the shop cum office was starting to get to Jim. Air conditioning had been forgotten about when this building was designed. Maybe it was part of the experience. Make it uncomfortably hot so people are more likely to agree to whatever it is you tell or offer them.

"How much do you want to borrow?"

Jim noticed the word "want" was emphasised, not "need". Ideally he'd have said ten grand, but he had to be realistic. The sign on the door said, "Borrow five to five thousand pounds". "Subject to Status", the small print added.

"Three thousand, please."

The man nodded, his well trained eyes giving nothing away. Returning to his screen, he tapped a few keys on his keyboard.

"Purpose of loan?" He continued to stare at his screen.

To carry on living he wanted to answer. "Buying a car. It's a small garage, cash only, you know." He knew how dodgy that sounded, but Philip nodded. He'd probably heard worse excuses. "It's a bit of a rush. My girlfriend's fallen in love with the car, you see. All my cash is locked into I-sa's." He'd never heard the word ISA said before, and noticed Philip's look when he said it. It was obviously pronounced differently.

"How soon would you be able to repay it?"

Jim looked at the ceiling pretending to work out the answer. "Um, well it takes three or four days to transfer the money, so I suppose a round week would make it easy."

Philip nodded. "We could make it over a longer term if that would help?" Jim reckoned that at the annual rate they charged they'd like nothing more than for him to take longer repaying it.

"Well, I've got the money here. It's just a timing thing, isn't it?" Jim pulled the ISA statement from his pile of paperwork and handed it to Philip. He looked at it, nodded and probably wondered what the hell Jim was doing in a payday loan office. After all, garages took deposits. No, the story had big holes in it. More seemed to be appearing by the minute.

"Okay, that will be fine. A week today then."

Philip typed more numbers and ran a credit check which came out as "Excellent". Jim couldn't believe how well this was going, but he knew it wasn't over yet.

"Would you like a coffee?" Philip stood up and pulled a strange vending machine key from his pocket. "It's not that bad, honest. I know some vending coffee is, well, rank to say the least."

"Yes please. Have you got tea?"

Again, Jim received that look when asking for tea. It was like he'd asked for a bag of crack or a syringe full of scag. Looking round while Philip went to the machine, Jim noticed the three CCTV cameras again. It was unavoidable. He'd tried hard to get the money without giving himself away, but as each day had passed the ante upped. When all this was over he'd head off to Wales or Cornwall, find himself somewhere to live, somewhere temporary to live, and maybe a seasonal job. After all, what was there for him in London?

His phone pinged. Charlotte.

What are you doing tomorrow evening? her message had said.

Nothing why? x, he replied.

His head went into turmoil as Philip continued his checks. It still wasn't too late to walk away from this. Sure, they had his picture but until the money was borrowed, and Raif was chased for it, no real crime had been committed. Doing this pretty much scuppered any chance of him staying in London. Realistically, he couldn't have stayed in London anyway. Why was he doing this? Why was he getting to know Charlotte just so he could hurt himself and her even more?

Do you want to come to mine for dinner tom evening? x

His heart leapt. Dinner at her place. Was that some London euphemism? Either way this was going from bad to worse, or was it getting better? The night before he was due to pay ten grand he didn't have, the night when he should be robbing and stealing, she wanted to cook him dinner. If he accepted he'd be dead the next day.

There could only be one answer.

Yeah, I'd really like to. What time? x

Philip nodded towards Jim's phone. "How did we survive before them?"

Jim smiled. "Makes you wonder, doesn't it?"

Seven okay? x she replied.

Fine x, replied Jim.

Philip went back to sipping his coffee and checking the bank statement and driving licence. "My bank card's in my other trousers," Jim had told him, which he seemed to believe.

"That all seems fine. I'll just print off a credit agreement, then the cars yours, so to speak."

"Thanks," said Jim. "She'll be over the moon."

The hotel seemed a lifetime away and every person looked like a mugger. Still, Jim knew that was the problem with having three grand in your pocket. He still couldn't believe how easy it had been. He'd been so worried about there being some kind of alert on Raif's name that he'd forgotten how little checks people actually do. All he'd shown them was a birth certificate, two bank statements and a false driving licence. He'd also written them a cheque for three thousand four hundred and eighty pounds, post-dated a week ahead. "If the cheque doesn't clear," Philip had said, "there will be charges, so keep us informed if anything doesn't go to plan."

Jim had assured him everything would be fine before he stuffed the wads of cash into his pockets.

Now on the street, all the cabs in London seemed to have disappeared. He thought of taking the tube, but what was the point? It was too big a risk to take. And for what? To save a tenner on cab fares? No, he'd get a cab. Assuming they weren't on strike or anything.

Eventually hailing one, the driver was more than happy to go south of the river in return for payment. Jim did wonder at one point if he was just very good at sarcasm. If he was, he was too good for it to be of use.

Halfway across the bridge he stared out of the window mentally counting his dough. He thought he now had six plus the builder boy's offer of another fifteen hundred. Jim hoped he wouldn't have to use their money. They were good lads and he'd never see them again. Taking their money would be difficult. He wondered if they were actually expecting it back, but that wasn't the point.

Two and a half or four left to get. Only just over halfway. And with a day left. He still had two iPods, an iPad and a few Raify bits. Five hundred tops for them. One and a half away.

As the cab stood still in heavy traffic, he wondered if he could keep his legs by offering them seven with another three next week. Of course it wouldn't be three; it'd be upped to five.

Another week, though. Charlotte. He'd never met anyone like her. She was unique, he knew that. Maybe everyone in London was, but she was the only person he'd met. Thinking hard, he knew she was different to other Londoners. She didn't have that closed off feel most had. She was friendly; she'd do anything to help.

"Maybe she'd lend me three grand?"

He caught the cabbie's eyes in the mirror. Shrugging his shoulders, the cabbie returned his stare to the road. Jim shook his head and sighed.

Borrowing money from her wasn't going to happen. How could he even ask? Just come out with it? No. Maybe he ought to do it by text. That seemed to be the London way. No, she was off limits.

Dressing into Raif's best suit, he caught a glimpse of himself in the mirror. Every day this past week he'd aged another few years. His face drawn and eyes black-ringed, he reckoned in real terms he was approaching mid-forties. If this wasn't sorted out this week he'd be drawing his pension by next Friday.

Raif's suit fitted him well. He almost felt a new man whenever he wore it. It seemed to add a certain something. He wasn't sure what that something was; maybe the sense of fitting in. However, he was using it to fit into places he'd no right to be in.

Leaving the hotel, he hailed another taxi and crawled across London to Leicester Square and his next port of call.

Chapter 20

Jim had always liked the idea of it. Maybe it was the tension or the risks involved. Shifty Ted was to blame. The way he glamourised Monte Carlo and the life of luxury. It had left Jim in no doubt that one day, when he had enough money, he'd do it too.

The casino was under exaggerated on the outside. According to the cabbie they couldn't advertise - it was against the law. The cabbie assured him this was a popular one with a good reputation. Jim wondered whether he was on a kickback. Everyone in London seemed to be.

There was a certain irony that Jim liked about spending Raif's money, while wearing his clothes, in a casino. He was sure Raif would appreciate the irony once he got over the shock of having his life stolen from him. That, of course, was the other reason he was here. His own life might be robbed from him so why not experience more of it before then? He was under no illusion of turning the five hundred quid in his pockets to four grand, but at least it was ticking off something on his life to-do list.

Inside, the exaggeration turned full track from under to over. Marble pillars led the way upstairs to the main entrance. The air cool and fresh, Jim walked up the velvet carpet to the top and the front desk. An attractive Asian woman, possibly Japanese, asked him if she could take his suit jacket. The air seemed over conditioned so he refused.

"Have you visited us before, sir?" she asked

"No, err." He shrugged his shoulders. Through the CCTV above his head, he reckoned they were already laughing at him, wondering how much he'd lose.

He listened and nodded as she politely explained how the casino worked. How to buy chips, minimum bets for each table, how to order drinks, she was very thorough. Though she'd obviously said the words a million times before, she'd recite them another million times before any hint of sarcasm or impoliteness crept into her voice.

"Thanks for your help." He turned and walked through the bouncer-guarded double doors into the casino itself.

His first thought was of an upmarket fairground. In a way, he didn't think it far from the truth. Coconut shies replaced by roulette wheels. Hoopla replaced by blackjack. Greasy hot dog vans replaced by a bar with restaurant attached. The roof overhead was partially mirrored making everything brighter and larger. A row of slot machines lined the walls each advertising thousands of pounds payouts. Turning round to get his bearings he eventually wandered to what resembled a post office counter, except it had glitzy tills and the biggest bouncer Jim had ever seen.

"Hello, sir, how can I help?"

Another attractive woman, this time Eastern European. Her English good, but with a slight twang on the h's.

"Er, can I get some chips please?"

"Certainly, sir. Cash or card?"

Jim reached into his inside pocket. The bouncer's eyes lit up, seeing and expecting all. Producing a bundle of notes, Jim laid them down. "Cash. Five hundred." What had seemed like a big deal, and a big wedge of cash to him, hardly battered her eyelids. She placed the cash in an automatic counting machine before pressing buttons on a till which released a combination of red, blue and green chips, each marked with a figure. Pocketing them, Jim thanked her then went for a stroll.

Early evening, the casino was sparsely populated. A few suited men, possibly bankers, sipped cocktails and talked loudly about share options at the bar. One roulette table with two hapless but smiling gamblers was in operation, while the croupier at a blackjack table stood, arms folded, waiting for someone to relieve his boredom. Jim settled on helping him. The place wasn't going to get busy for a few hours, but if he played it easy in the quiet he knew he'd look more of a pro when the crowds arrived.

According to his name badge the croupier was called Jason. Jim thought him a likeable and professional enough person. Playing slowly, with two hands, Jim bet barely above the minimum for half an hour. The tables and his luck turned regularly; at one point he was fifty up. By the end he was twenty down.

"Think I'll get a bite to eat."

The croupier nodded and thanked him.

Before eating he went to the roof terrace for a couple of cigarettes. The cocktail drinkers had moved outside, smoking cigars and discussing portfolios and Middle Eastern exposure. Standing at the balcony he watched the streets below. Cars still aimlessly going nowhere, people in a hurry to get somewhere and the odd beggar or *Big Issue* seller trying to make enough to get their mind off London for the night.

He sent Charlotte a message. *How was work today?*

Okay thanks. Still busy. Just going in shower x.

Sighing, Jim finished his fag and went to the restaurant.

Busier than he thought, it seemed most of the eaters were finishing their long dinners. Jim settled on the fillet steak. He'd never eaten fillet before and wondered just how it could be worth twice the price of other steak. Ordering a bottle of foreign lager to go with it, he sat alone watching others talk shop.

The fillet steak was twice as good as any steak he'd eaten. Ordering cheesecake for dessert, he couldn't help but feel like a death row inmate eating his last meal. Whatever he wanted was his. His life's dreams and wants served up in the next few hours.

Problem was, he didn't know what his life's dreams were. Life had been taken for granted. Ducking and diving all the way. Scraping from one disaster and prison cell to the next. What did he really want to do before he died? What made a life complete? Sighing again he paid the bill, adding a fiver tip, before heading back to the gaming floor.

The evening crowd were in. Most of them straight from a meal or a quick shower and change. Shifty Ted had told him of the three different types of casino crowd. There was the professionals - those that actually could beat the bank regularly enough to live from it. A dying breed, they drifted from casino to casino around the world, their luck on average never seeming to run out. Next, the fun lovers. People out for the evening with money burning in their pockets that would be the casino's by the end of the night. Among these, city folk were spending their hard-earned bonuses. Big bets placed for show with little want or need of a successful outcome. Lastly, the first timers. People stunned by the glitz, glamour and air-conditioned luxury. Maybe these would join the first group of winners. More likely, they'd lose all and never come back.

Jason, his previous croupier, wasn't at his table. Jim knew they rotated staff; the management always on the lookout for fraud and incompetence. Instead, a young woman with the name tag of Jessica played the banker to a group of three.

Hovering behind them, Jim realised the group was actually two groups. A man on his own, mid-fifties, balding yet charming sat beside a young couple full of smiles and awe.

"Mind if I join in?"

They didn't. The couple beamed as he sat. Parading their chips in front of themselves, Jim knew they were first timers blowing a wedge of money. The dream of winning big was in their eyes. The reality not sunk in.

He played a few hands at minimum stake. Each loss by the couple a huge disappointment, each win euphoria and surprise. The seasoned man at the end plodded on, steadily increasing his pot, slowly but surely. Studying him, Jim quickly learnt when to bet more or less. Of course it was random; no one knew what cards the dealer had, but it was about odds. Betting with the best odds would eventually see you into profit over the long term.

An hour later and a hundred quid down, he left the table. The couple next to him had slowly and steadily blown nearly a grand. Each loss made them keener to win it back. He'd half considered taking them to one side and offering them a deal. "You can lose all your money in the next ten minutes, and save a life if you want," he'd have said. That would have given them a better story for their night out. They'd have had something more human to chatter about at their coffee houses and dinner parties.

Realistically, he knew where tonight was ending. He'd walk out the door at two a.m. cashless and depressed. Just a quick go on roulette his head was saying. Just a little go. You might just be the one tonight that beats the odds.

The roulette wheels were busier and noisier. Jim settled on the quietest. A smallish group who definitely weren't bankers were blowing a week's wages and loving every second of it.

Taking his time, Jim studied the croupier's throw. He varied the spin length and the speed he hurled the ball. Some of them, especially inexperienced or just plain stupid, tended to get in a routine. Unconsciously, they'd allow it to spin the same time and throw the ball at the same speed. Not that it made it any easier to predict the number, but if you covered areas it lowered the odds.

Jim slowly punted his money. The drink now flowing, a few double whiskies had been quaffed and his problems forgotten. The woman next to him was idly talking, he wasn't entirely sure what about, but he nodded and smiled in the right places.

Down to three hundred quid he made his apologies and left to walk round the room.

Going to bed, night night x, said Charlotte's message.

Me too. Night x, he replied.

The busier roulette table beckoned him. Busier, louder, noisier, the croupier had his hands full. If any of the staff was going to cut corners or forget what they were doing, it was him. Stood beside the bankers and brokers, Jim bit his tongue as he followed the wheel and the bets, looking, searching for a pattern.

The croupier was good. Though his speed was regular, he seemed to vary his wait while the table was spinning with almost computer-like randomness.

Jim knew he had a choice. The staff were too good to make it easy so should he just lump all his eggs into three spins and hope for the best, or keep going for another four hours slowly flittering away three hundred. At least that was all he'd brought out with him. The thought of blowing his hard-earned six grand on one spin of the table may have been too tempting. After all, having no money was as near as having half the money.

He left the roulette and headed for the bar. He'd have two more large whiskies before he played it big. Ordering a fifteen-year-old malt, he sat on a barstool watching the barman wash glasses. In the bar mirror, he caught the eyes of two women sat at a table behind him. Working girls. He knew straight away they were, yet they were in a much better league than any he'd seen before. He remembered how he should have spent last Thursday evening after killing Geoffrey. How different things had become. He'd gone from near hero to zero.

Downing his whisky, he ordered another and took care of it before returning to the tables. His belly now full of fire, he headed for the first roulette wheel with the quiet-ish threesome.

The croupier had been replaced again - according to Shifty Ted this was normal to prevent any sort of relationship building up. Jim smiled at the previously talkative woman as he stood beside her.

"How's your luck?" he asked.

Turning, she smiled. Her face flushed with excitement and wine, she said, "Not good. Jeff's doing okay. We've nicknamed him Nostradamus."

Jim smiled back and watched as the croupier spun the wheel then the ball. Clattering round the outside, the woman next to him gasped as the ball rocketed into number four then back out, finally resting in two.

Jim ignored the moans and groans from the partially drunk group and tried to settle on his plan. Three goes at a hundred. Six at fifty. Ten at thirty. Maybe even up the ante. First spin ten, second twenty, and carry on. Yeah, that was the way. Whether to bet on the corners or the numbers themselves was a harder problem. It had to be corners; the chances of winning were slight anyway, but winning just based on single numbers? He wouldn't stand a chance.

"Here goes nothing," he said, partially to the woman but also to himself.

Ten pounds on the corners of twenty-three, twenty-four, twenty-six and twenty-seven.

The ball spun, teased for ten seconds then landed on six.

Again, the same corners with a twenty pound bet. The ball landed on fifteen. The woman next to him and her gang had stopped betting. Watching Jim lose all his money seemed more fun.

Forty pounds, same corners. The ball spun, shot round and dived into twenty-four.

"Woah."

The ball flickered and teased with the side but stayed there. Screams and hugs all round. Jim's heart was going like the clappers. It felt like it would explode. The croupier pushed over his winnings, a big pile of chips. He tried to count them but his head was spinning. He knew it was only about three hundred. Taking a deep breath he counted them. Three hundred and twenty. Still down on the night.

"Same numbers, eighty pounds."

His heart now pumping hard, the ball rocketed round and hovered over twenty-seven before settling in thirty-six. The woman next to him placed her arm on his shoulder. Just for a split second, he felt guilty. It wasn't fair on Charlotte. None of this was. He should have brought her here. It should be her hand comforting him.

They looked at him. Was he going to quit while still sort of ahead?

He took a deep breath. "One sixty. Same numbers."

Gasps all round. They could see his pile of chips and knew he was going for broke. Again no one else betted. Everyone keen to watch and see what happened.

Nearly shaking he watched the ball fly round and land in five. Again moaning and groaning and furtive looks at him as it seemed to dawn on the watchers that unlikely means just that. Looking at his chips, he had about three hundred left. Keeping back ten, he stacked up the rest. "All in. Same numbers."

The ball seemed to hang in mid-air as it swung round the side. Time slowed down and the laws of physics changed to allow the ball to keep swinging all night. He must have breathed six or seven times before the ball clattered down, flirted with twenty-seven, before landing in sixteen.

The world speeded up to a crescendo. His previous slow and immensely focused mind suddenly opened to take in the loss around him.

"Shit."

He looked to the mirrored ceiling and shook his head. He knew a CCTV operator would be looking down, laughing and calling him a tosser. Sighing, he looked back at the table.

"Sorry," the woman beside him said. She squeezed his arm gently. If it wasn't for Charlotte he'd have said something back; returned her friendship. Tried for more.

"Pick a number," said Jim. He held up his last ten pound chip looking at the croupier.

She shook her head. "I can't. Not allowed."

Jim nodded then turned to the woman next to him. "A number?"

"Four," she replied.

The wheel spun.

The ball landed on six.

The walk back was sobering. Despite expecting and almost wanting to lose everything, it was still humbling. Just a dream, nothing more. He could kid himself with "what ifs" all night, but the reality was just what he'd thought. There's only one winner in a casino: the owner.

The city now quieter; he walked for hours. He should have saved that last ten and got a cab. Maybe he should have split the last hundred into three goes. Would that have improved the odds?

Sliding back into the hotel at just after one and hitting his bed, sleep took time to come. The last full day was ahead. If it wasn't for Charlotte and the thought of dinner in her luxury apartment he'd do a runner. Yeah, he reckoned he would.

Chapter 21

His alarm went off at six. A headache accompanied him into the shower as he tried to wake himself up. Breakfasting at seven, partially raw sausage and burnt toast, he received the message.

Morning x.

Morning x. he replied.

He had no real plan for today. How do you plan to make four grand in a day? His mind was blank. Blagging and robbing would get him nowhere. Today had to be the biggy. It just had to be.

Returning to the room he ripped the gaffer-taped bag from the toilet cistern and lay on his bed. Gloves on, he unzipped the bag and pulled out the gun. The thing that had got him into this shit was getting him out of it. What else could he do?

After treble checking the safety was on, he unloaded the weapon. Replacing the bullets in the bag, he tidied up.

On the bed, the comedy mask, additional gloves, reading glasses, coat and weapon. Putting the coat on, he pocketed everything and left the room.

The air felt colder and more polluted. He reckoned summer had finally buggered off south leaving autumn and winter ready to wreak havoc. Walking south, he was conscious of his coat and whether or not the piece could be seen. It felt like six days ago except for the weather. But the anxiety, the nervousness, everything. Today was different though, the gun wasn't loaded. No one was getting killed today.

He hadn't killed anyone anyway. He never would have, he knew that. Knew it was a fact. If Geoffrey hadn't had his heart attack he'd have pissed around for two more days following him. The time would never have been right.

Through Kennington and Stockwell, Jim strolled mainly against the oncoming tide of workers rushing to their jobs. The time now half eight, he was far too early. A stop in a cafe yielded a tea and bacon sandwich. Looking round at the chipped Formica tables, grubby tablecloths and pepper pots that didn't have a grinder attached, Jim felt he'd returned to the pre-coffee shop age. It hadn't taken him long to get here.

It was just a case of picking the right area. Economists would no doubt call the area deprived because they sold fried food instead of muffins. To Jim, this was home.

A couple of builders opposite ate fried breakfasts noisily. Jim wished he'd found this place earlier. Just like the Queens Arms it was a home from home. A little place to unwind. There was probably a pub just round the corner he could have come to with its own Mick the Prick and Tim by Four.

He stretched the tea out for half an hour. The thought of what was coming wasn't the only thing that made him want to stay. Eventually leaving, he wandered through the streets passing shuttered shops, halal delicatessens and fruit shops selling weird shaped fruit he'd never seen before. Brixton, with its knife crime, hatred and diversity, was approaching.

Lurking round the back streets he looked inside a post office window. An early morning rush of two pensioners filled the little sub-post office. There'd be CCTV, he knew that. Plus a button to ring the police which would be pressed quicker than he could say, "This is a stick up."

"This is a stick up."

He'd always wanted to say it. It was just so glamorous and proper gangsterish. It was the very words Harry must have said before he robbed the security van and brained the driver with a crowbar. "Don't do it, son," he heard Harry say. "Don't end up like me. Don't spend your life in a cell."

Sighing, he turned and carried on. The post office wouldn't have got him four grand. No, that was a close shave. He'd have got five hundred or a grand plus the rozzers everywhere and his picture on the six o'clock news. That wouldn't have gone down well with Charlotte.

Charlotte again.

Tonight weighed on his mind. She'd become such a big part of his life he couldn't see how all this could possibly fit in with her. Or without her.

Walking back to the hotel he came across a small bookies. Inside, the smell of sweaty, unwashed man and stale cigarettes greeted him. The walls yellowed through smoke and lack of maintenance gave a good idea of not only the punters, but also the takings. Though still early, a few punters were looking at form and reading the papers ready for their afternoon bets. Again, aware of the gun in his pocket and his dire need for money, he considered it. There were two CCTV cameras, neither over the door. He could slip the mask on, no one had seen his face yet. The two oldies wouldn't put up a fight. One of them might be a have-a-go hero, but seeing a gun tended to relieve potential heroes of their bottle. He might get a grand, maybe two. Would they accept seven and leave him alone?

Of course not.

Jim looked at the boards. The day's races hadn't yet been chalked up, but a few old and long running bets were still there. White Christmas 10-1. Arsenal to win Premiership 8-1. GDP +0.5% 100-1.

GDP.

It hit him with a rush. This GDP thing he was supposed to be doing for the ONS would report tomorrow. Maybe that was the answer. A few of Charlotte's contacts would stump up four grand easily.

No, he wasn't going to use Charlotte.

But his life depended on it. Leaving the bookies, he made a decision he'd regret. One he knew would lead him down several dark alleys. One he hoped wouldn't ruin what they had, but also knew it would.

A newspaper shop supplied him with a *Financial Times* which had a GDP report inside. He wished he still had that laptop. He could have found out more on the internet, but he really was no computer whizz despite the courses inside.

Walking back to the hotel he'd no idea how to play it. Her words from the other night both in the taxi and at the Chinese were clear. She was after the information. What had she said? People would pay well for it.

Maybe he should just ring her now and say he could get the info if she was interested. No, he doubted she'd want that over the phone. It had to be face to face to know just how much information she really wanted. And, more importantly, how much he'd get for it.

One thing was determined, even set in stone. It wouldn't be her money. It would be her contact's money. If his prediction was wrong, which it would be, he'd offer to repay them. That would buy more time. He could carry on living at the hotel, or find a cheaper pad. Maybe a few card tricks. Yeah, he could do that. Maybe take a month or so to pay them back. He could do this.

But Charlotte. She'd be annoyed he'd got it wrong. How annoyed though? He reckoned this whole thing had gone far enough for him to talk his way out of it. Yeah, a bit of banter and she'd be fine.

He stopped and sighed at a pedestrian crossing. Cars whizzed by as his mind leapt from idea to idea. He knew this might just work. One day of course, he'd have to be honest with her. Tell her the truth. Or part of the truth. Hopefully, by then, he'd be sorted. A good enough story and a bit of cash to carry this on.

As the light turned green, he walked across the road. Halfway across the phone in his pocket buzzed.

Do you like Mexican food? her text said.

Yeah, really like it, he replied.

Entering the hotel, he hid the gun before making for the bar. Though open all day its customers were few and far between. Jim waited five minutes for the solitary barman to appear and unlock the bar before serving him a flat pint of lager. Sitting down with the pink paper he tried to read it, but the long words and complex explanations of things he knew nothing about weren't going in.

Drinking more lager, he tried again. As far as he could see, GDP was the cost of what the country did. It was like the gross pay on a payslip except for the whole country. Sure, he could see it was important, but he couldn't tell why people were so concerned if it went down 0.1% or up 0.5%. From what he could remember about maths at school, that was surely a rounding difference. Unless it fell by whole percents why was the whole country so bothered about it? And, how did these traders make huge sums betting on the outcome?

He read further, his mind taking more in, but he didn't feel confident to blag his way through. Another pint wasn't helping either.

Now sat outside in the concrete mini beer garden, he read again through the expert opinions and forecasts. Apparently two quarters of negative growth meant the country was in recession. Jim wondered why they just didn't say, "if it goes down for six months", instead of "two quarters of negative growth". He suspected big words were used to make a simple explanation appear more complicated. He knew most people would be bored shitless and put off by now. Maybe that was their aim.

It did explain the hoo-ha over the figures. Going into recession was bad news, Jim knew that. He remembered the last recession well. His own takings were well down; people's spending money disappeared. With that, the honest thief's earnings disappear too.

Most of the experts in the paper reckoned on very small growth. This seemed to be the consensus though one wild-haired doomsayer seemed to be arguing for a half a percent fall. Though Jim had little idea how the city worked he thought most people would bet with the majority. They'd be expecting an increase. Maybe he should say it's a fall. That half a percent fall the long-haired geezer reckoned looked a good bet. People, or Charlotte's contacts, would be more interested in a figure that was out of the ordinary. Four grand would be his by the end of tonight, he was sure of it.

He sent her a message, *These GDP figures are going to surprise everyone x.*

Really? Why? x was the almost instant response.

I'll tell you tonight x.

Chapter 22

He showered hard washing London from his skin. After walking past traffic most of the morning, he felt covered in a plague of soot. The time only five o'clock, he had considered re-hitting the square mile for one last look around. Maybe that stray set of Porsche keys would be dangling today. He didn't go. The only thing he was sure of was he'd get arrested if he tried.

Instead, he read and reread the paper. GDP wasn't that boring when you got into it. Actually, it was. But the interesting thing was a whole new world of numbers and new words had been invented to describe its smallest aspects. People devoted their whole life to the study of a three monthly press release. People were paid to give their opinion. If they were wrong it didn't matter. By the next release everyone had forgotten the last.

Choosing one of Raif's expensive polo shirts, Jim got ready. He felt light-headed and knew it wasn't the drink. There was anticipation over tonight. He was trying hard not to think about what may happen. Dinner. Just one little word, but the expectation was on what followed it.

Of course money was weighing on his mind, but Charlotte was close to pipping it and taking over. Not for the first time, he couldn't understand what she saw in him. She was perfect, intelligent and liquid. He was either a good liar or she a bad judge of character.

Finished work. On way home x, she said.

Okay. I'm already at hotel x, he replied.

It didn't help his butterflies. A couple of double whiskies in the bar might, but he knew turning up smelling of Scotland's finest was the worst way to ensure tonight went well. The fluttering was moving down his chest towards his stomach. He wasn't sure if he'd be sick before the night was out. Eating a hot chilli was going to be a test.

Laying back on the bed, he turned on the television. Some late afternoon quiz program was enough of a distraction. It reminded him of afternoon's inside. "Cobby Harris" would be playing pool with "Barney Barnsey". "Mad Luke" would be cheating at draughts with "Knifey Dave" and Jim himself would be sat on a plastic orange chair watching some afternoon TV drivel. Harry would be sat beside him telling a story about a robbery or a piece of gangland revenge usually involving hammers and kneecaps. Jim would have taken it all in. It'd been like a family party. He'd never been to any family parties because he barely knew his. But that's what it had always felt like. Like he belonged.

Approaching the high security front door of the warehouse flat, Jim's stomach once again leapt. It had settled down over the afternoon. While in the off licence buying a bottle of wine, it had almost been normal. The nearer he got, the harder it churned.

Pressing the buzzer, he waited.

A very long fifteen seconds passed before her voice came through the intercom. Crackly and devoid of any tone it was still recognisably Charlotte.

"Hi."

"It's me." He waited. "It's Jim," he added.

"Come up."

Heavy bolts dropped from their place and the door buzzed. Pushing it, he walked in. The fresh scent of pine and pot pourri was fighting for nose space with the smell of tomatoey-chilli. The combination smelt like an explosion in a Mexican air-freshener factory.

Legs like jelly, he walked up the stairs. Appearing round the top with a spatula in her hand, and wearing an expensive apron was Charlotte. Smiling, she said nothing but flicked her head briefly backwards.

Her face had colour. Jim wondered if she was as nervous as he, or whether she'd just tasted a too-hot chilli. Being normally so calm and unflustered he settled on the chilli. She wouldn't possibly be feeling as nervous as himself. She couldn't be.

"Sit down, it's nearly done."

Reaching the top of the stairs, Jim handed over the wine. A mid-price bottle of Australian white, the label said it was the perfect accompaniment to fish and meat. It said nothing about vegetarian chilli. She read the label, her face not quite turning into a frown, before she said, "I haven't had this. Looks nice." She offered her cheek for a quick kiss. Just a European thing, Jim told himself. It doesn't mean anything.

He walked past her. Being so near, within touching distance, every muscle in his body had clenched. Taking the edge of the nearest huge sofa, he sat, but cricked his neck round so he didn't break eye contact.

"Good day?" she asked.

"Busy."

He'd planned to say that. It was part of the GDP conversation he'd memorised. Now he'd seen her, seen her face and eyes and that smile, he was having second thoughts about the plan.

"Me too," she started. "Had another investor pull out today. Not what I need at this late stage. I mean, despite the meals and the bottles of champagne I bought him and his wife, it's not just that, it's the time wasted isn't it?"

He couldn't keep his eyes off her. She'd walked back to her island kitchen and was stirring chilli while delivering the rant.

"Trying to get a replacement at this late stage won't be easy. At least he wasn't a big investor though. That's the only saving grace."

His head was twisted almost one hundred and eighty degrees. Dressed in a knee-length skirt and blouse, she almost looked like she hadn't changed since work. Her still damp hair gave the truth away. She'd had a shower and redressed before cooking. Jim wondered if she'd change again after cooking. She walked towards the fridge. As she bent over, he turned and looked at the huge television screen.

"Put the telly on if you want," she said. "I normally just have the stereo on when I'm cooking. I mean you can't watch it and cook. It's just asking to burn something, my ..."

"No, I'm fine with the radio," he interrupted.

He briefly looked at the selection of magazines, papers and books on the coffee table. The business section from last weekend's broadsheet caught his eye. Having a quick look at an article on GDP, just in case there was something he'd missed, his eyes were drawn to the Blaupunkt stereo. He didn't recognise the music. A female solo singer. Quite relaxing and soothing. He thought it was Sade or someone else from the nineties. Mood music.

"Tea, coffee? Or do you want something stronger?"

"Tea please. Don't want to get," he paused and reworded, "Midweek isn't it? Don't want to drink too much." He turned round and smiled. She smiled back.

"Do you drink coffee at all?" She asked, almost accusingly.

174

"Never really got on with it." It occurred to him he was giving his class away. Everyone in London drunk some variety of coffee except the working class.

"Bet you're the only one at work who drinks tea."

"Yeah."

He should have thought that through more. Pistol Pete should have picked up on it too. She probably thought he was some heathen from the sticks. Too late to drink coffee now; she had his number.

"They think I'm some heathen from the sticks," he said.

She laughed, finished making the drinks then brought them over. Sitting on the other sofa, legs together, shoulders back, she sipped her far too hot to drink coffee.

"So, you need another investor then?"

Her eyes briefly lit as she took another sip. "Yeah. You don't know anyone do you?"

He couldn't tell if it was a joke or not. It was bordering on an actual question. Struggling for an answer, he shook his head.

Sat forward, cramped against the sofa and with his arms folded over his knees, he hoped she had no formal psychology training. Mind you, given her own clamped-in posture, Jim was sure her body language was as defensive as his own. Any psychologist watching would have enough material for a few books.

"Doing some homework are you?" She nodded towards the business section.

"You know." He shrugged his shoulders. "Hard to switch off, isn't it?" He could feel his cheeks going red.

"So, what's the GDP news then?"

He was surprised she'd asked so quickly. He'd planned to bring it up while they ate. He reckoned a mouthful of chilli was the best way of hiding his lack of knowledge should he get stuck.

"It's mad at work. Everyone's going out of their minds. Obviously, making sure it is actually correct is the main problem."

Her eyes were following his every word. He found it off-putting. The butterflies had returned and were threatening to make his stomach rumble. He took a sip of tea. Though hot, it was just the right strength. He wondered how she'd learnt to make such a decent cuppa.

"So you going to tell me or not?" As if on command, her dimples appeared. How could he say no?

"I shouldn't really." He smiled and wished he was closer and two six feet sofas didn't separate them.

"I won't tell anyone; honest Injun." She held up her left hand, thumb and little finger together leaving the remaining three fingers upright. He couldn't remember the last time he'd seen anyone do that.

"Yeah. But ..." He paused, trying desperately to think of something to stall. This wasn't going to plan. "Before that, you can tell me more about your deal."

"Tease." She stood up. "I'll just check the rice. She walked towards the kitchen, her apron flapping at her legs with each stride. "What do you want to know?"

He thought for a second. "I was just thinking the other day. I mean I don't know much about stocks and that, but the information you know must be worth money to the right people." He'd finally got his long-winded and prepared way of approaching things back on track.

She stirred the rice with a long-handled stainless steel spoon that Jim reckoned cost over a hundred pounds. "Inside information is the biggest problem if that's what you're getting at."

Jim nodded. It wasn't what he was getting at, but it would do.

"When the deal happens, such a large volume of buying will push the share price up. The FSA regularly investigate these movements. You know, see if anyone related had bought before the deal. They're really quite thorough." She replaced the lid and stirred the chilli. "I hope I haven't made it too hot."

"So," said Jim, "you personally couldn't buy shares?"

"God no. But ..." She paused. "The thing about this kind of work is you're remunerated in other ways, so you don't have too. Getting small investors into the fold is part of the way around it. They don't know exactly what they're buying until it's bought. Paper trails, everything's signed, trustee accounts, everything's documented."

Jim nodded, though with her back to him, she'd never have known.

"I wasn't sure whether to ask," she said, "but hey, I'll come right out with it. If you're interested, you could be part of it. Strictly professional obviously."

Jim's head raced. This wasn't going to plan. He needed money, and this was going the opposite way. Could he change the plan at this late stage? How about if he introduced Charlotte to the thug he owed money to? No, bad idea. He wouldn't let that evil bastard within a mile of her.

"What, er, kind of money are we talking about?"

"Usually it's minimum fifty thou. But there are a few who've invested ten. The one who's dropped out was fifty." Finished stirring, she walked back to the sofas wiping her hands on her apron. Sitting this time in the middle chair, she was now only ten feet away.

"I er, oh God." He paused trying to get his head round this. "Erm, I didn't realise it was that kind of amount." He noticed her face drop. "Problem is, you see, I'm still paying for the house. Not been sure whether to sell it or not."

"Not a good time to sell. I've got a friend in negative equity. Even if anyone wanted to buy she wouldn't be able to sell."

He nodded. He'd no idea what negative equity was, but it sounded painful. "To be honest ..." This was crunch time. He'd decided to go full-on with plan A, the only plan he had. "Money's very tight. It's London, you see. Work are paying for the hotel, but my wages aren't enough to cover everything." If he'd thought this through he'd have realised it was rubbish. Free food and board, they even paid part of his tube fares. He'd be much better off than back home.

The look of sympathy returned, the one he'd seen that first day, nearly a week ago. The butterflies made another attack on his stomach.

"Can't you rent your house out?"

"Urm." He paused while trying to think. "It's work you see. Only a temporary move at first. If I rent my place out and it goes wrong I'm homeless."

She nodded, the force of the nod causing her lump of hair to become detached. He watched it droop down, past her eyes and onto her nose. Her hand flicked it back up. They both knew it would only be a temporary fix.

"Sounds like you need a pay rise. I imagine in the public sector these days that's a swear word." She stood up and nodded towards the kitchen area.

As she walked he noticed the table. Set for dinner with a tablecloth, candles ready to be lit and napkins folded. This was another first. No plate on your lap in front of *Eastenders*.

"I need more than a pay rise." He tried to mumble but made sure it was audible. He was sowing seeds. Seeds that he hoped would root quickly and grow an idea in her head.

"So what's the GDP news then?" she called over while stirring the rice.

He was trying to hold out until the seedling had grown a bit. Currently, it had not even germinated.

"You're not going to tell anyone, are you?" he tried to sound nervous and thought his real nerves helped.

She stopped stirring and looked over. The lump of hair had dropped back down. "I'm selling it to the highest bidder." Though a joke she didn't look particularly amused.

He tried to smile. "It was only, you know." He stopped, took a deep breath then started. "We're pretty sure it's fallen by half a percent."

"Really?" She forgot about the chilli and rice. For a moment she just stared at him. "Recession then."

Jim nodded. "They're keeping a lid on it while they recheck. It's absolute chaos."

"I bet the government are all over you. Do you get all those spin doctors coming in?"

Jim nodded. He reckoned the ONS probably did have the government sticking its nose in.

"That's going to freak the markets." She looked back to her rice, deep in thought. "This could blow the whole deal," she mumbled.

"It's not final," he said, trying to reassure. "These things do change; fluctuate." He'd read that word earlier; remembered it sounded impressive.

She walked back to the sofas. The clump of hair had been joined by another. "If you were a betting man," she sat down, "what chance that's the final figure?"

Zero, he didn't say. "More than eighty."

She nodded. Her head seemed in a world Jim didn't understand. He thought he understood that a fall in GDP would mean a share price fall and hence would have an effect on her deal, but he didn't get the significance. "Would that not be good for you then?"

"No. People will start pulling out. Could be back to square one."

"It's not definite, don't forget that." He'd really messed this up. This should have just been dinner, heavy flirting and hopefully something more. He'd turned it into depression and everything off the menu.

"I suppose. It's about ready. Shall we eat now?"

"Yeah. Can I just use the bathroom?"

"Course. Just through the door on the left." She pointed to the back of the kitchen.

Besides everything else that had gone wrong at least he was going to see what was behind the door. Opening into a small hallway, a door on the left was obviously the bathroom. Another door on the right contained God knows what. He nodded to himself on seeing the door at the end opened onto a roof terrace.

The bathroom was small. Just a shower, small sink and toilet. He was pretty sure a bath would be upstairs in one of the larger rooms. Smelling sweetly of pot pourri, it was recently decorated, almost new. He felt guilty using it. Mind, he felt guilty of the whole way this evening was turning out. It was time for plan B.

It was just a shame there was no plan B.

Part Two

Chapter 23

Charlotte's head reeled as she gave the chilli another stir. She'd put so much into this evening, not just effort, but so much of herself. The chilli had dried out, and the rice had bloated, but that wasn't the problem. What did food matter now? He'd blown her head away, not for the first time this week, but this way was bad. The worst.

If trying to get enough people on board hadn't been hard enough, the spanner he'd just lobbed in the works would take her right back to the start. If he was right, of course. She wondered just how much information an ONS junior could actually get his hands on.

Apart from that she supposed it wasn't going too bad. Not the evening she'd planned, but that was life. One thing struck her more than anything else, and it even distracted from her own problems: he had money problems. She'd always had him down as well off. Not rich, just in good finances. He obviously wasn't. That had been a surprise. Hearing the toilet flush through the wall she started dishing up.

Pulling a metal colander from the stand, she drained the rice into the sink. She sighed as it fell in a lump to the bottom. Starchy white water dripped out, a sludge forming beneath. Rinsing with fresh water helped speed up the sludge, but the now cold rice didn't look appetising.

"Too late to ring for a takeaway," she whispered as the door opened.

He smiled as he walked back in. She smiled back and couldn't help but notice he'd washed his hands. The tap was powerful. He had that telltale splash of water on his shirt. She should have warned him. She meant too, but it had slipped her mind.

"Nice, erm, roof garden thing," he said.

"Terrace. Yeah. It overlooks a courtyard. Not private, but it's south facing so it catches the sun." She watched him as he loitered by the sink. Aware he was trying to look at the rice sludge she was hiding, she pointed at the table. "Sit down. I'll be two seconds."

He did as he was told. Should she come clean about dinner? It'd been ruined long before he'd arrived. Possibly from the moment she said, "I'll cook." The chilli was going to blow his head off. It was far too hot. How was she supposed to know tsp meant teaspoon. Surely it meant tablespoon.

"Nice picture," he called over.

Looking up, she saw him admiring the picture on the wall. "It's a copy, not the original." She wondered if he knew who the artist was. "Do you mind opening the wine? My hands are a bit full. I meant to do it earlier."

He stood up. "Of course not." Walking past her towards the small glass-plated wine fridge, she caught him looking at the chilli. "Looks nice."

She smiled and wondered just how polite he would be after a mouthful. "Bottle opener's next to the fridge." Pouring the lump of rice into a serving bowl, she turned her attention to the chilli.

Jim had seen people open wine bottles before. He wasn't that much of a pleb. The only problem was the cheap fizzy wine he always bought had a screw cap. The current bottle in his hands had not only a seal but a cork beneath it. Scratching at the seal with the end of the opener he realised just how hard it was.

The smell of dinner was making his stomach rumble. It was just a shame it was vegetarian. She'd gone to great trouble, he knew that. Not only kidney beans, but black-eyed beans, small corn on the cobs, French beans. It looked great. At least she hadn't noticed the wet patch on his trousers. That was the last, and possibly also the first, time he'd wash his hands after having a wee. She could have warned him about the tap.

Most of the foil off, he twisted the corkscrew inside. He favoured strength over technique and screwed the thing as hard as he could. He pulled at it and half the cork came out. "Damn."

Charlotte turned and looked at him. "Dodgy cork?"

He nodded. "Yeah, half's stuck inside."

Pouring chilli into another serving bowl, she said, "Just push it in if it's stuck."

Jim was not having that. He'd just spent money on a medium-high quality bottle. The cork was coming out. Twisting the corkscrew into the remainder of the cork it shredded into twenty pieces, each settling on top of the wine. "Erm. Bit of a cork situation."

Carrying some dips and a bag of corn chips to the table, she replied, "Doesn't matter."

It did though, it did matter. What kind of useless statistician was he? Unable even to open a bottle of wine. She sat down waiting for him to join her with his bottle of cork-flavoured wine. Pouring the wine, he said, "Got a sieve?"

Her laugh broke the tension slightly. He hadn't fully been joking.

"This looks great." He sat down and placed the napkin on his trousers.

"Dig in then." She sat back with half a smile. Jim thought it was probably polite for him to serve her then himself. This etiquette thing wasn't so hard after all.

"Rice?" he offered, wiggling the bowl over her plate.

"Just a little, thanks."

It was only when he tried to serve that he realised what a stodgy lump it was. The scoop he placed on her plate resembled a tennis ball.

"Think I may have overcooked it."

"No, it looks fine." He helped himself to a lump then picked up the chilli pot.

Charlotte was surprised he'd kept a straight face when he ladled out the lump of rice. Her domestic goddess act was unravelling line by line. He didn't look particularly bothered though which was good. Plus, the way he'd ruined that wine bottle hardly put him in the top league of culinary experts.

He seemed distracted. She couldn't put her finger on what, but something was on his mind. Though she barely knew him, over the last week he'd seemed more distracted and stressed each day. It had to be work. Tomorrow was a big day for him. It'd prove to be a big day for her as well if he was right. He was definitely on edge though, far too much to be healthy.

As he spooned some chilli onto his plate then took a bite, she was waiting for steam to come out of his nose. She'd poured sour cream on her own plate, and even then the small bite she'd just had proved the chilli hadn't decreased in ferocity. He nodded his head as he looked at her.

"Nice," he croaked. "Very hot."

"Don't eat it if it's too hot."

"No, it's fine. I like hot food. We used to have a really hot chilli inside."

She nodded, then did a double take. What did he mean inside? Inside what?

"What do you mean inside?"

She couldn't fail but notice his face drop. He seemed to cringe like he'd been caught out or was hiding something. He'd done that a few times before. She kept putting it down to nerves, but something inside her, just a little something, knew there was more.

"Er, inside the house. At home, where I grew up."

She nodded though she knew he was lying. Something wasn't right. She'd known that from the start, but hoped he'd tell her. They were getting close. Whatever the secret was she hoped he'd share it. She wasn't a monster after all. Whatever it was, it couldn't be that bad.

Dipping a corn chip in sour cream then topping it in salsa, she took a bite. She'd leave the rest of the chilli. It was just too hot. Looking at Jim she noticed his face had gone bright red. Whether from embarrassment or chilli she wasn't sure. She wondered whether to push this. Whatever it was, it was bugging him. A problem shared and all that.

"Is everything okay? You don't have to tell me, but maybe I can help."

She didn't expect him to answer. She half expected him to make his excuses and leave. She'd enforced crunch time without meaning to. He put his fork on the table, took a huge glug of wine and then spoke.

Plan B had crashed similarly to plan A. It was no great surprise, but Jim's new plan of extracting four grand hadn't started off so bad. It was obvious she knew something wasn't right. She knew something was bothering him and she'd given him the opportunity to try it on. Problem was, whenever he looked into her eyes and saw that lump of drooping hair, he wondered how the hell he was expected to rip her off.

He'd also said "while inside". That hadn't gone down well. He reckoned he'd got out of it, but wasn't sure.

"I'm in a bit of money trouble." He felt his face going redder. The chilli wasn't to blame.

She closed her eyes for a second then the smile half reappeared. "You don't have to tell me obviously, but you're not your normal self, not that I really know you all that well. I mean ..."

184

She'd gone into rant mode. Jim wondered whether to interrupt or not, but decided against it. It gave him a few seconds to work on plan C.

"... it can be tricky, living on your own. I know that. And, at the end of the day, it's only money."

She paused. He reckoned she'd finished. Time for plan C. "I owe ten grand to someone. He's, well, he's not the sort of person you borrow money from."

Her mouth opened, agape. Staring eyes bored into his. Maybe plan C was crap too.

"How? I mean, what?"

"Short story, I needed money. Urm, yeah, that's it. Tomorrow's payback day. I've got six grand, maybe seven and a half if I borrow from friends. But, well, you're right. I am worried. Terrified."

Her mouth was still open. Jim expected the words, "Get out and take that cheap wine with you," to come from them any second.

"Fuck."

He hadn't heard her swear before. He felt his own mouth opening. She'd shocked him. She hadn't learnt that word at finishing school. Maybe she had, but never used it. It rolled so nicely off her tongue as well. He half thought she'd fit in well in Coventry swearing like that.

She shook her head. "How?" was the word that came out.

This was where plan C failed if it hadn't already. Why the hell would an ONS statistician need to borrow ten grand from a leg-breaking loan shark? Gambling debts? Extortion? Either way, it didn't add to his charm as a potential boyfriend.

Charlotte could feel her blood pressure rising. The doctor said she was to avoid that at all costs. Unfortunately, the doctor hadn't said what to do in this circumstance. Was Jim for real? She was having doubts. She regretted asking what the problem was, but she was also glad she knew. He couldn't be lying now. Things had been going so well, too. Right up until ten minutes ago. Now they'd turned as shit as her cooking. She wanted to tell him to leave, but something inside made her say, "Why did you borrow ten grand?"

He looked lost and red-faced. Truly a pathetic creature. Was he worth it? She'd asked herself that a few times this week. Now though, with this included, he didn't have much going for him.

"To lend to a friend." He struggled to get his words out. "He needed money." He looked at the picture on the wall. "His house was going to get repossessed. James, his name is, got a three-month-old kid, lost his job last year. James lost his job, not the kid."

She nodded. She'd understood despite his poor wording.

"I thought I could get a loan from the bank, repay the shark and he could pay me back over time, but the bank wouldn't lend to me. This last week I've been going mad trying to get money from everywhere."

She sighed. What a mess. At least he'd borrowed for the right reason, to help out a friend. A friend in real need by the sound of it. "I take it James has already paid the money you lent him off his mortgage?"

He nodded back.

Filling a taco shell with a small amount of chilli and a lot of sour cream, she bit into it. Her initial rage had subsided. She could help him out, that wasn't a problem. It'd be barely noticeable. The question was, should she? Was he worth it?

Jim thanked God for both plan C, and also that she hadn't read the business section he'd just been reading. He'd only read the one story: a man out of work was about to lose his house after taking a loan from a loan shark. She seemed to have bought the story.

Okay, so he'd lied. He'd involved her. All the things he wasn't going to do. He really was something different. An evil, manipulative bastard. The worst of the worst. Lowest of the low. She didn't deserve this.

"Where does he live, your friend?"

"Newport."

"Did you work with him then?"

"Yeah, he got laid off. Mortgage was too big. Can't sell the house, you know."

She looked puzzled. "Don't the benefits people pay your mortgage if you're unemployed?"

Maybe plan C was as bad as the rest. Perhaps he should come clean. Just walk out. This wasn't her mess. She didn't need this. "He's been in trouble for a long time." Jim nodded hard, hoping it would stop further questions.

"I suppose his wife or partner must have stopped working too." She nodded. Apparently, she'd convinced herself it was believable.

"He's married. It's his wife."

This didn't fix anything. All that had happened was he had taken a romantic date and turned it into a begging match. Any moment now she'd show him the door. He wouldn't blame her when she did.

"Just, erm." Though this was mightily planned he tried hard to make it look otherwise. "The GDP figures. I'm thinking. All I have to sell is knowledge. Do you think anyone would pay to know what they're going to be?"

He winced as he looked at her. Direct eye contact was becoming hard. Her eyes had darkened and were half closed. He wondered if she would start crying. That would finish him off.

She shook her head. "Are you serious?"

No, he thought of saying. Shrugging his shoulders, he replied, "It's all I've got."

"My God you are serious." Her eyes opened, but she was looking at the wall behind him. "I know people who are always on the lookout for tip-offs. One in particular would pay that kind of amount if the figures are right. How sure are you they're right?"

He noticed her change. She'd become what he could only describe as cold and professional. This was her day job. It was what she did. This was how she did it.

"Fairly sure." He paused. "As I said though, they're trying desperately to prove it's wrong."

She leaned back in her chair. The flop of hair flopped down.

"The problem is," she said, "if the prediction is right, I stand to lose a great deal."

Though pissed off, extremely pissed off, there was something about him. She still didn't know what it was. It wasn't his looks that was for sure. Nor his honesty. Perhaps she saw some of herself in him. Maybe just lust or hormones. Either way, she knew she was going to help him.

"Sorry," he said.

She shook her head. There was no need to apologise. It wouldn't help or change anything. As he took another mouthful of chilli, she was again surprised he found it edible. What was it he'd said? "We had it like this inside". Inside where? The only inside she could think of was inside prison. He'd backtracked from that comment. Regional dialects are one thing, but using the word inside to mean home? No, he was holding back on something.

It came to her suddenly. Was this a scam? Was he after money? Was he some fleecing gigolo going from woman to woman, five grand here, ten there. His face made him more *piccolo* than gigolo. Some women would fall for it. She knew that from experience. He was charming in his own way.

She breathed deeply. This was crunch time. She was no fool. Whatever it was that had built up between them this last week could be destroyed by this, but bearing in mind the last half hour it'd probably already been ruined.

"What's the real story? You can barely look me in the eye." She sighed. "I know when someone's lying. So, what really is going on here?"

Plan C had let him down. There were no more plans in the box. He'd blown everything, but she seemed to be giving him another chance. This was it, no more lies. The truth was the only saviour here.

"It's me in trouble not a friend. I owe ten grand." He fought to get the words out. Why hadn't he just let whatever happen tonight happen. He could have died a happy man in the morning.

"Keep going."

She was strong, much stronger than he thought.

"I don't work for the ONS. I recently ..." He paused. He really didn't want to say it but knew he had to. "I was in prison." He saw her face fall. "I was wrongly convicted though. But now I'm out I'm tarred with that brush. I had the chance of this job, but I blew it. It went badly wrong. They want compensation from me for messing up. I'm halfway there, but they aren't the sort to accept part payment. Sorry I've dragged you into this. None of it's anything to do with you."

She didn't look as shocked as he'd thought. The tears hadn't come either and she hadn't yet checked if her purse was safe. She also hadn't thrown anything.

"What did you go down for?"

"Selling and receiving stolen goods." He shrugged his shoulders. "I didn't know they were stolen. Wrong place wrong time." This wasn't entirely a lie. He'd got caught by being in the wrong place at the wrong time. It didn't make him innocent.

"What was this job you had to do?"

She really was taking this well. However, he couldn't tell the truth about being a crap assassin. That was asking too much.

"Geoffrey. He owed a fortune to a drugs dealer. My job was to make sure Geoffrey learnt a lesson." As he spoke the words, Jim only just realised the coincidence between Geoffrey's predicament and his own. Life was cruel at times.

She folded her arms backing slightly away from the table. "You didn't hurt him did you? The heart attack, that wasn't your fault?"

"No, God no. I literally was about to scare the life out of him when he had it. It wasn't my fault."

"I wondered what you were doing behind those cardboard boxes."

Jim felt his mouth open. She'd seen him hiding. Why hadn't she mentioned this before? Did she see the gun too? She couldn't have.

"You saw me?" This was bad.

She nodded. "I thought at first you were the police hiding, but then I sort of forgot. A few days ago I remembered. To be honest I'm still not sure if you are the police or not."

This floored Jim. She looked less upset the more he revealed. She was almost smiling. What the fuck was going on?

Charlotte actually started to feel relaxed. She finally knew the truth. It must be the truth. He wouldn't lie about being in prison. She took a deep breath. This was probably the hardest thing she'd had to do, but it needed doing. He was in pieces there. What must he have been through the past week? The stress, searching for money, and on top of all that, they'd got close. She wanted to walk over and hold him, but it was too soon. Things needed to be said.

She still had to have her say.

Chapter 24

Jim was still wondering why she hadn't kicked him out. What did it take to annoy her? Instead, she cleared her throat and started speaking. "As it's Honest Injun night," she said, "there's something I need to say." Her eyes found his. The sparkle had returned. He knew his mouth was open; virtually dragging on the floor. All he could do was nod. "You're definitely not a policeman are you? Because if you are, this won't be admissible."

The nod turned to a sideways shake.

"Okay." She licked her lips. "My name isn't Charlotte, it's Teresa. I went to prison four years ago for fraud. I was innocent too, if you know what I mean." She winked. The butterflies returned. He felt physically sick. "The deal I'm working on is, er, you're really not the police are you?"

"You were in prison?"

She nodded again. Was she winding him up, having a bit of fun before kicking him out?

"Holloway at first but they moved me to Askham Grange. Askham wasn't too bad. It's an open prison. White-collar crime, you see. Easier time."

He tried to speak but only, "Bleugh," came out.

"I met someone inside. Another inmate. She looked after me."

Jim felt his eyes bulge and nearly pop out.

"Not in that way." She was smiling now. "Like a mother. She looked after me. She used to work in the city; brokered deals from the Emirates. This was her idea. It's her money." She pointed to the walls and the flat. "I'm like, ticking her business over, so to speak."

"Wha?"

"Is this too much to take in?"

"But?"

She stood up and walked round the table. Kneeling beside him, she placed an arm round his shoulder and muzzled her head next to his. Her earring scratched the side of his face as it passed.

"I knew something wasn't right," she said. "Normal people don't stop when someone collapses in the street. This is fucking London, after all."

Despite his chilli and wine breath, she could have stayed there all night with her arms round his head. Various grunts and other confused noises kept coming from his mouth, but overwhelmingly the silence was golden. There was so much to talk about. She had many questions. She felt she only knew half his story. But, she knew the rest would come. For now this was perfect.

"I'll sort out the money. Don't worry," she said.

"Th-hanks," he stuttered. His voice seemed to have returned. "I still don't get it."

Standing up, she walked to the kitchen and opened a cupboard. Pulling out two bottles, vodka and whisky, she nodded to the sofas. "Think this needs a proper drink." He nodded and walked to the sofa, plonking himself on the edge of the furthest one away. She decided to sit on the same sofa, but kept a fair distance as she poured two very large neat drinks.

"My parents did really die when I was younger," she started. "Thirteen. I went off the rails and ended up in care. We used to go out blagging. You know, just nicking chocolate and fags at first, but it escalated." Picking up her glass, she knocked back the vodka. "Jesus. I got caught a few times, bound over to keep the peace, fines, that sort of thing. It kind of carried on until I was eighteen. That's when I met this guy."

She could see Jim was still shocked, almost comatose. Deciding quickly to carry on talking, she hoped he'd come out of his shell. "They call them grifters now, don't they, like it's some fucking romantic proper job. Reality is, as I'm sure you know, you're constantly at poverty's door. Always looking over your shoulder in case the last bloke you ripped off is coming after you. We cleaned up in Bristol. He took the divorced women for a ride, and I the young, shy, rich men. We moved to Plymouth, but got caught out. He fled with the money and left me alone and penniless."

She poured and drank another vodka. It wasn't working.

"I moved to Birmingham and managed to get a proper job in an office through an agency. It was only temping; the gift of the gab helped but soon I ended up in the finance department. I'd never worked before, but it wasn't as bad as I thought. I started to make plans to buy a flat. Even take exams to get a better job. I kind of realised you can't carry on grifting forever. Guess I grew up."

She noticed he was following her words better now. The staring eyes were focused. Maybe even his smile was returning. He hadn't touched his whisky, but she thought that was a good thing. He'd obviously been drinking again today, just like every other day since she'd met him.

"I was doing well in this job. Just had a promotion, pay rise, everything was going well. The past has a habit of catching you out doesn't it. Someone I'd blagged from Bristol had somehow become a bank manager and visited the office. I didn't even recognise him in the two minutes I saw him. Unfortunately, he recognised me. It only clicked when the police smashed down my door later that night. The rest, as they say, is history."

He'd calmed down. He still wasn't sure if she was taking the piss. The story seemed good. Too good to not be true. He hadn't suspected anything. Not a glimmer. This bugged him more than anything else. How could he not spot a conner?

She seemed more relaxed talking about her past than he could remember. The front was gone. He knew keeping secrets made you desperate for someone to share them with. The only problem was, did he now tell her the full truth about Geoffrey?

"So," he said, "I take it there's no real investment then?"

She laughed. "Welcome back. No. Greedy people think they're getting in on a hush-hush get-rich-quick scheme. I haven't even got a proper office. I just go from bar to bar, restaurant to restaurant and find people who look slightly drunk and corrupt."

"No office? What if someone wants to visit where you work?"

"I've got a serviced phone line and address. They take messages and pass on calls. You can hire rooms by the hour too. Brenda taught me how to do it. She got ten years, but she'd hid a lump of cash. I'm just borrowing and reinvesting part of it, so to speak."

Jim shook his head. "What made you go back to it?" He blinked and shook his head. "Once a con always a con."

She nodded. "I knew I could never get another job in an office. That was the end of it. I decided while inside it was either a life on the dole or go back to my old ways."

"This city blag. When was it going to happen? I mean, there must be a day when you collect in the money and scarper?"

"Next month. You scared the life out of me with your GDP figures. I imagined everyone pulling out. This place isn't cheap to rent you know. If I blew all of Brenda's dough she wouldn't be impressed."

She poured herself another vodka, pulled her legs onto the sofa and turned towards him. "Your turn now. Full story from the start."

He decided whisky was a good idea before he started. He took nearly ten minutes explaining his childhood, teenage years and the ins and outs of prison over the past decade. Now arriving at his leaving date, he had a huge choice. Tell the truth about contract killing or a lie.

"Harry, my cellmate, offered me this job when I left. I say job, it was more a contract. You've got to understand this, life just wasn't going anywhere. I was in and out of nick all the time. I was the hooky-goods man, the Del Boy of Coventry. I knew it'd only be a year until I was back inside. It's no life. I wanted more." He drained the whisky. Fire burned his throat before hitting his stomach. "I got talked into it. Caught up in the glamour and money. I forgot what the job actually was."

"What was the job?"

He knew this wasn't a good idea. She definitely wasn't a cop, that wasn't the problem. Taking a life is so different to taking possessions. A different league of crime. He knew that even the most messed up person offered the largest sum of money would still have the moral dilemma that killing gives. To just say you'd forgotten. No, it wouldn't wash.

He had to lie.

While he paused, she reached over and touched his shoulder. Her warm hand made him flinch. Once again, he knew he couldn't risk losing this by telling the truth.

"Kidnapping. Well, 'adultnapping'."

He turned and looked in her eyes. Her face had changed. He'd expected that.

"I was desperate. That's what I was doing behind the cardboard box. The plan was to jump out in front of him, wave a replica pistol in his face then escort him to a van parked round the corner. We'd take him to some waste ground, scare the Bejesus out of him then let him go. Then, he'd find the money to pay up."

She'd folded her arms. Had he gone too far?

"What you've got to understand," he said, "is that was the third day I was there. I bottled two other chances. I would have bottled that day too, even if his heart wasn't dicky. I couldn't do it. Replica gun or not, I couldn't do it. I sell stolen gear. I'm a thief, a crap one at that, but I'm not a murderer." He quickly backtracked. "I'm not a murderer or threatener or bully-boy or whatever. I sell wallets and laptops."

He waited.

She was regretting asking for the truth. He couldn't hurt a fly. She could tell that by looking at him. How hard up do you have to get before you think it's an option? She'd been hard up. Lived in squats, stole food. Physically hurting people never registered. It was just wrong. There were moral boundaries. She knew where hers were. Where were his?

Shaking her head, she said, "How did you convince yourself it was an option?"

Taking a large glug of whisky, he shrugged. "Prison. It does things to you." He sighed. "I was banged up with murderers and thugs. Life like that, it just ... I don't know the proper words, but it becomes normal. You forget yourself, get drawn into their world."

"Desensitised?"

He nodded. It sounded like the right word. "The other times I'd been inside there were the hard bastards and the petty thieves like me. We stayed out of their way. If you made the mistake of talking to them you regretted it." Charlotte's flop of hair had pounced down, but she didn't seem to notice it was there. "The last stretch was different. I was in at the deep end. Sharing a cell with Harry, the only people I ever saw were hardened and serial GBHers. My head got lost, stuck in this world of violence and retribution. I guess I knew it was wrong, but ..." He thought she seemed convinced. He had many other questions he wanted to ask her, but couldn't begin to order them properly. One question though stuck out.

"Were you planning on fleecing me?" He tried to word it as a joke, but it was deadly serious.

It was a fair question. She'd been wondering the same about him. Was his plan to rob her or her flat if she hadn't agreed to his GDP scam? Something told her not. He'd had opportunities this week if he was after money. He'd been so wound up earlier though; a doomed man. God knows what he would have done if she'd said no. That didn't bear thinking about.

"I could ask you the same question," she replied.

He shrugged his shoulders. She knew what that meant.

He'd been a mark from early on. She didn't just give her number to anyone. He didn't match her normal mark though. Too caring. Not full of himself. Deep down, she knew that although she'd have taken his money, it would have kept her awake at night.

"Stalemate?" he offered.

She nodded. "So, when do you have to pay them?"

"I've got to ring a number. Are you sure this is okay? I mean, I'm quite attached to my legs and that, but, you know."

She flicked her hair back onto her forehead. The floppy fringe was fucking annoying. She was never getting her haircut there again. It's all the rage they'd said. They didn't say how annoying it was. They didn't say how many times it would get in the way.

"It's only money. Money versus a life isn't close. I can get it first thing when the banks open. Four gee, yeah?"

He nodded. "I'll get the rest together. Some of it's in the East End. I got a lock-up there. Don't ask, it's been a busy week."

"I bet it has. You've done well though. Six in a week. How did you do it."

"Well," he started, "I had a bit of luck."

Chapter 25

Time had flown by. Raif's watch said eleven and he didn't doubt it. It seemed like they'd been talking an hour, not four. They'd been laughing at one point then it got serious again. She kept returning the conversation to thuggery. He was glad he'd held back on the real reason, but wondered if it would return to haunt him.

"The problem's prison," he said again. "It puts you in situations that seem normal, but aren't." He didn't know if his repeated argument was winning or not.

"That's not what I meant." She took another sip of vodka. Jim himself felt plastered after all the drink. His last walk to the toilet had been a trial. Apart from her red face, Charlotte didn't look drunk at all. "You grow up with inbuilt morals. Deep down, you know if something's right or wrong."

He shrugged his shoulders. "I'm not proud of many things I've done. What I do want, more than anything, is a different life. A chance of something better. I had this plan you see."

He looked away from her towards the stereo. She was looking at his face, following every word. He needed distracting from her eyes. "A couple of jobs, earn money then retire. Get myself a little farm or smallholding or something. When I was in Scotland, I saw places that go for nothing compared to down here. Or Wales for that matter. It wasn't long term, it was the means to an end."

"I didn't think being a bovver boy paid that well."

He knew she'd got him again.

"I'd have done other stuff too. One last blitz then retire. Or at the least get enough to get me settled and start again. What I did to Raif, you know, the broker?" She nodded. He had tried to bring Raif up as much as possible. She seemed to approve of that particular blag. "Yeah, Raif was sort of planned inside. Not the ins and outs and who. But, I knew people like that existed and were heavily insured. There's a lot of thinking time inside. You know that."

She sighed and poured another round of drinks.

"So," she said, "Is that it then? No other lies or things I should know?"

He shook his head. Then, remembering something, shrugged his shoulders. "Erm, yeah, just one thing."

"And what would that be?"

Should he tell the truth or not? He opened his mouth and left his subconscious in charge of what came out.

"I'm not vegetarian."

She laughed then threw all available cushions towards him. "You absolute bastard. Why?"

"Sorry." The cushions were quite firm. Especially the pointy leather corners. "It was that restaurant. It was so expensive and I thought we were going halves."

She looked at the ceiling, apparently deep in thought. "Of course." Shaking her head, she leaned over to the other sofa for another cushion. "You could have told me after."

"Stop it. Hey, look, what could I do? I was in tofu up to my eyeballs. I had to keep the lie going. I'm sorry."

"Do you know how much effort I put into that bloody chilli?"

"It was nice."

"No it wasn't, it was fucking horrible. It was burnt."

Jim laughed. "It was hot though."

"Just like inside?" She laughed. "I can't believe you lied about that."

After everything else he'd lied about, Jim thought it small in comparison. But maybe she had a point. Up until an hour or two ago she didn't know anything about him. It was all fake. Similarly, his view of her. He supposed it was like meeting all over again. Either way, she was laughing which was better than the alternative.

"Are you hungry?" she asked.

"No. Why, do you want me to go and get a takeaway or something?"

She shook her head. "Just asking. We didn't really eat much. I made, well bought, a vegan cheesecake. I wasn't sure just how strict you were on the whole milk and cheese thing."

"No, I'm not hungry, thanks." He wanted to say yes. Food might soak up the whisky trudging through his veins, but he got the impression food was the last thing on her mind.

With the time getting on for half eleven he was waiting for a sign that she wanted him to leave. So far, it hadn't come. Just a yawn or a long check of her watch would do. Of course he didn't want to force it from her. He was kind of hoping to spend the night on the sofa. If he left and went back to the hotel she might change her mind by the morning.

Camping out for the night in her front room would make it harder to not lend him four grand.

"I really am grateful you know. I'll pay back every penny. I don't know how, but I will. Maybe street entertaining. That's fairly respectable these days. I could make four grand in a few months."

"Not if you live in a hotel paying seventy quid a night you won't. Look, it's not a loan. I said earlier. I'm helping you out. Don't worry about it."

He shook his head. "That's not right. I can't just let you pay."

"Ooh, look at Mr Work Ethic. Where did that come from? Harry?"

He thought that was harsh. Maybe she thought it funny or it was the drink talking. He looked at his shoes nestling in the huge piles of carpet beneath them.

"Sorry, was that a bit much? Truth hurt?"

He mumbled something but couldn't get the words out. She faked an east London accent. "Always look after our own, guvnor. And we're good to our muvvers. Sometimes you gotta be harsh to be fair."

He shook his head. "Don't give up the day job."

"I'm offering to give you money. For the last week you've been robbing people blind. Just take it."

"As you said in your great accent. You're like me. A lot like me. I'll pay you back one day, I promise."

Her smile had returned, if anything, cheekier than before. He thought the last few glasses of vodka had gone to her head. Her cheeks were flushed and the lump of dangling hair no longer seemed to bother her. He looked at the bottle. She'd finished it. He was surprised and impressed by her ability to drink.

"I'll tell you what," she said, "you could help me. When you're not doing card tricks that is." He wasn't sure if he fully liked the drunk Charlotte or Teresa, or whatever her real name was.

"How?"

"Get me some marks?" She stopped and looked at the empty bottle. "Don't know. I haven't thought that through, have I? Have you made any contacts in the bars?"

"None that wouldn't have me arrested on sight."

She smiled. "Burnt all your bridges for a wallet full of cash."

"If I'd have known you were pulling tricks, I'd have played the last week differently." He felt himself sobering the more she talked. Maybe he needed more whisky. Maybe that was the answer. It hadn't solved anything this past week, but maybe it would tonight.

"*Touche.*"

"That reminds me." He downed his whisky. "Where did you learn to speak French? You were flawless with that waiter the other day."

"A year in Provence. Well, four months in Paris. We hit there between Bristol and Plymouth. I did quite well in French at school, when I bothered to go to school that is. I quite liked it over there. Different pace of life, different attitude. I took a GCSE inside too."

Jim nodded as she poured him another whisky. He was still miles behind her; his bottle just under three quarters full. "Had me fooled."

She screwed up her nose while pouring herself some whisky. "You don't need to know much to get by in a restaurant," she laughed. "When I told that waiter you didn't eat meat I got the words mixed up."

"I won't ask what you actually said."

She sighed. Jim wondered whether a yawn would follow, but it didn't. He liked the idea of working for her, or with her. They could have a lot of fun. Sure, there were a few people he'd have to avoid, but the supply of greedy fools wasn't low. He knew with the right suit and look, he could bring in some cash.

"What you thinking about?"

"I'm thinking," he said, "that I'd really like to work for you."

"More with me than for me. Saying that, I'd be able to boss you around wouldn't I?"

"I'd take you to a tribunal if you did."

"Cheeky sod." She looked for a cushion, but none were to hand.

Her head fell towards his. Though still four feet apart, Jim was convinced they were inching towards each other. Those few kisses over the days seemed miles away now. Like two different people. He supposed they were.

"It really is a different kind of game to the one you've been playing." She rolled her head around and seemed to move another fraction of an inch closer. Though her make-up was starting to wither, he still couldn't believe how attractive she was. He wasn't sober, that was a fact. But if she looked this good when he was drunk, and only half as good sober, he was onto a winner.

"I've got all the right skill sets for any sort of blag you know."

"Skill set?" She shook her head. "You sound just like a banker."

"Is that an insult? That tribunal's getting nearer."

She leaned forward and sipped from her glass. When she sat back she was another inch nearer. Jim knew at this rate, within an hour, they'd be side by side.

He turned slightly. "I'll tell you what. Someone I do know. Raif. If anyone deserves more pain, he does."

"Raif? Oh, him. That's cruel. Haven't you done enough?"

Jim shrugged his shoulders. "I wouldn't be able to do it though. He's bound to remember me. You, though, you could get away with it."

"Too risky."

Jim leaned towards her. However this night was going to end, he was determined he wouldn't leave before getting the money. Whether he was on the sofa or in her bed, that was the only question. He thought the odds were favouring the latter; after all they were mutually inching towards each other. They were actually taking it in terms. If they had spent an hour planning it he doubted they'd get it this subtly.

"I suppose. Plenty more fish in the sea." He stopped and thought.

She briefly held his arm with her right hand. "I'm gonna enjoy this."

When the clock struck one he was so close he could almost feel her. He was reluctant to make a move. The evening, though starting off poor, had become perfect. It didn't need ruining by clumsiness. Charlotte seemed to have gone through and out the other side of being drunk. The past half hour had seen her reflective, almost philosophical about life. She had dreams too, similar to Jim's in many ways, though they contained less farm animals and more yachts.

The plan for the next few weeks was clear though would no doubt be refined tomorrow when sober. Jim would hit the bars and cafes of the city's heart, and smooth talk his way into the hearts of anyone affluent and greedy. Charlotte would continue to play the role of the deal breaker. Jim himself would be an investor singing her praises throughout and maybe even referring to the last deal that had made money. She couldn't overstress the importance of being subtle. This was a long game not a short wallet-stealing grab. You had to win their confidence first. Jim told her he was the perfect man - the phrase confidence trickster was invented with him in mind.

"That was just corny," she said.

She was right. Problem was, he was drunk and getting more hammered by the minute.

"Sorry."

"Don't need to apologise. I was just saying, it was corny."

"Maybe. I'm not much into egos and that, but I surprised myself this week how good I was."

"I don't doubt that for a minute. You had me fooled, remember?"

"And you me. The perfect partnership, eh?" He smiled, but knew it must look like a drunken leer.

"Not sure about partnership, but yeah, we'll work well together."

He yawned. An involuntary action. The combination of alcohol and lack of sleep, but it was the last thing he wanted to do. She looked at her watch. Damn, he'd done it now. In a second she'd yawn too and say, "Well, it's been a great night and all that, but ..."

"Am I keeping you up?"

"Sorry." He knew he had to stop apologising but couldn't. "Haven't slept well lately. Feels different now though, like a weight's been lifted."

Her hand moved towards his. He placed his hands gingerly on his thighs unsure where else to put them. Grabbing his left hand, she squeezed it. He turned towards her, licked his lips and moved his face nearer. Squeezing his hand tighter, she moved herself.

Minutes seemed to count down until their lips met. He gasped a breath before starting what he knew would end the night one way or another.

Chapter 26

Coming out of the hotel bathroom, Jim turned the kettle on. With everything that could have happened last night sleeping in his own bed was the last thing he'd suspected. Sometimes he was glad he didn't bet. Rolling his head round he looked out of the window. Though dull and fuzzy, his head didn't have the hangover it should have. The whisky had flowed like a river. He'd been drinking all week, but the combination of chilli, Charlotte and a possible increase in his longevity had made alcohol more potent. How the hell did he end back here at the hotel though? He couldn't remember that.

"Mine's a coffee," said Charlotte.

Turning round, Jim saw she'd woken. Her bouffant-like hair was tipped at right angles to her head. The make-up smeared around her eyes and lips made her look ten years older.

"Morning. Did I wake you?"

She yawned. "Do you know where my clothes are?"

"Half of them in the bathroom, the other half down there." He pointed to the floor.

She scratched a hand through her hair. "Why did we come here?"

"Don't ask me." He looked round the room half expecting to see a traffic cone or a pile of wallets. Two half-eaten kebabs in the bin gave the only clue to the venue change. "Apparently we ate kebabs?"

"No wonder I feel like shit." She paused. "Urm, any chance you could, er, get my clothes?"

"God, yeah. Sorry." He felt himself blush. Though why either of them should be embarrassed was beyond him. It was obvious by the location of both their clothes they'd seen it all before, and possibly more. He knew deep inside that much had happened last night. Three years in prison gave a strong yearning. You knew when that yearning has been fulfilled.

Picking up the pile near the window he deposited it on the bed. Then grabbing the bathroom pile he did the same. The two piles of clothes seemed to be conflicting, the order of removal impossible. Returning to the bathroom, he said, "I'll, er, brush my teeth or whatever."

He locked the door and sat on the toilet with the lid down. He remembered the gun behind him in the cistern. He hoped he hadn't told her about that. Who knows what he'd said. He could remember much about last night, but it just seemed to go blank. They'd been sat on the sofa, next to each other. Kissed. Then, nothing.

He thought again of the gun. She'd be in the bedroom now quickly throwing clothes on then running out the door. Desperate to get away.

"You can come out now." She knocked on the door.

Okay, he was wrong. Was the loan still on though? That was the question.

"I'll finish that coffee." He walked towards the low-powered travel kettle and willed it to hurry up.

"Is it really only seven?" she said. "Seems much later." She pointed to the window and the sounds of traffic tearing by.

"Yeah, it's a great alarm clock." He poured two coffee sachets into a cup and plonked a teabag on a string in the other.

"Just, er." She pointed at the bathroom.

"Yeah, sorry."

She smiled as she closed the door.

Please don't look in the toilet cistern was his only thought as the kettle started to warm.

"Ralph? It's Jim." He could hear the knuckle scraper's heavy breathing in the background. Those steroids must play havoc with sinuses.

"Yeah."

"I'm, er, I'll be ready about two this afternoon."

"That's good. We were getting worried."

"Nothing to worry about. Nothing at all." Jim paused. Charlotte, squeezed beside him in the phone box, made the okay sign with her fingers. He nodded back. "Where shall we meet?"

"We'll pick you up from your hotel."

"Okay I'll be outside at two."

The phone went dead.

"Okay then? Really?" she asked.

"Yeah, fine. Bit nerve-racking, but he sounded fine."

"Do you smoke?" said Charlotte.

"Occasionally, why?"

"I thought you did. I've got a half smoked pack of fags in my pocket, but I gave up three years ago."

A titbit of remembrance returned. "We went out for them last night. You smoked most of them, too."

She shrugged her shoulders and handed them back along with a lighter.

"Do you mind if I have one now?"

She shook her head.

He lit one and exhaled noisily. For all his worry last night that she'd kick him out or ignore him this morning, the reality was the opposite. He'd treated her to breakfast in a cafe then watched her telly while she showered and changed. They seemed to be inseparable. She wasn't going to be there when he handed over the money though. That was definite.

By the side of the road, next to the rare telephone booth that was both working and accepted cash, they waited while he sucked the fag. She'd dressed down compared to her normal attire. Jeans and a t-shirt. However, he knew the jeans were as expensive as her normal clothes. Her hair still damp, but drying in the wind, made her look even more attractive. He had to constantly kick himself to make sure this wasn't a dream.

Crushing the fag under his foot, he said, "Taxi to the East End, Madam?"

"You know how to treat a girl, don't you?"

The cab slowly worked its way through London, its driver the font of knowledge of every news event and traffic delay. His own driving was beyond reproach. It was always everyone else's fault.

"You 'eard we're back in recession now?" he said.

Charlotte sat forward. "The GDP figures? Are they negative?"

"Yes, love. Half a percent fall. Cor blimey, this government, I ask you. I dunno what the world's coming to ..."

Jim could only look at Charlotte and smile. She wasn't smiling back. "You sure you don't work for the ONS?"

He shook his head. Remembering from last night, a recession was bad news for fake takeovers, he tried to take her hand. She shrugged him off.

Stopping the cabby's rant, she said, "How's the market reacted?"

"Footsie's down a few percent last I heard. You into shares then? I tried a few years back. Dot com and all that. Never again. Never again."

She was silent until they reached the lock-up.

"You sure this is the right place?" asked the cabby.

Apparently he didn't go south of the river after ten so his near reluctance to go this far east at this time of day wasn't a huge surprise.

"Yeah," said Jim. "I'll just be a minute. It's a friend's lock-up. Just keeping an eye on it while he's away."

Charlotte smiled at him as he left the cab. Unlocking the garage door, he went inside.

The rolls of cash fitted nicely inside Raif's old briefcase. Jim thought it made a fitting end to the last of his possessions. The other items left, an iPod he'd forgot to sell and The Clash CD, were tossed in the briefcase too. Back outside, the taxi was still waiting. The driver, though interested in the briefcase, made no comment.

Traffic was heavy leading back to the city. Charlotte, who still seemed bewildered by what Jim could only imagine was the GDP news, directed the cab towards a safety deposit storage centre.

Taking the case inside with her, Jim waited in the cab. The driver's stock conversations on the weather, traffic and the mayor soon dried up. Before five minutes was up, just the radio filled the cab.

Jim had never been in a safety deposit stronghold, but he imagined the obvious security plus waiting would make this at least fifteen minutes. He could almost see her inside handing over her ID, typing in security codes and eventually being given a key to a box.

When ten minutes had passed, the cab's fare ticked to thirty-five quid. Charlotte had already handed the cabbie three twenties when explaining the unusual route they were taking. The cabbie wasn't too bothered; he'd seen it all in funny old London. However, he was now eyeing the meter. They'd promised to pay him handsomely for the waiting and messing round. Jim pulled a twenty from his pocket and passed it through the hatch.

"Cheers, guv."

Another five minutes crawled by. The smallest doubt, that he kept trying to push away, was growing. He'd seen her go in the building with his five grand, but she hadn't come out. Maybe, just maybe, there was another exit.

He shook his head. This was Charlotte, or whatever her name was, not some common criminal like himself. They'd spent last night together. They were close. Besides, what was five grand to her? She was loaded. At least she would be after this job.

He sighed. The money wasn't hers. She was borrowing it. She wasn't loaded at all. Like him, she had nothing. The payoff was ages away, and the surprise GDP figures had probably messed everything up.

"Shit."

He felt sick as if he'd been kicked in the stomach.

"You alright, chief?" asked the cabbie with genuine concern.

"Not sure." He didn't want to panic the cabbie. They had CCTV after all. If he suspected any sort of crime he might report it. He seemed the sort. A bit of cash in hand work himself was different. It was everyone else who robbed from the taxman.

Another ten minutes, and he was sure she wasn't coming back. It surely wouldn't take nearly half an hour to get cash out of a box. She'd blagged him. Pure and simple. A sickly feeling rose up his throat. He had to control his breathing to make sure the cab wasn't going to get pepper-blasted with last night's chilli and kebab. How stupid had he been? He'd got so close too. They might have taken five grand if he'd begged. But now, just to make it worse, they were expecting him in an hour with ten grand. They were going to be disappointed.

"I don't think she's coming back." He knew he'd said the words, but they seemed so distant.

"How d'ya mean, pal?"

"I think she might have dumped me."

The cabbie looked at his meter. "Still a tenner left if you wanna go anywhere."

Jim shrugged, pulled out his mobile and dialled her number. Dancing Queen, her ringtone, started playing from down the side of the cab seat.

The cab was just indicating to pull into traffic when she walked out the front door.

"Stop."

The cab did, nearly taking out a car with it. The cabbie muttered something Jim didn't recognise.

Letting herself in, she looked awkwardly at Jim. "It was busy."

He shook his head and whispered, "Sorry. You left your phone here, down the side of the cab."

"That's where it is. I thought I'd lost it."

The cabbie, his eyes heavily on the rear-view mirror, drove back south towards the hotel.

"Sorry," said Jim again.

"You will be."

Though she was sitting on the hotel bed, Jim had nothing to smile about. She had the briefcase too. The briefcase that contained ten grand. The ten grand he needed to pay for his life in less than an hour.

"Is this what it's going to be like?" she said. "Every moment you're wondering if I'm ripping you off?"

He'd messed up. What could he say to convince her? Sorry just wasn't cutting it.

"Look. My head's all over the place. In less than an hour I'm dead if I haven't got the money." He looked again at the briefcase.

"Oh yeah, the money. It's all there. Do you want to count it first? Or make sure I haven't replaced your five grand with cut up pieces of paper?"

He didn't need ideas putting in his head. Maybe she was working for the big man. No. Of course she wasn't. He breathed deeply.

"Christ, I've messed up haven't I?" He tried his puppy dog look. It didn't work.

"If there's no trust this ain't gonna work." Her perfectly tutored and practised voice slipped. The black in her hair wasn't the only roots showing.

"Once this is done," he said, "it'll be different, won't it? I've spent the whole week thinking I'm dead. I even gave away two bags for life the other day. That's how convinced I was. This has happened so quickly. I just ..." He paused. "I want this rod off my back."

Her face moved into something approaching a smile. "You gave away a bag for life?"

He nodded. "I pawned that stolen laptop and iPad; told the pawnbroker to keep the bags. Look." He changed tact and spoke softer, his eyes pleading with hers. "How many opportunities have I had to rob you? Ask yourself. How many times did I look after your bag when you went to the toilet? Or when I was in your flat, your laptop was there wasn't it? I could have had that, and a hundredweight of stainless steel out while you were having a shower." He shook his head. He wasn't sure this new tack would work but he'd tried everything else in the last ten minutes. "I panicked. Can you seriously tell me you wouldn't have?"

She sighed and picked up the briefcase. "Call me when it's over." She threw the case into his lap.

"Charlotte." She was heading for the door, but turned round as he said her name. "I won't let you down."

"You better fucking not."

The blackened-windowed Range Rover arrived on time. Jim thought it might. Money had a habit of making even the most tardiest punctual. Not that the front seat passenger was tardy in any way.

The door was held open for him by Ralph the knuckle scraper. Placing the case on his legs, he waited for the car to tear off at high speed.

"Good afternoon," the man in front said.

"Afternoon." Jim had been unsure whether to reply or not, but politeness couldn't possibly cause harm or offense.

"I hear you've been busy." He paused briefly, though he definitely didn't want a reply. "One of my little birdies tells me you done well. I'm very nearly impressed. You see, hard graft's something I respect. We're all in this boat together, aren't we? It's hard enough getting by these days as it is. I respect hard graft. It'll always come through in the end."

Jim remembered how much he liked his own voice. Also, given the cost of the car, he wondered just what his experience of being hard up was.

"Anyway, down to business. If you hand the briefcase to Ralph, he'll count it. It's not that I don't trust you, I'd just hate for anything to be realised later that could be sorted now."

He handed the briefcase to Ralph. He'd counted the money four times and it was bang on. He had a feeling Charlotte had counted it a few times too. His heart was still in his mouth as Ralph opened the case then flicked through the wads of cash.

"As I believe I said last time," he continued, "it's a shame our business relationship had to come to this. However, I'm not in the habit of making enemies. They cause such time-consuming complications as I'm sure you'll agree."

Ralph was nearly halfway through counting. Though he'd run out of fingers a long time ago, Jim thought he was doing a great job.

"Similarly though, friendship is something that I believe should start correctly. Therefore, assuming all is correct with the case, I think our parting of ways should be permanent. If ever I see you again, I will have no way of knowing whether you are intending to recollect the compensation or not. So it stands to reason that, should I see you approach my businesses, my home or any part of London that I, for want of a better word, control, I will have to assume the worst. Is that clear?"

Jim had lost him halfway through, but he had a feeling the phrase, "don't come back looking for your money," would have saved him some wear on his vocal cords. "Yes," he croaked.

"Good."

He turned and looked at Ralph counting. Jim guessed the speech was over. In a perfect world the car would pull over and he'd be turfed out. However, the Ralph factor hadn't been taken into account.

He knew an embarrassed silence would fill the rest of the short journey. But for the first time in a week, he felt free. The week that might have been the last he'd ever see had been and gone. As long as he kept out of east London, he could live to a ripe old age.

"It's all here, boss."

The man nodded at the driver who pulled into the kerb. "Well, that concludes things nicely. As it's such a lovely day, I'm sure you'll be glad of the walk. Goodbye. It's been a pleasure doing business."

"Thanks." He wasn't sure why he thanked him, but he had to say something.

As Ralph let him out he took a deep mouthful of clean, fresh London air. Coughing slightly, he looked round to get his bearings. The West End. An Irish themed pub on a corner looked inviting, but there was something he had to do first.

Chapter 27

"Hi, it's me," he said to the voicemail. "Just to let you know, everything went well. I'm off to get changed then I'll head for the square mile." He wasn't too bothered she hadn't answered the phone. Her phone had been ringing all morning. Clients wanting to meet to discuss things they couldn't on the phone. The GDP figures had messed up the plan. Jim only hoped some punters were left in by the end. If not, then Charlotte would end up owing money to Holloway's answer to the big man.

Sat at the bar of the fake Irish pub, he knew he'd help her. He'd rob every twat in a suit in the square mile for her. Every last one.

"Pint of Guinness, pal," he said.

The barman nodded and poured an unfeasibly slow pint.

Business was slow. A few drunks and an American couple taking in the delights of a traditional London Irish pub. Jim considered the man's wallet. No doubt it was heavy, almost sagging with the brown and blue notes that weren't dollars and who's value was confusing. A week ago he may have followed them, relieved them of all that funny money. He smiled, glad all that was over. He'd never felt comfortable wallet snatching. It had just been a means to an end. Turned out he hadn't needed to rob anyone. That was life though.

The pint slipped down in two gulps.

"Another?" asked the Australian barman.

"Please."

Street robbing and buying and selling wasn't his game anymore. He'd joined the big league. White-collar crime. City crime. Stealing not from under people's noses, but over a period of time when anything could happen. That took *cojones*. Large *cojones*. He had to do his bit not only to repay Charlotte, but to win her back after this morning. How could he have thought she'd fleece him? After last night too. Not that he could remember last night, but he knew it was special. No, he'd let her down but he'd make it right again.

The pint disappeared in three mouthfuls. Making his way to the hotel he had to get dressed and hit the city in time for the end-of-day trading pub rush.

Before that, there was one other job from his past to finish.

He reckoned he looked alright in a suit. Not a natural banker or whizz kid, but he felt he fitted. His face looked drawn and aged though. Like he hadn't slept for a month. Last night hadn't helped. Maybe he'd catch up on a few hours tonight.

Walking into the bathroom he pulled the top from the toilet cistern. The unused shooter was still inside almost begging to be used. How close had he come? Just how close? Not just Geoffrey either, but the other day. He'd been close to robbing a post office or that bookies. All the time, Charlotte was waiting with money in the bank.

He shook his head. He couldn't help but smile. Today could have gone so differently. He couldn't even remember how he and Charlotte had discovered they were doing similar jobs last night. It was just a blur.

Gloves on, he pulled out the pistol, took it from the bag then wiped at it with a towel. He'd been so careful not to get prints on it, but double checking never hurt. His plan for disposal was clear. Walk to the river and chuck it in. Though crowds were everywhere, no one noticed anything in London. No one ever noticed anything.

He felt conspicuous alongside the Thames. He knew no one could see the gun lurking in his inside breast pocket, but that didn't matter. Paranoia was back in town. The fenced-off shoreline was busier than he'd expected. Groups of tourists taking pictures of the Millennium Wheel and the skyscraper-filled skyline. South of the river was apparently good for something: taking pictures of the other shore.

Jim wandered for ages, possibly a mile, until the river and tourists calmed down. A few launches were at the north side, taking trippers for a tour, but the south side was clear. Taking a deep breath, he looked round one last time. No one watching. Removing the gun from his pocket, his gloved hand dropped it in the river. He expected it to ignore the rules of physics and just sit there atop the water, floating away towards the nearest police boat.

It didn't.

It sunk. Quicker than a stone. Quicker than he would have with concrete wellies on.

It was gone.

The last reminder of that failed mistake, gone. He sighed heavily then headed for the tube.

The tube network was quiet waiting for the five o'clock rush. Alighting in the heart of the city, he made for a bar avoiding a few he'd previously done his own form of business in.

A wine bar. It too was preparing for the rush. Champagne and Chardonnay was on ice. Jim bought a bottle of Mexican lager and stood near the bar, sipping it gently. The past week had been a mess of alcohol. He needed a few days from it. Rehab. That was what he needed. Alcohol seemed to go with this job though. His new job for his new employer.

He smiled. After what had happened last night, most of which he couldn't remember, being classed as her employee gave him a chuckle. He had to be careful though. He'd already upset the boss today. Anymore messing round and he'd be fired. With no severance.

An hour and two bottles of lager clicked by before the hoards entered. Being Thursday, more than normal hit the bars and restaurants for their near weekend snifter. The pub was soon full, albeit temporarily. Jim surveyed the potential quarry. A gaggle of blokes, similar shirts and ties, all sipping the same lager. A swanny of girls, glasses of white wine in their hands, talked above the din sharing tales and smiles. Small groups from the same office stood round, a misfit of people desperate to go home or drink with their friends instead.

No group looked too appealing. From what he remembered of Charlotte's advice in finding a mark, it was best to go for the boring looking ones on the outskirts. Of course, Charlotte had an advantage; she was an attractive woman. Befriending men was easy for her than women would be for Jim. He reckoned most of the women were too savvy here anyway. They weren't greedy enough either. That was more a male trait.

The group beside him had two outlying males. Smaller and uglier than the rest, they may just be the ones. Jim moved slightly towards them, pulled out his mobile and rang Charlotte.

"Hi Charlotte," he said in his best Home Counties accent.

"Bloody hell," she said. "Have you been drinking?"

"Crazy day, Charlotte, crazy day. Reuben made a mint today. Absolute mint."

Her laughing was almost hysterical. He hoped the two guys couldn't hear it.

"Uh huh, yeah," he said.

The two were interested in him and his call, though he could tell they thought him the very sort of upper-class twit they normally avoided.

"I hope you're not making a twat of yourself," she whispered.

"So then," he paused, "how are things in Dealsville US of A. Any news for *moi?*"

They were definitely taking interest. If only to watch a twat make a bigger twat of himself.

"Do you really think," she said, "that I'd deal with someone who sounds like that?"

"Ya, ya."

"I hope whoever you've got your eyes on is worth it. God knows we need some help now."

"Really? Some space for investment has come up? Oh, let me think ..." Jim nodded at one of the men in front, the one who was most obviously taking it all in. The man turned to his friend, eyebrow raised.

"Keep thinking buddy. What do you fancy for tea tonight?" she said.

"Mmmm. Can't really say now. Johnny might be up for an investment opportunity. Seems to have his finger in many pies."

"Steak and Kidney?"

"Ya, ya. Look gotta split, Charlotte. I'll ask around. Let you know if anyone's interested." He snorted, really loudly. "Ha ha, you'll be paying me commission next. *Ciao, ciao, ciao.*"

He pressed the red button and ended the call. The two men in front, still smiling to themselves, were definitely interested in his little show. It beat listening to their boss moan about targets and future prospects.

"Alright, lads," said Jim in the Coventry accent he now rarely used. "Financial advisor." He pointed at the phone. "Don't want her knowing I'm a brummie, like."

"Excellent," said the most smiley one. The other shook his head.

Jim reeled in the net.

The long game was hard. Jim wasn't sure if it was him or not. Just gaining friendship, contacts, with no mention of the scam or anything financial was almost killing him inside. His heart wanted to offer them the chance to be rich. The chance was for one day only. They'd have to sign now.

It didn't work like that.

The hour he'd just spent with Dave and Gary, technical assistants on a trading desk, could have been wasted. He had their numbers stored in his phone and some vague promise of meeting again for a drink one evening.

It seemed a waste of time.

During the hour, he'd spotted two wallets practically begging to be popped from pockets. He'd also pointed out to a young woman that her Blackberry had fallen from her handbag.

It just wasn't right.

Halfway to the next pub, he checked his phone.

Home now x. How's it going?

In hindsight, his phone call couldn't have worked out better. The messiness and betrayal of earlier seemed forgotten. Jim knew forgotten was the wrong word. It'd been pushed under the carpet, stored somewhere mentally ready for the next time he fucked up. Was she really cooking him dinner tonight? He wasn't sure. He really wasn't sure.

Not bad, I think x, he replied.

Two more pubs brought one more contact. The brokers and bankers, now either homeward bound or half drunk, wouldn't have remembered him the next morning if he'd robbed them. A middle-aged man, Robin, propping up the bar with a seemingly iron liver and an unlimited wedge of money was the only person he talked to. Jim quickly learnt to ask first where they worked. He'd nearly been caught out by pretending to work for the same company and on the same floor as someone. A lesson learnt.

The time quarter to eight, he sent a final message, *Coming back now. Shall I bring a takeaway?* Both cheeky and to the point, he'd soon find out not only where he was spending this evening, but also, tonight.

When he got off the tube in south London, her reply arrived. *I've cooked. It wasn't a joke x.*

See you in a minute x.

He stopped at the off licence for a few bottles of spirits. Just in case.

Chapter 28

The sofa was uncomfortable to sleep on. Given the cost and the sheer amount of leather involved in its manufacture it wasn't unsurprising. As Jim woke he heard movement from above. Charlotte was getting ready, maybe having a shower. Putting the kettle on, he made her a drink. He still had some making up to do.

Looking refreshed she came down the stairs. "Morning."

"Hello." He pointed at the steaming mug of coffee.

"Ta."

Jim thought the good news from last night was only two people had pulled out. Another had reduced his stake, but overall the fallout was less than Charlotte had expected. Jim had suggested they celebrate with the bottles he'd bought, but Charlotte didn't feel like celebrating. They had a lot of work to do. Also today was Friday, the last day of the week. She'd said there'd be plenty of time for drinking at the weekend.

"Sleep well?" she asked.

"Fine." He grimaced slightly and felt the small of his back. Her smiling face showed his lack of subtlety was appreciated.

"Look, I was thinking last night," she started.

Jim felt his face drop. This was it. Her next words would be, "You're really nice and that, but ..."

"Don't look so worried. I just thought, it seems silly you paying for that hotel. I mean, it's chucking money away."

He felt his face move back up. Though not as bad as it seemed a minute ago, this could still go either way.

"There's a spare room back there. She nodded towards the downstairs toilet and so-called laundry room opposite it. You could keep your stuff there and, you know."

Jim did know. He really did. He winced and felt the base of his spine again, while trying to stop smiling.

"And you're gonna have to be more subtle if you're going to drag any money in."

He nodded. The point taken.

Last night hadn't gone so badly. They'd sat together, watched a documentary on Al Capone and even kissed a few times. The next stage never came. It was as if neither of them wanted to rush the way they'd obviously rushed the night before. He still couldn't believe, when looking at her, that he even came close to her radar, let alone fitted it.

"Thanks." He sipped his tea. Either it had got hot, or his face was reddening. Hers was too. "What's today's plan then, boss."

She sat at the breakfast bar and twisted her cup round. "I've a few meetings; doubt anything will come of them, but you gotta try. Bars are always busiest Friday night. I reckon we'll get a few contacts if we work at it."

Jim nodded. He still didn't fully understand how this worked. People were going to pay thousands of pounds of cash, or straight into Charlotte's bank account which would be transferred to Switzerland. It got confusing then. Apparently, she'd withdraw it, buy gold bars then store them in a different Swiss bank. With no passport and still wanted for his release violations, Jim knew the last stage was beyond him. Whether she'd return to England after, he didn't know.

"I'll sort out the hotel room then hit the pubs lunchtime," he said.

She nodded, her cheeks full of colour. "I'm free between two and four if you fancy a spot of lunch."

Jim smiled. "That'd be nice. Like old times."

Her piece of hair flopped down over her eyes. "I'm paying so you can eat meat too."

He laughed and took a large swig of tea. "I'd better get ready, you know." He pointed towards the bathroom.

"Want another cuppa?"

"Please."

He was surprised when she gave him her spare key. He shouldn't have been surprised. How else could he move his stuff in? There was no fuss or embarrassment just the simple handover of a small piece of shaped metal.

Back at the hotel, he felt a stranger. He'd barely been there to sample their wonderful food or service the past few days. Settling his bill and carrying his suitcase out, he half expected a Range Rover to offer him a lift. He'd been warned off the East End, but not the city. He kind of knew they were keeping an eye on him; anyone would. He just hoped they didn't involve Charlotte. If they did, it was going to get messy.

Back at the apartment, he realised the spare room cum laundry had a guest bed. Just a single, unmade, foldable bed, but it was a bed. He wondered what her idea of the sleeping plan was. Remembering back, she hadn't actually invited him to sleep there just leave his stuff. She could hardly expect him to sleep there amongst the mountain of her underwear and skirts. Could she? If so, why all the red faces earlier?

He made a cup of tea and put the stereo on. He found nothing he really liked amongst the Enya, Jazz and Tracey Chapman ones. Getting The Clash CD he'd bought, he blasted out "I Fought The Law" and settled on the couch. He still couldn't believe this. Realistically, he should be dead. Charlotte had saved his life. No two ways about it.

And if she wanted separate bedrooms, that was fine by him.

For a day or two.

Chapter 29

Lunchtime brought another contact. A monotonous-voiced trader from Northumberland. He'd latched on to Jim a but quick for his liking. He was after fools with money not friendless losers. He took his number anyway. "You never know" had become his new phrase for the week.

Charlotte looked flustered over lunch. Her phone barely stopped ringing through the soup and main course. It had been her idea to eat three courses. "It'll soak up the drink you have later," she'd said.

Jim had agreed and laid off the wine choosing coke instead. In the pause before the main course, she said, "Two weeks on Monday. I can't risk waiting longer. There are more stats out from the ONS on the Wednesday as I'm sure you know as you're working there."

Jim poked his tongue out, but she didn't smile back.

"I thought this would be it, you know." She looked philosophical. Jim wanted to stand and walk to her, put his arms round her.

"You mean the last one?"

"Yeah. Exactly what I mean. After costs and the rent on the flat, sorry, 'apartment', there's nowhere near enough to retire on."

She spoke clearly, yet quietly enough so only he heard. He didn't know what to say. This was the only job she'd be able to pull in London for years, plastic surgery aside. She'd spoken last night of Switzerland or Monaco. There were some seriously rich people there. But, she'd have to use almost all this money for a future blag. If it went wrong she was back to square one.

Jim didn't envy her the decision. He knew what he'd do with the money, but it wasn't his. They hadn't talked of a share or wage. She'd given him five hundred last night the leftovers of what she'd drawn from the safety deposit box. When that ran out, he'd have to go cap in hand asking for more. He hoped she'd bring the subject up before then.

He shrugged his shoulders. "This is your game, not mine. I couldn't possibly think of an idea of anything this size."

"You could." Her voice was much softer; he could barely hear. "You just need practise. Start at the beginning."

He smiled. "It would take me months."

"I didn't do this overnight, you know. I spent months researching markets making the whole thing believable, yet just secretive enough. Literally months."

"I can believe it."

"It's never too early to think of the next one."

"It's putting up money that would worry me." Though the alcove felt private, he kept checking round. Just in case.

She shrugged her shoulders. "Speculate to accumulate. I bet you're useless at poker, aren't you?"

"Not if I cheat I'm not."

She smiled. Her piece of hair plopped down. He wondered again how she put it with it. Surely it was annoying?

The work conversation ended though Jim had an unasked question, and he thought she did too. He hoped she did. But there was plenty of time for that. No point worrying over what may or may not happen in the future.

They chatted about music, which pub or bar they hated the most and just why was everything so expensive. Jim had fillet steak for the second time in his life. Though nice, it still wasn't worth the extra money.

Parting, he headed for the same bar as the previous day. Still an hour before knocking off time he thought he'd grab a bar seat. Drinking expensive Mexican bottled lager, he thought again of Charlotte and the unsaid next job.

When this ended, he'd be skint, homeless and still a wanted man. Never a great combination. He had to follow her. He had to work with her again. What use was he though? A bit of cheeky charm and the ability to steal wallets or do card tricks wasn't going to make him indispensible. He needed a plan. The next job. He needed to come up with something big.

A big scam.

"So then I said to Yolanda," said Jim, "you might have three letters after your name, but some of us will have four letters before it one day." They didn't laugh. Jim thought on reflection it wasn't funny. It'd seemed funnier in his head. "Lord? The four letters before?"

The two men smiled. Though the joke had sunk home it didn't make it funny. Jim thought the pair would have been easy when he first saw them, but they were hard work. A skinny, twenty-something from the Wirral, and a balding thirty-year-old from Essex. Both brokers but definitely not broke.

"You're not are you?" the younger one asked.

"Course not." Jim took another sip from his bottle. "Do I look like a lord? Worked though, I got her phone number."

The elder one smiled. Jim had him down as the younger's boss. Maybe they'd come out for a quiet after-work drink to discuss a raise or bonus. Either way, Jim had hijacked their quiet drink with his badly thought out ranting.

"Where was it you worked, again?" the younger one said. He was full of questions. Jim wondered whether he should have planned these rants more. His throat was dry from all the talking and he didn't seem to be getting anywhere. This was supposed to be a long con, but he felt he was trying too much too quickly.

"Small brokers. Palmers and Son." The previous person he'd annoyed had worked there. These two were from a large multinational bank so they'd no chance of knowing anyone who worked there. The elder one nodded. Jim was wariest of him. He seemed to digest every word without comment. Probably had a brain like a computer. Every word noted in case it was needed. "Hopefully I'll be retiring soon," said Jim. "Working on a few deals of my own, know what I mean?"

The confused look on the younger one's face meant he didn't know. Jim fancied getting the lad on his own, away from the boss. The boss seemed to have an iron bladder though. No trip to the toilet in over three bottles of lager.

"A lot of people retire young, don't they?" he said.

Jim nodded. "Stress. Biggest killer in the city. Takes years off your life. What you need is an exit plan. You don't want to still be here in twenty years time." Though talking to the younger, he looked at his boss as he got to the end of the sentence.

"How exactly do you mean?" the older one finally said.

Jim suggested they find a table before he continued.

Half nine and most of the brokers were either bladdered or tucked up in bed. He saw no point lingering further. He was just wasting time he could be spending with Charlotte. They'd texted a few times since leaving the restaurant, but her meetings had ended over an hour ago. His brain wasn't quite functioning right to continue lying anymore. Finishing his lager, he headed for the station.

Three new contacts. That's all a hundred quid and an evening talking to twats had got him. Two via business card and one email address. Emails still baffled him. Apparently they'd changed the world; made business so much easier. When someone earlier had asked for his email address he used the advice Charlotte had given: "It's a very secure network. Give me yours and I'll send you one from my home address." He was surprised it'd worked so well.

Just leaving. Be back soon x, he typed.

Okay x, the reply,

The tube was standing room only. Prime time thieving ground. As people bustled into him and apologised or just shrugged, he found himself checking his own pockets. He was more than surprised when the suited man next to him, his hand hanging from the roof support, actually fell asleep. He woke up in time for his own stop too. Jim guessed some natural homing instinct had kicked in. All in all, he found it impressive.

Nearly there x, he sent as he left the tube.

Okay. I'll order takeaway x, her reply.

Want me to pick it up? x

No, it's okay x.

Shrugging, he walked past the takeaway. The server was answering a phone call. No doubt Charlotte. She'd fitted into London well. Shaking his head, he walked past the old cinema and towards the luxury apartments.

"Hi, honey. I'm home."

He walked through the cow-sided room and smiled as she turned from the island kitchen.

"Busy day?" she asked.

He nodded. "Have I got enough time for a shower before it arrives?"

"Yeah. Usually takes an hour or so for delivery this time of night. Cup of tea first?"

Jim nodded again. He thought of pointing out he walked straight past the takeaway but it didn't seem important. Butterflies had ripped his stomach apart again. She was dressed in jeans and a t-shirt. Still smart but very casual. Her hair recently washed and her face without make-up.

He sat down while she made the drinks. Taking off his shoes, he sighed and shook his head. "Don't know how you do it. It's exhausting."

"You get used to it. You've just got to keep seeing the end of the tunnel."

"Just feels like a dead end at times. You can talk for an hour and get nowhere."

"Bigger picture." She brought in two cups and sat next to him. "You've got the weekend off now. We can relax."

Jim watched as she tucked a leg underneath herself and flicked the wayward piece of hair onto her head. She was relaxed. Much more than relaxed. If there was an on off switch for work it'd been pressed. He smiled as she sipped her coffee.

"What?"

"Nothing. What's the plan for the weekend?"

She shrugged her shoulders. "Meeting Sunday evening. Apart from that, I'm all yours."

He felt his smile grow further as he grabbed his tea. "We could go out tomorrow." He shrugged his shoulders. He didn't know where they could go. A million things to do on the doorstep, but after spending all week on tubes crushed by others none of the million things seemed appealing.

"See what happens."

He sipped his tea. Too hot to drink. "Got a few names earlier, and an email address. Don't know what to do with that."

She nodded though he didn't think her heart was in it.

"Anything wrong?"

"No."

He reckoned the switch had flicked back to work. Something was troubling her.

"You're worried about the recession thing?"

She nodded. "If it falls through, I owe a shedload of money with no way to repay it."

Jim couldn't help but laugh. "I've become an expert in that lately. We'll sort it out, whatever happens."

"Yeah. I'll get the plates ready." She stood and went to the kitchen. As Jim drank his tea then headed for the shower, he wondered just how much she'd borrowed from the Holloway Queen. He'd earn her every penny if he could.

Chinese and a bottle of wine led to laughter and smiles. Though his head was still full of the sleeping arrangements he was determined not to make an issue of it. After all, she'd saved his life. He'd sleep in the dog kennel if she had one.

The television, playing some half-funny comedy program, was getting half their attention. Occasionally, Charlotte would interrupt and tell him a nugget of news, or occasionally mention the other night and how funny it was on reflection.

"The funniest thing," he said, looking at her flopped down lump of hair, "was when you accused me of being the police."

She shook her head. "Crazy isn't it? I don't know how we didn't suspect each other earlier." Finishing the last of his wine, he offered refills.

"Go on then."

He looked back at the television. The program hadn't got funnier. "Where do you want to go tomorrow then?"

"Dunno. There's museums, art galleries. Anywhere you've always wanted to go?"

He thought for a minute. A million places and ways to spend money. None of them appealed. London Eye? No. Just looking at London from high up wasn't him. He'd seen enough of London this past week. Eventually he shrugged his shoulders.

"Just a lazy day then." She twisted her legs round then laid them on his lap as she turned on her side. "Do a bit of washing. Bake a cake."

"You bake cakes?"

He watched her nose screw up. "I can cook a bit. Okay so chilli's not my strongest point."

"I wasn't having a dig. I just, you know." He stopped before he said something he might regret. Despite her legs being on him, he couldn't help but feel this was awkward. Not remembering how they'd ended back at the hotel was the possible reason. Her legs felt relaxed plonked on top of his jeans. They weren't tense like his own. He wondered if he should feign a sore leg. It'd be an excuse to lie next to her.

"Legs are a bit stiff. Can I just move?" He kicked his feet round and onto the sofa, laying his head on her dressing gowned arm.

"Get comfy, won't you."

He thought of apologising but didn't. It was light-hearted. When her hand appeared on his head, ruffling his nearly dry hair, he finally felt something close to relaxed.

"Victoria sponge or muffins?" he asked.

"Eh?"

"Cake. What cake you going to make me?"

She moved her head and faced him. "Something with a file in. Remind you of inside won't it?"

Chapter 30

Coffee, morning newspapers and a warm Charlotte nicking most of the duvet: Jim couldn't think of a better start to a Saturday morning. When he thought back to all those years inside, slopping out and eating rancid, cold breakfasts, he wondered why he'd kept offending. Of course he'd never met her, but a similar life was always available, though with poorer quality coffee and papers.

As he yawned and tugged on the cover, he caught her eye. Reading some piece in the glossy supplement on Gil Scott-Heron, she looked for all the world an angel. An angel with ruffled hair and bags under her eyes, but still an angel.

"What you thinking?" she said.

"Nothing." He closed his eyes and spread himself out, starfish style, in the ample bed. "Suppose we ought to think about getting up." He yawned again. He'd had a couple of catnaps since waking at six but still felt tired. It'd been a long week. At many stages it'd been his last week. Maybe another hour or two extra sleep wouldn't hurt.

"It's only eleven." She yawned. "Are you hungry? Cooker's downstairs if you are."

His eyes pinged open. Breakfast in bed. What more could he want? Just maybe someone other than himself making it.

Bacon, scrambled eggs, toast and The Clash were cooking in the kitchen. Jim thought she needed some more CDs. He couldn't keep playing the same one all the time. Still, she'd been inside herself. Started afresh. Possessions always got lost.

Two plates on the tray and more coffee, he took it upstairs. Filtered coffee wasn't that bad if you had it occasionally. Of course it didn't beat tea, but coffee was easier to drink cold. Lying there, with one of Raif's shirts on, she looked a million dollars. He smiled again. How had this happened? How had he wormed his way into this?

Handing over the tray, he took his own plate and splattered it with tomato sauce before offering her the bottle.

"Heathen."

He shrugged his shoulders. Years of tasteless food had made him act on impulse. Bacon needed tomato sauce though. Everyone knew that.

Breakfast finished and another hour of snoozing and schmoozing flew by. Jim finally persuaded her to get up. She'd become a different person in bed. Lethargic, pouty and demanding. He wanted to get up, go see things and celebrate this new life he'd been given.

Downstairs and with The Clash on again, he watched as she applied a layer of war paint. It was the first time he could remember her putting it on in front of him. He wondered if that meant anything. Maybe she felt comfortable around him. Or she was just past caring what he thought.

Another hour and cup of coffee disappeared before they left. Outside, the weather was still good. Warm but cloudy. They'd chosen to go coatless which seemed the London way. A sudden shower and they'd grab a coffee or taxi.

Heading for the tube, Charlotte asked him for the twentieth time where they were going.

"I told you, it's a surprise."

"You mean you don't know. You're just making it up as you go along. Dragging me out through the shitty city when all I wanted to do was ..." She leaned close to him and whispered a word.

"Please." he said. "Don't. You'll like it when we get there. Honest."

She shrugged her shoulders and retook his hand. "I hope so. I've got big expectations you know."

The tube network was busy; teenagers going shopping, tourists sightseeing and the station teeming from the plod of cricket fans heading south for a test match at The Oval. After they changed at Victoria, Charlotte's face seemed to show some recognition of where they were headed.

"Either you're not very original or you spotted something last week."

Jim shrugged. He supposed it wasn't original. Millions of things to do and he'd picked the same area as last week. He thought back to that day. Pulling faces at her through the tunnel reflections. He looked at the floor and wondered if he was still a mark in her eyes at that point.

Catching her eye he smiled. When did he stop being her mark? Has he stopped being her mark? Thinking back to his own head and state over the past week, he reckoned deep down she'd always been a mark to him. She'd paid up too.

She was still paying up. It wasn't like that though. He wasn't after her money. He was after something different. Much different. That's what this afternoon would be about.

"Penny for them?"

He smiled again. "Found a penny one day. On a tube floor. I picked it up, too."

She grabbed his arm, her cold hand finding his. "History now, isn't it?"

He nodded. She was right. It was history. The future was important now. The future.

"Are we really going to the same gallery as last week?"

He shrugged his shoulders. "Yeah, but it's a different display or whatever they're called."

"Fair enough."

They walked by the side of the Thames towards the galleries. He knew this could have been done anywhere, but doing it here made the impact greater. It also brought them back to this place. The place of their first sort-of date. He kept telling himself he wasn't terrified of losing her. He'd been alone most of his life so why would he be? No, it wouldn't matter if this job was the last and they went their separate ways.

He turned round to catch her looking at him. "You're very dark and moody today Mr Mysterious."

"Sorry. I'm trying to work this out before I start."

"Start what?" She turned to face him twisting his hand the wrong way.

"You'll see." He smiled, more at her serious grin than anything funny.

"Keep a girl in suspense why don't you."

As they walked the rest of the way in silence, he finalised the plan. Obviously, he'd wing it. No big speech had been prepared, but he thought he knew the main points well enough.

"Oh," she said as she saw the new exhibition sign.

Jim read the sign again, but couldn't believe it. "Porn through the ages. A history of pornography."

He shook his head. "This isn't it."

"I bloody well hope not. What kind of girl do you take me for?"

"Sorry." He turned to her. He reckoned her face was as red as his own. "I had this idea for a scam."

"I'm not taking my clothes off." She looked away, towards a boat chugging down the Thames.

"No. It's nothing to do with this." He grabbed her arm. "Come on. Let's go for a walk."

Her arm felt stiff, cold. As he walked towards the river, he said, "Last week's exhibition. It gave me an idea."

"Just keep talking."

He stopped and leant against the guard rail. The murky river below, he wondered if he would have jumped in it two days ago if Charlotte hadn't helped. "That famous artist that no one's ever seen."

She shook her head.

"Fairly young, I think. One of his pieces was in that exhibition. Looks like graffiti but somehow it's actually art."

She nodded. "I know who you mean."

"Well. I haven't fully thought this through, but there's that place in Cornwall. Loads of artists and that live there. Art galleries, you know." He took a deep breath. If she was planning on dumping him after this scam he'd probably just brought the dumping date forward a few weeks. "We hit the town. It's far enough away from here. If you stroll into a shop or art gallery constantly on your phone, talking loudly about a certain artist, hopefully you'll whip up some intrigue."

He looked at her face; she was taking it in. "Then I appear a day or so later with you dressed like a scruffy urchin with spray paint on my hands. Act a bit eccentric, swear a lot, you know. Before long you'll have people offering you thousands for a bus ticket I've wiped my nose on."

"A scam?"

He scrunched up his nose. He'd no idea if she'd laugh or even cry. This was probably the peak of ideas scamwise he was going to have. If this was laughed out he might as well give up.

She started to nod. A smile broke through her lips and the flop of hair flipped down. "It's got legs. Needs tweaking a bit. But yeah. I can see that. It's St Ives, isn't it? Little coastal town. I've read about it." She turned and looked over the water. "That's not bad. Could be pretty quick too. Whoever the mark is, they're going to want to buy your bus ticket or whatever before anyone else knows you're around. Lack of time makes people panic; do things they'd otherwise think through."

He couldn't help but feel relieved. His stomach was churning again. It wasn't just the job. It was working together. Being together for longer. He wondered if he ought to think of the job after that quickly too, but realised maybe he didn't

227

need to. Perhaps if he'd said rob the crown jewels she'd agree. Smiling, he put his arm round her shoulders. "The world won't know what's hit it, will it?"

He felt her arm move round his waist ending up on his hip. "I wouldn't go that far, but I reckon we could do some damage."

He looked at her and smiled. "Come on. Let's go to a museum or something."

Though the dinosaur skeleton was impressive, Jim found himself wondering whether she truly thought the art scam was a good idea or she was just humouring him. He'd find out soon enough. He knew he should just take each moment for what it was. Charlotte herself seemed more interested in the Eskimo pieces. Despite the odd not very funny joke, Jim had been quiet throughout.

After a sandwich in a cafe they meandered home. Jim thought it the lull before the storm. The tempestuous scam Charlotte was pulling was on the horizon, the ship that was Charlotte and him idling towards the eye of it. Some bollocks or other like that anyway.

"You okay?" she said.

"Yeah, just thinking."

"Share."

"Nah. Nothing really."

"You're getting this mean and moody thing off to a tee. Good practise for Cornwall."

He shrugged his shoulders and took her arm. "You wait until I get my crayons out and really get started."

Early evening slipped by with alcohol and a just in date vegan cheesecake. A Hollywood action film, which they both hated but couldn't stop watching, took care of the rest of the evening until sleep beckoned.

Chapter 31

Waking to an empty bed, Jim went downstairs. Ten in the morning and with a slight hangover, he still felt tired. The last week was to blame for that. He reckoned it'd take a full week of sleep to catch up.

Charlotte was sitting at the breakfast bar reading a broadsheet.

"Morning," he tried to say but just a grunt came out.

"Hi." She smiled but it wasn't convincing. He looked at the broadsheet. Pictures of city institutions and graphs that headed downwards in red ink. He reckoned he knew what the problem was.

"Bad news day?"

She nodded. "Going to pull it forward. This Friday or next Monday. I've got to before it's too late."

Jim leant against the granite worktop and poured a coffee. "What can I do?"

She shrugged her shoulders. "Probably not much now. Get in contact with everyone you've met. You never know. They might be really greedy."

"Or stupid?" said Jim. He knew this was bad. Probably just damage limitation now. Whether she'd be able to repay what she'd borrowed was the question. It was a question he wasn't going to ask. Four grand of that had been to bail him out. If all this news had come out a week earlier he wondered if she would have done it.

"I think most will cough up. A few might struggle to move money around short notice. Hopefully, it'll be enough."

He put his hand on her shoulder. Tense; stiff. It wasn't the time to offer a massage either.

"We'll do the best we can. I know it." He wasn't even convincing himself let alone her. "Is there anything I can do? Dress up as an Arab?"

She smiled. "I don't think that would work. You might ..." She looked into the distance. Jim thought a plan was brewing. "Maybe it wouldn't hurt to bring you along to a few meetings. Some wouldn't like it though."

"Breakfast?" he asked.

"Yeah, go on. I've got a feeling today's going to drag."

The phone calls lasted forever. One after another she rang them arranging meetings for the next few days. Watching it, Jim was amazed how cool she was, but also what an excellent liar she was. In another world or life it might have bothered him. In this one, it added to her charm.

He rang his own short list of four contacts. All bar one couldn't remember him let alone want to meet him. The one who did, James, was overkeen too. Still, it was only money he was after. They arranged to meet for an afternoon drink in Covent Garden. Jim had suggested there as he sort of knew his way round.

He sent an email to his final contact. Jim didn't think it would come to anything. He'd be like the other non-desperate ones who'd forgotten.

Charlotte was still making calls so he opened a Facebook account and tried to look up old friends and lags. As most were inside, he didn't get very far. Looking at the clock, eleven, he knew today was going to drag for him as well as Charlotte. He didn't feel comfortable sitting round. It just felt and looked like he was doing nothing. Of course, he was doing nothing, but he needed something constructive.

"I'm going to pop out," he said. "See if I can't find anyone or anything to fleece."

She smiled. Between calls, she was making another pot of coffee. That's all today had become for her: coffee and calls.

Saying goodbye, he left and made for the tube.

Halfway to the station he realised this was their first time apart, work excepted, since that night three days ago. It'd flown by, no doubt about it. Time took a different concept when she was around. Part of him thought a few hours apart would do them good. After all, they weren't joined at the hip. Another part of him missed her already.

He broke from his normal route and headed west at the cinema. He knew where his legs were taking him. He wasn't sure why, but he guessed the thieving scrote buried deep down was doing its own talking.

Outside the block of apartments he looked at the windows. He still didn't even know which flat it was. Pressing the buzzer that hadn't answered four days ago he waited.

"Hello?" A woman's voice.

"Is, er, Geoffrey in?"

"Ur, no. Who is this?"

Jim looked at the electronic keypad. A small recessed camera aimed at his face. Of course, Geoffrey would probably still be in hospital. The woman in the flat was probably a girlfriend or his ex wife. No doubt, as she was alone, she'd be reluctant to admit he wasn't there.

"I'm a friend. Is he still in hospital?"

"Yes he is." The voice firm but hiding something.

"Okay, I'll see him there. Visiting's afternoon and evenings, isn't it?"

The voice buzzed off without an answer.

Jim headed for the tube. Another example of London's friendliness ringing in his ears. What was this place about? The tube network was busy again. Hundreds more cricket fans with bags and England shirts headed for The Oval. Staring at the tube map for the fiftieth time in a week, he wondered if the test match had been last week whether he could have pulled some scam from it. Late evening in a pub near the ground, there would be all sorts of drunken fans. A day on the piss for people not used to it might have got him more than a wallet or two.

At Covent Garden, he walked around a few shops. The amount of money some of them charged was exorbitant. He realised that last week he'd been walking round in a daze. He'd missed most of the sights and feel of the place.

Half an hour early to meet James, he bought an expensive bottle of lager and sat outside a pub. All coffee tables and fenced-off bar areas the whole place was trying too hard for a European cafe culture. Add that to binge drinkers, serial fighters and an already overstretched police force and the result was chaos. He thought in hindsight he should have spent most of last weekend working nights. The amount of wallets that wouldn't be missed until the morning was tempting.

James arrived ten minutes early. Jim barely recognised him in his weekend clothes: smart jeans, t-shirt and light coat. Nodding at each other briefly, James asked if he wanted a drink before heading to the bar.

Jim had no idea how to play this. Just come straight out with it or wait and see how things went. Sending a message to Charlotte, *He's here, speak later x,* he then put his phone on vibrate and waited.

James was overkeen. No two ways about it. Brought up near Carlisle, he'd ended up working for a stock brokers after university. Jim reckoned hundreds must find themselves in similar positions. Without old school friends or being in the right gang, London sounded a lonely life.

"Same with me," said Jim. "Come from a comprehensive in Coventry. Half the people at work seem to know each other from school or whatever. Don't bother me though. It's all about money, isn't it? Work for five years and make enough to retire."

He watched James nod though he seemed distracted by the table next door. Jim wasn't surprised why. Two young women drinking expensive wine and wearing expensive short skirts. Suntanned faces, though obviously via a spray gun, pristine hair and Gucci shades. Jim reckoned they must spend hours each day on their appearance. Wags or wannabe wags, he wondered just how much money they had and where it came from. Perfect for a scam.

"Has benefits living here, doesn't it?" said James.

Jim nodded and tried not to smile too hard. He supposed his mark thought of him as single like himself. Why else would he be out alone meeting some stranger on a Sunday afternoon? Maybe that would help if this idea somehow worked in three days.

"Did you go out last night?" Jim eventually said. Small talk was difficult especially when you had so much to hide and the person you're hiding it from is distracted by two blondes.

"Nah. Rarely do on a Saturday. What about you?"

He finally looked back. Jim held his gaze for a few seconds. "Me neither. Early night, couple of tinnies. I mainly go out Friday after work." He watched James nod. That seemed to be the single thing to do. "Like a couple of fifty-year-olds, aren't we?" Jim smiled at his drinking companion but he'd gone back to staring at the fake women with fake tans and God knows what fake else.

"Do you go back home much?"

Jim shook his head. "About six months since the last visit. You?"

"Once a month."

Jim knew this awkwardness could only end one way. Serious amounts of alcohol. Being a Sunday afternoon though, it'd get messy by five if they really went for it. He leaned forward and whispered, "How about we sink a few quick shorts then try our luck?" He nodded his head backwards leaving, he hoped, little doubt at what luck was to be tried out.

James' smile said he agreed. Standing he said, "I'll get them in. Vodka okay?"

Jim nodded thinking back to that famous saying, "when in Rome" and all that.

The double vodka had barely touched the sides so Jim bought two trebles. Sitting down he couldn't believe the dent it had made in his pocket. It was like money meant nothing in this part of London. The two girls were finishing off their wine, their spirits now higher with giggles replacing their previous chit chatter. Jim didn't relish the thought of trying to chat them up. He reckoned when you've got fillet steak at home you don't play around with suntanned mutton.

"Down the hatch," said James, his face now reddened and full of smiles.

"So then, who's going to start, me or thee?" said Jim.

James downed the triple in one then gasped. "Jeez. I'll launch the attack. You play the wing man. Wish me luck squadron leader, I'm going in."

Jim hid his face behind his glass and quaffed the contents.

"Good afternoon, ladies," he heard James say. "I wonder if you would like to join my friend and I for a drink?"

Jim didn't know what was worse, the initial deathly silence or the looks they gave them. The looks could kill cliché only went so far. Maybe another cliché existed for this sort of event. Something about looks ripping your heart out, feeding it to a pack of angry wolves then transplanting one of the wolves' hearts in its place. Then, getting a bigger wolf or a bear, to rip it out again and again.

James was trying his best, but as his wing man Jim could only smile at the bronze-skinned football wife wannabes and laugh at his jokes. Less than a minute of making a fool of himself was all the lad could handle. Walking to a different pub, Jim slapped him on the back.

"Ten out of ten for effort, mate. Like a dog with a bone you were."

He shrugged. "No chance though, was there? That sort." He shook his head. "They don't go for the likes of us."

"I don't think anyone in London goes for the likes of us, mate," said Jim.

"Lonely old place, isn't it?"

"Yep." Jim opened the door to a much cheaper looking bar and walked in. "My round. Lager okay?"

James nodded and sat at the remaining table. Through the mirrored bar, Jim saw that beneath the bravado, James was maybe more hurt by the incident than he'd seemed. Lonely man disease, that's what Jim had always called it. The circle of despair. Once you get down about being single it makes you less of a catch. That makes you even more depressed. A never-ending downward spiral.

Taking the drinks over, Jim tried to lighten the mood. "You're better off out of there I reckon. Imagine what they must look like without a vat of make-up and spray tan. There's no ..." He paused, trying to word it right. "You won't ever see them later and be surprised by how good-looking they actually are. It's downhill forever." It made sense in his mind, but he didn't think he'd got the gist of it over.

James just shrugged his shoulders. "Suppose. It'd just be, you know, nice to actually meet someone."

Jim reckoned this was as good a time as any. "You know, that's sort of why I came up with the glorious ten-year plan."

James shook his head then supped on his pint.

"Seriously. Work for ten years. No more. No burning yourself out. Always have a goal in the background."

He looked up. "What sort of goal?"

"Very early retirement. Secret is not to blow it all on plastic birds and expensive lager." He sipped his pint. His head, already light-headed, welcomed more alcohol. He didn't like to think what Charlotte would make of things when he staggered back later.

"Can you really save enough to retire that early? I know we're well paid, but most of it just goes on rent and that."

Jim took another sip of lager. "There are other ways."

"Such as?"

Jim smiled and shook his head. This was going too well. "You're not the police are you?"

He shook his head.

"Just kidding. No, just finding correct investments that's all."

James whispered, "Insider?"

Jim shook his head and leant over the table. "Insider's an ugly word. No, what you want is something safe. Safe as houses, or apartments or whatever the phrase is now."

James nodded. "You're not the first to mention it. I just worry about getting caught. I've never fancied porridge."

"No risk though. My broker deals in cash, gold or Swiss accounts. No trace, plus it's technically not illegal. She's got a big one coming up." Jim took a big glug of his pint. "Like I say, I'm just thinking long term. It's not huge amounts of

234

money. A little nest egg. You do this game for too long and you die young with nothing. It's like a pension, that's all."

James shrugged his shoulders. "Fancy a bite to eat? This drink's gone to my head."

A chainless burger shop three streets from the heart of Covent Garden made do. Jim thought it had aspirations to be more than it was. The prices were very aspirational. Nearly twenty quid for a burger and chips. They weren't even called chips either. French Fries, the bane of all British men.

"What's your week looking like?" Jim took another bite of the burger. Good quality meat and interesting sauce. Not tomato. A cross between thousand island and salsa.

"Same as usual." James had sobered. It was obvious to Jim. His face had lost its red sheen, and he was more reserved. Back in his shell again. The investment hadn't been mentioned since the pub, but Jim reckoned that's what Charlotte would have wanted. Plant the seed and wait. In a few days, after waiting on stifling tubes and drudging through the crowds, Jim reckoned he'd get a call.

"All work and no play, eh? I might nip out for a midweek drink. Depends how it goes of course." He took another bite of burger. Not worth twenty quid, but definitely good quality.

James nodded. "Give us a shout. I might join you. Don't want to drink too much midweek though."

Jim smiled. "Yeah. Probably ought to knock today on the head soon. Otherwise, I'll be a mess all week."

"You read my mind."

The burger gone and a coffee to help sober them up, they left. James lived in north London so wanted a different tube. Jim said his goodbyes, trying not to sound too desperate, and made for his own tube. The alcohol now soaked up, he felt the onset of a headache coming. Taking out his phone he typed, *All done. Think he might be a goer x.*

Walking down the escalator, he noticed someone familiar. He'd robbed so many people the past week they all kind of merged into one. Bar one person.

Raif.

With a woman who Jim thought was actually a lot better looking than Raif had given the impression of. He was carrying shopping bags from an expensive tailors. Though he was smiling at the reason why he had bags, Jim also felt a dread come over him. Less than ten feet in front, a bloke that could put him inside was standing there, and occasionally looking round as other women went past on the up escalator.

His heart sunk as he turned round to read the adverts. He was wearing the bloke's clothes for fucks sake. Jim realised just how stupid this had been. He shouldn't be out tempting fate. He should be lying low.

At the escalator bottom, Raif and wife headed for the north-bound line. Jim turned and went straight back up the escalator. Emerging onto the street, his hands sweating and shaking, his phone pinged. *Good work xxx.*

Just had a nightmare. Nearly bumped into Raif.

He leant against the station wall for a second. His heart pounding through his chest and the very nice burger threatening to re-emerge the way it'd gone down. He shook his head. That could have been the moment he lost everything. The problem was the everything he could have lost had become just one thing. And it was a someone, not a thing.

Ooops. I'm in between meetings. So far so good x.

He sighed as he typed, *Well done x*, then walked back to Covent Garden. Though Raif would already be on a tube north, Jim didn't want to go anywhere near the station.

Halfway to the river, and with the afternoon still only half over, he didn't fancy being home alone. Or Charlotte's home alone. It just didn't seem right if she was working. Finding a pub he ordered a pint. The pub, a chain that was trying to be traditional, was doing a good trade. The beer garden, with barbecue, seemed the reason. Jim sat at the bar taking the place in. Families out for the day seemed to be the stock trade. Kids eating mini-burgers in between tears, fizzy drinks and running around. Adults drinking a pint with far away looks, no doubt remembering the pre-kids time when they'd have spent the whole afternoon getting wasted.

Jim sipped his beer and nodded at the glass-wiping barman. "Busy in here."

"Always is, mate." Another Australian. Jim wondered just how many were left in Australia. "Two for one Sunday dinners, plus the barby."

Jim nodded. "You here for long?"

"Knock off at six."

Jim shrugged his shoulders and smiled. That wasn't what he meant, but he reckoned the barman knew that. "What part of Canada you from then?" His smile was matched then beaten by the Australian's.

"Good one. Little town near Perth."

Jim nodded. "I've never been. Maybe one day I'll go."

"You ought to, mate. Don't worry about the flight. It just takes a day or two to get over it."

"I suppose it does." He'd somehow finished his drink so he tried to order another. The barman had three others in the queue before he got back to Jim.

"You living nearby?" Jim asked.

"South London, near The Old Kent Road."

Jim nodded. He had no idea where it was, but knew it was the sort of place anyone who lived in London would know.

"What about yourself?"

He shrugged his shoulders. "Apartment just south of the river. Mate of a mate's pad, you know."

The barman went back to serving and wiping as Jim quaffed his second pint. His head now back in the land of the drunk, he pulled out his phone. He typed, *Just stopped at a pub* to *find new recruits,* and pressed send.

A little phone icon on the screen was flashing. Jim had no idea what it meant but it definitely meant something. Opening the menus he realised it was a missed call. Dave. Some bloke from the other day. The one he'd rung earlier who barely remembered him.

Jim nodded at the barman and went into the beer garden. Lighting a fag, he dialled Dave's number.

"Hello, Jim?"

"Alright, Dave. How you doing?" He looked at the punters sat on wooden seats. All seem to be enjoying themselves with their half cooked sausages and burgers.

"Not bad. Look, I'm out with a few mates and they're heading off soon. So, just wondered if you were still around?"

"Yeah, I'm out and about. Just in a pub near the river, I think." He pulled another cigarette from his pocket and searched for his lighter.

"I'm in a bar just off Leicester Square. I could meet you at the tube if you want?"

"Um." Jim paused. The bloke sounded very keen. He could barely remember him, but thought he hadn't got that far into his ten-year plan patter anyway. What did he want? "Yeah, go on. God knows where the tube is from here."

"Lost are you?" Dave laughed. A bit haughty, but Jim realised it went with the job round these parts.

"Yeah. I was walking home and found a pub."

"You could be anywhere, mate. Ask the barman or something."

"Yeah. I'll ring you when I get off the tube."

"Okay."

Jim lit his fag and shook his head. Maybe the bloke was just bored and lonely. There seemed to be a lot of it about. He looked round the garden again at the adults drinking, while the kids played on swings and tried to climb the slide backwards. They seemed happy enough, both adults and children. He did think though that each was more comfortable with their own age group.

Stubbing out his fag, he went to the bar and caught the barman's eye.

"Where's the nearest tube, pal?"

"What line do you want?"

"Leicester Square. Don't know which line."

The Aussie thought for a minute; scowl on his face. "Kind of between two stops. Probably best to go to Green Park. Saying that, you could probably walk it quicker."

Jim shrugged his shoulders. He just wanted directions, he didn't care walking or not.

"Out the door, turn right, then left, then right again at the traffic lights. Tube's just off to the left. If you want to walk it, right then right then sort of carry on for a mile or so. Can't miss it."

Jim thanked him, left, and flagged down a taxi.

"You see," the cabbie said, "that's what they never thought of when they wanted the Olympics. They can put more tubes on, can't they? But they can't just hire more cabbies for a month. Knowledge, mate, the knowledge. That's what it is." The cabbie shook his head while Jim looked out of the window. "They always say, 'what are you worried about? Be more overtime, won't it?' Well it won't. We'll still be driving the same hours, but we'll all be stuck in traffic outside the frigging venues. Chaos it's gonna be, chaos."

Jim looked back at the driver's head and neck. Strong, possibly bulletproof plastic separated them. He wondered for a minute if robbery wasn't the only reason they were protected. "And what's worse." He paused before continuing. "How many of your foreigners and day trippers aren't gonna come at all cos the Olympics are on? Eh? Didn't think of that, did they? Gonna be quiet all year we reckons. Barely be able to make ends meet we reckon." He paused again then pulled in to the kerb. "Here you are, squire. Eight pounds eighty."

Jim made a point of paying the exact fare before he walked to the station foyer and dialled Dave's phone.

"Be there in two minutes," he said.

Jim smoked another fag while waiting. Just as he stubbed it out, a young man appeared on the opposite side of the entrance. Jim thought he looked familiar but wasn't sure. Maybe he needed a carnation for his lapel or something. He smiled before walking over.

"Dave?"

The young man nodded. Jim barely remembered him. Friday night, definitely, but what pub? Where did he work and what job?

"Sorry," the man said. "Barely recognised you."

"It's the suit," said Jim. "Makes me almost respectable." He pointed towards a pub. "Shall we?"

Chapter 32

Dave was from Derby and overall fairly decent. Probably too decent to rip off. Jim had noticed an occasional flourish from him when speaking. His voice sounded more than a bit camp too which for a moment worried him. He wondered if he'd inadvertently picked the bloke up or been flirting without realising.

"Have you got a girlfriend then?" asked Jim.

He shook his head. Again, flamboyant, almost theatrical. Perhaps he'd just got into the wrong job.

"I have." Jim realised he was sounding desperate. Or like a thirteen-year-old trying to impress.

"Quite hard to meet people, isn't it?" said Dave, swigging from his pint.

Jim nodded.

"The only time you ever meet people in this city, you're rushing about, trying to get home. The rest of the time you're at work or trying to forget about work."

He knew, like James before, that this was rapidly becoming a shorts situation. The problem was he'd already drunk too much. The train to pissedville was already out of the station. He looked at the young man for a minute. Realistically, how much did he have? If anything, was it enough to make him gamble his future, and possible freedom on some bloke he'd never met?

If Jim had worn a watch he'd have checked it. He settled with, "Do you know what the time is?"

"Half five."

He nodded. "So, no girlfriend then?"

"Nah. Been here a year now. A few dates and that, but you know how it is."

"I only met Charlotte a few weeks ago. Nice girl, she is. You'd like her." He wondered why he said that. He barely knew who this person was let alone what tastes he'd have in other random men's girlfriends.

"How did you meet?"

Jim laughed. "You won't believe this."

Jim realised not only that he'd been talking about Charlotte for half an hour, but also Dave was the one checking his watch for his own benefit. He'd gone into some unstoppable rant about her. Of course he'd left out most of the story, but the meat of it was there.

He paused and shrugged his shoulders.

"You're lucky," said Dave. He nodded a few times as if trying to think of something further to say.

Jim shrugged his shoulders. "Probably ought to, er." He pointed at the door. "One more for the road?"

Dave stood up. "Yeah, my round."

As he walked to the bar, Jim pulled out his phone. Charlotte's last message, *Last meeting of the day, then home x,* had been an hour ago. He guessed she'd be nearly finished. If London were smaller, they'd probably bump into each other on the tube.

Just about done myself x, his reply read.

Back with two pints, Dave talked for a while about football before they parted. Another midweek drink arrangement was made, but Jim didn't feel fully into it. There just wasn't enough time to befriend someone enough to pull this kind of blag. He thought deep down Charlotte must know it too. He was being put out to pasture for the week. She was keeping him near, but giving him a useless, unfeasible job.

The tube packed, he stood and swayed as it travelled south. There were at least eighty people on the tube. He reckoned most would have a grand they really wouldn't miss. Eighty big ones. That's all Charlotte would end up getting for all her work. He shook his head. Maybe they were both missing a trick. The old cream off the top blag. How many millions lived in London? Even ten pence off each person would solve both their money cravings for a long time.

How did you do it though? Ten pence from each person. "Excuse me, mate. I haven't quite got enough change for the tube. Can you spare ten pence?" He quickly realised you could only get fifty, maybe eighty people an hour at most. No. The ante would have to be higher.

As the tube pulled into the station he thought he'd work on the plan during the week. The week he knew would seem so long while Charlotte was running around doing all the work. A kept man, that's what he was. She paid the rent. He remembered an old Pet Shop Boys song about that. At least he thought it was about that. What was that song called?

He shrugged his shoulders as he walked past the cinema. Life could be worse. He had some sort of mid-term future with Charlotte and her scams. His own idea in Cornwall, despite needing work, wasn't bad. A little fill-in job maybe.

Letting himself into the empty apartment, he turned the kettle on and checked out the fridge. Charlotte had eaten too, but he thought a little snack wouldn't do any harm. Ham salad with those expensive little tomatoes and the curly salad stuff in a bag. Nothing like the salads he'd had before. The ham was actually carved straight from cooked pig instead of the watery, compacted slices of waste cuts he was used to. He'd still cover everything with salad cream though. The habit was too hard to break.

Charlotte wasn't far behind, though well after he'd finished "cooking" the salad. Appreciative, but tired, she ate hers without salad cream and with few words.

"So it sort of went okay then?" Jim was far from giving up. She seemed too quiet, lost in a world of numbers, profit calculation and planning tomorrow's meetings.

"As well as it could I suppose. First one's actually paid. Well, they will tomorrow when the bank opens. Ten thousand pounds."

Jim whistled. "Something to celebrate?"

"Not really. Need another nought on the end before we start that."

Though glad she'd said we, he wondered about the apartment she'd chosen to rent. It seemed superfluous. None of the duped bankers had ever seen it or been there. She could have rented a bedsit in north London and been thirty grand better off. He thought maybe she was still learning too, like himself.

"We'll get there." She smiled. He thought it was because he'd used the word "we" so quickly and added, "You'll get there anyway. I'll probably be lucky to repay what I've borrowed."

She took another bite of salad, or rocket as it was apparently called, then said, "It wasn't a loan. We've been through this."

Jim thought about pushing this further but didn't. She didn't look in the mood. Nowhere near the right mood. He took another mouthful of salad cream and ham then looked at his plate while trying to think of a different subject. Prodding a tomato with his fork, he wondered if there were any other subjects. This scam had become their lives like some all possessing demon. He couldn't remember the last time something had consumed him as much.

Crunching on the tomato, he remembered. Last week. Ten grand, yeah, that pretty much became an obsession.

"How are your plans for tomorrow?" He knew she'd reply with busy, but it wasn't really a question.

She shook her head. "Rammed. Seeing four people. Two at lunch, two after work. Have to make some calls too." She looked up. The piece of hair flopped down. "Should calm down by Wednesday. Then, it's just a case of waiting for the money and running."

He wanted to ask run where, but knew he couldn't. Some of the money would end up in Switzerland and she'd have to go there, swap it into gold then reopen the other account. He knew he'd be staying here, probably camping in Devon the way things were going.

"Just hope it's worth it." She pushed the plate aside having barely touched his carefully arranged salad. He didn't feel too hungry himself. He supposed all scammers must feel this way. The lull before the storm.

"Want me to run you a bath?" he said, trying hard not to grin.

She shook her head. "I'm not that tired. I think I can manage to turn two taps on."

He stood and picked her plate up. "I'll wash up then. Give me something to do."

Chapter 33

He spent the evening fiddling with the laptop while Charlotte took and received what seemed like hundreds of calls. Despite finding what appeared to be a convict-reuniting website, his heart wasn't really into it. The thought from earlier kept pounding back into his head. A few million Londoners, fifty pence each, problem sorted. How though? He wondered if every entrepreneur came across the same problem. Probably marketing or something would do it. Fake charity? No, that wasn't fair. They'd have to willingly give it without any expectation of it doing some good to anyone but himself.

Bed came all too early and with it came sleep for Charlotte. Jim found himself lying awake and going over and over the same thing. Redistribution of wealth in a way Robin Hood wouldn't have agreed with. Was it possible? Maybe a hundred thousand at a tenner each?

By three o'clock, sleep came. The alarm woke him at six, dog-tired and groggy from the previous days drink. Charlotte seemed well rested. Eager, determined and with a purpose, she made toast and coffee as Jim slumped at the breakfast bar.

"Didn't you sleep well?" she asked.

He shook his head. "Not really. Something going round and round."

She poured a coffee and sat opposite. "Care to share?"

"Kind of a plan, but it's half-hearted. Possibly half-arsed."

She smiled. The first one of the day. He was expecting her lump of hair to fall down but it'd just been cemented with half a bottle of hairspray. "Go on then."

"It's going to sound stupid, but ..."

Her eyes seemed to gloss over halfway through as he told his modern day inverse Robin Hood idea. Maybe it was stupid, infantile even. She nodded in the right places, but he could tell her heart wasn't in it.

"Sorry," he said, "here I am babbling on about a hare-brained job and you've got a hectic day."

She shook her head. "Not at all. There's just so much going on upstairs it's hard to concentrate."

He left it at that and made another coffee. The time nearly eight, he knew she'd be leaving soon, but it was the thought that counted. Half a caffeine boost was always welcome especially in a rush.

A goodbye kiss and she'd gone. Jim cleaned up the breakfast bits, played his Clash CD then got dressed.

Emerging onto the street at eleven, he looked both ways. This week was going to drag. He was little more than a spare part, but he knew there must be some way he could pull his weight. He'd pester his contacts again later, but they'd probably come to nothing. Maybe a few grand if he was lucky. No, this was Charlotte's big one, not his. He needed his own blag. Sitting around all day moping or cleaning wasn't cutting it. He had to physically do something; get some money in.

On the tube he sighed. Another hour spent underground going back and forth to the city's heartland. The ten pence idea was stupid in hindsight; he couldn't believe he'd told Charlotte about it. That was stupid. She'd probably change the locks while he was out. Deep down he knew she wouldn't. Okay, she was the boss, more than in charge of both this scam and everything, but he knew she needed him too. This world was scary alone. They both knew that. Finding someone alike was a one in a million chance.

The city pubs and restaurants were only just opening as he hit the square mile. Checking his phone, he retrieved a message.

Can we meet later, about threeish? x

Okay x, he replied as he ordered a tea.

He wondered for a minute what she wanted to meet for. Probably a gap between meetings. Maybe they'd have a bite to eat.

As the first lot of city workers came for their lunchtime drink, he took a deep breath and looked around. Couple of blokes together. Similarly, a couple of women a few paces behind. He realised they weren't together, but noticed the difference in what they did. The blokes headed straight for the bar, no messing. Drink came first. The women, however, found a seat, took off their jackets then ummed and arrred before one of them went for drinks.

Sat on his barstool, both groups either side of him, he smiled politely at the woman. A curt smile back. Functional but no other message. That was her intention and she succeeded.

Turning to the blokes, they were trying hard to sink their bottles in one. As Jim had noticed the past few weeks, bottles made for seriously slow drinking. Not like a pint where you could just tip it down, bottles had to be sunk between gulps and breaths. He nodded at the nearest bloke and got a nod back. Again, nothing more. None of these were up for friend making or opening themselves to being ripped off. Just a quiet drink, that's all they wanted.

Jim sighed and looked at his phone. He wondered whether he should ring James or Dave from yesterday. No, that stank of overkeeness. They had to come to him. He'd laid down the bait, but were the rats biting?

The bar soon filled. Monday seemed to have that effect in the city. Most were bored of it after four hours. After a couple of false starts with single drinkers, Jim moved onto bottles of lager offering the bloke on the seat next to him one.

"Cheers, mate," he said, taking a sip.

"Amazing, isn't it?" said Jim. "You could spend all weekend on the sauce, but after three hours at work on a Monday it feels like you've been sober a month."

He smiled and nodded. "Charles, Charles Harker." He stuck out a hand. Jim shook it not failing to notice the little finger twiddle Charles did. He'd no idea if it was masonic, but it seemed in the right area.

"Jim, Jim Trott," he replied. It was Charlotte's idea to use a false surname. She'd got the name Trott from a comedy series, but couldn't remember which one.

"What you in, Jim?"

"The shit mainly." He laughed and shook his head. "Brokerage. Small firm, we don't launch rockets or anything."

Charles nodded. "I'm over the road." He pointed in the direction of the huge bank dominating the skyline. "Wish I was in a small company sometimes. You're not even a number in a big place like that. No chance of ever meeting the boss or impressing anyone."

Jim nodded. "It can have its advantages. There's no chance of getting on the wrong side of the boss if you never see him."

"Tough morning, eh?" He finished his drink and nodded at the barman for two more.

"You don't want to hear my problems," said Jim.

"Go on, problem shared and that."

Jim sighed. "Well, bit of a misunderstanding with his daughter. Long story, short version is, next round of redundancies, I'm top of the list."

"Business and pleasure. Don't mix, do they?"

Jim wondered if this Charles was only going to speak in *clichés*. "Yeah, learnt the hard way. Just need to ..." He paused then shook his head. "Doesn't matter."

"Go on, what?"

"Not much really. Just got to try and make myself indispensable in a week. I've got a plan, but it's not very good."

Charles checked his watch. "Love to hear it, old chap, but was only supposed to be nipping out for a sandwich." He pulled a card from his pocket and shoved it in Jim's hand. "Give us a call after work, about sixish. Go for a proper drink if you like."

Jim nodded. "Okay. I'll give you a bell. Enjoy your afternoon."

Charles shook his head and smiled as he left. Jim folded the card into his pocket. Maybe this week wouldn't be wasted after all.

A different bar then lunchtime was over. The clientele had been quiet and not interested in his attempts to make friends. Jim thought through the plan for Charles and this evening. He'd claim to be a good friend of Charlotte and would put through similar trades in the hope of keeping his job. Hopefully, pound signs would flash in the bloke's eyes and he'd want in too.

Buying a coffee, he walked to the river and looked across. The time just after two. He had an hour before meeting Charlotte. He knew that hour would drag in the now nearly deserted streets. He sighed, thinking back to this time last week. What was he doing then? Selling Raif's stuff to Terence or maybe hitting the pawn shop with the raver's electrical goods.

He thought back to Raif. The bloke had paid enough, but was there some other way Jim could rifle a bit more from him? No, he doubted he could. He'd be on the lookout in his newly acquired wardrobe for thieving scallys. Yesterday had been a close call, but would he really have recognised him? Jim thought not.

The girls on the other hand. He regretted that. They hadn't deserved half of what he did. Possibly the only friendly people he'd met in London and he did that to them. Charlotte hadn't been too impressed when he told her about that blag. It takes a certain type of low life to rob someone's house, she'd said. His argument about his life depending on it seemed to sway her a bit, but no, it wasn't his finest hour.

His phone buzzed. He knew who it was.

Finished early. Where are you? x

By the river drinking coffee. Where do you want to meet?

The coffee was still nuclear hot but he forced another mouthful. Scalding hot on a warm day. He knew he'd be sweating within minutes, but still tried to force another mouthful down. He wondered why he'd bought coffee instead of tea. He'd always been a tea man, but Charlotte had got him into drinking it. He found the caffeine boost intense, a real perk-up.

I'll be in the wine bar opposite the bank x, her message read.

Binning the rest of his drink, he walked the few hundred yards to the wine bar. He didn't know why he felt nervous. Maybe it was her first message, "can we meet". Maybe he was reading too much into that. Shrugging, he went into the bar.

Looking round, he saw her. Sat in a booth, her floppy bit of hair was flopped down. Her face looked fresh yet flustered. Busy, yet sort of approachable.

"Hi." She smiled as he sat down.

"You okay for a drink?" He pointed to her glass. She nodded and took a sip of the lime with ice and something else, possibly vodka.

"You not thirsty?"

He shook his head. "Been drinking all lunchtime. Don't want to get sloshed." He looked again at her eyes. More with it than this morning. It seemed half the world's weight had been lifted from her shoulders. The smile was back too. It reminded him of the art gallery.

She nodded downwards at the next seat. A black briefcase, not her usual brown leather bag. He looked at her then shrugged his shoulders.

She mouthed some words which to Jim looked like "Someone's made a dash." He shook his head. Leaning nearer, she said, "Cash. Can you take it back to the flat? I don't want to carry it around."

He looked back at the briefcase and felt his eyes nearly popping out. "How much?"

248

"Ten big ones." Her voice still a whisper but it seemed too loud for his ears.

"You leave it with me." He winked which made her smile grow.

"Some's arrived in the bank too. Kind of feels like it's coming together."

Jim nodded. It explained her enthusiasm. He couldn't help but smile himself. She trusted him with ten grand in cash. That was more than a good sign. He had wondered whether to expect the worst of this meeting, but once again she'd proved more than an angel.

"I'll get a taxi, I think," he said. "Don't want to mess about with tubes."

She nodded, though her face said it was more obvious than a good idea.

"You got many more meetings?"

"Few more. After work, I'm going to dinner. That's a big one. Just shy of fifty. Don't know if he'll pull out or not; always been a maybe that one. The other one's in about an hour. Meeting for a coffee just round the corner. He's a bit creepy though."

Jim nodded and hoped he didn't look angry. He supposed he was jealous. He knew from the start a certain amount of flirting would go on. It had to, the scam demanded it. But where was the line drawn?

He took a deep breath. "I take it there are no women on your books?"

"No. Men are the greedy ones. Any woman with half a brain would see right through this."

He nodded. She had something there. Women just weren't stupid enough to be conned this way. There'd be one or two ruthless and greedy enough to chance it, but finding them would be so much harder than men.

His smile returned as he sat there, one eye on the case, the other on her.

"Finally feels like this is actually going somewhere." She sipped her drink again.

He wondered if she'd had too many today. She certainly looked a bit giddy. Maybe it was life giving her that high. He realised life was the wrong word. Money, or the knowledge that money would buy a better life, that was the reason.

He looked up at the ceiling then back at her. "Maybe I will have that drink."

They toasted success before he drained half the large malt whisky. As the fire burned in his throat, he reckoned he should have eaten earlier. Running on nothing but beer and toast for breakfast was asking for trouble. Charlotte's phone had buzzed and, as she looked at the message, Jim picked up the wine bar menu.

"I wouldn't eat here," she said, without looking up. "Over-priced crap."

He nodded. "That's London all over, isn't it?"

She smiled. "He's ready. I ought to get going." Flicking her lump of hair back, she made for the toilets.

Jim stared at the case. A week ago he would have run. Hell, yesterday he may have ran. Something was stopping his deep urges from their normal path. That something told him there was more where it came from. It was also telling him something else. She was worth more, way more than a briefcase full of twenties. Anyway, why would he run? She was giving the bloody thing to him.

Returned and looking heavily made-up, she stopped at the table and picked up her own bag. "Wish me luck."

"Good luck." He stood and kissed her. Just briefly, he caught her eyes and smiled.

"See you."

He decided to make the whisky last ten minutes before leaving himself. The road at the top of the pedestrianised area was busy. He'd grab a cab there. He didn't really know why he was waiting. It just seemed the sort of thing you did with a briefcase full of cash.

Holding the case tight, he finished his drink.

Ten minutes became five as time seemed to drag. The whisky gone and his head lighter, he left the bar. There was no point hanging around. No one would be watching or waiting. Every other person had a briefcase. It wasn't unusual.

Outside the sun beat down on the streets. Walking at a fair pace, he turned the corner and headed for the bus stop and cab ranks. It'd just be his luck he wouldn't find a cab. The one day he needed one there would be none around.

Someone brushed past as they tried to overtake him. He turned to look but knew straight away something was wrong. He seemed to be falling, heading face first towards the floor. His arm was being pulled too. More behind his back than away from himself. The briefcase. That was in that arm. He tried to force the arm back. His other one was out ready to break the fall but the other was still twisting away.

His arm crashed into the pavement breaking most of the fall, but his cheek also crunched into the ground. It didn't hurt, he thought it should, but it didn't. His other arm was still twisting. That hurt more than both his other arm and his face. He let go his grip on the briefcase. He had to, his arm would break otherwise.

It was then he saw him. Young lad, hoody covering most of his face. Baggy jeans riding halfway down his arse and trainers without laces. He didn't see his face. He just saw him run, Charlotte's briefcase in his hand.

"No."

He tried to stand but his arm hurt. Real serious fucking pain. Throbbing, shaking, the pain seemed to hit his head at once. His eyes seemed to be closing too. He wanted them to stay open. He had to get up and run after that little shit, but his body wasn't having it. As he lay down, resting his head on his good arm, he saw other people, frozen to the spot, staring. A few of them had phones out, a few just carried on walking, but none of them went after the briefcase. Not one.

Chapter 34

At first he wondered what the fuck was going on. A policeman kneeling down looking at him. He was lying on the floor.

"Can you hear me? Don't move, the paramedics will be here soon."

He nodded.

"Don't move your neck or back, you might have an injury."

He nodded again. His arm ached. Felt like it was in two pieces. Pain shot through his shoulder every second or two.

"The case," he said.

"Try not to speak or move."

Jim blinked then looked again at the policeman. Badge numbers on his lapel. Earpiece in his left ear. Shirtsleeves on a summer's day but his belt still had all of its Spiderman-style implements of incarceration.

"The case."

"It's okay, we're looking for it. Try not to speak until the paramedics get here."

He looked round. A crowd of onlookers, one of them phone out, maybe filming the scene for posterity. A few others looked concerned, but glad it had happened to him and not themselves.

"Try not to move your head."

"I'm fine. Just my arm."

He moved it. Jabs of pain raced to his brain. It didn't look broken. Just battered, maybe twisted or whatever, or popped from its socket.

"What's your name?" the policeman asked. "I couldn't find a wallet or ID."

He sat up instantly. The copper had been through his pockets. How long had he been out. He thought back. Was there anything incriminating there? No, just phone, key to Charlotte's flat and a hundred quid or so.

"Don't sit up. Your neck, you might ..." The policeman gave up and looked into his eyes. "I'm sure I've seen you before. What's your name?"

Jim saw the look in the copper's eye. Recognised it from his past. There was only one way he could recognise him. Wanted posters circulated round a nick.

"Raif Mortimer," he said, instantly regretting it. In a split second it had seemed a good idea. It was anything but. If the copper searched he'd see the outstanding crimes.

"Name rings a bell, too."

Jim looked round. The onlookers had parted to let a green-suited female paramedic through.

"Have we got a name?" she asked the policeman.

"Raif, Raif Mortimer," he replied. His face had changed again. His mind lost going through some internal database trying to get a match.

"Any pain in your back or legs?"

"No." Jim shook his head causing his shoulder to move again. Shit, it hurt. "Just the arm."

She squatted down and looked at his arm. He turned his head; it didn't look right. Not in its socket. He closed his eyes and shook his head.

"I'll check on the ambulance," she said.

Jim opened his eyes. He thought she'd come in an ambulance, but when he saw the motorbike parked he realised she was some speedy paramedic thing. Rapid response he thought they called them.

The policeman, now stood up, seemed to be on his radio. Jim caught the odd word, heard the name Raif Mortimer said a few times.

"I've got to go," said Jim. He tried to stand but the paramedic held him down. She seemed strong for her size, not that it took much to keep him down. The pain from his arm was restraint enough.

The policeman moved forward again, his arms out. "Where are you going? Stay still. You can't go anywhere with your arm like that."

"I've got to go. My arm's fine." He winced while saying it. It so obviously wasn't fine. He wanted nothing more than to go to hospital. But, what about the briefcase. Shit, he'd lost all the money. He'd lost Charlotte's money.

"Can you send a picture through," he heard the policeman say. That settled it. He'd been rumbled. Any minute now his good arm would be cuffed and he was going back down. Taking a deep breath, he tried to stand. He could probably outrun the copper. He had to, his free life depended on it.

He made it halfway up. The policeman had his big hands around his good shoulder. "Sit down." It wasn't a question.

Jim struggled again, but the copper's hand was too big and powerful. A few people in the crowd were talking to each other, nodding accusingly. The policeman now had his other hand around the scruff of Jim's shirt. He wondered if he'd get another chance to escape. He had to at least try.

"When the ambulance arrives we'll give you something for the pain." She looked at the policeman after saying it. He recognised a knowing look when he saw one, but didn't know what that one meant.

"It's okay," the policeman said. "They'll be here soon."

Jim knew he wasn't imagining the copper's hand grip his collar tighter. He knew all about having his collar felt, and knew just where this was going.

The ambulance arrived with two young, but male paramedics. They diagnosed a possible elbow sprain and gave him gas and air. Apparently his shoulder was fine, just bruised. As Jim sucked greedily on the tube, he thought the mixture of alcohol and gas wasn't going to help any potential getaway. The first paramedic had now sped off seemingly after not doing anything. He wondered if it was just some scam to get callout times down or something. The whole world seemed obsessed with figures and targets.

When the policeman's Blackberry beeped, Jim had thought little of it. Now, after he'd opened the email, Jim wondered if he'd missed his chance. Pulling cuffs from his Spiderman belt he stared at Jim.

"Well then, Jim." He snapped the cuffs over his good wrist. "Who's been a busy boy then?"

He tried to stand but his legs weren't moving. Just one thought in his head: this was it. The end. The end of what, Charlotte or freedom? He tried to stand again, but his legs had turned to jelly in some gas and alcohol reaction.

As the policeman snapped the other end of the cuffs to his own hand, Jim knew it was over. In some ridiculously stupid way, he felt relieved. He supposed it was relief at not having to run or hide. But he'd been enjoying being on the run. The hiding at Charlotte's gaff hadn't been too bad either.

After the paramedics helped him up he walked towards the ambulance, the policeman attached to his right hand side. He looked again at the built-up crowd. Some of the original lot were still there. Their big event of the day was Jim getting mugged then arrested. He supposed it must have looked odd. The disgust on their suntanned faces was clear. No smoke without fire he imagined them thinking. He must be guilty of something bad. Really bad.

One face stood out as he reached the ambulance door. Clear complexion, early thirties, floppy lump of hair that had given up and was drooping over her eyes. He looked hard at her, his eyes pleading for help. She brushed the hair aside, her cold and hard eyes catching his.

She mouthed two words. They were either, "Sorry, mate," or "I'll wait." He wondered if he'd find out what they were.

Chapter 35

The hospital visit was soon over. The X-ray was the only time the copper left his side. Jim didn't mind him so much. The bloke was only doing his job. He'd chosen a crap job, but it was still just a job.

Bruising was the full diagnosis, and with that a squad car rushed him to a central London station. Booked in and fingerprinted he was led to the cell. As the door slammed shut, he looked around. Eight by six cell, brick-lined walls, no windows. Home, or the nearest he seemed to have to one.

Sitting on the hard bunk, he sighed. He'd had it all two hours ago. Ten grand and a good woman. He'd had a future. Now, he'd lost it all. And why? Some little thieving scally on the rob. He shook his head and wondered if the little shit would ever get caught. Wondered how far his little eyes would pop from his head when he opened the briefcase and saw the wad of notes.

And Charlotte. He wondered what the hell this would do to her. Would she have to go to ground, call the scam off, or would she see it out on her own. He reckoned she'd probably see it out. She'd have to be careful though. They'd been seen together. CCTV would probably have hours of footage of the pair walking around or sharing a drink. If she was smart he reckoned she could get away with something. He hoped she could.

He lay on the bunk. They'd leave him to sweat for a few hours before the interview. That was the way it worked. Some people after just a few hours would sing like canaries. Jim knew he wouldn't. He'd been here too many times.

The only good thing he could think of was at least he hadn't shot Geoffrey. At least he wasn't a murderer.

They made him wait four hours before the interview. He declined a lawyer; didn't need one. He'd just keep quiet or deny everything. He was hardly going to confess and plead leniency. Anyway, what good was a lawyer when you knew what to do? They were just a waste of everyone's time.

The CCTV pictures they showed him in the interview were unreal in quality. Hard to believe they'd been taken in packed bars in the evening rush. A few showed him taking wallets, the mobile and the Blackberry off the women outside a cafe.

And Raif.

Stills of him talking to Raif, spilling his drink then rifling through his plane ticket and copying the address into his phone.

"Doesn't prove anything," said Jim. "Whatever might have happened at his house, it's nothing to do with me."

The detective across the table, some seventies throwback that refused to be pensioned off, smiled. He pulled another set of photos from the buff file and threw them across the table. CCTV footage from the cheque-cashing shop where he'd cashed Raif's cheque.

"We got some DNA at the flat too. I don't think we have yours on file." He turned to the officer next to him, a young and wide-eyed woman. "Maybe we should take some. What do you think?"

She looked at him, nodded, and then looked at Jim. "Of course, we think the break-in couldn't have been just one person. Maybe with DNA, we might find who else was there, unless ..." She left the sentence hanging as they'd probably been practicing for two hours.

Jim looked down at his unshoed feet. Tim by Four and Mick the Prick. Decent, hardworking, dodgy geezers. He couldn't drop them in it. Tim had just got out, on licence. He'd be straight back in. Would they have his DNA on file? He couldn't remember the exact date of his offence. Chances are they would.

Another thing was bugging him. Once they started digging, who knows where they'd stop. Charlotte would be next. They were bound to have pictures of them together. If they started digging and asking her questions it didn't bear thinking of. No, he couldn't do it, not to the lads. Charlotte though, she hadn't exactly rushed to his aid had she? She'd just stood there, watching them lead him away. Did he owe her anything?

"What you thinking about, Jim?" said the man.

Britwell was what Jim thought his name was. Some dinosaur still lurking round the ranks getting his full thirty years service for the maximum pension. He'd have seen the dark old days of beatings and forged confessions. Probably a few skeletons in his own closet. If there was a deal to be done, he was the sort to do it. Jim sighed. He was going down, that wasn't in doubt. Breaking parole and the pictures made sure of that. The only thing that was in doubt was who was joining him.

He looked up at the old-timer and shrugged his shoulders. "Okay. Maybe I will have that lawyer."

Ten a.m. the next morning, the magistrate sent him back down. Breaking his release terms, it was just a formality. The hearing itself had lasted barely ten minutes. The case would take weeks, months, to prepare, despite him admitting to gutting Raif of his worldly goods and fifteen other offences to be taken into account.

The converted transit van that took him to Brixton took its time crossing the river. Some private security van converted into mini plastic cells with a couple of security guards on board. Only one other occupant was in the van and he spent the whole journey protesting his innocence. Jim wondered how quickly the man would learn that everyone in prison is innocent. Everyone.

Booked in, Jim put on his new attire. Luckily he didn't get the jump suit with orange flash his co-prisoner got. Those on remand were kept separate and wore distinct clothes. Jim knew that as he technically wasn't on remand, but was awaiting another trial, he'd get shoved in with a separate lot. The inbetweeners. Both guilty and innocent until proven guilty. Porridge without the fun. Separate landings, isolation from other prisoners, slopping out and an hour a day solitary recreation. Sometimes they'd move prisoners around, but Jim knew he'd be in London until the trial. They were keeping him close to the city, close enough to be interviewed as and when needed.

Waiting to be taken to his new cell, he sighed. Fitting in was always hard. He hadn't been to Brixton before, but had heard stories. Not many of them good. It didn't sound as bad as the old days. The riots over the years had made it slightly more bearable.

Everything was so slow too. The whole system was designed to wear you down before you even started. With nothing to do but stare at the wall, he allowed his mind to drift off and wonder about Charlotte. Just how pissed off would she be? He'd lost her not only ten grand yesterday but also four from last week. He hadn't added anything to the deal. The only actual work he'd done was cook for her a few times.

Had he cost her more though? Had she pulled the plug? Had he cost her the lot?

He hoped not. Sure, he'd made it hard, but he reckoned she could salvage something from the pile of shit he'd left behind. He hoped she could.

The first night dragged on forever. Lights out at nine when the sun was still shining through the high, barred windows didn't welcome sleep. Hours seemed to pass as he went through the last few days. Maybe if he'd waited just that bit longer in the bar the kid would have mugged someone else. He should have caught a bus or walked the other way.

As the hours ticked on, his mind took a different route. Was it a set up? Was Charlotte in on it? He'd never checked inside the case. How did he know there was actually ten grand? Maybe she got the kid to mug him. Why though? What was in it for her apart from getting rid of him?

He also wondered about the two lads, Mick and Tim. Maybe he shouldn't have coughed so quickly. Chances are the coppers were bluffing about the DNA. Had they conned him? He'd have gone back down anyway for a few months, but had he messed up by protecting them?

When sleep eventually came, his mind was exhausted. Someone a few cells down seemed to be pacing his cell all night too. Jim knew it wasn't the innocent one he'd shared a ride with. It was someone else recently re-imprisoned. Someone else remembering how shit life was inside and why had he gone back to his old ways. He knew the real problem though. When your old ways are the only ways you know you're fucked before you even begin.

The days dragged by. A meeting with his young solicitor revealed the trial would be in about three months. The solicitor asked if he wanted to change his plea, but Jim shook his head. He was reminded he could get a much smaller sentence with more co-operation, but that wasn't the way things worked. Everyone knew that. Apparently everyone except wet-behind-the-ears solicitors.

Prison itself wasn't too bad. The cell larger than the previous one, the bed nearly comfortable. After a few days, sleep came naturally at nine until he woke at seven. As he was awaiting trial, he had the cell to himself. In some ways he preferred that, but twenty-three hours a day on your own brought its own troubles. The hourly exercise was the only chance to meet others. Most of them in a similar situation, it was the only thing they all looked forward to. Though they'd very little to talk about, that hour each day spent walking round in circles was all that kept him, and he knew the others, going. That and the two trips a day to the canteen where they'd pick up trays of slushy food and take them back past the other permanent guests of her majesty who were only too happy to wish them a fair trial.

After a month, he got the trial date. The end of November, the start of the season of goodwill. Jim wondered if that goodwill would extend to judges but decided it probably had an adverse effect.

Though other prisoners came and went, Jim got on best with a south London small-time wide boy called "Lanky Dave". Dave had been released a year early and promptly went straight over the Channel to France on a false passport. Returning with thirty thousand fake cigarettes, customs had him in no time. Dave's story that he'd been doing it for his kids to give them a Christmas to remember had struck a chord with Jim. He did, however, admit he'd been stupid to get caught so quickly. Very stupid.

In the fourteen hours a day he was awake and alone, Jim read. He'd never been big on reading, besides the newspaper, but with so little else to do he did it to avoid climbing the walls. Starting with Dickens, he went through other classics. Though the prison library was limited, he was soon up to half a book a day. His other reading comfort was occasional newspapers. Usually old, he tried for the London one whenever he could. The story he was searching for never appeared. He didn't know if that was good or bad.

His solitary visitor while on remand surprised him. His sister. Not seen or heard from for nearly eight years, he was surprised when she answered his letter to her. After a few more letters changed hands he applied for a visiting pass wondering if that would be the end of their reunion.

It hadn't been. In that hour of embarrassed silences, talk of growing up and hearing about her life as a waitress, he wondered why he'd taken the route he had. She had the same start as him, but had never once lived outside the law. It had to be something inside you, he was sure of that. Something bad inside that you were born with.

She promised she'd still write, but with her forthcoming marriage it would be harder. The man she was marrying sounded like a good man. He knew of Jim's incarceration and, though not said, he knew as well as she did it was nothing to boast about. When visiting time had ended he made her promise to stay on the right side of the law. She just shrugged her shoulders as if to say she wouldn't have broken it anyway.

The days dragged as the trial approached. Put back another week at the last moment, it was even harder to stomach. His young and perky solicitor was confident of doing the best for him. They both knew he was staying inside. The length though, that was the million dollar question. The solicitor reckoned he'd get a year at the most. Time served, admission of guilt. It all added up to him being out by next Christmas. The night before his trial sleeplessness returned. He knew what the score was and how it worked. This was going to be his thirteenth appearance before a court. Not usually superstitious, that fact alone couldn't fail but play on his mind. The solicitor assured him that wouldn't come into it, but he knew when it came to sentencing the judge would know all the details.

The judge wasn't lenient. Four years. Six months ago Jim wasn't sure if he'd have known what habitual meant, but he knew now. The judge was right too. That's exactly what he was. His only mitigating factor was the guilty plea. Jim knew with good behaviour he'd be out after three. But, three years is still a long time.

Something about those two months he'd had outside had changed him. He tried not to think too deeply about what it was, but with so much time to think it rattled round his head. He was getting too old for this. Prison gave its own cosy feel especially on long stretches. You got used to it and it seemed a better life than outside.

Things had changed. He'd seen life outside under a different cloud. A good woman, or a bad one in a good way, made the difference. He wondered why the hell anyone would feel better off inside with its lack of freedom, lack of companionship and lack of hope.

He was more than surprised when they carted off him off to Onley, a category C prison in the West Midlands. He'd been expecting Wormword Scrubs and all the delights held within. Prison overcrowding and the guilty plea had been the only reason him or his solicitor could see for the slight reprieve.

Not that the porridge wasn't tough, but at least he didn't have to share a cell or slop out. A few of the other lags on his floor were in similar circumstances. Lifelong repeat offenders determined they wouldn't get caught again. Either they'd go straight or be more careful from now on.

A dicey moment came after three months when, while the screw's backs were turned, two Londoners from a different floor appeared in his cell.

"We've to give you a message," said Chocker, the larger of the two by a good foot.

While the other watched the door, Chocker grabbed Jim by the throat and smashed him into the wall. Breath unable to go down, he tried pulling at the tree trunk arms holding him but Chocker was built like the toilet Jim was next to. He tried to speak but couldn't. It didn't really matter if he had spoken. Chocker didn't seem the listening sort.

"Someone in east London admires your sense of discretion. He was watching your trial with interest. I think you know who I mean."

Jim nodded as best he could. The wannabe Kray with the Range Rover seemed the best candidate for this.

"But he says don't get any ideas about squealing. True, you might get out a year or two earlier. But ..." He moved in closer. "The life sentence you'll get from my employer won't be as easy to shift."

He removed his hands and straightened Jim's collar. Looking him in the eye, he nodded before leaving the cell. It took ages before he could breathe properly. Even then, he was sure the red marks round his neck would be permanent.

He saw them every day at breakfast and dinner. Every day without fail, Chocker would nod a greeting at him, his eyes heavy. Every day, Jim would return that nod.

Chapter 36

Aside from the usual fights and disagreements time plodded on. He kept his nose as clean as he could and took an interest in a cookery course. The kitchen beat sewing mailbags, and as his time progressed he ended up on mashed potato duty. This in itself, although repetitive, bought him a certain amount of respect from the other prisoners as he tried hard to remove the stodgy lumps others didn't care about.

Another year and an NVQ in food hygiene later, Jim was leading the kitchen. He'd never considered it as a job before, he'd never considered any job before, but he found something enormously satisfying about creating an edible meal from basic ingredients.

Another few months and talk was of early release. He'd kept his nose clean, taken exams and read books. He'd learnt his lesson. Plus, a local hotel was after a kitchen assistant and, as the enhancements paid to the hotel for employing ex-cons were huge, they were interested in him.

A visit to the hotel, prison guard attached, told him the real reason why the hotel was so keen. The entire staff except for the chef were from either Poland or Romania. "No one'll work for these shit wages," the chef said. "Just can't get the staff."

With a month to release, the job was accepted and a bedroom in a halfway house obtained by his case worker. He knew he didn't have to stay there forever, but was also more than aware his history would follow him around like a bad smell. He knew it was a start though. And what came of it was up to him.

The letters from his sister had all but dried up. He still wrote occasionally but guessed she had a new life, and if anything was worried she'd become his next victim after release. He told her of cooking and of the hotel and suggested she visit it sometime.

The last month dragged. Friendships made inside wouldn't carry on no matter how much they insisted they would. It was known by both sides too. Little more than saying what they thought should be said. With three weeks to go, he was moved to the releasers wing. The prisoners in the last few days of their sentences tended to be calmer. Avoiding anything that may hinder their early release became a way of life.

As he ticked down each day to go, he had a different feeling to the other times he was awaiting release. This was it now. The start of a new life. A second chance. He was going to take that chance and see where it took him.

Epilogue

The prison gate opened. Stepping forward, he crossed the line that separated being inside and being free. The air tasted sweeter. Just under three years of breathing that foul air had made him yearn for this moment. The grass looked greener than the last time he could remember seeing it too. The trees taller, they appeared to swish more in the wind.

He turned round and thanked the guard.

"Don't come back," he replied with a smile.

Jim shook his head. "This time, I won't."

He walked to the front gate past the gatehouse that inspected cars coming in and out. One final wave and he was out. Traffic sped by on the road. People in cars looked round and saw a man in jeans and coat. Jim wondered if they'd mistake him for a guard, or could everyone tell straight away he'd just been released.

Heading for the bus stop, he breathed in deeply. Traffic fumes, but they were familiar. The taste of freedom. The taste of free England.

He knew the bus would arrive in ten minutes. The timetable had been scoured every day for the past week. He'd get on and ask for a single to Dunchurch then change there to Rugby. He'd find the halfway house easily then nip to the shops for some food and maybe a couple of cans of lager. After that, he'd go back to the room and sleep. He'd an early start in the morning. Four a.m. Half a mile walk to the hotel to help cook breakfasts for its guests.

He looked round at the car slowing on its approach to the bus stop. Range Rover; new model. Black with blackened windows. His heart sunk as it pulled up beside him and the passenger electric window wound down.

The man he expected to see wasn't there; the passenger seat empty. The only seat occupied was the driver's and that wasn't him.

It was a woman. Mid-thirties, maybe older but heavily made-up. Red hair, sunglasses and a very familiar look to her nose.

"Fancy a lift?" she said.

Opening the door he got in. Fastening his seat belt he turned to her. The years had been kind. Her face seemed smoother. If anything she looked younger. Jim wondered whether a surgeon had a hand in it.

"You okay?" she asked.

He nodded. "Not bad. I take it I didn't ruin everything?"

She took her glasses off as she pulled away. "No, God no. Worked out just fine in the end. Sorry I just..." she paused, looking back at the road, "left you."

He was going to say I'd have done the same but didn't. He didn't know if he would have or not. "I'd have got caught eventually."

She nodded. "So ... Fancy a drink? There's a little pub up the road."

"Charlotte, I ..." He stopped, wondering what her name was now. "I've got a job and somewhere to live. It's only a hotel kitchen, but it's a start. I ..." He looked out of the window as the trees rushed by. "I'm getting too old for this."

"That's a shame," she said. A smile he'd never forgotten reappeared. "I've got this thing going in Manchester, but I really need some help. How about we have a little drink and I tell you all about it."

The End

Lightning Source UK Ltd.
Milton Keynes UK
UKOW040711310513

211555UK00002B/7/P